EL TAJIN, NEW MEXICO

2/9/19

For Lynne,

Fondest regards,

Robert

El Tajín, New Mexico

A NOVEL

Robert MacIsaac

EVERY BOOK PRESS

MMXVIII

ISBN 978-0-9837714-3-2

Book Design by William Bentley.
Cover Photo by Radu Sava.

for Michael Eroy

On Gods or fools the high risk falls – on you.

Rupert Brooke

Coming he is not seen, departing he is not understood; he who while he is present, and only while he is present, is light to soul and mind. In that light, invisible he is seen, inconceivable he is understood.

Guerric of Igny

···· **1** ····

ONE TASTE was necessary, just one pure taste, before invention
left another scar. When he slid back the bolt and popped open
the hatch door, the rush of dry air was so sweet, so warm, his heart
swelled with confusion. He pulled himself up through the hatch and
sat on the concrete rim, keeping his feet on the topmost iron rung.
Not far to stray, not this night, this moment. He placed his palms flat
on the cool paving and stared eastward. Here he could sit a while
in the predawn air, to drink in the desert and await the first halo of
morn.

Silence, and always silence was the language of this place. The
deep darkness of the land revealed in only the vaguest bulges and
outlines perhaps a shrub or cactus, or pile of boulders, at depths or
proximities uncertain. In such absence of definition one could suppose the desert aswim with life and mischief. To walk out into this,
the Colonel thought, would gear with caution every step in dread of
some crawling fang or treacherous claw. But here atop this bunker,
a few short paces from duty, the life one fancied moved or reveled
out on the midnight plains dwelled rather in the flitting ether, spirits
colliding wayward on the mild wind, looming eyes and voices never
heard, now pausing in their play to hover before him and hark to his
curious musings.

No less, the silence above. The sky just now was thick with starry
clusters, the blizzard of light more fervent and vast the deeper he
strained his gaze, yet it was a blizzard absorbed, surrounded in, a

black and limpid void equally as deep and endless. The Colonel let his line of vision caress the quiet spectacle, absorbing its suggested forms and their almost insights, seemingly apparent but really more elusive than the fleetingest memories of youth. For a moment or two he attempted to deny the stellar world so carefully mapped by astronomer and nomad, to see mere chaos in the night, like the wild play of flame about a candle wick. But Orion's yearning chase, with Sirius at his footfall, the cloud of Seven Sisters, the upturned Dipper, and all the other named and nameless visions of the sky, imposed on him again their story, a tale at once incessant yet with meaning vaguer than the layers of shadow that unfolded round about him.

He looked ahead of him again and from the hooded land inhaled long fragrant draughts. Hints of pine and sage, occasional lilts of seared sandy crispness, then once or twice a bloom of darker traces. But the deepest sweetest scent of all was the odorless stream of clean, untamed atmosphere, scrubbed by rock and whirlwind, and by laughing days of sun and nights of stellar weeping. The wind lifted a little. He closed his eyes and let its warmth invade his face and hair and neck. A short bath in Nature's innocent arms, before the end of innocence.

Then the sound of steps and voices in the corridor below disturbed his reverie.

He dropped down a few rungs of the ladder and called into the lamplit tunnel. "Gray? Are you ready?" No reply. The murmurs continued, further off, there seemed a short laugh, and then all was still.

No matter. Colonel Andrews hopped back to the surface and gazed anew above him. He started to think.

No change upon this night, save his own agitation. Those voices reminded him of what was to come, and now the stillness sharpened rather than soothed the worm of his anxiety. The only test this year, not technically allowable under the current negotiations with the Soviets, but – as it had been originally planned – since it was an "underground" blast the indiscretion of a nuclear rumble would cause merely the usual outrage among the press and diplomatic corps. Then soon the shouting would subside, the president and secretary of state could dust off their image, and so back to more talks and treaties and state dinners. So it had seemed, and so the State Department and Pentagon had worked it all out between them. "But how," the Colonel said aloud to the group of elves gathered in the near darkness to hear his complaining, "how describe, let alone comprehend, the genius of human error." It had started with his own unit, so the Colonel was not waxing censorious at a carefree remove. But the astounding snowball that followed afterward still left him silent with amazement. Curiously not unlike the amazement he now felt gazing overhead through the patterns of order, an order that surely found no like reflection on this roiling, crazy globe.

The way Robson Andrews saw it, he had simply been instructed to dig a tunnel. The depth and dimensions told him it was for underground blasts, which seemed odd since there were two operational tunnels already. What was even more odd was that everyone emphatically denied that this was its purpose.

"Keep the boys busy," General Morgan had said.

"You mean the tax collecting boys," the Colonel had quipped, since the outrageous sums required were way beyond any budget he had previously been assigned. The money arrived however, the drilling began in earnest, and Congressman Whiting, while pleased with the local commerce, had a bank of phone operators working until evening day after day fielding complaints and allaying fears.

But phoning the congressman's hotline would not have dismissed Colonel Andrews' misgivings. He had stopped tunneling only a month into the project. Sanderson, the lead engineer, had been sending him weekly updates of the soil and stress analyses, and each new report confirmed more explicitly what each previous one had predicted.

"We're heading into muck, colonel," Sanderson told him.

How splendidly ironic, Andrews thought, to have the earth underline for him what was already evident politically and emotionally.

"Stop at once," the Colonel said. Both men grinned, and the engineer put their mutual feeling into words, "Would it were always so simple."

General Morgan, though, never had a problem with simplicity. In this case General Morgan wanted a tunnel, so General Morgan was going to have a tunnel.

The Sisyphean boulder was set rolling downhill the next morning in the General's office. Robson walked in without an appointment but with the naïve confidence of common sense. Ten minutes of dire consequences spelled out billboard style, and they would both be taking a leisurely stroll over to the canteen for a long lunch and breezy discussions of how to carve up congressional pork.

But the Colonel neglected to remember the basic rule of rushing the quarterback he had once mastered so well as an all-state linebacker.

His broad shoulders and long muscular arms well managed their rugged work shoving and elbowing between stubborn linemen. Then his greatest asset, thighs and calves of quick elastic steel, reliably held him upright or – his signature move – helped him feint inside, then out, then back in again, his opponent often expecting the outside end run. Now and then a pylon of a guard was able to hold him in check at every move, and that happened whenever he forgot the basic rule: Do not underestimate your opponent, do not exaggerate your own abilities.

And so his dark, close-cropped hair and high forehead never broke a sweat as he walked down that cool corridor and knocked on the General's door and went in. Measured Reason, say hello to Brick Wall Decision.

Paul Morgan was sitting behind his desk, arms in his lap. The General's nickname was "Big," for breadth rather than height. His wide red face exhibited two noticeable scars, on forehead and jawline, and the tinge to his flesh, amplified by a helmet-like head of iron-grey hair, looked less like sunburn than a fastidious wide-eyed attempt to hold his breath well into zones of discomfort and unrest.

He stood up briefly as Andrews entered, the width of his stout shoulders continuing straight down his body, trunk of oak grasping hard whatever it claimed as its own.

The General (unbeknownst to the Colonel) had himself been a right guard, for two years only, and never once in his brief career did a defender knock him off his feet. And it did not happen here. The on-rusher feinted left, right, left again, and was soon haplessly gazing at the ceiling.

"Rob, do you realize what Whiting did to lobby for that money?"

"Money can always be spent, sir. We could use a few hangars."

"How much further to our destination?"

"It's virtually quicksand, sir. It's impossible. A mile, two miles, of concrete wouldn't help."

The General traced his fingers along the map due north of where the dig had stopped. "You can go this way, up towards Pale Moon. We've never dug that way before."

"That's because it's brutally solid rock that way, general. We would have to tunnel considerably higher, but that would put us dangerously close."

"Dangerously close to what?"

"An explosion from such a site would be a surface explosion, sir, not an underground test. A mushroom cloud, seen for miles."

"No it won't."

The land was so quiet. The desert breeze stirred no dust, and the only visible motion was the occasional streak of a meteor across the darkness. He had counted five already. Here was respite, Andrews thought, but not a way to live. Despite the clarity and the closeness to wider mysteries that the nighttime gave, one could not lead a life in the dark. Had anyone tried? The fury of the day ever remained one's teacher, and its absence was not peace. There was no real peace, only different lessons.

So the tunnel was completed. It took fourteen months. Fourteen months! He remembered one of the last days, he was in mid-sentence explaining to Sanderson and a few others about a road he wanted cut "when this was over," and he had wanted to stop, to stop before getting to "was over," but he did finish the sentence, and they left, and he closed the door of his office. And the sentences stopped, including the ones in his head. He remained there the rest of the afternoon, spent long hours looking at his hands, looking at the walls, his desk, determined not to do the next thing once the last thing was over. He remembered most of all, from that afternoon, how good it felt to take off his shoes. Imagine going to a weekly briefing without your shoes on. Just imagine that. The next thing, always the next thing. Could one even imagine, much less know, a life where there was no "next thing"? What would you do... next? He had not had the luxury of contemplating this possibility at any length, since the phone rang just as he had prepared to leave, with his shoes on.

It was Morgan. "Rob, the first trucks are arriving a month ahead of schedule. A month! Can you believe it?"

"Trucks, sir?"

"With the detonator frames and casings. They were assembled in West Virginia..."

"For...?"

"The tests. Well, probably only one test. In your new tunnel."

"Detonators? Tests? Sir, begging your pardon, sir, but we've been over this, sir. This tunnel was not built for tests, sir. Not to mention the full-blown treaty violation."

"Then what the hell is it for, mining gold? Of course it's built for tests, the specs are no different."

"I told you! – sir – we went too near the surface, sir. I will tell you again. You–"

A court martial, a transfer, just a dressing down, all would have been preferable of course, to what Morgan did do after Andrews proceeded to utter every conceivable street and gutter spawned epithet that four hundred years of modern English usage had contributed to the vocabulary of an American Army colonel in the latter half of the twentieth century. He put him in charge.

Feldon Whiting came to see him a week after the trucks arrived. He wanted to be "absolutely clear" on what he needed to do to "protect his constituency."

"That's simple," the Colonel answered. "Order 237,500 lead-lined suits and helmets. And oxygen tanks." The man from Washington even had the nerve to tell him that the population of his sector was "well over half a million, and growing" before they began the process of carving up the albatross that would adorn both their necks. Andrews described the technical aspects of the explosion to the congressmen, which included a lengthy explanation as to why "pointing the thing downward" would not make the mushroom cloud "go in reverse."

"It is, congressman, going to end up a surface blast. Over a hundred square miles of desert will be destroyed. And there may be fallout."

"That's not so much, colonel," Whiting said with the most genial and comforting tone of obstinate defiance Andrews had ever witnessed. Such was the innate contradiction of this servant of the people, with his perpetual unassuming smile, squeaky voice, and happy gleam in his hazel eyes. Robson noticed once again how that gleam persisted, decorating rather than obscuring a wily audaciousness, coupled with an intelligence that perpetually probed the nuances of an endeavor for the most optimistic way of getting what he wanted. To others, however, the precision of Whiting's carefully parted dark blonde hair, starched cuffs, polished shoes (and polished belt!) conveyed a sense of organization and refinement that gave everyone on first meeting a feeling of assurance. This was a feeling they might have hesitated to embrace had they known the schemes and ploys the hidden mind behind them was constantly entertaining. Though, in his defense, the well-meaning impetus that drove him was always sincere.

Whiting became more convinced of his reasoning when he was shown the blast's location and the probable range of surrounding havoc. He saw it would be necessary to "move Brandonville a bit east" by buying up the affected half of Jackson Monroe's ranch, and stop construction of the Hacienda industrial park scheduled to begin in less than three months. And he would work hard to clear the blast area of "our precious wildlife." All this maneuvering needed to take place without the least suspicion that any testing was in progress, indeed that the military intended to explode a nuclear device ever again. At least not in New Mexico. To this end the congressman gave a speech three days later at a luncheon for the landowners in his constituency, "to open our strategy of concealment" as he termed it to Andrews. The Colonel read a fax of the speech the following morning, and he could not deny the superb cunning of this three-term member of the House of Representatives:

"Ladies and gentlemen, I believe the end of the nuclear age is at hand," it began. "We may even see it in our own lifetime," provided, Andrews gathered from a careful reading between the lines, the US military stopped spending money on bombs and started applying advanced technology to peaceful land development. Brilliant. He laid the groundwork for pushing all forms of registered voter life out of harm's way and at the same time placed the blame for the blast that was to come squarely on the shoulders of the personnel at the Silas Testing Grounds, more specifically, on those of Colonel Robson Andrews. "I am in touch with Colonel Andrews, who is in charge of testing, on a weekly basis, and we share this vision of the future. Our future…" Why was this mention of his name necessary? "Because, Rob," Whiting explained over the phone after Andrews tore the speech asunder and rang him up, "I'll need you to make a few speeches in the local communities. We'll need some military clout to handle Monroe."

Why Jackson Monroe acquiesced so readily to selling off half of his property was never made clear to Andrews, though a mixture of blackmail and concessions was no doubt involved. What proved far more difficult was persuading General Morgan to pay for it.

"We don't need any more rattlesnake turf. We should sell off half of what we've got now."

"The cloud is likely to drift that way, sir. It must be viewed by the public as part of the testing grounds."

"The public will not be invited, colonel."

"I mean, sir…" It did not matter what he meant, of course. Robson Andrews could not but marvel at how the General, through all of this, never referred directly to the impending explosion, much less its aftermath. He passed on reports of supply levels, deliveries, supplementary personnel, enemy satellite maneuvers. But it was all in the abstract, as though finding office space for a physicist or signing the order for a battalion to clear five acres of underbrush were actions performed in the same spirit as quaffing an ale. Now you drink this, now the drink is gone. Any notion of consequence, of one action having an effect on something else, did not seem to enter his mind. Perhaps, Andrews thought with some irony, this is how one escapes "the next thing" syndrome. Just don't think of consequences, just do what you do, and when it's over, or gone, do something else.

Another shooting star. Six. "Did you see that one, guys?" he asked his spirit friends, now certain they were bouncing about the air in sympathy with his ruminations.

The funding became a nightmare, and he could not see the end of the tangle. There was plenty left over from the original monstrosity of a budget, but this was for "tunneling" and only tunneling. Repairing most of the roads, sprucing up the Information Center, even installing new flagpoles was somehow "tunneling." Whiting would not go to Washington for more, so Morgan appealed to the Governor.

"I'll buy it," the General kept saying while asking for the credit to write the check. The Governor acquiesced, he wanted more Defense Department "presence," and he just loved halving Monroe's holdings. The state's budget was not tampered with, however. There would be a new property tax, "proportional acreage" something or other, meaning the more land you had, the more you paid, meaning Monroe was buying his own land for someone else. As this tax would raise havoc with those paying less (albeit proportionally more, since they had less), the legislation was pushed through in conjunction with "education and rehabilitation services," which funding Whiting and a few others were somehow able to cajole out of the Federal government. The purchase, and its attendant dominoes, went ahead even though all the proposed legislation from which the check writing came had yet to pass through the House. Only Whiting seemed to understand the situation. "I don't like Jackson's silence," he said to Andrews on the day the property was signed over.

The promise alone of cash is usually enough to get out the checkbooks and purses, and these days the currency of promise tended to empty its billfold on what everyone assumed would be the next savior of mankind: computer software. Once the savior is declared, one must follow its holy edicts. So no one objected to the extra complications, extra personnel (including, by necessity, civilians), extra office space, extra hardware, and extra funding necessary to design, write, and install a system that would do much more than touch off a nuclear blast. Somehow it was concluded that testing a fully automated monitoring and firing package would save the Pentagon millions in future. Even though, as Andrews saw it, once this project was over, the system was bound to become the same old past, the aged, aged man that no one ever learns from. Why using software to send the signal and ignite the blast rather than a conventional charge was never considered. Here, as far as he could see, was the seed of real chaos, that goes by soberly about its havoc. Question it at your peril.

Erecting a fence proved impossible. Morgan was happy to give the battalion something to do, but Monroe refused to grant access to his land. This curious legal conundrum was a needle's eye no one seemed able to thread. Building a fence on the border between the two properties meant that half the fence (half its width, or approximately three quarters of an inch) rested on Monroe's side. This he called trespassing. But if it was built entirely within the perimeter of the testing grounds, then what was left outside was in effect land ceded to civilian personnel. This violated innumerable Federal regulations. To construct something precisely on the edge for the entire seven miles was an engineering feat that would have surpassed the digging of the tunnel. And the men would not do it anyway. So Morgan enabled what he saw to be the two soundest follow-up initiatives: a fleet of helicopters that patrolled the unfenced purlieus day and night ("Special delivery invoice to the congressional wags," he asserted to Captain Gray as he banged his rubber Approval stamp over his signature); and an elaborate publishing endeavor from the Information Center of maps of all sizes and colors that delineated the "vital unimpeachable borders of our most important national programs," etcetera more of the same, followed by an elaborate circulation and mailing to every library, civic center, and bookstore in New Mexico, Arizona, and western Texas, affirming in print what belonged under the Silas jurisdiction.

The bunker Robson Andrews sat upon was the last bit of construction completed before the green light for the blast was given. The silence among his men that followed the order from the Joint Chiefs was telling. Cups of coffee began to be passed with careful politeness, office doors closed with a hush, desks and typewriters hummed with mere efficiency, no gossip or ribaldry, no idle chat. Everyone worked toward the moment they dreaded, a relentless march to a precipice beyond which plummeted no one knew what depth, but fall, fall they would. How far, how far. "Even goddamn Brandonville was moved," the Colonel said to Jupiter and sniggered. What people will do for a swimming pool. He knew as well that the president and his staff were informed only yesterday of what would really happen. He had prayed for a last minute reprieve, a final stay of execution. But why pray, why expect anything but madness.

There is that first moment, the moment when we awaken each morning, when we realize that at some time hours previous we had dropped off in the darkness and ceased thinking, feeling, knowing. And in that first moment, when the phantoms flee and the dreamy bliss dissolves, you see the world had never ceased its movement and purpose. So dawn broke. Suddenly his reverie absented itself enough to taste the change in the air, to see a pink aura steal about the plains and hills. The shadows lifted, light revealed the land in tones of red and tawny mustard, the shrubs were real shrubs, the twinkling pupils in the heavens one by one their eyelids dropped as deep azure filled the eastern sky. His companion sprites were gone, or maybe just hidden in the "broad daylight" men so often overlook. Now more steps sounded in the corridor, and this time they grew loud and urgent in an instant and a voice as urgent called out, "Colonel Andrews, sir. We are at the hour, sir."

Andrews clambered down without a final look, slammed to the hatch, brushed past the two men and hurried toward the elevator down to the Action Room. He called back orders and demanded updates all in one breath, but he did not heed their replies and he did not care. They would do what was needed, he knew that. Authority alone was necessary, a man in front, an axis round which whirled the step by step precision of levers pulled, panels watched, buttons – a button – pressed.

As he came off the elevator he asked, "Where is General Morgan?"

"In Florida, sir."

"In Fl... .What is our countdown?"

"Forty-four minutes, sir."

"Excuse my absence, captain. We are clear of overhead observation?"

"First Soviet satellite not due until 0700 hours, sir,..." Captain Gray hesitated, biting off what he wanted to say next.

Andrews eyed him frankly. The "biting off" was seldom figurative with this thin slip of a captain, given the man's habit of making a continual snack of his lower lip. Yet set within a frame of thin wispy hair that never seemed to have known a comb and pale skin drawn a bit too tight around his cheekbones were a pair of shrewd blue eyes that often made more sense than his artless attempts at conversation. "Yes, captain, they will no doubt experience considerable difficulty photographing through the cloud we are about to throw up." And those shrewd eyes replied with one quiet wink of acknowledgement.

The countdown continued. Tenths of a second fleeing wildly in unison from every digital clock face. Men and women sat dutifully at their computers and consoles. A long fax spilled along the floor. Someone passed around a few morning rolls and coffee.

It was all so mad. Such sobriety, such intelligence, at the service of a juggernaut no one even thought of stopping. They had managed to bring in and assemble a nuclear device under everyone's nose, even as our own U.N. ambassador demanded yesterday that Russian and Chinese testing cease this year, nay, this very month. Andrews could see the futility of such posturing, a gnat upbraiding the sun. Orders were given, orders were followed, progress was obeyed. And anyway, the ambassador did not believe what he was saying. Such palaver was only another dial turned, the next lever that opened the next circuit.

"Fourteen minutes, sir."

Fourteen? Where did the half hour go? But of course, he was reading reports. All animals and birds had been cleared from the area, except for the hapless wild few who would die untamed. There were weather reports, community updates, a congratulatory letter from Whiting. All of it conveyed the unstated belief that everything would be just fine. The right thing was taking place, and Colonel Andrews had everything he needed to complete a successful operation. He had everything he needed...

He reached out and grabbed Gray's frail arm even before articulating to himself what the impulse told him.

"Sir?"

"Captain Gray, what would it take...?"

"Sir?"

"To stop it."

"You would have to tell us, sir."

The Captain's tone of voice said that he would be more than happy to hear just that. How suddenly the possibility pressed up against him! There was no opposition at all. He could walk over to the microphone, open all channels, and begin something like, "Attention all personnel, there is a slight change in schedule." Why didn't Gray argue? He did not, and no one else would either. He could stop it.

But not just with his words, for the hierarchies would make him pay, even if everyone, right down to the last intelligence operative were as relieved as he would be. There is always a dripping head. Life had taught him that much.

"Nine minutes, sir."

Why was someone calling out the time? "Who said that?" No answer. He looked around the room again. A corporal was cleaning his monitor, otherwise not a single pair of shoulders stirred. This end of the tunnel was poised and ready, and at the other end, deep in the starless night of concrete and plutonium, sat an obedient array of human engineering, not a whisper of a soul, no conscience, no fear, only minerals and metals hewn and drawn like giant steel coils into excruciating tension. A millisecond of electric impulse would shoot along a gold expressway and trip the hair-trigger system. What was a millisecond? A blink? He blinked. No, half a blink. Which half, upper or lower? His eyelid fluttered. It was hard, a millisecond was hard.

"Attention, all personnel," the mike slipped from his wet hands. He grabbed it in a white fist. "We have, we are going to experience a change in schedule." What a choice of words. Highlight, delete, highlight, delete. "Begin close-down procedure, code five, seven, one, niner, niner, eight."

Captain Gray rushed toward him, but he saw only one head look away from the video game to gaze at him. "Colonel, sir, we are beyond the code's threshold." He paused, but this time there was no hint of unstated agreement.

"What is the code then, captain?"

"You remember, sir, it is the Atlas code. I have one digit, you have three, and then we open General Morgan's envelope."

"Damn my digits. Get him on the phone."

"We are one minute thirty, sir."

"Get him on the phone, captain."

"One minute twenty, sir."

Andrews wondered why he had never noticed the scar under Gray's left eye before. Then the answer was obvious. He had never needed to look for anything on that psychological terrain. Now he looked in earnest, scanned the mouth, nostrils, calm blue eyes for some trace of that gentleman whose tone of voice had said, "Yes, colonel, do it, please, please, do it." But it seemed that gentleman had gone to Florida too.

Robson Andrews resolved not to speak. It will happen, *it will happen.* He would stand there, maybe even tap a key or two, but it was going to happen without him. He would not go away, he would watch every final tenth of a second depart, he would even feel his toes crammed into his black lace-ups, but it was just going to happen.

"One minute and counting."

Gray became Gray. "Wheel Lock Maneuver, colonel?"

When someone speaks to us and we answer, they walk off with whatever bone we throw them, however disagreeable or absurd. But when we give them naught, they are at liberty to imagine any and all menus.

The Captain paused but a fraction, then took up the microphone. "Begin Wheel Lock Maneuver." He looked again at Andrews. "We're on our way, sir."

Where?

He opened a folding chair and sat down. He took up his coffee. Simple actions are the stuff of ritual. What is it made one action a ritual, and not another? As a boy he fancied that the Church fathers of medieval times had sat around a large stone table and decided, "Right, lift up the chalice two times." "No, three. You know, Holy Trinity." "Oh right, three. And then turn around—" The acts of ritual were private and personal, but took place before the crowd. So perhaps the crowd always decided. Behold this man, this private act that he performs not in his bedchamber but on the podium of our time. Let us always remember, and so as always to remember, let us always do, and redo. Now there was a question. Remember what?

The efficiency of the maneuver was appallingly impressive. Three men inserted three keys in three locks, all turned in unison, then the final twenty-second countdown monitored on the "Bang Board" as it came to be called. He stared at it now. A descending light bar a la Times Square marked off the brutal moments; at ten the "Cyclops," a single red bulb ("Damn these nicknames") would illumine – then ignition, and Cyclops goes out, shutting his eye on what shall happen.

But it was happening! He was dreaming it, anticipating how it would be, but there it was, now, Cyclops glowed, Gray pressed the button!

"Ignition!"

Cyclops glowed.

No one moved except Robson, who did what seemed to him the right thing to do. He took his last gulp of coffee.

"Colonel Andrews, sir, ignition malfunction. Shall I order backup maneuver?" If that second press had worked, and a flash of sunlight ruptured the earth, and a terribly blazing globe had billowed and risen and spread in meticulous fury, then maybe his silence would have been silently ignored.

Gray glanced over at him, ordered the manual backup, which was duly performed, someone gave the oral countdown, and the captain this time heaved his full weight onto the button. Cyclops leered on.

"Colonel Andrews, sir, we have serious ignition failure, sir." It was the ghostly aftermath of that detonation, there in the Action Room, without the detonation itself. Or perhaps *this* was the blast, this was death, silent, glowing, naked and exposed, all eyes aware, beholding what you, supposedly the one in charge, feel, think, are, will. Every-one now joined with Cyclops and stared, not at their consoles, but at the Colonel. The absence of mystery, the lifted veil, more blind-ing and unspeakable than all the sealed riddles writ in flesh. No one moved, and no one understood.

Gray strode across the floor and nearly stood on Andrews' shoes, this despite the fact that Robson was almost twice his size and prob-ably three times his strength. Emboldened by his superior's inaction, he trembled with fury, "Colonel Andrews, sir, request permission to remove ignition panel and check wiring." Andrews barely suppressed a grin. When did an angry man not appear a fool.

The Colonel did not look away. He was far too fascinated. Who was this man standing over him? He felt for his personnel, he felt for Gray's dilemma, indeed he was in full sympathy with it. Unreasonable behavior was, after all, unreasonable. How great the yearning to explain, how deep the urge to stand up and take charge. He could just do it. He knew how, it was his job. Everyone respected him. Just stand up, remove that panel, shout at the men. His throat and tongue were so dry. Another coffee, perhaps. The pain, such pain around his heart. Yet how curious it is. This had never happened before. Taking charge had happened before, always. But not this. The next thing, what would the next thing be?

Captain Gray scanned the room for the one dependable person he knew would follow an order without getting a cup of coffee first. "Private Stephson, come over here please."

A young athletic blonde was before them in an instant. Captain Gray remarked once again, not without a certain wry envy (once again), the golden tan and honest blue eyes of this Southern California native. An unfair distribution of gifts had paired his alarmingly good looks with a perpetual competence in all tasks tedious and complex, which made his name many an officer's substitute for "hammer," "pliers," and most other implements of construction and repair. Yet over time some had noticed, Andrews especially, that Stephson's ingenuous nature competed with a constant internal distraction, the young man seemingly watching at all times for something no one else could see.

"Check the wiring, Stephson, and give us a status report as soon as possible."

"Yes, captain." The private looked at Robson for confirmation of Gray's order. He then looked at a few of his comrades, and then the Bang Board. Perhaps it was that red eye that persuaded him to grab his toolbox and crouch before the panel. He had the metal plate off in a wink, and his flashlight beam was soon probing the multi-colored wiring and gold and silver circuitry. Robson finally stood up, to get another coffee, but his movement set everyone in consonant motion back to their respective tasks, and one must always obey one's conscience, even when it contradicts what it just told you.

"How are we, Stephson?"

"It seems, colonel, that everything is secure, but I could try tweaking the main leads. Of course, sir," he turned about to look up at the Colonel, "if I did that it might give us instantaneous ignition."

"Then that is what will happen, private."

"Yes, sir." Stephson grabbed his pliers and reached under the board. Andrews, Gray, and a few others winced as the private gave a few short tugs. With each one they glanced at the red bulb, but it never wavered.

"What if we cut the power to the signal light itself?"

"I doubt it would help, colonel, but I could do it."

He did it. Cyclops went to sleep. There was a pause, the stillness between two breaths. But there was no tremor, no graph readings, nothing. Robson could hear the computers hum.

The Colonel asked to see printouts of all log reports up to a full half hour before the Wheel Lock Maneuver began. He and Gray consulted the original blueprints, and after an hour of study he took Gray aside. He wanted to know everyone's movements while he had taken his break up on the bunker. The Captain was taken aback, but it was an appropriate request. They went over everyone's duties, checked all comings and goings, and Captain Gray dictated all that he remembered of that fifteen or twenty minutes into a pocket recorder. Stephson and a few others did the same. Their testimonies formed part of the overall report, but it was evident that neither sabotage nor human error were to blame. In the meantime the entire team of physicists and engineers who had worked on construction or testing had all been roused from their beds, or ordered to fly in from wherever they were stationed at once. Faxes streamed out of numerous Washington offices, Colonel Andrews finally got General Morgan on the phone, and over his sixth or seventh coffee he summed up for him the dilemma they confronted.

"We have pulled the pin on a modern hand grenade, general, and hours later we're still holding our ears."

"That's a ridiculous thing to say, colonel. Has Stahlbergen arrived yet?"

"Yes, sir. But no, sir. He's mystified."

"Convene a meeting for 1600 hours."

The meeting provided a forum for elaborating in great detail on how incomprehensible the situation was. Engineer after engineer and staff member after staff member stood up and cogently explained how what was happening could not be happening. The General lost all patience somewhere into the second hour and swept several glasses and a water pitcher onto the floor. "Well, dammit, don't try figuring it out! Just make it work!"

Though many in the room were as uneasy about Morgan's explosions as they were about the one waiting to happen in the desert, engineering knowhow had to win the day. It started with the meteorological reports, which definitely ruled out another try for at least two weeks. Then came reports of unexpected Soviet satellite maneuvers, a reminder about the Vice President's speech before NATO next month, and then someone even had the temerity to say that soon it would be the Fourth of July. Morgan went purple.

"You can't... I'm sorry, sir... but, well, it is the Fourth, sir. The American people would object."

What topped off the absurdity of this remark was how true it was. Only the General's silent rage prevented it from bringing the house down. Andrews and Gray exchanged a smile for the first time in what seemed to Robson like years.

Private Jack Stephson managed to save the moment, but in so doing he started Robson Andrews on a long, long journey from which the Colonel never really returned. "I think, general, it becomes more a question of making sure it doesn't work. We had explored that possibility from the start..." He went on speaking for another few minutes before anyone registered the incongruity of that statement.

Then Stahlbergen stopped him with his usual imperious tone and asked what he meant by exploring not having it work from the start. Stephson stared at the aged Swiss scientist, with his long narrow face and perpetual grimace, which conveyed the contradiction of intellectual haughtiness coupled with a thin frail body that had no business taking military personnel to task. But as the professor had caught out the awkwardness of his words, Jack maintained his poise and did his best to step around the question with a summary of the last half hour of the countdown. He spelled out the procedures that the firing team had gone through, procedures he knew by rote, but when he came to that last two minutes he could not recite the steps because, well, it didn't happen that way, and he could not forget, and no one could, the Colonel at the microphone, and he and Gray squared off, and there he was sipping his coffee, but the circuits were fine and maybe bypassing Cyclops might have worked. "It should have worked." He paused, then hoped formality would save the day. "Sir. Professor. Gentlemen."

Honing the guillotine blade has a way of wresting certainty from the most unsolvable of dilemmas. Every hand holding pencil or pen or tumbler froze. Stahlbergen went into suspended animation. As impassive as the General appeared, a careful look into his grey eyes would have revealed a fervent desire for the roof to collapse. Again a silent bomb discharged, again the shards and fragments flew. After a few millennia, the orderly switched off the overhead projector and politely sat down, as if intuiting an entire change in the proceedings. Will the defendant please stand.

Colonel Andrews did not wait to be addressed. He broke the stillness with an acknowledgement of Private Stephson's report and a reminder that the testing grounds were still in serious danger. He underscored this point with his own rapid review of the ignition procedure and equipment status. All monitoring devices still, up to this very moment, registered live activity. No circuits were disabled – the power had not been cut to the warhead – and no Level One errors were being returned by the firing mechanism. That megaton monster was out there trembling to unleash its sunburst. Wild maddened horses tethered and barred, and banging at their prison gates.

"Why did you begin a close down, colonel?"

"Because, sir, it would be a surface blast. A mushroom cloud."

Preludes and postscripts to this bald statement would have been but window dressing, and no one would have been fooled. He watched his sentences float across the room like a display banner above a holiday shore, ends curling and the middle section of the strip – "surface blast" – bulging forward in the mild breeze. What confirmed for him the futility of all argument was that those two words still stubbornly refused to come out of anyone's mouth but his own.

After the banner was well out of sight the General put his papers together in a neat stack and commented that at least part of the mystery was solved. This met with murmurs, coughs, and raised hands from all corners. Captain Gray, as second in command, was allowed to speak first, and he asserted that no close down procedure had begun as the order was given too late, and he did not agree with it anyway. Three other officers on the firing team confirmed this. The General, and even Stahlbergen, who was now clearly in earnest about his own credibility, posited the theory that the order, even though not carried out, might have influenced the sequence of maneuvers. "One wrong button pressed is all it takes, captain," Morgan said. This met with more coughing and raising of hands, and someone voiced the common consensus that the entire sequence had already been charted in detail, going back well over thirty-five minutes before ignition. But Stahlbergen propped up the new party line by saying that they had gone over all the logs and listened to all testimony from the point of view of *firing* the weapon, not from the point of view of *not firing* the weapon. A miraculous coughing cure manifested itself, and all those healed let out a general moan. The water pitchers were refilled, the projector went back on, and all reports were reevaluated over the next two hours from the point of view of not firing the weapon. Professor Brandt, Stahlbergen's second, tried to inject some levity by saying that after all, it hasn't fired, but stone does not laugh.

Nothing was resolved that night or the next day. More personnel flew in from Washington and, much to General Morgan's annoyance, they were joined by officers of the French and British nuclear missions. The only saving grace in the whole affair, and it was truly a miracle, was that not a whisper appeared in the press. The U.N. ambassador parried a few Soviet insinuations with a speech about "prosperity versus slavery." Morgan's men deftly handled the entrances and exits of advisers to and from the base, and Whiting handled his colleagues on Capitol Hill. He remained the only politician to know of the disaster, and Colonel Andrews had to admire the way the congressman managed to keep his head on his shoulders.

Not so the officer in charge of Blast IN-417 in Tunnel Number 3. Stahlbergen pressed Morgan to begin court martial proceedings. It was fair, the scientist reasoned, and they had what amounted to a public confession during the debriefing. And there were witnesses. General Morgan balked at the idea for fear of the attention it would arouse in the nearby towns. Andrews was a respected public figure, there had been all those speeches of his in favor of appropriating the Monroe ranch, and because of Whiting the Colonel was even viewed as an anti-nuclear advocate. To court-martial him for undisclosed reasons would stir far too much controversy. Anyway, the people were not stupid, they would draw a clear enough outline of what was happening without needing to know the details, and then details, both speculative and absurd, would follow in torrents. So no, not a court martial. A promotion.

"To the wilderness, general?"

Morgan's logic in matters retaliatory persisted. "No, doctor. The front lines."

The morning Andrews was called into Morgan's office he had been working out a plan for defusing the device. With Jack Stephson's help he had devised a set of programs to be downloaded to the

EL TAJIN, NEW MEXICO

firing mechanism that would render inactive all code loops awaiting a detonation instruction. The Colonel was confident that once the warhead's computer was no longer polling for something to happen, then the power could be turned off and the device dismantled without much risk of a last minute software brainwave. Stephson, following the conclusions of Stahlbergen and Brandt during the briefings, had convinced Robson – though not anyone else – that cutting power without first stopping the software sequences could abruptly trigger the warhead, since it remained unclear how the firing mechanism would respond to an unorthodox power down.

Captain Gray passed out of Morgan's office just as Andrews was about to enter it. The Captain saluted but kept his eyes to the floor and did not return his Colonel's hello. Andrews watched him disappear down the corridor, and only much later would he know that this was the last time they would ever meet.

General Morgan had no doubt had his eardrums surgically removed. He took Andrews' document and placed it in the In-tray, but his gaze did not leave the man opposite him. He was brisk and authoritative, and all of the Colonel's pleas to consider the importance of a careful shutdown review were ignored. "Gray is in charge. He knows the game back to front. And we're not shutting down, we stay on yellow alert until the smoke clears," staring over the lip of a billowing volcano and waiting for sunny weather as Robson completed the image to himself. The only subject discussed was Colonel Andrews' promotion to head one of the ICBM stations in North Dakota. "We are engaging in a new joint effort with the Air Force, colonel. You'll have five silos under your command. Each one packed with a ramrod that could blow a hole in the moon. They only tolerate one hundred percent accuracy on launching procedures, colonel, if you know what I mean. One hundred per cent." The necessary training would take place in Virginia, but as Colonel Andrews was a top man this would need no more than a couple of months. Since the debriefing on Andrews' last assignment had already taken place, there was nothing further to go over. Gray knew the rest. The Colonel was to be ready to fly out at 0800 hours. Robson stood up to leave, but Morgan had one more thing to say.

"I can't get out of my mind, colonel, a picture of you opening a folding chair and sitting down while your men spun the Wheel."

"Neither can I, sir."

This could become a dangerous habit, Robson thought as he walked back to the office, stating the truth sans embellishment. Not a good idea either to use the truth as a weapon, but he had felt no wish to score points. It was just that that moment had not left his mind any more than it had the General's. A simple intentional action, a private decision taken. Was it a blessing or a curse? The price of that decision had revealed itself in private one-on-one opprobrium – he was going away, things were going to happen without him. Without him and to him. What could have been different? Only, he concluded, not attempting to act differently. But the ignition still would have failed, the mute acres of uninhabited desert, where barely a wisp of dust stirred in the brutal daylight, would still entomb dreadful lightning, in a moment blinding white chaos, all would shudder and melt…

These fears needed to stop. It was no longer his business. Anyway, it was only a stretch of cactus and scorpions. Who cares. Let the congressman and the General take the flak. His reputation was secure. He would actually leave the Silas Testing Grounds with an unblemished record and a modest public following. Who knows, maybe he would have lunch with Feldon in a congressional lounge some day and talk over "old times."

Still, these were the "old times," and despite his safe exit he felt the presence of unfinished business flitting about the shores of his future, just as he had fancied those midnight imps cavorting in the dark. There was unfinished business underground, there had been jarring discords in his partings from both Morgan and Gray, and his internal vow to "let be" had yet to see circumstances play themselves out into anything resembling finality. He was forced to conclude, au contraire, that maybe his departure was not the luck of riding one giddy wave to momentary safety, but rather the early hints of a reeling vortex that would pull him and those about him into a maelstrom of unimagined consequences.

Jack Stephson made some excuse to accompany him to the airstrip. The two men were silent as the small private jet rolled to a halt on the runway and the cabin door eased open and down, but the Colonel was so only because he could not find a way to express his gratitude. He looked over this earnest young man with his intelligent blue eyes, and was again intrigued by the way those eyes seemed to be watching not just his surroundings but the overlay of some invisible curiosity. Awkward formality ruled in the end, his hand went forward to take Jack's, they grasped and ungrasped, pulled back and started out again, then Robson snapped his hand to his cap brim for the final salute. He stepped up the stairs without looking back, and the hatch slammed to. The plane was aloft in minutes. He looked out over the golden plain dotted with clumps of brush and deadwood. Miles and miles of it. He squinted at the crystal blue sky and remembered his friends that predawn hour on the other side of daylight. To move, and to be moved.

Night came to the desert and no one will ever know if pairs of silent eyes were looking for a comrade atop a hardened concrete shell. And the land was silent, and some stars glow bluish and others are red.

EL TAJIN, NEW MEXICO

···· **2** ····

T HE NEXT day General Morgan wanted the flagpoles moved. A detail from the Action Room was put to the task, since only a core group was needed at this stage to "keep an eye on the beast" as he put it to Gray. The men in their boredom did not notice how wide a hole they were digging for the first pole and, before they could react, it came sailing down like a well-cut redwood and smashed through the roof of Major General Osbourne's new sports car and savaged three other vehicles. Both forward doors were ripped off the hinges of Osbourne's beauty, and the ball of the pole landed on the radiator of a visiting doctor's sedan, sending jets of water in every direction. The sudden bang of metal on metal had so startled Morgan back in his office that he dropped a mug of coffee in his lap, and the men, hearing distant howls of pain, believed for one horrible instant that some innocent civilian had been snoozing in one of the victimized vehicles. The ensuing mayhem saw two privates trip over the pole, one fracturing a wrist, and a nurse stumble headfirst into the hole and emerge all mud and sorrow. Osbourne bellowed like a bull elephant for what seemed like an hour while a backhoe arrived and dragged the pole away, in the process smashing two other windshields. The Action Room boys were sent back to their underground cell, the flagpole was tucked away in a hangar, and the hole stayed a hole.

Experiments in human resources were set aside in favor of status quo maintenance. Morgan did eventually look over Andrews' and Stephson's report, and passed it on to Stahlbergen for comment. The latter, as scientist and architect of this canker in the earth, would not hear of any shutdown procedure, though he did acknowledge that in the event of a "change in strategy," these recommendations for a software solution were "reasonable and sound." To Morgan's frank question about the risk of the bomb going off at any moment, Stahlbergen replied that it was "far higher than a yellow. We'd have to call it a red alert, because we just don't know what's going on under there," and it was too risky to send anyone in to find out. The General, not fully satisfied, sent back another memo wanting to know if "reasonable and sound" meant that a physical disconnect might trigger the thing if nothing else did. Stahlbergen wrote back a one-word answer and the paper shredders hummed alongside the coffee makers. By some unstated consensus a plan was devised whereby an undated confidential memo was prepared in electronic form and planted on the computers of a few unwitting personnel stating all the particulars of the test. The blast area would be kept on high alert and clear of all wildlife, trespassers, and flight paths. If the bomb went off, the date and time would be inserted in the memo, a general wringing of hands would accompany the fervent apologies that this memo had not been more widely circulated, but secrecy was essential, and so on and so on, and hopefully off. An official date for the blast was set for the end of autumn after Whiting's re-election, and the General assured the Silas brass that the diplomatic corps were clearing the air of "opposition to a possible test," a turn of phrase that evidently caused not a ripple, ironical or otherwise, since the public memorandum that went around with details of the new plan bore the heading Operation Light of Heaven.

Feldon Whiting, though, had little time to spare on further back room camouflage. Without warning his campaign was in jeopardy. His opponent, Dresden P. Pondhurst, had managed to elbow his way into the political center with a series of speeches in front of supermarkets. It was basically one speech, which came to be known as the "Supermarket Manifesto," that declared that the people's land was not lined up on so many shelves with bargain basement price tags on display for the government's shopping pleasure. Stamping his foot on the asphalt, Pondhurst would proclaim in his shrill alto, "Where's the sticker on this parcel? Show it to me!" The crowds would laugh in simple merriment, and Whiting had laughed at the absurdity of it all. His dismissive response to these histrionics was a poster campaign with a picture of himself with clenched fist alongside the caption, "We'll Bomb Dresden – Again!" Pondhurst responded with television ads showing black-and-white film clips of his urban namesake in flames from '44 and a deadpan voiceover totting up statistics on people killed, square miles destroyed, and the carpet bomb equivalent in nuclear warheads. Amid a skyline of smoking hulks the rhetorical "Again?" materialized in ghostly letters. The nonsense worked, partly because it provoked nonsense from Whiting's camp. And Pondhurst had plenty of Jackson Monroe dollars behind him. The rancher took to the stump with his "true confession" saga of Pentagon arm-twisting. Whiting argued ferociously that Mr. Monroe wanted the money and was only too glad to part with his "rattlesnake turf." This colorful phrase now passed well out of a general's private office and onto billboards all over the district. "This is what your congressman thinks of your land," and more and more of the like. Monroe and Pondhurst further countered with an exposé of the tax legislation that Congressman Bluebeard had proposed "to pillage and pilfer your profits." Here Whiting was most vulnerable, and he appealed to the Governor for extra support. This request, however, was side-stepped with a slickness that impressed even the hapless congressman. A letter over the governor's seal was published on page 3 of all the major dailies declaring that the ebb and flow of federal and state property depended on the tide of the people's will, and that the people should always let their voice in congress know which way the waters churned, while they should also acknowledge that an ocean was an ocean and land was land. And, oh yes, the legislation would be reviewed in the new year. Whiting was forced to agree with the idea of a review, further dwindling his credibility, while the opposition seized the momentum to publish their own "shopping list," which included not only Jackson Monroe's moiety and Brandonville's "true home," but several square miles of turf that was currently occupied by a few snakes of the button-pushing variety. The Governor's one speech on Whiting's behalf tried to portray him as the new compromiser, with his finger constantly on the community pulse. "To see if it's stopped yet!" one heckler shouted back, setting the crowd aroar. As the weeks passed and his desperation mounted, Whiting felt his only chance was for Colonel Robson Andrews to join him on an eleventh hour swing through the entire district, the two anti-nuclear comrades setting their agenda for a clear and peaceful future for the Land of Enchantment. General Morgan at first refused to say how and where Andrews could be contacted, as he was on a top-secret assignment. "Anyway, Feldon," Morgan said, "if the next try at this succeeds without another hiccup, I want to push for an enlargement of our program. Lots of money could come this way, Feldon, lots and lots." A tacit agreement to this proposition was Morgan's price for allowing Whiting to send Colonel Andrews a fax. As he himself fed the sheets into the machine that evening, the congressman reflected on that time bomb in the desert and wondered whether failure would be such a humiliation after all.

The Colonel faxed back a reply during the night declining to participate. In a single terse page he said he was too busy, but wished Whiting all the best. The congressman's campaign strategists plotted out the town-by-town assault nonetheless, and his writers peppered his speeches with excerpts from the Colonel's arguments in favor of ceding land to the testing grounds while at the same time continuously making the transition from military to commercial nuclear technologies. There were also passages reminding the constituency of those days not long gone when Feldon Whiting and Robson Andrews showed how the people's will extended even into the corridors of power in Washington. "I assume he is with us in spirit," his head speechwriter told him.

The "non-foreboding" of his wife Ethel's musings remained a lasting taste about his heart, not unlike the charm of music that still delights long after the notes have faded. That final afternoon they spent together before he set off on his last campaign she had stepped away from her drawing table and wrapped a towel around her otherwise unadorned body, and lifted a single rose to his lips and nostrils.

"You see how full and strong it is, darling," she said as she took it away. "Such has been your political role, and as such that role has absorbed, encharmed your constituents. But now, breathe again. What fragrance there?" She tilted her head as she held it up to him a second time, and swayed gently in place. He inhaled and sighed, the taste of the rose not half so delicious as the sweet allure of her light brown hair resting carelessly on her bare shoulders, and her clear brown eyes smiling up at him as lovingly as her soft pink lips.

He was used to her ways and responded in kind. "There are two kinds of nothing, my love. What I no longer feel, and what I may yet embrace."

"Why embrace anyone but me," she said. "Life has taken enough of you. And 'nothing' is as unreliable as it is reliable. And you know, I still want a child – I am yet ripe enough, and you, my not so senior husband, are yet not so old." And so he did embrace her warm and delightful body, and over her shoulder he gazed back at the recent past and dreaded what that past had delivered over into his present life. For, no, he was not yet so old and she was yet so young, and he did too want that child, that unknown person who would hopefully one day run delightful havoc over their leisure and their duties.

The campaign blur that followed left him a mere handful of memories. There was the continual placing of something in his hand, a phone, a pen, a flower, a cup, a microphone (especially the one that did not work because he was not so told until his speech was over and the crowd, attentive throughout, roared and clapped anyway), hamburgers, cake (far too much), and hands, especially the one, and only helpful one, offered to him by Thomson, his campaign manager, when he stumbled on a stairwell. All the other hands at all the other events extended themselves in oblique rows like open sunflowers that he pressed and pressed as he tightly held up the corners of his mouth. Where were the eyes, the faces of those hands? He could not recall a single one. He did remember a little girl at one of his "save the jobs" speeches out there in the crowd, staring into her mother's hair, fascinated no doubt with its black gloss, the minutiae of strands, how she could bury her little face in it. Her mother never flinched or scolded, which so absorbed Feldon that he said "Hair" in the middle of his tax cutting proposals.

The blur slowed to a frieze the day General Morgan joined him on the platform. It was the final, and largest, gathering of his campaign, and Feldon's heart swelled with hope as in the distance he watched more and more cars arrive. So many individual shirts, thermoses, banners could he see in this expanding pool, magnified in high relief in the clear dry sunlight. Despite its size there was but the merest rustle of talk, like winds shivering the sagebrush.

At a certain point Feldon leaned over to ask Thomson to choose the right moment for Morgan's introduction, and he could feel eyes and ears, and more eyes, upon him, Argus after breakfast, every lid agape and wondering. The stillness unsettled the campaign manager a little. He looked at his watch, looked out over the rolling waves of silence heading his way, looked at his watch again, and decided to wait until eleven sharp. He could not. Seven minutes to the hour, why wait seven more, he stood up and said ladies and gentlemen it is a great honor for me to introduce General Paul "Big" Morgan of the Silas Testing Grounds.

Morgan stood up, tapped the microphone once to test the pickup, arranged his speech on the stand, cleared his throat away from the microphone, moved close to it and began, "Ladies and gentlemen," and only then realized that something was well amiss. He was too uneasy to stop speaking, but he tried formulating what step had been omitted as he charted the brief history of the atomic age, which saw its travail and miraculous birth take place right in this very state, "the blessed Trinity." Then he realized what it was. He had expected to come to the podium and spread out his sheets and prepare his voice amid a roar of applause, and his fussing about and non-acknowledgement of it were intended to heighten, by subtle counterpoint, the no-nonsense demeanor of a man who understood what perils hung in the balance and what vigilant overview was required to weigh present burdens against future wishes, but it did not work for there had been no applause at all. He went through to the end without stopping, as nothing and no one stopped him. His voice rose and fell with the prearranged cadences, he rose mightily on a crescendo of daring to trust in a nuclear-free world and glided down on a solemn and serious coda that began, "Life, a breath we take everywhere with us, a swell and fall that we never do without...". He did not write and did not quite understand "swell and fall," so what came after "do without" seemed to him an airless muddle, and he finished without knowing what he said.

It was like shouting himself awake in the middle of the night. Nothing answered. He heard a dozen clapping hands behind him. The midnight hush of walls and drapery that the crowd before him resembled were still and mute. He looked at his pages and wondered if Thomson or someone had put swear words in it. He went and sat down. Whiting waved off an introduction and went straight to the microphone with his text. "Fellow members of this great state, of this greatest of nations, of this glorious land. Whenever I behold a crowd of free Americans, as I do now, I cannot help but think of," so far his team's invention, but Feldon scanned ahead over the bombast and further anecdotes concerning a certain colonel and decided that he had belched enough platitudes for one lifetime, so looking away from the script and squinting at the face here and clothing there of person after person he did not know and never would know, "the multitude of stars in the heavens. You've seen them, I'm sure, on black cloudless nights. We've got plenty of them. Shining way up there. Well, I'm not a poet, nor a scientist, but I'll tell you this, I can't quite fathom how they could be so many million miles away. Light years they call it. Meaning you'll be dead and buried and born again twelve times over before you get there. But they don't seem so far away, really. They're like our friends, always there, and they make these great patterns, people, animals, gods. Maybe things are only as far away as we imagine they are. Take you, for instance, and me. I don't know any of you personally, maybe I never will. All the same, you could tell me, right here and now, what you think, what you wish for, what you feel. Feel. You thought you'd listen to a couple of speeches, already thought out, the usual bows and scrapes, but instead I want you to tell me what you expect from me over the next two years. Or just tell me your name. Hey, sometimes that's enough. You there, sir, I'm Feldon Whiting."

"I know."

It was dubbed political suicide, but Feldon, despite begrudging monosyllables from the four people who bothered to speak back to him, trembled that afternoon with a giddy new delight. What a different world stood on the other side of convention. The elastic rise in his head, his heart, the moment when a cluster of impassive onlookers near the edge spluttered in spite of themselves at his jokes (and Morgan too!), the taste of the air, an ugly building he noticed for the first time and pointed out to everyone, "We'll tow that thing to the testing grounds for target practice." Of course, that evening when he drank in those memories along with bright washes of champagne while sitting on the bed of his motel room, he had to acknowledge that next morning he would be target practice for the columnists. Along with a careful scrutiny of his faux pas, and an interview with the architect of his clay pigeon, they would no doubt pillory him with the firmest of manacles: his own words. He had foregone promises, and parry and thrust with Pondhurst's allegations, for a simple appeal. It was the iron wall of unresponse that had prompted him to it, and all his efforts to move the crowd had moved only himself. So what. Despite the silliness of his words, this was his personal satisfaction to savor, but there would be no proof of it in the press. He would read about "pedestrian trivia" and "desperation one-liners," and no hue of wafted colors from an unseen spectrum would glow from the black and white.

There had certainly been no aureole emanating from the crowd. Masses turned and shuffled off while he spoke. Thud after thud of car door and whir of starting engine spread open a vacancy in his heart that was then filled and reignited as each of his inspired improvisations was answered by the sound of another set of tires on crunching gravel disappearing into the distance like the hiss of sea foam. One of the last things he had said, and perhaps the microphone was not working for no one that was still around seemed to hear it, "I guess moments when you understand something new get coupled, maybe against our will, with being humiliated, feeling that way."

"But was there any understanding?" He jumped up and shouted into the darkness of the room. He stared at the telephone. Who would he call? "It was absurd, what I said," came out loud. This was necessary, to voice the antithesis. He was really persuaded to this thought by the silence of his peers after they all left the platform. He shook the last drop from the champagne bottle into his glass and quaffed the remains, while calling up further memories of the day. The silent ride back to campaign headquarters with Thomson, the General's polite nod of the head and shrug of the shoulders to Captain Gray when he thought Whiting was not looking, the downward look of most of his staff, as though searching in unison for a paper clip among the leaflets, or was it a swizzle stick among the coffee cups. Damn people's reticence. The silence of his colleagues was far worse than that of the crowd. And what did all and sundry expect? If they expected nothing, why come at all? And if he had not said the right thing – then what was the right thing? What did he not say?

To fall asleep amid a hail of questions. Now there was an achievement.

Whiting was trounced, and Andrews sued. His lawyer's letter arrived the day after the election results. "Self-interest is punctual, Feldon," Thomson said. The now former congressman's concession speech spoke of "reassessing the past in order to reassess the future," since it matters not "how deeply we bury a mistake if we spend all our latter days tramping down the earth on top of it." A reporter asked him what he meant by this, and Feldon's "we all need to find this out, sir, but in this case I hope you never do," was italicized in a leading article, and the sharpshooters went to work again. Pondhurst's victory party had been held at Jackson Monroe's ranch, and that evening the two men had begun to map out a strategy for readjusting borders that, as far as they were concerned, existed on paper only. Over the next week Whiting, the speechwriters, and his lawyer drafted a long refutation of Andrews' allegations. Feldon was flush with energy over this exercise, as he felt the old wiliness and one-step-ahead calculating return to him in force. "One last battle, one last back room brawl won – and decisively," he said to Thomson. He decided – and told Ethel so – that there would be no vacation until Andrews was beaten. As he anticipated the letters that would fly forth and back, he realized that here was where his talent truly lay. He was not a leader, he did not like public speaking anyway, it was rather the quiet corner, with writing pads and water tumblers, the rapid conversations in the corridor as he hustled from meeting to meeting, the phone calls, faxes, and follow up phone calls, this is what he knew and what he was. He moved hundreds of people in his own way as surely and effectively as General Morgan's vein-popping tirades ever had. There was no need for him to consider a different future. He was his future, he could do as he had done. And he defied convention by knowing it thoroughly and mastering handshake and sidelong glance and agreements unagreed.

The one moment arrived, however, in Feldon Whiting's life when he did not think through the ramifications of a decision, either then or at any time thereafter. His secretary placed the final draft of the six-page reply to Robson Andrews on his desk at nine-thirty a.m. He remembered that she wore a dark blue skirt. "How well it suits her," he thought. At one in the afternoon a sealed envelope went off to the Colonel at an address in Washington D.C. The envelope contained a check for the amount of money specified by Andrews to avoid litigation, folded into a one-sentence letter that read, "Why didn't you speak to me?" The six-page draft was dropped unread into a hallway waste bin.

In the weeks that followed General Morgan became a very quiet man. At first it was mere sullenness. He hated making speeches, and he knew Whiting was going to lose. If somehow that day had saved the congressman, or at least made his loss a respectable one, the General had hoped for a fair share of the credit and, nurtured so secretly that he barely felt it himself, had prepared to bring forth into the world the newest of his psychological brood: Paul Morgan, Politician. But that young personage was killed in its cradle, buried deep beneath folds of withering spite and bland irony. Still, his hard feelings could not prevent him from marveling at the curious anomaly of that moment at the podium. All of his previous speeches had been to obedient rows of scrubbed cadets, or attentive rows of wiry troops, or modest groupings of the maimed. Never a shout, no clapping, not a murmur, and certainly not an en masse search for the nearest exit. The silence of those immobile faces always satisfied him as his words boomed forth around the auditorium or out into the fresh breezes. Yet this time he expected noise, he wanted it, cheering, laughter, an eager phrase shouted out here and there for him to take in and respond to. Isn't this what politicians did? That crowd had been as silent as his brigades, but it was a silence without respect, without regard for who he was. They did not know who he was. What could they notice squinting in the sun, getting drunk, chasing after the kids? And they certainly didn't hear much of anything, or the clapping would have drowned out even his vocal authority.

These and similar ruminations had come in fits and flashes as the days hurtled by. The sameness of routine had become a renewed solace, as it had when his beloved Kate passed away nearly a decade ago, his companion for life and the only woman he had ever known. This time around, instead of a regimen of quiet walks and quieter fishing, he would barrel down the corridor and into his office, never sure if anyone had been there for the salutes he returned. Coffee and newspapers followed, then reports, dictation, lunch, and tours around the grounds. His silence had everyone hopping, though it took him a while to notice this. He had wanted not to think and not to feel, a rigid stare anchored this intention, which only let up when his dentist observed that he was grinding his teeth. He liked the afternoon tours best of all, to draw in the dry air and stare long and long at the distant hills. So as to conceal this quiet pleasure from his aides, he would often have them make calls from a satellite phone while he stared and stared. Perhaps he had hoped his mind would drain into clear, crimped lines like those etched into the brown ridges against the flame-blue sky. Perhaps he hoped that nothing more would happen to him, that he would wake up each morning and plow through his tedium to reach these few precious hours, and then return to his end-of-day briefings pervaded by a warm silence that kept at bay the annoying habits of his staff, like Gray chewing his lips, and the ponderous ache, concerning that other ache in the northern desert, that yet refused to part from his breast.

That last feeling was the difficult one, and the General did not like to pursue it. "Until things happen they haven't happened," was all he would allow his mind to utter. He was eventually forced to, however, through a sequence of curious events, some with massive repercussions and others of significance to himself alone.

"Something else happened," his secretary Miriam said to him one morning in her pleasant artless accent, as she tried to explain why there was no coffee. She was still wary of his rages, though the volcano had been dormant for some time, and she was helpless just now to defend her neglect. Morgan looked at his diminutive Hispanic assistant of many years, and for the first time noticed strands of grey in her long black hair. A wave of guilt washed away his anxieties as he noticed the nervousness in her dark eyes, and realized that above all else he needed her tender attentions and easy confidence more than he needed a hot drink. He waved her off with a smile and told her to take the day off. He then went straight to the canteen, and over his second cup her words helped him formulate what was going on. Something else was indeed happening to him other than the numbing ambivalence he had wished for. He had the lieutenant bring the jeep around an hour early and had him drive far out into the desert. To think, and think again.

He realized that instead of devolving into a rock, his afternoons in the desert had set his inner world burgeoning with sparks, glimpses, and eventually long meandering panoramas of his many rallyings of the troops and pounding of conference tables; but they always ended with a return to that moment before the void of that crowd, upon which had depended both Congressman Whiting's and his own political hopes. The ranks and clusters of censors in shirtsleeves, staring at him, staring. Just staring? Or waiting? What had they been waiting for? Sometimes the bitterness of it all made his eyes wet, and the bowels of the volcano would rumble and spew up an angry hail of ordnances and overtime. And sometimes, and gradually more often, the one perception he refused to confront refused to let him alone: they would have surely applauded if they had listened to what he was saying, but they never did.

"And they never do. Never."

"Sir?"

"Nobody ever pays attention to anybody else. Have you ever noticed that, lieutenant?"

"No, sir. Yes, sir."

"What do you think about that?"

"I don't know, sir. I guess everybody's too busy." After a pause he added, "I must confess, general, I did not hear what you said before."

"Before what?"

"Before you said, 'they never do'."

"Well, it's all right, lieutenant. You were on the phone. Let's turn around now."

That day mattered a great deal to General Morgan. It was, in fact, the first time he had ever accepted that an idea could be a defining moment in his life. As the jeep headed back to the barracks, he made a decision. His silence would continue, he would connect the dots of tomorrow's routine the same way he did today's, and color it again in grey until he snored off. But from now on he was going to enjoy the slumber party. No more the ranting fool who railed against communism and roused his legions to wrap their fingers around trigger and pin and button. The legions were all the same person, and that person was permanently out to lunch. This decision came coupled with a growing awareness of the way his taciturnity sent the aides and orderlies scampering. How curious, to watch them react to an imaginary "Big" Morgan, who glowered at their inattentiveness and threatened court martial if a door was opened a trifle late or a salute was returned without the proper crispness. Not only did they not listen to his words, they did not even see him! He decided to indulge a fiendish amusement. The morning after his "realization" in the jeep he sauntered coffee cup in hand over to the officers of the Information Center. After a brief wander around the complex, he sidled up to desk after desk and stared. Sure enough, at each of his stops he received a stream of explanations from the occupant of the desk as to what he or she was doing and why. A grim nod of the head or a quick smile was deftly returned, and so on to the next bedchamber. Major O'Connell, the officer in charge of the Information Center, soon appeared (as Morgan knew he would once word got around), all thin-haired, hundred-sixty pounds and thick bifocals of him, and accosted the General in the corridor.

"Yes, sir, we'll have a new imprint of full-color maps of our grounds for the civilian community ready to go in a couple of days."

"Very good, major."

"The timing's perfect since Mr. Monroe's making noise again."

"The man's a fool."

"Shall I send him one directly?"

"Of course, and our new congressman, too."

"And would you like to review our tourist brochure?"

Morgan gave another nod and walked off. So little to do, really, as, wherever he went, the cogs and pulleys of industriousness clanked ahead. A little oil, a little encouragement, what more was needed? What, indeed, was there to do all day long, once you realized the wheels turned all by themselves? Something did nag at him a bit as he walked back to his office, and just before he rose again from his desk to head for the cafeteria, it came to him.

He reached for the phone. "Miriam, when is my next scheduled visit to the Action Room?"

"Friday afternoon, general."

"I'll go down today, after lunch. Tell Captain Gray."

For some time after the election Whiting had made a nuisance of himself, calling on the phone and stopping by to demand assurances about "the bomb." "What about the bomb?" he would say. "What about it, Feldon? It's going to go off. It'll roar like a vengeful tornado, and the world will tremble. It'll flood the midnight sky, light up like a furious miniature sun in the lonely desert, eclipsing that Pale Moon jumble of hills right out of existence. The sun always beats the moon. You've got to assert yourself, Feldon. Authority is what matters." Whiting had continued to mutter about "unnecessary rages" and "nobody could control such an event," to the point where Morgan barred his entry to the base and refused to answer his calls. It was risky to appear short with him, since Whiting was privy to a secret that silenced even the White House. The General well knew the man's powers of manipulation, but reasoned that the trail of serpent skins he had left behind on Capitol Hill would not endear him to investigative committees, many of which would have gladly dug their claws into the ex-congressman's own hide. Whiting had lost, and losers are not believed; a month later Morgan learned that he had moved to New England, and someone quoted him as saying that he wanted to know what snow was. In the interim the rescheduled date for the blast came and went without anything taking place. So another date was set. Ahh, the future... No one knew how to tell Pondhurst about the whole thing, or even if they should. Washington was curiously silent, and Morgan sometimes imagined them all under their desks fingers in ears and eyes shut tight. But he was not going to make the first move. True, very few knew of the plan for playing Pontius Pilate to this inferno in the sky; so then, he concluded, why should I make noise when someone else, at much further remove and therefore more knowledgeable, could come to us and offer a new proposal. He and his men were playing their part. They watched. The ogre slumbered with his red eye open, and when he awoke – and he could only awake –

There were other things to think about. But he wanted to give the Action Room the same treatment as the Info Center people.

Captain Gray greeted him on the surface. "General Morgan, sir, are you coming on Friday as well?"

"A question like that is usually asked at the end of a visit, captain."

"Yes, sir. Our routine would be in better shape at that time. I would want you to see."

"Routines do not change, captain. That is why they are called routines."

"We've done some probing, general, which required changes in procedure. No, not changes. Additions, additions to procedures."

"Probing what?"

"The firing mechanism came alive, sir. A request to initialize appeared out of the blue on the Bang Board."

"Someone fooling around perhaps."

"Negative, general. We've checked all the logs, all personnel gave us reports –"

"Yes, captain, I know about logs and personnel reports."

"We theorize, sir, that a polling loop somehow came to the end of its sequence at last. Took it near on ten months, after we first sent it out the morning the test was supposed to succeed, to go through every sub-routine and decide to let us know it was ready. Imagine –"

"Plain English, captain. Computers are not my domain. And captain, you're going to bite your lip off if you keep chewing it like that."

"Sir, the problem is, sir, that if it took the software this long to respond to the first stage of the firing request, and since last spring it was sent all requests and clearances in proper sequence, including Ignition, then –"

"How many stages are there?"

"Eleven, sir. But we cannot be sure that each one will take as many months to clear. It might all happen right away."

"Sabotage?"

"Impossible, sir. As you know, it's a closed circuit operation. We're not linked to the outside world."

"The world is lucky. You were intending, I presume, to inform me of this."

"I wanted to be sure that there was a problem, sir. Didn't want a false alarm. I was just not satisfied that there is indeed a problem when you called. Coincidences do happen, I suppose, sir."

The General had grown feverish about the neck and ears during this exchange. He became aware that he was still holding his coffee cup and flung it against the concrete wall. He only became aware a fraction too late that it was half full, and its contents splattered him and everywhere.

"Oh damn! Never mind! Show me all this!"

Down they hurried through dim corridors and low ceilings, and then the long elevator descent. The Action Room hummed with its usual efficiency. Banks of computers blinked and clicked as was their wont, operators surveyed rolls of paper and stared at lines of equations on green and blue monitors, the occasional sandwich wrapper and soda can betraying a mild untidiness, and long hours at the terminals. There was only the slightest studied murmur among the men and women as Morgan entered, but the keyboards rattled a little louder. And the General knew that behind the efficient lighting and rows of cabinets, behind the chilly conditioned air and shiny linoleum, behind the neat stacks of perforated paper and plastic sacks of shredded confetti, lingered chaos and murk, and all the moles bumped their noses in the dark.

"I want everyone in this room at attention! Now!"

He had expected a docile row of alert faces to materialize before him. Instead everyone froze in place, gradually getting up out of their chairs or putting down pen and paper but not otherwise moving from where they were. Morgan swiveled on Captain Gray and for an instant his left arm flickered as though he would knock the man's head off. Instead he cleared his throat in loud snorts, and the Captain called on everyone to come forward.

Gray asked everyone with a share of responsibility for the device to brief the General on what they knew about the unexpected firing request. Morgan remained outwardly composed, though toward the end of the briefing his face took on a cast of purple when it became clear that behind all the computer talk they told him no more than what the Captain already had. Gray did not help matters by frequently interrupting his subordinates and telling them to speak more clearly. And while they spoke he still chewed his lip.

A red alert was initiated, and a team was assigned to simulate the entire firing sequence on another computer. While thus occupied Morgan would convene a meeting in the coming weeks with Stahlbergen and the other engineers. It was all given top secret priority, and no one outside the Action Room was to hear of this development except from the General himself. As a precautionary measure the lieutenant who drove Morgan's jeep had to stay below, and the unfortunate fellow was handed a mop and a broom and directed to a labyrinth of corridors.

The first person General Morgan called was Colonel Andrews. He wanted the Colonel to come down to the testing grounds, but tried to persuade him to it without telling him why. The Colonel, unaware of all the goings on after he left New Mexico, suspected that the bomb had not been dismantled and now assumed that a new blast date was set, and Morgan either wanted to put him in charge again or was even considering promoting him to the General's own job so that the old warrior could retire to his marlin fishing before the desert sands gave birth to sunlight. Andrews declined, and Morgan almost broke the phone receiver as he knew there was nothing he could do.

Colonel Andrews had been wrong. The General was going to ask him to come clean with the public and Congress about the whole affair. He began to feel there was going to be no way out of this but through the bog and briars of a frank exposé. He was prepared to grant the Colonel anything he wanted in exchange for making the first announcement, giving the required interviews, and appearing before whatever tribunal the Senatorial Inquisition came up with. Morgan would be there with him, but after his last failure at public speaking he no longer trusted his own artlessness. Neither did he trust his temper, which left privates dry in the mouth but made all species of pundit gloat with ominous delight as they circled overhead. He would not have involved Whiting, since the man was bound to be overly clever, and in the end would probably apply more creative engineering than Stahlbergen's gang to fashioning a tale that cleared him absolutely and labeled the testing grounds a den of vipers. No use gambling that Whiting would drown in his own artifice. Such people were always victorious. Honesty could only lose.

What was he to do? He wandered to the window and lowered the blind. Between the slats he gazed at the black tarmac oozing liquid heat waves, fence and signpost dancing under a hard unrelenting clarity. A private passed by walking his girlfriend to the parking lot, his arm around her waist. The man was supposed to be on duty, the woman had no right to be there. Here was something he could control…

If the meeting with the core team yielded no solution, he would have to go to North Dakota and plead. His revelation still held sway with him – that sleepwalking prevailed wheresoever he looked – but thrashing the minions awake would only make them turn on him. There was, in any case, much that he himself never paid attention to, wasn't there? And did he care? Would those in Washington believe him when he picked through the knots of decision and accident that led to this absurdity? They would not. They would send a few congressmen down to investigate, the journalists would follow them, and the TV people them. The web would spin thick and fast, every thread yanked at would bind up the truth in further speculation and acrimony. Yet maybe that was just as well. If all the encrustations were scraped clean and the bare truth addressed, then to where would all the frightened minnows scurry? Much better, he concluded, to live in a Tower of Babel. So, Alexander, resheathe thy blade and hie thee by the Gordian knot.

The private passed by his window again. He rushed to the intercom. "Miriam, I see Private Spooner returning to Surveillance. Could you catch up with him and send him to me?"

Private Spooner blinked a lot, which made him appear nervous on first appraisal. His head rested on an unusually long neck, and he had a funny habit of holding that head tilted slightly upwards, as though he was constantly looking just over you. He was tall and gangly, with thin arms and legs but disproportionately large hands and feet, which made him appear self-consciously awkward, on second appraisal. But a few appraisals further on and one began to notice that behind the incidental twitching and clumsy movements lurked a profoundly defiant attitude, of which the General was aware and which intrigued him no end. He stepped around from behind his desk and faced Spooner as he entered.

"Remain at attention, private, I have only one thing to ask you. Did you know that we were readying a new device?"

"Is that what all the movement was about last spring, sir?"

"I could probably guess at your answer from what you just said, private, but perhaps you could save me a little energy."

"No, sir, I did not know."

"In your opinion no one else in your unit knows of this?"

"I don't think so, sir. Though the women sometimes perceive things."

"Meaning what?"

"Well, I mean, sir, they all admired Colonel Andrews."

"I see." Morgan paused a moment and stared at him, not knowing whether to take this remark as a poke at his authority. Then he stepped up quite close to the young man's agitated countenance, such that they were almost nose to nose. "What if I told you, private, that this test was going to be a surface blast. A mushroom cloud."

Spooner stopped blinking. He gave the General a shrewd look. "Why, sir?"

"Why am I telling you this, or why a surface blast?"

"Both, sir, since you mention it."

The General after all liked this fellow. He paused a few moments before replying. "The answer in both cases, private, is, I don't know."

A shade of a smile appeared on Spooner's face, and Morgan saw the man's eyes searching for permission to show it.

"You may go now, private. But keep this to yourself."

"Yes, sir."

"Or you will be shot."

"Yes, sir."

He turned around and made for the door, but the General stopped him. "What is your friend's name?"

"Caroline, sir." Their eyes met, and the private understood.

The General waited until Spooner passed by the window again, then he called Stahlbergen. He wanted the meeting moved forward to next week, and he wanted the venue changed. There were to be no recording devices, not even pen and paper. General Morgan wanted to talk, and General Morgan wanted everyone else to do nothing but listen to him. He did not want statistics, and he did not want to read any more reports or meeting minutes.

"That's it," he said out loud after he hung up, "we turn the damn thing off."

The locals called them "the streaks." Most people who now lived and worked in that part of the state assumed that the phenomenon was no more than a decade or two old, but Captain Gray, a local boy, claimed he saw it several times in his childhood and adolescence, and was told by his elders that its appearance was said to have been made manifest since time forgotten, even predating the Indian migrations. The simplicity of the name fostered an atmosphere of intimacy with the strange presence, as though it were another rock on the land-scape. No one could recall the first time it was spoken of in public or written about in the science periodicals, and no one ever claimed credit for its naming. Inexactitudes were understandable, since in the given moment an observer, especially a novice, might assume the streaks were but a mental projection, or a purely subjective trick of the eyes, like seeing spots after staring at a light bulb. What mainly dispelled doubts about these visions was not everyone's agreement that they were there, but rather the lingering spell of their beauty. When you saw, experienced rather, the streaks, you above all wanted them to be there. Others having experienced them deepened the mystery but did not confirm it. Confirmation was not needed, not even wished. There was, in fact, something isolating about this communal event, whereby everyone had their own private moments with the manifestation, but since everyone had them, everyone understood each other's private moment.

The streaks were both a natural and a personal phenomenon. In Nature, they appeared as pale bands of translucent purple high in a cloudless sky. The bands were thicker than jet streams and stretched from horizon to horizon. One usually counted about a dozen of them at any one time. They only appeared at twilight, and therein lay their magic – while they persisted, twilight persisted. Time would seem to stand still for an hour, or even up to two or three hours, with a truant sun refusing to dip below the horizon. At such times a tranquil film infused the air, violet and amber highlights seemed to aureate both plant and beast, men and women moved through an atmosphere not so much of half-light as supplemental light, a mellow ether almost tactile in the way it charged the senses, touch more keen, sight more sure, even one's feelings both sexual and emotional fuller and untrammeled.

Such sensuous enchantments were not felt as drug or hypnosis – effect and cause knew naught of each other. What was known, with sudden and inarguable immediacy, was oneself. When the streaks appeared, you in the same light-pulse appeared – you were suddenly inside and outside yourself, your thoughts, eyelashes, hands and fingers, smiles and anecdotes, as curiously alien and familiar as pinkish cloud swells forming into figures that dispersed in their very recognition. Tourists and jaded sceptics could deny what was happening, not see nor succumb to what enwrapped them, popped them into momentary dazzle before the innocuous. But lack of denial, a simple inner ease that inhaled this nuanced illumination of beholder and beheld, was the silent secret portal any person could peer into for as many minutes or seconds as circumstance and one's own attentiveness permitted.

And a curious psychology left its impress. For while these heightened moments kept people more in touch with, more satisfied with whatever was before or around them, the eventual departure of the phenomenon into dusk and night took the memories with it. The bright desert mornings seemed dull by comparison – but comparison to what? Both local citizens and military personnel felt it as vacancy only. Something beautiful had appeared, and then the beauty was gone. What remained was what remained, and it was everyday life. The experiences and understandings that people had during the streaks were not completely effaced, but their traces were ephemeral enough that any reminiscence about a meal shared or walk in the park while they were occurring made one feel as though one were recounting a dream, but a dream in which all parties concerned had mutually partaken in another place, another time. And then, for some, finding one's way back to that place and time became the concern of all their waking life.

The streaks had taken somewhat of a hiatus over central New Mexico, "Two months or more, I'd say," came from Captain Gray the evening they did appear again, three days after General Morgan's unexpected decision against rescheduling the blast in favor of an all-out effort to shut the project down. (He was going to stop the ignition, cut off all electricity to the tunnel, a tunnel which only a handful of people even knew existed, and then plug it with as much concrete as he could find the budget for. "Five football fields worth, heck, a mile if we can get it.") Late that afternoon, as the streaks made their unheralded return and the clear reddish sky began to filter into its crepuscular enigmatic aura, Colonel Andrews eased into a tight parking space just across the street from the Summit Bar and Grill.

He had come by commercial aircraft, flying into Albuquerque and driving all the way to the environs of Silas in a rented car. He put up at a motel on the outskirts of town, and drove in for dinner just as twilight settled in. The dining room was full, and quiet, everyone staring out the large windows at the majestic bands of purple celestial lines drawn by a steady celestial brush stroke, stretching toward a motionless sunset. The Colonel found a table by himself and ordered a drink, but he was soon noticed by Jack Stephson and his girlfriend, and they called him over with happy surprise.

"I guess this is the streaks at work," the blue-eyed young man said, springing up out of his chair and extending a congenial hand.

This time the Colonel took his firmly and smiled. "Tough calluses you got there, private. Looks like you've been busy."

"Actually, corporal now, sir. And busy? Yes, I am, and will be."

"So shall we all."

Jack's companion rose from her chair and held out a fine slender hand. "Monica, Monica Dearborne. I have heard only admirable things about you, colonel."

Robson smiled and held her soft palm a lingering moment as he looked over her graceful abundance of dark curls, quick perceptive brown eyes, soft mouth, and smooth olive complexion. Their glances lingered another moment after they released each other's grasp.

After an exchange of pleasantries the three of them ordered, dined, and sat with coffee without much anecdote or chat. Their silence was anything but uncomfortable, for all of them had had enough experience with the streaks to know not to resist the half-light spell still at work. This evening the swell of emotion and tranquility was particularly clear and deep, and they each felt and persisted in the elastic pleasure of simply being together, unneeded words necessarily avoided so as not to disturb a silence that gave them so much more.

As the hour approached eight, the sunset finally dimmed and departed along the rocky horizon. The eye adjusted to the lamps and neon banners inside the restaurant, and soon the chatter from table to table increased in volume. The three remained silent a while longer until Jack mentioned that Monica, though a civilian, had become a managing consultant for the emergency project now underway.

"You know, colonel, she's a programmer, and a poet."

"Hey," Monica poked him in the arm.

"Sorry, sweetheart," the corporal grinned. "Poetess."

They both looked for a reaction from their guest, but Colonel Andrews did not reply at once. He was still staring out the window, into the now impalpable darkness. Jack thought he had not heard him, and though just an idle remark, he began to say it again. The Colonel finally stirred. "You can still see into the land. The Pale Moon range due north, that runnel lying westward. It has seemed to me lately that even in what seems the blackest pitch there is light somewhere. Light is never really absent, you know, but sometimes we have to look at it backwards in order to recognize it. Don't you think?"

"Backwards?" Monica asked. "What do you mean?"

"Recognizing what gets removed, to see what remains."

Jack agreed with him because he saw no reason not to. He still wondered if the Colonel had received his bit of news about the "emergency project," and the corporal's silence now prompted Robson to reply. "I am sure, Monica, that, if not already, you will soon win the trust of the Action Room team. They are all great people. It is the same group, isn't it?"

"Minor changes, colonel," she replied. "I guess you will notice who's gone when you meet everyone."

"Oh, I will not be meeting them. And I am sure I will not be missed."

Jack was a bit surprised. "The General just wants to brief you?"

"He's here?"

"Yes, sir. He wants to run the operation himself."

"What operation is that?"

What startled Jack was not so much Andrews' seeming lack of knowledge of the project, but the innocent way in which he asked his question. He was unsure where to go next. "I guess, sir, that if you do not know, then I cannot tell you."

Andrews smiled. "What I have always liked about the streaks is that they change things, and don't change things. How far our personal feelings and insights influence anyone else, or anything else – well, I guess we can never know that. I now assume that it cannot be 'nothing,' but we always tend to overestimate our own epiphanies."

Monica spoke up. "You've had one, colonel?"

A moment's hesitation. "Yes."

"If you tell us about it, then maybe we can tell you if we're affected. And in what way. If you don't want to say anything, well then, I'm affected already." She laughed, and the Colonel did as well. Jack remained silent because he expected Andrews to fill in the obvious blank space looming over the table. An empty coffee cup later the space was still blank. A larger blank, if that were possible.

They all rose to leave, and the Colonel politely extended his hand to Monica. "A real pleasure. And corporal, I'm glad we could get acquainted like this."

Jack replied with similar sentiments as they exited the restaurant, and added that he hoped they could meet again, while he was here.

"You will be staying a while, sir?"

"Not sure, corporal. Not up to me." Colonel Andrews started crossing the street and looked back for a final smile and farewell. Jack and Monica watched him get into his car and drive away. Jack did not move.

Monica put her chin on his shoulder and nibbled at his ear. "What's the matter?'

Jack did not reply. What had Robson said – changing things and not changing things? He took her hand and they walked out into the warm night. The blank space followed him all the way to Monica's apartment.

In all of his years in New Mexico, General Morgan was scrupulous about avoiding the streaks. He did not hate them, he did not deny their existence. He just made sure he was doing something else. This often simply meant long hours at his desk, shades drawn, radio up loud. As such, he appreciated the phenomenon in a way no one else did. He was productive, and he always remembered what he was doing. No ambiguities to worry about; because he was the man in charge, he could not afford ambiguity anyway. He even learned not to get annoyed with his staff the following morning when they wandered in, often late and often in a daze. The only real problems were with his secretary. "Did you manage to make those calls to Hawaii, Miriam?" "Does it matter, general? I'll do it today. But even another day won't matter." He would then receive another lecture from her about the need to paint the offices more interesting colors, and why don't we have spicier food in the canteen. All the more reason, he felt, to stay clear-headed. Someone had to be the watchdog.

The evening of Colonel Andrews' arrival the General was down in the Action Room getting a briefing from Captain Gray about a proposal for new computer equipment. Someone came off the elevator and mentioned that the streaks were here. This stirred Morgan out of his chair, and he tossed aside Gray's forty-page report.

"Does anyone know if Stahlbergen arrived yet?"

"He is due in at 19:15, general."

"Good. When he lands, send him down right away." He began dragging folding chairs toward one of the trestle tables used to sort through faxes. "Roll this stuff up. Get it out of the way. We need seven chairs. Eight."

Captain Gray attempted to turn into a concrete pylon. It always avails nothing to say it could not be, when that "it" is and will. And he knew it would not help to say he was hungry.

"Are we going to start now, general?"

"The only way to start, captain, is to start."

"The staff were probably going to break for dinner soon."

"Get pizzas."

Stahlbergen was greeted at the runway by the General's lieutenant. His willful response to Morgan's call for the impromptu meeting was met with a threat from the lieutenant to carry him bodily into the elevator. The professor grumbled that he had had dinner with Congressman Pondhurst only two nights ago, and the lieutenant, intent on misunderstanding him, said that the local pizza was far superior to anything in Washington.

Once the team was assembled and the scraps of their meal removed, Morgan looked around the table and began. Never before, everyone later recalled, was he as soft-spoken, as deliberate as then. "Gentlemen, when something goes wrong we always blame ourselves. We get like the superhero that couldn't, but should have. When something goes well for us, only then are we willing to bow to our compeers, to accident, luck, to fate even, and let someone else take home the Oscar. Why is that? Why is failure such an assertion of individuality, and success a willingness to relinquish it? It would seem as though, when something comes our way, we act like we don't want it, or want everyone else to have it instead. Or maybe we feel we were up to the struggle to achieve something, but not up to the unforeseeable struggle of having achieved it; because, what happens after the blood is drawn, the sweat sopped and cleaned? Do you think that is it, that success cannot be handled? I would say 'yes,' and I would say 'no.' Because there is something else again at work here, and it is this: a success, an achievement, goes right past our ego and straight to the real person that we are, a person that sees more and knows more. What does this person know? That everything moves along, that there are wheels and wheels, whether we go left or go right, it does not matter. The wheels turn and we cannot stop them. The curious thing is, when the wheel moves our way, when it lines up with our own wish, we can see it. We can see that the wheel did it, and not us. What fool would claim otherwise? Did I become a general simply because I wanted to be a general? Well, many think so, and let them so think. I hopped on a certain merry-go-round a long time ago, and I'm still on it. Heck, I'm not sure now I could get off if I wanted to.

"So, who is this real person? What does he do, if he is not doing everything else? The only answer I can come up with is the simple one. Nothing. He is not someone who works; he is someone who sees. And much of the time he is hidden, which is the way he wants it. I would also say this: when he sees something, it doesn't mean that that is when we see him. No, it means that *he* sees, *instead* of us. We step out of the way, or disappear. And that, gentlemen, is the moment of success. When we are not there to take the credit."

Morgan stopped. Three sounds – the irregular click of a computer reel, a quiet hiss of air in the overhead duct, the slight gurgle of a coffee maker in some unseen alcove – ornamented the crystal stillness, making of it an envelope that held each person in his chair, each barely willing to take an audible breath. No eye contact followed, no awkward noise or shuffle of feet. Motionless they sat and looked at their leader. Even incredulity would have been excess.

The General looked at his watch for a full minute, and then resumed in the same quiet manner as before. "Silence bothers me, gentlemen. It really does. Especially other people's. But I cannot deny that it's how things get done. We have a sleeping leviathan out there, and he's been poked with a lightning bolt. God only knows why he has not wakened to it yet. I have no idea whether it is within our power to return him to perpetual slumber, and whether the wheels are going to turn our way... are turning our way. We only know by trying, so let us do our damndest." He paused momentarily. "Now I'm sorry, I know the official meeting is thirty-six hours away. But here we are, and respecting an artificial future seems preposterous before our, dare I say, terrifying present." One more pause. "Does anyone else want to say something?"

Gray raised his hand. Morgan stared into a corner of the room looking for a gnat. Moments went by and the hand remained aloft. "Gray."

The Captain cleared his throat. "As you can see, sir, we cleaned the Bang Board. Everything is clear and sparkly. We wanted to be sure that we know what we're looking at. Those digital displays in particular. An eight looks like a zero. Sometimes."

Morgan followed the gnat to the Bang Board and squinted. Several moments went by. Then without looking away from the console he said, "Why is Cyclops out?"

"We cut the power to the light the day of ignition, sir. Just the light."

The General turned and stared at the gnat on the tip of Gray's nose. "What was that supposed to do?

"It seemed like a good idea in the moment, sir."

"That is our final signal, captain, before it happens. Our parting wink. We went to a lot of trouble to arrange it that way. Don't you remember."

"Yes, sir, and we can fix it sir. Well, better if Corporal Stephson fixes it, since he did it, and he knows that thing best."

Morgan looked around the table. "Where is Stephson?"

Jack lay awake long into the night. He enjoyed the cool draft of air entering through the just opened sash, and he enjoyed listening to Monica's quiet breathing. The streaks' magic was at him, and he knew it. Had he had dinner with Colonel Andrews? Of course he had. Nothing to doubt there. And their prolonged silences over dinner were special, very special. He had never experienced such abandon to the phenomenon as he had those few short hours ago. Those few short hours.

He reached over and placed his hand on her soft back. Her gentle respiring continued as before. The clear night sparkled with silent gems. Jack closed his eyes.

The Colonel. Something was unexplained. As he thought it over, he kept returning to the obvious conclusion, that the streaks had made him see something in Andrews that was not really there. But no, he had lived here long enough to know the difference. The difference in the way people speak and behave when the twilight spell was upon them. And something had been occurring with Robson Andrews tonight unlike anyone he had ever been with during the streaks appearances. In fact, that was the point, that was the difference, and as he gazed back in his mind through the time warp of before and after sunset, he remained sure of what he felt. Somehow the Colonel was not affected. The streaks did not change him. He experienced them, yes, but he did not change. How that could be he did not know, but he was sure it was true, despite the fact that such perceptions of another's inner world offer but the most ephemeral hints of what other people within themselves really are. An epiphany, he said. Well, admitted to when coaxed…

He must have dozed off only briefly, because when he woke to the light rain tapping against the window pane, his first sight was of the stars, still unmoving, still staring at him. They did not sleep. The rain increased a moment, seemed to die down, then came again a little too insistent. Then he realized that this was impossible, the sky had been cloudless for weeks, he rose to see what the sound could be and then heard the doorbell, and heard it again and again and again. He threw open the window and looked down to see two shadows with handfuls of gravel, ready for the next toss.

"General wants you, Jack," came from one of them.

The turmoil in the Action Room was teetering on chaos as Jack and the others emerged from the elevator. Morgan was standing in front of the Bang Board with the rest of the team facing him. Everyone was talking at once. The General had been trying as hard as he could to maintain the atmosphere of patience and composure that he had created with his opening remarks around the table before they all set to work, but as the next hour went by he only just kept the fury out of his voice as he asked over and over again why the electricity to the device could not simply be cut off. A new Guinness world record for saying the same thing in different ways was probably achieved in that hour, but the decision to disallow any record of the proceedings prevented the Army from collecting the prize.

"One more time, Stahlbergen, why not?"

"It could go off. Remember, it signaled us. It finally replied to the start of Wheel Lock. Remember, it signaled us."

"You don't have to repeat everything! But if there is no power, how can it go off?"

"We can only cut the power here. There is no full shutdown mechanism. Something is still active out there, so a sudden signal loss could…"

"Then shut it off out there."

"General, as I said…"

"I heard what you said, damn you!"

"…we can only do it violently, by destroying the cables, probably other things, and that destruction is just out of bounds – destruction can only lead to destruction." The professor quietly made the point he wanted to make all along, not so much from defiance as from a fatigue so deep that it could do no other than unravel itself until his breath was gone.

The General looked around and noticed Jack among the new-comers. He gave him an almost grateful look and motioned him over. "Corporal, get Cyclops back on."

Jack had his tools with him, and he had the panel off and the light back on in a few moments. A palpable silence reigned as he screwed the panel back in place. He stepped away from the Board and looked around him. Everyone remained standing but no one spoke. For a moment Morgan seemed not to know what to do. And he probably did not know what to do. So after a few more moments of no one daring to speak up, he formally asked Captain Gray and Corporal Stephson to talk everyone through the firing sequence as it had happened that fateful morning almost one year ago.

Everyone moved around to stand and face the two men. Gray led the presentation. The Captain was patient and methodical, and if anything his detailed recollections threatened to try everyone's patience ("…the Colonel opened that chair, the one with the bent leg. You see it's still bent…"), but after sixty-five minutes of painstaking review everyone present was able to settle into two equal and opposite emotions: satisfaction, of understanding in full what had transpired and why; and despair, from realizing in full that every square inch of possibility had been studied, every door, alleyway and cul de sac had been sounded to its labyrinthine conclusion, and there remained only walls.

The digital clock silently churned its milliseconds to and past 1 a.m. The other displays stared motionlessly, except for the occasional flicker of a single number to mark some recalculation of some unknown algorithm deep in the bowels of circuitry. The entire cluster of digits and small yellow lights surrounded the red glow of Cyclops like a newborn galaxy emerging from some starry tumult. The cooling systems hummed, the lone computer reel continued to click obediently, the air ducts continued to hiss. Someone sniffed. Someone else coughed.

Cyclops went out.

Silence screamed as eleven men stared in horror. Jack heard someone slam a duffel bag to the concrete floor just behind him, and the next moment he expected rifle fire to savage the console. He wanted to look at General Morgan, but before he could move the lieutenant pushed him aside and rushed toward the duffel bag on the floor, which, when he looked around, he saw was Stahlbergen, pale and crumpled, blood flowing from his face. Three more men came to help the lieutenant, and the scientist was gently lifted and placed on one of the tables. Someone brought water and towels. No one among the group was a physician, but it was soon apparent that despite the nasty fall the professor had not broken any bones.

All of this concern strangely obscured the event that started it, and it was Stahlbergen himself who, when he felt revived enough, sat up and called out, "My God, did it happen!"

Then everyone noticed that the General had not moved. His feet had grown claws that grabbed the hard concrete under him and held him firm. His eyes had never left the Bang Board. The lieutenant started to walk toward him, concerned that Morgan might himself collapse at any moment. But then he stirred. "Did anyone feel anything?"

There were several murmurs of "No," and before the General could ask a follow-up question, Gray rushed to review the latest readings, even though he had not heard the printer start up and the other displays stared back unchanged.

"Nothing, sir," the Captain said. "Nothing happened."

Before anyone could ask, Jack opened the panel and looked at the wiring. "Sorry, sir, but everything is solid. No frayed wires. Nothing." He heard no reply, so he again screwed it shut. He looked around at everyone, and saw only helplessness and the silent shroud started to descend again. Then he had an idea.

Jack went over and looked at Cyclops itself. He undid the casing surrounding the bulb and unscrewed it. He held it up to the fluorescent glare and turned it over in his hand. "The damndest thing," he said finally. "The bulb is burned out."

What should have been greeted with mild amusement, or at least relief, only cast a shadow of defeat over the larger defeat. The General murmured a command to replace it, though he and everyone knew that no such replacement existed and it would be weeks before they could get another. Jack, realizing this, attached some wire to Cyclops' socket and hooked a desk lamp up to it and placed it on the floor. The vigil of the sleeping giant would continue, ad absurdum. Despite the ridiculousness of it all, Jack called out to the room at large, "Remember, don't turn off this lamp." But everyone was shuffling toward the elevators, and he watched the exhausted bodies enter the cars and the doors close. His last impression was of a haggard General Morgan, more defeated than if he were leaving a pockmarked battlefield, bleeding limbs unhinging his conscience.

And all through those agonizing hours in the Action Room, over one thousand feet above them Robson Andrews had sat in his car and looked out into the desert shadows and up into the gleaming night.

···· **3** ····

FOR THE next two days the pool of programmers and engineers, led by Gray, brainstormed new ways of attacking the crisis. The freedom with which they threw out ideas and ran test scenarios was aided by the good fortune that no one was looking over their shoulders, with the General at home recovering from exhaustion and dehydration and Doctor Stahlbergen having every whim attended to in the infirmary. Somehow word got around that the professor was on close terms with Congressman Pondhurst, which engendered in the medical staff a respectful caution whenever anyone brought him a meal or reviewed his vitals. This was due less to any complaints on the scientist's part – he was intentional about thanking each of the men individually who had helped him recover from his fainting spell – and more to the fact that no one on the base knew much of anything about the congressman.

Since the election Pondhurst had not so much as telephoned the General, or even sent a letter of formal greeting, much less visited the base. How different from the animated personality of Feldon Whiting, who had been on a first-name basis with so many of the personnel. Morgan had had little spare time until now to concern himself with the shadowy representative, and his need for rest stirred him into speculations that for the moment led only to mild curiosity followed by bland indifference. But that was soon to change.

Jack and Monica were also busy over these two days. Monica had been contracted to help devise a software model that could undo the existing program for the firing sequence – in effect, download a virus into the system. The idea was to monitor the pollings between the Action Room and the device, and to isolate each of these call-and-response exchanges as a separate incident. Once the pattern and number of incidents was established, each call from the device would be answered with a viral upload that would erase the call while using dummy code to keep the trigger thinking that the Master was still present. So little by little they hoped to eat away at the connection between button and burst. Once all the incidents were erased, and the deadly mechanism was in effect talking to itself, they were optimistic that a solution to the second, more delicate task of actually sending in a shutdown command would present itself. And even if the second phase solution was months or even years away, at least the Serpent would be happily coiled up in its programmed dream.

Monica's presentation on the morning of the second day went well, and the final proposal was typed up, signed off by all the engineers, and sent to Morgan's desk for final approval. Jack was now in charge of all hardware in the Action Room, and with so much design work going on he was free to run diagnostics on all circuitry, just to confirm that every pin, socket, lever, and button was fluid and secure. The monotony of these tests left him time to pursue his more urgent concern, which was going through the phone book line by line and calling every motel in the county. Also on the morning of the second day, he began to wonder whether on a whim the Colonel had registered under an alias, but his persistence was rewarded at 11:20 a.m. when a bored desk clerk put him through to Room 112. Jack let it ring twenty times before hanging up, and then informed his staff that he would be on an extended meeting over lunch. The tests could continue without him.

The Rise and Shine Inn sat on the single road that led north to Brandonville and beyond. Jack pulled off onto the shoulder about fifty yards from the complex and waited. He gazed ahead along the asphalt strip that disappeared into a flat blue and brown horizon. It was out there, a few miles northwest of his line of sight at the foot of Pale Moon, buried under sagebrush and cactus, boulders and valleys, where hawks circled and desert rats scurried, and the winds swirled and died and no one heard a sound. How could it all have happened, he wondered. The two tunnels that everyone knew about ran south and southwest, so this folly of an excavation, under which an electronic behemoth now ruminated over God knows how many commands and counter-commands, had no influence over a happy couple's drive along a picturesque canyon, or weekend rock climbing parties, or glider tours of the low-lying peaks. Life wanders where it will, and only unawareness keeps some of us happy. What else do we not know of what we should? Where else the ticking time bomb?

As these thoughts began to wheel too tightly about him, Jack leapt out of the car and dashed across the road and into the parking area. He gazed along the row of pale green doors until he found the number, strode up to it and knocked, then pounded, then pounded again. He had to go into the lobby to borrow pen and paper, and he slid the note under the door face up without folding it. He turned the car around without another look north, and once back in the Action Room he worked until his eyes would no longer stay open.

The General entered the base at 9 a.m. the following morning, and went straight to the infirmary to see Stahlbergen. The scientist was still under pampered surveillance and showed no desire to escape his fate. The two men exchanged niceties in front of the medical staff, but they managed to pass back and forth a subtext that was clear to the two of them without pricking up inquisitive ears. A translation of that dialogue went something like this:

"The new design sounds promising, doctor. I'll know more within the hour."

"So I understand, but we should not get any more civilians involved."

"Their involvement is done. We can manage the details."

"I would like to see the design myself."

"Later today then."

"Well – not so urgent, I guess."

Morgan grunted and started for the door. The aroma of another memory stopped him... something else he wanted to say. Stahlbergen spared him the divining and said for all to hear, "We've had no time to discuss Dresden's paper, general. I had it sent over to your office."

"Oh yes, doctor, your dinner with the congressman. Yes, that was on my mind."

Back at his desk the General could not now avoid what he so often managed to avoid: lengthy careful reading. Miriam brought him a thermos of coffee and he settled in for two hours, reviewing Monica's designs and the commentary from the rest of the team. Their collective confidence above all reassured him, and he initialed and signed each page with a degree of relief he had not felt in many months. He asked for lunch to be sent in, then started on the curious document that Congressman Pondhurst had delivered via the scientist from Switzerland, the scientist who had become so indispensable to the current dilemma. Strange, he thought, how quietly the unexpected inserts itself. A man I hardly ever expected to interact with, except at the other end of an audio-visual aid, speaks to me as an equal, a superior it sometimes seemed. But asserting a defiant authority would avail nothing now. Circumstance ruled, and it dictated to all what would be what, who would be who, and when they would each enter and depart.

But the nerve of this congressman. The thick manila envelope with its red ink scrawl: "General Paul Morgan, Personal and Urgent." Who addresses a parcel like this? And why the circumspect behavior? It appeared as if this newly elected official was going out of his way to avoid any semblance of his predecessor's amiable personality. Well, he had succeeded, as if that meant anything.

The document began with a legal summary of all the federal government property holdings in the state of New Mexico. It then went over in what seemed to the General unnecessary detail about the transactions that Congressman Whiting had overseen last year regarding the relocation of Brandonville and the acquisition of lands previously held by Mr. Jackson Monroe II. Some of these details made him wince as he recalled the level of dissembling needed to clear away a perimeter that he could somehow live with. (But could he live with it?) Only Feldon could have managed a thing like that. And that fence business. How absurd it was not to have one in place. He sighed deeply at the cost involved in maintaining helicopter patrols instead to protect the perimeter. It had to be done, and there was no end in sight. How many other projects had to be postponed, or written off, because of this. But how long could he justify it to state officials and the local police? For now only their own indifference protected him, protected them.

By mid-afternoon he had ploughed through fifty pages of enervating legalese, and it looked as though the congressman's only intention was death by boredom. He was about to put it aside when one more turn of the page brought him to the concluding remarks. And the bold black title that heralded those remarks stared at him with a pronouncement so ominous that he thought it must be a joke. He scanned the first few paragraphs, felt sure it could not possibly be, then turned to the end and read the final two pages. He put the document down, picked it up again, and read those final two pages once more.

Morgan stared at the wall opposite. His collection of framed photographs, medals, and citations that crowded every corner always served to reassure him, no matter how agitated he was about to become. A leisurely scan of those memories and triumphs had always helped him remember who he was and what he had accomplished, and so helped him dismiss whatever threatened to undo his disciplined balance. But now it was not agitation he needed rescuing from. It was despair. Cold, abject despair. And the trophies and pictures were suddenly empty things, so many pieces of wood and metal and glass hanging ugly and useless, belonging to some other person living some other life.

A near simultaneous rap and opening of the door startled him out of his cloud. The lieutenant was brisk, and seemingly a bit confused.

"Sorry, sir, but the patrols caught someone out in the northern limits. They should be landing with him momentarily."

"I have no time for this now, lieutenant. Have them fly the fellow to the border and let him go. I hate having to deal with those damned immigration people."

The lieutenant's confused manner did not abate. "Sir, it's Colonel Andrews, sir."

Every question rose and fell, the more willingly since the General was still too benumbed to rouse himself even to disbelief. "Send him here as soon as he arrives."

"Yes, sir. Right after we book him in and assign his cell…"

"Immediately, lieutenant. No write-up, no arrest."

The man appeared to suppress a spurt of anger and awkwardly turned to leave. Noticing this Morgan added, "And no escort either. He is just our guest, like Doctor Stahlbergen. You can tell Miriam to make more coffee."

The lieutenant left pale and lifeless, and closed the door without a whisper. The General almost chuckled. He turned in his chair and pulled the blinds all the way up. The afternoon light cast a mellow haze over his private garden, the arcs of irrigation spray just now painting rainbow shimmers in the clear air that lived and died with every pulse. How generous Fortune can sometimes be, he thought. The Colonel literally drops out of the sky just when I need him most. He will know what to do. And my welcome should make him at least a little grateful.

He continued to sit and enjoy the late afternoon sunlight play on the bushes and flowers. The colors were so pleasing. As the fog around his heart started to lift, he wondered why he did not do this more often, just sit and look out. He had always fancied this as one of the "pastimes to be" in his retirement. So why not "to be," now.

Soon he heard the murmur of Miriam and the Colonel in the corridor. He could not distinguish their words, but the happy Latin music of her voice told enough of a tale. Andrews' deep monotone rolled on for a minute or so, then Miriam replied with a series of excited giggles that somehow managed to convey enough of a story that they were both soon laughing out loud. Then the laughter subsided, but their murmuring continued. Morgan began to get a bit vexed. So they were not through talking. Don't they realize I am waiting? He stood up and started for the door, but then it suddenly opened and he was summarily greeted with an extended hand from Robson and a mug of coffee from his secretary.

"Impeccable timing, general. How did you know? Miriam says you seem to have grown antennae lately. A compliment, of course."

"My radar seems not to catch compliments unfortunately. I'll have to do more meditating," the General said, giving her a curious eye. Miriam smiled through her blushes and closed the door again.

The General regarded this intruder from the desert. He was obviously still strong and healthy, but he was surprised, first of all by his dirty clothing, and more particularly by an air of casualness that seemed to pervade the man's demeanor. He did not conclude that the Colonel's attentiveness was as casual, and he offered him a chair with the intention of getting to Pondhurst's document as soon as possible. But first, curiosity had to be put to rest.

"You seem to have brought some of the land indoors, colonel. Were you climbing, or just lost your way?"

"A lot of this came from the helicopter kicking it up around me. You've got an efficient team out there."

"Sometimes I think they are the only thing that works properly around here. Of course, we had no choice about that."

"Beautiful land, anyway. I had to experience it."

"You could have been shot."

"That Pale Moon range is not so large up close, but the charm is still there. Actually yes, I was intending to do some climbing, had I had the opportunity."

What was this evasiveness all about? "Colonel, I hope you understand that I have made an exception for you. I did this without explanation – it is all off the record. So if some corporal aspiring to greater things wants to put it on the record in some way, I am not sure I can protect you from a court martial."

"Thanks, general, I do appreciate that. And as for a court martial, well, to let you in on a little secret, I have just been through one."

"Oh?"

"And I was discharged. That's right, I'm a civilian. The judicial panel decided to keep all records pertaining to my trial sealed, which means I am officially still a colonel, headed for early retirement rather than lasting ignominy. So really, you are now the only person outside of that courtroom that knows. I trust I can burden you and you alone with this."

"It ends here – colonel."

Andrews laughed. "Yes, I admit, I like the title even more, now that it has no meaning. Funny how that works. You are given some-thing and you claim it as your own. Then it's taken away, but then given back to you to use again for appearance sake. Suddenly it is no longer your skin, but a coat you can put on and take off." He paused for a moment and looked down at his dusty trousers. "And the salutes from all the men as I made my way here. I had to wonder what they really saw, and who they were saluting. It wasn't me – not the person I feel myself to be now. Made me feel invisible. You know what I mean, general?"

Morgan grunted assent. Deep gold started to fill the room. Both men sipped their coffee, while a horde of thoughts and reactions came and went through the General's mind. That feeling of despair started to show itself again, but he saw at once that he could not let it prevail. He had to push ahead with his original intention, even though it meant sharing one of the highest-level secrets of govern-ment with unauthorized personnel. But then, how "unauthorized" could he be? He knew everything. If the General allowed himself to dwell on it, he *started* everything. But that was no use.

"I suppose you are not at liberty to say what happened?" the General asked.

"A series of unexpected events. I am still trying to fathom it all. And I guess that sounds like déjà vu."

"You have a way with unexpected events, Rob."

Andrews laughed. "North Dakota did not share your method of dealing with the person responsible. Good thing, or I'd be on the Joint Chiefs by now."

"We can't all have a politician's luck. Some of us have to pay."

"Well, we don't know yet who has to pay for what. I am not supposed to ask and you are not supposed to tell, but what is happening down in our favorite subterranean lair? Have you guys figured it out yet?"

It poured out of him. A passing wave of guilt rose momentarily, but the deluge of frustration, feeble successes, and blind hope led the General to chart the course of every turn in the chaos of their battle with that infernal Titan, from the unexpected response to the initial firing sequence to the latest proposals by the small design team led by Monica Dearborne.

"Gray remains an irritant, but he keeps it all together. I can't do anything without him right now. Him and Stephson. It was through the corporal that we got the girl. Beautiful and brilliant. Though I guess I don't know how brilliant, until we see if it works. Do you like the idea?"

"It looks like a good shot. As you say, you can't back down. You have to see it through. And, just so you know, I am having dinner with them tonight – Jack and Monica. But no worries, we have plenty of other things to talk about."

"And I have one more thing to talk about." And with that, the General handed across Pondhurst's paper. "Page sixty-one."

This time Morgan got what he half-expected, though he still could not believe it. Andrews opened to the forbidden page. His first reaction was to squint as though suddenly myopic. He brought the document closer and read, then quietly turned the page, read on and turned and read several more. His expression did not change, except that he appeared to grow more and more interested in the details.

Then he actually settled back into a quiet study as though he were alone, turning pages back and forth, and the General was tempted to blurt out that he had not just lent him the Sunday sports section. Minutes passed in silence. The General had been arranging the points he wanted to make when Andrews finished. He was not sure what the most important one was, but he was sure that he was going to be stern, aggressive, really get out what needed to be said and done. As Andrews continued to read, however, the General began to drift away from these thoughts and turned to look again at his framed pictures and glass display cases. There he was with his son and their prize marlin catch seven years ago. There were his many trophies for golf, including two first place finishes. And the pictures of him with all the governors, senators, and congressmen that have come and gone. He looked from photo to photo, almost caressing each image with his eyes, and the light in the room seemed to enhance his sight as it began to adopt a curious lens-like aura, as though the ether itself were charged with a clarity that made everything seem bigger and closer. He grew giddy at this new-found perception, and gazed deeper into several of the poses of friends and acquaintances he had known. He could see lines and grimaces in faces that he had not noticed before. And the eyes. Why had he so seldom noticed people's eye color? Then there was the tale, the mysterious, hidden tale, nestled deep in the dark recess of those little orbs. It was almost not there, yet somehow very definitely there. How fearful some people actually were, though the carriage of their posture was making a different statement altogether. And some now seemed angry, really angry. What had imprinted such a look upon them? Others clearly just dead asleep. Mind somewhere else. Yes, that NATO official was probably dreaming about what he was going to have for dinner that night. He always ate more than he should.

Morgan spoke up, almost in spite of himself. "You know, colonel. I mean, Rob. Ha, Colonel Rob. Anyway, when you get your picture taken you almost always think you know what you look like. Then when you see the picture you realize for a moment how different you must look to others, but then something inside corrects it. You know what I mean? You forget that instant of shock at who you really are, and see what you always expected you were. Does that make sense?"

Andrews put down the document, leaned on one of the armrests, and propped his chin on his hand. "True of most men perhaps. But women are more realistic about these things."

"Mmm. Yes. Sensitivity. Or maybe vanity. But I guess I'm as vain as any diva. I just don't notice myself. Do you notice yourself? You see yourself in a picture and sure enough, you were there. But more than half of these pictures I now can't remember standing in front of that camera. I remember other things about the day. Like dinner. Or lunch. Ha, ha. But what about right then, in front of the camera? Well, it is only a second or two. Not like the old days, where you had to stand for an hour. Was it an hour? Seems impossible. How could you breathe? But at least such people knew they were getting their picture taken. Couldn't help it if they tried. But people always act like they know everything. Yeah, I guess you're right, especially men. Especially the other officers. Gray told me the other day that he knew the Action Room like the back of his hand. And so I looked at my hand, and you know what, I don't know the back of my hand at all. Does anybody? Does Gray? Makes no sense, that expression. Here, just look at it now. Like I never saw it before. Heck, I know more about my ass."

He ended with a guffaw that made him cough and clear his throat. It was then he noticed that Andrews was still sitting with his chin propped up by his hand, his fingers covering a mouth that was show-ing distinct signs of mirth. Morgan looked in his eyes. The one-time colonel looked back at him, then looked above him out the window. Suddenly the General noticed the tinge of violet in the afternoon light. He groaned and swiveled around to face the window himself.

There they were, the "dreaded" streaks, thick bands of pale purple high in the clear sky through which one just noticed Venus and one other heavenly body peer back steadily at the silent desert. The burnished halo of a half-sun sat resplendent amid a gravure of rugged hills and silent stone. The roses and flowering shrubs in the near garden glowed motionless in the limpid twilight.

Morgan reached for the blinds. "Oh, those damn things…" But Andrews' hand was there to stop him.

"Leave it, Paul. They've been up for several minutes already – working a little mischief over you, as it seems. Why not come along with me to the Summit? I believe Jack and Monica want to meet with me privately, but we can see what Miriam is doing." He took up the document and placed it intentionally on the desk. "As for this issue of the Monroes taking back the land around Pale Moon, I was planning to call Feldon Whiting tomorrow anyway. I think he'd be willing to go to DC and talk to Pondhurst. I have a few ideas that we might try out."

"You, talk to Feldon? Didn't he make you rich?"

"I gave it back. He is still our man. Let me call him at least."

The feeling of having everything decided for him was now remarkably pleasing to the General, and he rose without another word and put on his jacket. He led the way to his office door, and just as he was about to open it Andrews said one more thing.

"Those photos of yours. They say a man notices more when he is near death. So maybe it is life that we see in those photos. Just life, life without death."

"I think you're right, Rob," Morgan said, and they passed out of his office and into the hallway. The General fumbled for his keys but quickly gave up the idea. "Miriam," he called out. "What are you about?"

Jack Stephson had arrived early at the Summit to secure the one booth that guaranteed privacy. He was gratified to find an electrical outlet at the base of the wall so that he did not have to rely on batteries for his tape recorder. He was able to relax with a drink while the afternoon was still golden and, to his surprise, and then mild consternation, he watched several fingers of sunlight emerge out of the clear sky, separate into distinct bands, then shift their glow from gold to orange to pink to clear violet. And there the color locked in place, along with that just perceptible feeling of time stopping – movement and sound, people chatting, glasses tinkling, laughter and pause, all suspended in the amber of an ageless feeling of now, of only this.

The waitress passed by and smiled. Jack had been watching her as she moved about the dining room with a curious delightful lilt in her step. He enjoyed her friendly demeanor and long blonde curls, and he smiled back in hope that she would linger for a moment. Which she did.

"Everything okay?" she asked with eyes as blue and merry as his own. "You seem to be looking at something, here in the booth, or maybe on the table. Can I help?"

He smiled back. "Oh, a little habit of mine, nothing important. But did you see them appear just now? I never saw that before, the actual start of it."

She turned toward the windows. "The streaks? They are in 'full bloom,' aren't they. And to have them again so soon – they appeared just a few days ago, didn't they?"

"Yes, that's right. And I was here that evening also, though I don't remember seeing you."

She raised her eyebrows. "No, I wasn't here. And no, I didn't see them start… but you know, I've been told that people only imagine that. You feel like you saw the beginning, but you couldn't really."

"Why not?"

She laughed. "When you're in something strange and new, you always want to know how it started. Does that matter? If you think about that, then you will want to see the end. But why want something that just came, to end?"

"But I wasn't analyzing it," Jack started to protest. "I was just telling you my experience –" He managed to interrupt himself, and fumbled into a sheepish silence.

"Oh!" she giggled and started to walk away. She stopped and turned to him again, "I'll be back when your friends get here," and off she went with that charming lilt in her step that allured him almost in spite of himself. Only then did he realize that he had wanted to order another drink, and that he felt he had more to say to her.

The appearance of the streaks was usually always welcome to him, but Jack's consternation came from the feeling that it might affect the coming interview. And affect him. Could he say what he wanted and ask what he wanted without lapsing into an attitude that saw all his curiosities melt away? He smiled to himself over the satisfaction of the effect his note under the motel room door had produced: "You must tell me what is going on with you." Andrews called him at dawn and agreed to talk. "It needs to be confidential, for now. But don't get too excited. It has nothing to do with military secrets."

"I didn't think so, colonel. Not the way you seem to be floating around. Just my old journalistic instincts at work."

"You, a journalist? What don't you do? Now that you say that, it gives me an idea. Something I want to try out today."

"Well, I'm not going to take any blame."

"No chance of that. See you tonight." Robson then did a curious thing, calling back a few moments later to ask if Monica could join them. That had not been Jack's plan, but she was delighted when he asked her later in the day.

He watched the passersby outside moving slowly through the liquid atmosphere. The absence of hurry, of coming from somewhere or going to somewhere, was palpable, the milling crowd – and there were many people out this evening – behaving like an enormous cocktail party, everyone ready to stop and chat, curious about their immediate surroundings, but not so curious as to dispense with the private pleasure before them. Dalliance was now the rule and not the forbidden indulgence that stayed man or woman from their next important moment. And suddenly, as never before, Jack was struck by this seeming lack of busyness, the un-need for something else to happen. The next important moment. Was there such a thing? How do you get there… and if you got there, what would it be? Better to think of it as The Next Moment Plus Now – there was an equation to live by.

After a while he thought he must have been staring too strictly in one direction, because he noticed a burly man with hard grey hair who looked a lot like General Morgan make his way through the crowd and toward the restaurant entrance. Of course that was not possible, until he saw the man stop and laugh out loud, and then saw that Miriam and Monica were just behind him and were joining in the laughter. Then the tall frame of Robson Andrews emerged from the crowd and ushered the merry group inside. Morgan seemed half-embarrassed, half-unconcerned as he entered the dining room and looked around. He spied out Jack and gave him a genial wave of the hand, which was almost as surprising as then seeing Miriam take his arm and start to lead him to a table. Monica and Robson shared a few final words with general and secretary, then came over and sat down.

"Who is that impostor?" Jack said.

Robson laughed. "Our 'Big' was just telling us how he 'finally remembered' the photo of him and Congressman Whiting. It was for the congressman's re-election campaign, and it went out to all the papers in advance of the day Morgan shared the podium with him. The photographer had insisted on many shots and poses – jackets off as casual chums, jackets and ties on in official business mode. Anyway the shot that went out shows them in jackets all right, but they inadvertently had each other's on. You can miss it at a glance, but a closer look shows poor Feldon swimming in hulking shoulder pads. Poor guy, no wonder he lost."

"So much for celebrity endorsement. But, 'Our Big'? Has it come to this between superior officers?"

"For tonight anyway. I suppose he will regret it tomorrow."

"So what's your nickname, sir?"

Andrews raised his eyebrows but had no other reply, and in that momentary silence Jack looked across the table at his two friends. And was surprised at what he saw. He looked directly at Monica, trying to fathom a trace of discomfort, and evasiveness, that he detected in her. She noticed this, and leaned across and gave him a belated kiss.

"Beautiful evening," she said briefly.

"Many kinds of beauty," Jack grunted as he fumbled to insert a cassette and press the Record button.

"Like witnessing a sweet kiss," Robson offered. "That's real beauty."

Jack gave him a sharp look. "I guess so...sir." He paused and collected himself. "I was about to say – 'Shall we start' – but since I'm not sure what that starting point is, please feel free to lead us where you will."

The unmistakable belly laugh of General Morgan erupted through the murmurs and background music from across the room.

"Looks like Miriam is in for some particular attention tonight," Monica said with a smirk.

"She's too fond of him to get embarrassed," Andrews said. "I would rather say her real challenge tonight is keeping her delight to herself." He looked across at Jack. "Okay then, a preamble of a story is in order, although along the way I am probably going to feel as much led as anyone else. But before the preamble..."

Somewhere during the start of their dinner, with the streaks still blazing their quiet presence, Captain Gray passed the Summit on his way to a night shift in the Action Room. He wore sunglasses to ward off a light he knew to be anathema to his duty. With mild irritation he slipped past person after person on the crowded sidewalk, wondering only briefly what all the aimless chatting and lounging around was about. He glanced through the big windows of the restaurant as he went by, and saw through his darkened gaze what you always see when you look through a restaurant window, food and talk, laughter and smiles. Nothing special, and always more talk than food. He shrugged and hurried along to his car. Half an hour later, on his way down the long elevator ride he realized that he thought he had seen General Morgan back there amid that food and talk. An impossible fancy that would not easily go away. Yes, that light, that surreal unnatural light, even a filtered taste of it, was treacherous.

$$\cdots 4 \cdots$$

"N O COFFEE at the moment, sir. We have bottled water."

"Can you make coffee?"

The secretary, a tall grey-haired woman with the bearing of an aristocrat, gave him a well-practiced look of indignation. "Someone will."

"Water then. Thank you." She turned about and walked off, and Feldon concluded he was not going to get water or coffee.

He sat back in the leather chair and looked around him with a mild sense of triumph. Ethel's reserved design and exquisite taste had survived where he, the politician, could not. The chairs, sofas and desks, the half-wainscoting, the carpets and curtains in understated tones of grey and green, her entire vision as intact and crisp as the day it was completed. How curious, what endures. With a modest sense of individual purpose and social concern, he had planned to create a life for himself as a servant of the people, a cliché he had fully embraced. Ethel had complained at one point, "Sweetheart, no one notices a man who acts out the complete stereotype. You will become invisible." "Me, perhaps. But not what I do. And invisible gets more things done." "Recognition is not a crime, Feldon." "Many a flameout would disagree." But she was not entirely wrong. He did enjoy going unnoticed. His co-authored bills were all a success, every one. His Yea and Nay votes were all on the side he wanted them to be, and every one of them received either praise or no comment at all in the press. His private negotiations in favor of one or another expenditure or appointment usually went the way of his party or constituency, and always because he worked through meetings, dinners, and conference calls with the air of one indifferent to the outcome. No one had to deny him in order to spite him, because the congressman did not seem to care. And therein lay both the germ of his success and the canker of his final demise. He did not care. Or, to be a little more fair to himself, he cared but for the few inches that his third of the state could nudge itself above the status quo without arousing the world's curiosity or enmity, which often attended too much conspicuous success. The people and the land could have their few inches without his personal stamp besmearing modest gains, as he himself did not feel the need to add to his glory with what glory others had a right to. Anyway, there was no glory, and not to seek what was not there was his great accomplishment.

Yet while anonymity by its very nature could not be praised, it could be blamed, and eventually it was. It still startled him whenever he relived those furious days and weeks that led him from behind the polished walnut desk that Ethel had found at an estate sale in Georgetown – and that Dresden was no doubt sitting behind right now – to the dry arid plains and parking lots that became his last stand, his last "office." He never came back here after the day of his defeat. He did all his final meetings by phone, and he absented himself from the remaining floor votes, none of which were of any consequence. He had let his wife arrange the packing and moving of all his personal effects, and even the selection and purchase of their new home on Cape Cod. He had met his staff for a farewell lunch at their favorite bistro, and then he had tunneled inside himself, ignoring requests for interviews, television spots, even a book deal. What would he have written about? The one thing worth writing about, that would have easily landed him a seven-figure contract, was the one thing that had to remain more silent than the still point between his breaths, the one thing that did not and could not exist, and hopefully never would. But how does something like this not exist? Its immense silence, its week after week after week of not being what

EL TAJIN, NEW MEXICO

those who knew dreaded, remained the most dreadful thing of all. An irony too inscrutable to resolve: something that is not there, yet never goes away. Something that if it were to exist would exist for a single moment only, a single moment that would last years, ages beyond the ten thousand chronicles of night and day.

He was gratified to receive Robson Andrews' call two weeks ago. It at once brought him out of the self-imposed exile of his confused feelings, and flooded his heart with new purpose. Such a curious frankness pervaded their talk, given that they had not spoken since the weeks leading up to that fateful blast date, when all the silent machinations Feldon had set in place would have left the Colonel in the solitary cross-hairs of near-treasonous culpability. There were moments since then of the darkest self-loathing, where a remorseless clarity glared through the baffles of his justified feelings and set in high relief the terribleness of self-preservation and how one's own survival had to become another's destruction. How had Robson been able to forgive him? But he had, as Feldon again recalled the moment he opened that envelope with no return address, slid out the simple white card with no image or quote, only a blue ink line that in a sure firm hand said, "You are right," which he read as he watched his returned check flutter to the floor. He left it there for more than a day, his tears and heavy waves of guilt unwilling to give him peace until exhaustion made him surrender.

The now absurd whitewash that was Operation Light of Heaven remained sequestered on hard drives throughout the military's networks, but where and how many he was quite sure no one knew. Perhaps the memo would not ever be found were it really needed. Needed? How would it change anything? How would telling the world, "We did not expect this," have any effect on public opinion? And opinion would be irrelevant anyway. What solace could there be in everyone patting him on the head as they stared together into the radioactive cavern that was once the northern desert. Strange, the holes we dig for ourselves, how we can say it is not so and believe it is not so, as long as it is not so.

All the same, the unwitting folly that Pondhurst and Monroe were engineering had to be stopped. Another bitter irony in a litany of such events this past year, the political activism of Dresden's supermarket heroes, together with the bankroll – and righteous indignation – of Jackson and Alicia, was about to send a thousand well-meaning citizens marching into the yawing maw of a beast that waited upon God knows what inconsequential sequence of bits and bytes to rouse its million degree rage.

Feldon stood up and sauntered around the anteroom. He did not want to walk into the congressman's office trembling with these thoughts. Instead he looked about him and realized the final consequence of no longer working here. Real anonymity. Unlike the private toil that gave him personal satisfaction – the shadow that got things done without leaving behind his handprint – he was now a shadow that people barely noticed. The several colleagues he passed in the hallways on his way here hardly acknowledged his presence. What does it take to exist in a world like this – or rather, to not exist? He now knew. Remove the title, and all that comes with that title wisps away. You better have something else to call your "self," or you will shrivel away too.

He glanced over at the secretary. She gave a hint of a turn in his direction and went back to her binders. He realized he was indeed growing a bit thirsty, but no use showing it. He returned to his appreciation of his wife's thoughtful décor. Only the pictures and paintings had been replaced, and he allowed himself an internal cringe or two at the mediocre taste of the new designer. But then, he saw them – where they had always been. He eased over to the far wall, and sure enough his two favorite period engravings, matted and framed to his own specifications, still nestled side by side in their quiet corner. A wave of possession swam over him. These were his, he was sure they had not been purchased, somehow they were overlooked by everyone. He surveyed the office again, and now he could not help but succumb to the feeling that had smoldered in his heart from the moment he passed through the metal detector downstairs. This was his, all of it. Different people sat in the chairs, answered the phones, breezed in and out the door, but everything was as he left it. Suddenly it felt like an occupation, a usurpation of the life he had so carefully and unobtrusively put together. His eyes attempted to engulf all he saw and paste his personal ID into every corner. How very strange, this world of rule by public opinion. The law said that now you are here and you can adorn it as you please… and now you are out, there's the door and thanks for the paint job. He swallowed dry and hard. It had all slipped away from him. Could he go over and fire the secretary? Could he do it without knowing her name, because he did not. And maybe demand a nice hot cup as she cleaned out her desk and bagged her knick-knacks. Almost on queue she stood up and walked over to him. Yes, Madam, your services are no longer required…

"Congressman Pondhurst will see you now."

"Thank you, you have been very kind."

He walked the length of the anteroom, his anteroom, and across the threshold of the office, his office, and without waiting for a word from his host closed the door.

Pondhurst stood up in the midst of cleaning his glasses and made an awkward gesture with both hands. "Feldon Whiting. So sorry it took a couple of weeks to get us to this moment. Please, have a seat."

Balding and bespectacled, and perpetually nervous, the new congressman was one of the more unassuming politicians Feldon had ever encountered. But he beat him outright, and would probably beat him in a rematch, so he knew better than to raise the subject of his visit too abruptly. Instead he marveled for a moment at the mountain of clutter on and nearly hanging off in several places from the desk. Something he would never understand, how anyone worked amid a tangle like this. Wasn't life enough of a mess?

But oh, the desk. How beautiful it was. He was tempted toward a self-criticism that he had never truly appreciated it when it was his. But he had appreciated it. He had always given it at least a moment's regard each day, and not infrequently he took the time to linger over the carefully rounded edgings, the evenly cut borders, the smooth contours of the spiraled columns, the high immaculate luster of dark golden tones and swirled patterns of grain that resolved before the eye into magic symmetries. The moment of loss bit hard, but it was followed by a pleasure he had never really known, because as supplicant rather than master he could avail himself the pleasure of viewing the elaborate floral design that animated the entire outward base. No wonder his visitors often seemed so preoccupied. Well, now it was his turn.

"Good of you to see me, Dresden. I am no doubt interrupting something or other."

He gave Feldon a cheery smile. "We learn to get used to it, don't we. One thing interrupts another, and somehow they all stagger toward some kind of solution. How it feels anyway. I am still waiting for that firm control of events, when it goes when you say go and stays when you say stay."

"Enjoy the wait. That is part of the secret."

Dresden eyed him for a moment, watching the direction of his glances. "Don't worry about this baby, Feldon," he said and patted the surface of the desk. "She is well cared for. Pampered almost to shame. She is dusted every day, and gets at least one oiling a month. And as you can see, I keep the armchairs a shade back, just a bit shy of stray kicks and scrapes."

"No avoiding intentional ones, though, unless you manage to have everyone walk out smiling."

"That's part of the job. Smile and smile. So what can I do for you? Though I believe I can guess."

"If you can do that, I will campaign for you next year."

Pondhurst laughed, and took a moment to picture such a scenario. "You know, they might end up voting for you instead. Political usurpation via write-in. If anyone could pull that off, it would be you."

"Dresden, really, it is too early in your tenure for paranoia. The world is not that clever. And I assure you, I am not that clever."

"Never mind. My office owes you an apology. We overlooked the Italian engravings in that splendid corner your wife so beautifully conjured into being. I asked only this morning that they cut you a check. I want to be generous." He paused for a moment. "And how is Ethel?"

"She still looks great naked. She often does her design work naked. Did you know that?"

The congressman coughed. "No need to be hostile, Feldon. When our battle was over, and the election results were conclusive, I suddenly had a bit of an epiphany. Everything, it seems to me now, moves in a larger orbit. There really is a 'big picture,' you know, and sometimes we have glimpses of it. The excitement of that campaign did it for me. How you feel yourself a cog in the wheel – a willing cog, O so ready to turn as you must turn. And as you turn in your appointed place, Ah, the revelation of those larger cogs and pins and meshes. How strangely it all fires and spins and trundles, every lever leading its own life while it serves that marvelous higher, collective life."

"I used to regret not seeing this big picture that everyone talks about. But I no longer look for it. The 'not seeing' – that is what interests me."

"How so?"

"A 'big picture' surely has little room for us. No matter how humble we try to be, it is hard to avoid feeling that at least a couple of galaxies in this universe orbit around our self-importance. But, they don't of course. So what picture are we really looking at? A mirror, more like. 'Mirror, Mirror, on the wall/I am still the best of all.'"

"All is vanity. Whatever. I still don't see how your 'non' business gets you anywhere. We have to keep our eyes and ears open."

"Yes, my own eyes and ears. And yours. You cannot take yourself out of the picture. That would be lunacy. But you can put yourself into it. And when you do, you realize how much unknown surrounds you. It is marvelous really, don't you think? Like the people at our rallies. How many did you ever talk to at any one of them? Ten?

Thirty? But all those others, the hundreds and hundreds you never met. Remember, many of them checked a box for you. Why? You see, it's overwhelming. We swim in an ocean of unknown. The more you look, the more you see you will never know, so you have to be satisfied with the seeing."

"I like carving out my nook of reality. That is our duty. You build your known world – since we are using your lingo – out of the chaos. How else does a person get on?"

"Sure, everyone has to manage somehow. But it is not chaos. We are chaos."

"Speak for yourself, my friend. This detour of ours into philosophy is not going to have us agreeing. We will have to keep to our own conclusions."

"Okay then, so you at least agree to that. Not knowing becomes the bottom line."

They were quiet for a few moments. Feldon wanted to settle into admiring the desk again, but Pondhurst looked at his watch. "Donna probably has your check."

Suddenly he realized that his satisfaction over triumphing in their little debate put him dangerously close to neglecting his entire mission. "Actually, Dresden, I did not come about the engravings. I do need a few more minutes."

"So out with it." He quickly interjected, "Morgan send you?"

"No, I don't communicate with him anymore. But you are right, it is about this reclamation project of Jackson's. Surely this notion of returning Brandonville to its 'honest origins' is just a cover for the Monroes' buying back their land."

"How could you possibly know about that?"

He never considered this. How could he know. He could not. He stood up.

"Let me try something, Dresden. Humor me, and I will explain it all. Let me sit behind the desk there, and you come around and play the part of visitor. Just for a minute, for one last time." He walked around as he spoke without waiting for an answer.

"Feldon, if I weren't so tired I would have you out on the Mall by now. Well, let us be merciful to our one-time adversary." They switched places and, to his surprise, Feldon suddenly had a twinge of concern about the congressman scuffing the polished wood. Why had that never bothered him before?

"Well?"

Feldon placed his forearms purposefully on the desk, and took a moment to let that familiar sense of control and oversight return to him. During his time in office, this had always been the posture that suited him best as he was about to press home his point to whatever adversary or constituent sat opposite him. "It's too dangerous, Dresden. We cannot know what the Army has been up to over there, around Pale Moon and the nearby plains. There might be land mines or something. Or target practice for tanks. They might have destroyed large swaths of that place. I always tried to keep on top of what those guys were up to, you know, just hanging around and looking for any signs of a death ray or something. Okay, so that is not so amusing. But you see my point. You can't expect civilian life to thrive there again. In fact, it never did."

Pondhurst stared at him. Moments went by and the stare continued. Ordinarily that would have unnerved him, but the thrill of sitting on his little "throne" again absorbed Feldon so much that he leaned back and regarded with satisfaction the conquest of ownership. No matter that this elected official would sit here every day for two years, maybe four or six or more. Look how it all stayed the same. As he and his wife had designed it, fashioned it, left it. This was an achievement. Your vision accepted, embraced by others. And it appeared as though this new tenant did not have a clue about what he had tacitly yielded to.

"All of these issues are being dealt with, Feldon," the congressman said finally. "But that is not the bottom line. The new tax was illegal, unconstitutional if we have to fight it that way. It was outright theft as far as I'm concerned. Jackson kept his anger to himself at the time, because he wanted to come back at them in a big way. And I was part of that way. He wants to move Brandonville back, sure. But that is not a 'cover' for getting his land. Neither the military nor the government ever really bought it. You can check that yourself. There was no transfer of ownership. Ever. I proved all of this in my report, and I know Morgan read it. But did that stop them from collecting taxes? It is nonsense to argue otherwise."

"Well, I knew Monroe was up to something back then."

"He was not 'up to something.' Silas was. He just bided his time to take back what was his, both land and money. And he is going to succeed, make no mistake. Anyway, why do you want to support the Army? How can it possibly matter to you now?"

"Right or wrong, the military does not believe in resets, not when it is against their interests."

"What interests? Where is the fence? You should hear how Jackson and Alicia laugh at those chopper patrols. They have literally had picnics out there."

So Andrews was right about that. "Are you sure there is no fallout? People get radioactive sickness without realizing what is happening."

"From what? The tests were all miles away to the south, and all underground. There have been no tests for years, and Brandonville was never in any danger before. You know we and the Soviets agreed some time ago to stop all of that. The land is the same. It just sits there useless, when it could be home to hundreds, if not thousands. That is Jackson's new vision, to build a brand new modern village right there, just at the foot of Pale Moon, and I fully support him. I know you preferred to work in modest increments, and I admire that. I do. But after a few years of normal growth you sometimes need a major initiative. It gets people excited, and gets the economy really humming."

Feldon had to suppress several waves of sarcasm over Dresden's "full support" for something that would no doubt keep him in this room for the foreseeable future. But after the snickers and jokes came and went, he was bereft of replies. Offering land concessions elsewhere in the state, though feasible, did not now seem realistic, especially since he was not authorized to promise anything definite. Andrews had said that if nothing else worked to make him reconsider, then he should be told the truth. Just tell him. But Feldon now felt that this could not come from him. To do so, he would have to unfold countless layers of deception, double-speak and outright folly, and Feldon could hardly bear to think of it all himself, much less lay it out in stark detail to this righteous standard bearer. The revelation, if it was going to come at all, would have to come from the General and the Colonel. It could not be otherwise. The real hope remained that it would not be necessary. They will stop it, they will surely find a way. There was no monster. It was a switch, or a line of code. Nothing else. Find it and turn it off. And everybody go back to bed. Nighty-nite.

So instead of baring his breast in lurid confession, he leaned back into the plush leather and put his hands behind his head. "You got to admit, Dresden, you have some nice digs here."

"Careful with your shoes, old boy. I'm sure you have something just as nice up at the Cape. Are you really going to retire?"

"Yes. Altogether. Good-bye to it all."

"I envy you, but we all have our duty."

"But before my final farewell, what do you say you let me be acting congressman for a day or two."

"What? What are you talking about?"

"Get away for a few days. Go to Brandonville, have a picnic with your deep pockets. I will take care of things. Make a speech, sign a bill or two – Ethel taught me how to forge signatures – field local complaints. I was always good at that, you know."

"That's enough, Feldon."

"And that secretary of yours could use a few lessons in etiquette. Also a coffee maker in the far corner would be an improvement."

"Out you go. If you liked it here so much, you should have worked harder last fall, when it mattered." He got up and turned toward the door. "And why did you close this door? I always leave it open. It only closes for senators."

"I am a senator."

"Out!"

He barely suppressed a laugh over the congressman's look of indignation as he passed back into the reception room. The door closed behind him. At least he did not slam it.

The room was empty. No visitors, and no Donna. He walked over to her desk, and there indeed was a check in his name sitting on top of a stack of sealed envelopes. Should he be still more impertinent and take it right now? He looked at the engravings again. How special they were. They looked so well in that corner, but as he now thought about it, he had never agreed to a sale. These were his, and this he could do something about. He strode over and took them off the wall. Out into the hallway and down the stairs he went. Now it helped to be a shadow. He could act the stereotypical thief while not being a thief; unlike many who did not act the stereotype but certainly were thieves. And as he passed through the lobby and out of the building, this seemed to him now the real stuff of life indeed – do not look like what you are; in fact, look the opposite of what you are. That is how we all get on in this world.

He took a taxi back to his hotel. He drank two full tumblers of water, and then called Morgan's office. Hopefully the General would not ask too much about what had transpired. For now he just wanted to warn him about people wandering into that forbidden zone.

Miriam's friendly voice filled his heart. "That's Mr. Whiting. How wonderful to hear you."

"Come on, now, Miriam, I am Feldon, if not Feldy. Remember?"

"Oh, yes, of course, I'm sorry. And I need your sanity right now. There is just so much going on here. Everybody wants me to do what I can't do."

"What's the matter? Where is the General?"

"Oh, General Morgan, he is in Florida. He took some time off while we have the offices painted. It is looking very nice –" She broke off for a moment, and then suddenly raised her voice to a curious moan. "Oh, but I can't enjoy it! Listen! Do you hear them? It has been going on for almost an hour." He had indeed noticed a lot of background noise while she spoke, and now discerned the distant shouts of troops on the move and the muffled pounding of copter blades.

"And that poor Ms. Dearborne," Miriam continued. "They are getting her now. I don't understand why they send her up there."

"Who? Sending where?"

"The occupation. They say there are a hundred people or more crowding under Pale Moon. Could it be true? They say Mr. and Mrs. Monroe are holding some kind of rally about taking back what is theirs, or something like that. And they are willing to die if our men try to get aggressive. It's so horrible, Mr. Feldy."

Feldon looked out the window at the Capitol dome in the cloudy distance. Now he understood why Pondhurst met his first remarks about the land with a silent stare. He knew about this "occupation," or whatever it was, and had been calculating whether it had already begun. So this is how things get dealt with.

"I am very sorry Miriam. I hope that the General can fly back there as soon as possible. I am sure he will know what to do. Please tell him I called, and send my regards."

Her innocent pleas for help continued as he slowly set the receiver in its cradle. A twinge of guilt almost prompted him to call her back, but something else was more important. He sat on the floor and took up one of the engravings. Now, to take it apart, feel that soft, supple handmade paper. He always enjoyed rolling it through his fingers. It was a prison, this frame. A prison. How smoothly and expertly it was fashioned. He did not want to break the glass, so he started to cut the back. It resisted his letter opener, so he took a corkscrew from the table. He caught up a corner with the sharp tip, but just a little too much pressure tore a jagged line through the board. Never mind. Tear it, tear it up. Get it out. It is mine.

EL TAJIN, NEW MEXICO

···· **5** ····

NO ELEVATOR ride ever felt so confining. It was not only because of the three men in full combat gear crowded around her
as they quietly ascended from the Action Room, but the uncertainty
coupled with the lack of choice. They had surrounded her desk,
seeming to materialize out of nowhere, and the terse request stopped
all thinking, "Please come with us, Ms. Dearborne, we need your
help." Need and coercion. How brutal it felt compared to how ironic
it sounded. Where was she going and why was she suddenly singled
out? She kept trying to dispel the feeling that Jack was behind this.
But he would not do such a thing. He had taken their break-up with
such dignity, she almost wanted him back when she saw how deeply
he understood things. But something else was happening to her. It
probably was not fair, but it was right. She knew it was right.

The ascending elevator came softly to rest. The doors slid open
and the men remained perfectly still. The discipline impressed her.
She was not touched, no one spoke, but as soon as she stepped out
they were around her again and the group walked in brisk unison
down the long corridor. As they neared the sliding glass doors, she
could hear the tak-tak of helicopters ready to ascend. Just before they
reached the exit a soldier leaned over, "Please cover your face, ma'am,
it gets pretty windy out there." And so it did. Her jacket was over
her head, and they trotted out to the pads, her blouse and trousers
shuddering in the turbulent dry air. A door opened, an arm reached
out, and a powerful hand gripped hers and lifted her deftly into the

rear cabin. She barely settled in and had headphones placed over her ears when they jolted aloft, the sudden rise away from solid ground startling her momentarily into a nervous gasp and giddy stirrings as she looked down to see the grounds and buildings recede rapidly to toy models. Far below the copter silhouette glided rapidly over brush and plains, hills and prairie. She sat back and took in the confines of the cabin. Captain Gray was in the passenger seat in front of her; the pilot, and the soldier sitting next to her in the rear, were unfamiliar. Through the far window she saw two large transport helicopters keeping pace with them, both filled with armed infantry. Gray finally turned and acknowledged her with what seemed like a propped up smile, which accentuated the tightness of his pale skin. "Thank you for being here," came through her headphones competing with the propeller's continuous thud. "They wanted to see someone neutral. Miriam was not good enough for them."

"Are they expecting me?" she asked, with a newfound tone of certitude as she realized in a moment, from what Robson had told them, what was about to happen.

"You are not one of us. That's all they care about."

"How would they know that?" Her sharp reply was not directed against the people waiting for her on the ground, but at the Captain's presumption. As though he had the slightest idea who I was and what I thought about. She stared at him, ready to challenge him again with the same question. But he unfolded a map and looked it over in silence without another remark. She continued to look in his direction until the comprehension gradually emerged that it was he who had singled her out for this "mission."

She sank back into her seat and stared through the thin wall of glass that separated her from a thousand foot drop. This crazy day was so much like every day since that "interview" dinner at the Summit, that in spite of herself she had acquired the habit of no longer resisting the virtual disappearance of her orderly life. As she thought back over the past two weeks it appeared to her as one interruption after another, each of them moving her curiously closer to her feelings and away from concerns about the success or failure of each little incident that presented itself. But the project was succeeding. Several uploads of dummy code had been carried out without a murmur, though she held her breath even now as she recalled that first nervous press of the Enter key when they sent off the initial payload: that long infernal pause before the blank screen, it was blank and blank and blank. Had she mistakenly cut through all those interrupts and loops? Set that wild horrid banshee shrieking violent rages into the desert sky, white hot tornados of dust charged with singeing electric horror melting rock and flesh! Then the simple line of green text acknowledging success. She had almost swooned. The other uploads were not so dramatic, but she never quite looked straight at the screen again. She slept two nights in a row on one of the trestle tables in the Action Room, just to be sure the work was going smoothly. The meetings were never-ending, Gray constantly looking for updates, updates, yet every presentation always went off into digressions upon digressions as his team wanted to dangle out into the ozone every remote consequence they could think of, and then wait for her to explain how she would solve it. She smiled to herself again over the moment when she found a way to stop these infernal hypotheses, as she interrupted the lead programmer in mid sentence one afternoon and said, "If you thought of it, you know how it ends. So why don't you tell me."

And Jack. After the recording and dinner were over, Andrews said he needed to leave at once in order to make a few calls back East. She impulsively got up and followed him out into the night while Jack was still packing up his equipment. The Colonel showed no surprise and did not speak, and he walked at a moderate pace to his car, she by his side. Before he opened the door he turned to her, and she was at once drawn toward a deep and distant look in his dark eyes, like a midnight sky whose stars had not quite yet appeared. He put his powerful arms around her for a moment, arms that could crush her like a twig but never would, instead trembling a gentle hairsbreadth from her. Or rather she trembled. "Give Jack my best," he said and in a moment he was in the car and drove away. Bereft of word and habit she walked back toward the Summit and somewhere came to a halt. She waited for Jack to appear. What seemed like several minutes went by, though it could not have been more than one, and he was not there. She looked in the direction of the restaurant, and there he was, or his shadow rather, several yards away. Silently they beheld mere outlines of each other in the dark. She knew she had been a bit unfair to him all evening – but not really, she countered to herself, because something else was happening to him too. She finally yielded and walked back to him, and they continued in silence to her door, a silence only broken by her repeating Robson's farewell, words leaden and hollow though she had not wanted them to be. And then reaching for her key, and the need to say, "I think I will be alone tonight." He kissed her goodbye and departed without a word. She listened to his footfalls recede as the tears began, and continued all the way upstairs and until she fell asleep.

And Robson. Earlier that evening, when she left the office and started walking to her car for the drive to the Summit, she took the time to gaze long into that surreal sky and absorb the streaks and their gorgeous twilight magic. The streaks! How they had overwhelmed her! Each quiet step across the parking lot became an eternity of giddy, delicious tremors of the heart, a canopy of amber enveloping not just sky but time itself, suspending her between her own Death and Life, twin lovers of this eternal second. For a moment she could not tell if she was moving at all. And suddenly, there were Andrews, Morgan, and Miriam. At a distance she was at first curious, then, as she drew nearer to them, surprised by the General's jocular behavior. His boyishness grew quickly infectious and in spite of herself she could not help but smile as, with raised eyebrows and delicate hand gestures that seemed incongruous coming from his thick powerful fingers, he described how a certain senator kept insisting on having his picture taken and retaken from various angles. "And then he said: 'Send me the best five, and I'll pick one for the newspaper article.'" Morgan barely got the words out amid gasps of mirth, and she laughed out loud for a moment, only to quickly feel the need to collect herself. Often during the streaks a delicate hum of pleasure bubbled beneath the surface of her emotions, as it did then, a fineness of feeling attuned to the nuanced changes in the moment-by-moment shift in the impressions around her or the thoughts that passed unexpressed through her mind. And all of this sensitivity rooted in the heightened awareness of herself, of who and where she was. Eventually she learned, as many others seemed to do, to guard against disturbing this pool of sensitivity, treating it rather like a frequency or medium through which she moved and communicated with others during this enchanted suspension of time and duration. And such a curious delight it was, to see that recognition in another's gaze, of an almost mutual "death" to one's own persona given over to the still point of Now. So she well understood the General's exuberance, akin to splashing about unrestrained in an ephemeral bath that knew no law save its own existence. But she also understood the necessity of not lending simple pleasures like his humorous anecdotes unnecessary wealth of feeling, wit untrammeled at wisdom's expense. She therefore tried to reclaim her internal poise by looking to Robson, who, though obviously enjoying the General's tale, was showing only a reserved smile. She met his gaze, and the tenderness she found there surprised and delighted her. She got in her car and followed them to the vicinity of the Summit. Parking was difficult on that crowded evening, so they ended up several blocks away and walked to the restaurant together. The General kept up his stories of politicians off camera, but the whole way she engaged Robson in quiet conversation, looking into his eyes now and then to see if that touch of intimacy was still alive. It was. By the time they sat down with Jack she felt her world start to change, and the rest of the evening only elaborated this feeling.

The copter's momentum slowed noticeably, interrupting her reverie, and began to dip down toward the wide plains that halted at the foot of Pale Moon. Ahead and below two semicircular crowds of people were separated by an open space the size of a football field.

The modest expanse of the range cast a crisp line of shadow through the center of the circle they formed. Though little more than a cluster of hills that stretched no farther than half a mile across, its enigmatic presence cast a benevolent majesty over the petty strife taking place at its base. At this moment in their descent they were level with its peaks, and so she briefly shared in the vision of One who sees and knows the to-ings and fro-ings of life, and therefore knows that the to and the fro are naught, and that when you are above it all, then down is only down.

What was immediately striking was the lack of movement among the crowds, as though all concerned were waiting for something to happen. On the near side were arrayed a contingent of soldiers and police, standing around a few cars and two helicopters. On the far side of the open space, right at the foot of Pale Moon, were a large number of passenger vehicles of all types and sizes. The crowd of civilians standing or leaning among them were of all ages, including many children, all of silent innocence. Several turned-up faces watched as the copters commenced a vertical descent, whirling up huge clouds of desert dust as they came to ground. Monica's copter bounced awkwardly as it landed, and everyone sat motionless for several minutes as the propellers whined to a slow loping halt. She watched the men in the transports leap out quickly and hurry ahead to the perimeter already formed, but she and the other passengers remained seated in silence for several more minutes. When the engine was completely at rest, Captain Gray motioned for the pilot and soldier to exit. Once they were alone, he took off his headphones and turned around to face Monica.

"We were worried that we would find full-blown chaos up here. Thankfully the boys have kept things in order."

She was still too angry. She was not even sure she was going to get out of her seat. And this transparent attempt at casual banter, after basically commandeering her credibility to keep blood off Silas's hands, was too much. "How do you know they are the ones in charge? I would hardly call this 'order.' Just because we don't see people running around and bodies writhing on the ground? This is anarchy at its most sublime, captain. No one has what they want, and no one can walk away."

Gray was clearly not expecting an argument. He looked out the window for a moment. All was as tense and motionless as on their approach. Evidently everyone awaited their emergence. He turned to her and tried to be the captain he assumed he was. "Right now it is a simple matter of obeying the law. Can't we just look at it that way, and argue principles later? Look, I am a career military person, so perhaps I have my prejudices. One agrees in advance that rules have been established so that things can function properly. Function at all. Some of us give orders to follow those rules and others enforce the rules when they are broken. And some of us follow the rules."

"Some of us? So the enforcers and commanders don't follow the rules."

"No, we all follow the rules. But different rules apply at different levels. Right?"

"That's the carrot to get ahead. So you can escape rules – and enforce them on everyone else."

"I am trying to state things simply, Ms. Dearborne. I can't argue with you; I am sure you would always win. All I know is, if we woke up one morning and General Morgan said that we all could do what-ever we wanted, then there would be chaos."

"Funny definition of chaos, captain, that people do what they want. I could picture the staff dragging their feet for a bit. But surely people would continue about their business. That is their life. What would they throw it over for? Sounds like you are saying we need someone around to tell us how to breathe."

"Everybody lives in their own private chaos, don't they? But here we are, and the military rules apply."

"And if the people win in court and in congress? Then their rules would apply, and Silas would have to follow orders."

He stared at her for a moment and then looked down at the map which for some reason was still in his hands. He started to chew his lip. Eventually he said, "I am sorry for my manner. This whole thing is so unexpected. But we have to get them out of here. You do realize that."

Monica gazed at him a bit more closely. Despite his thin reserved features (except for that lip) his eyes showed both panic and uncertainty. Being in charge, above ground at least, was obviously not his calling. It was true enough in fact: without the General everyone was at sea. The entire atmosphere of this standoff reeked of indecision. If it continued like this, accident would decide, and then everyone and everything other than accident would be held accountable. And she was touched by Gray's apology. How men get larger the moment they permit themselves to get smaller. After these reflections she said, "We all have to get out of here, captain. In fact, you and I are probably more terrified than anyone else. The soldiers are protecting military property. The police are enforcing what – trespassing, incitement to riot – whatever law they think is being broken. The people want this land because, I assume, they consider it theirs. Only the two of us know that none of those arguments matter."

"It's the Monroes. Jackson and Alicia. Not only do they want to move Brandonville back to its previous location, they actually want to establish a new village right here, at the foot of Pale Moon. As far as I can see the whole thing is based on hatred of the General and Whiting. They hated the tax and they hated giving good land for nothing." He sighed. "I guess it all was for nothing."

A moment of quiet despair. And it soon enveloped her as well, because suddenly the weight of her project washed over her in solemn waves of dread. It was not just a consulting job, or a technical challenge, that she was managing. It was a desperate battle with brutish, mechanized malevolence, tinkering ingenuity that reproduced boiling ions from out of the silent void of space – where they belonged – and set them upon the surface of our delicate respiration of water, sunlight, air, mineral, and organism. How did it ever get here? Why would divinity permit the reshuffling of its spheres of harmony, where greatest and most sublime annihilates, by its pure manifestation, densest and most helpless? Was this the gods' intent, or defiance thereof? If the former, then harmony and order in the universe destroyed as much as it praised.

"What do you want me to do?"

He started in surprise. The map rustled in his hands, and in an amusing moment of self-irritation he crumpled it and chucked it away. She suppressed a grin. He composed himself a bit and then said, "Invite them to the base for lunch on Saturday with General Morgan. You will be there – if you would be so kind – myself, probably Jack and a few others. Please do not share details with them now, but the General intends to make them a generous offer of Army holdings further east. He will also support the repeal of the tax, which, of course, makes no difference in fact, because it is going to happen anyway, but politically he needs to be on record as saying so." He paused. "It goes without saying that we are going to do everything we can to avoid discussing what is going on beneath the surface."

What goes on beneath the surface of an individual life is seldom discussed, she mused to herself. That is why so many things exist there. "I am sorry, captain, but do you really think the promise of a free lunch is going to send them all home? Alicia and Jackson are not going to offer to bring a bottle of wine. They are going to demand that the troops leave. Now. Can I tell them that?"

Gray knew she was right, and for a moment he wrestled with the twinge of vanity that recognized the superiority of someone else's common sense. "Yes, tell them that. I will speak to the team leaders while you are speaking with them."

"Fine, but if, while we are talking, we do not see troop movement back into the choppers, there is little I can do. They will just ignore me as a military apologist." To herself she concluded that this is how she will be seen no matter what happens.

"Thank you, Ms. Dearborne." Gray opened his door and stepped down, then opened Monica's door and helped her out.

The sun blared down on the open windless plain. Monica tossed her jacket into the copter and looked into the distance at the crowd of civilians. She tried to pick out the Monroes, or some indication of a spokesperson, among the tiny figures, and indeed in a few moments one of those figures separated itself from the rest and started walking out into the center of the wide empty circle. Monica took one more look at Captain Gray and started off. She only went a few steps however when he said from behind her, "It's really too bad that it came to this. Who would have predicted what Colonel Andrews' decisions led to."

She whirled about. "What? What do you mean?"

He waved his hand at her. "Never mind. That is confidential. Sorry."

Monica stood her ground. "Tell me what you mean, or I go back."

Gray stared at her. He looked down and ran his hands through his hair. He looked up again and saw her unmoved. "He was in charge of the blast and gave the order, too late, to stop it from happening."

She pored over every word. But was unconvinced. "If it was too late, then how did that influence things?"

He shrugged. "I suppose I don't know. But what happened, happened."

Her anger started to rise again. She wanted to keep after him but realized, from all they had exchanged so far, that winning another verbal battle would avail nothing. And she could not turn back now. The standoff around the silent circle, and the solitary figure walking to its center, beckoned with undeniable inevitability. She turned about and walked forward, not knowing what to do or to say. The infantry parted to let her pass, then closed up behind her. As she walked on she heard Gray's voice call out to some of the men, and concluded that he would at least keep to their agreement.

Her heart was in turmoil. She no longer cared about these people and their villages, or saving face for Morgan, or repealing taxes. Silas saw Robson as the real villain in this drama. It explained his reticence about hearing details of her project, and perhaps it explained why he involved himself in this Brandonville mess at all. But what are they going to do to him? What if there were an explosion? Would he be arrested and tried for treason? Why doesn't he flee the country? I would go with him. To hell with the bombs, and their masters. I would go.

She suddenly became aware of the incongruity of walking out into this huge empty space, all eyes upon her and the striding figure, now discernible as a woman in white, coming toward her. She had an impulse to take her clothes off. She felt so naked and vulnerable anyway, it hardly mattered what a few threads of costume were supposed to conceal. And then she marveled at what convention concealed from us. Certainly she seldom knew how powerless she now saw herself to be. What could these crowds possibly expect from two women? If everyone here was waiting for the solution to manifest itself at the center of this circle, then, like every other achievement they had ever dreamed for in their life, they had a long wait.

The woman stopped about thirty yards away from her. Monica kept walking and took in her appearance as she got closer and closer. She was about sixty years old. She wore a white tunic that ended at the knee, white trousers, and simple leather sandals. Her long blonde hair streaked with white was bound in a ponytail that dropped straight down her back. But it was her unusual amber-colored eyes that were most prominent. Like two suns settled low on the horizon surrounded by streaks of black wayward cirrus, the deep creases surrounding her eyelids framed a steady gaze at once defiant, proud, curious, but also a shade melancholy.

She approached, extending her hand at once. "Monica Dearborne."

A leathery palm pressed against her soft flesh. "Alicia Monroe. Well, you are certainly non-military. Where do you come from?"

Her hand was indeed tough, but her question, though direct, quivered with the sadness Monica had suspected. She tried to be casual, and not betray what she saw. "Oh, I happen to be doing some consulting this month at Silas, and basically got myself hijacked up here. So I guess we can say I was either in the right place at the right time, or the wrong place at the wrong time, depending on what happens now."

"Do you have an expectation?"

"I do not. Do you?"

The amber eyes widened but were otherwise unmoved. "You spent rather a long time conversing with that officer in the helicopter. What did he say to you?"

"He said people who follow rules live in chaos."

The twitch of a smile trembled at the corners of Alicia's mouth, somehow catching the intended irony. She took in a breath and looked Monica over. "You intrigue me, Ms. Dearborne, chatting with the brass while everyone stands around wondering whether that chaos is imminent. And such a smart outfit for this wasteland." She paused and looked her over a second time. "You don't look the type to be coerced against your will, so something motivates you to be here."

Clearly a platitude would not work with this woman. Perhaps a role-play would. "The men at Silas seem at a loss with their General away. Inevitably they looked to the few women that were on some project or other, and I got the short straw, so to speak. I also had to agree with them that I have the least attachment to what goes on around here. I'm from back east."

"Does that matter? All right then, let us call you emissary. What have you to offer us?"

"I know no 'us,' Mrs. Monroe. I can only say that I refused to walk out here at all unless they agreed to start moving back some of these troops. I think I am not overreaching to assure you that there will be no violence."

Suddenly Alicia's impassive demeanor contorted into a scowl. "They wouldn't dare. No, they wouldn't dare. I wish you could see through the illusion of these theatrics." A note of sarcasm escaped her as she threw out a disdainful arm. "This looks like a standoff, but it is not. The authorities feel obliged to put their emergency drills into practice, since they all have nothing better to do. That wall of men and armor over there is as much a sorry excuse for a fashion show as anything else. It is too bad they sent you out here, because I would like nothing better than to walk straight over and through that mirage of menace." She scanned the line of men as she spoke, almost as though she were about to set her words afoot.

"Then maybe you should…"

A movement in the civilian crowd interrupted what was about to be a probably unwise challenge from Monica. Instead she pointed to three men starting out toward them. "I am soon to be outnumbered it seems."

Alicia turned around. "Oh, my husband and our boys. Not to worry. Jackson no doubt wants you to pass a message back to Morgan." Her curious gaze fell back on Monica once again. "Do you have any words from him?"

"He's expected later today. That's all I know, though the idea of a lunch or dinner was floated."

"Ha. We are through with social and political posturing. And I don't eat when I'm angry." She continued to glance back at her family as they approached. "We will have our case heard very soon, and before anyone knows it, we will be holding our groundbreaking ceremony right on this spot."

These last words compelled Monica to look down at the dry red earth. It was right here. She had seen the maps, she knew the designs. It was straight down there, right under their feet. Silent, unsleeping, humming along byte after relentless byte as it had been told to do, its pressurized payload awaiting the pinprick of voltage that would yield up white hot destruction. A cascade of boulders hurtling down that mountain range right now would not be half so deadly.

She sighed, and a new feeling suddenly invaded her heart. *Maybe I should just tell her, and her family. Maybe that is why the Fates have dropped me into this absurd dramedy. How could I not tell them? How could I stand here and exchange nuanced parleys with this dignified woman, saying everything but what should be said? At no time in her life was it more true to say that those before her were* her equals. Here was a moment not unlike the streaks, where only Now mattered; but instead of euphoria, this time the touchstone that anchored her in this feeling of no past or future was the realization, the taste, of potential nothingness, an instant of sensation, emotion, words, thoughts that in the very next instant could vanish into an oblivion they would not even have time to register. She glanced around, at people, children, vehicles, then at the hills and the shadows they cast, the hot sun that forced her to squint, the wisps of dust that sprouted and died on the empty plain. Here, then not here. What would it mean to not exist?

"Who is your man?" Alicia abruptly asked. "Does he work on the base?"

Monica choked back an attempt at a quick reply, as a sudden hot flame licked her eyes. She trembled and blushed for a moment, and just restrained her tears enough to compose herself and say, "No man. Not now."

Alicia looked away, but a sense of sympathy emanated from her that seemed to draw a circle around them. Monica was gratified by her silence, and watched the approaching Monroe men, who were now only yards away. The sons – twins, as she now saw – were in their early twenties. Their lanky frames towered over that of their father who was, or appeared to be, much older, a dignified man with white hair and an intelligent but flushed face. He strode at the young men's pace with the help of a cane, but as Monica eyed him more closely she sensed that Jackson struggled mightily to keep up, though he tried not to show it, his body more fragile than his broad chest and arms would seem to indicate. As they joined the two women the old man abruptly stopped and leaned on his cane, which trembled imperceptibly under his grip. Several rapid quaffs of air kept him from speaking, but one of the young men, who seemed the more authoritative of the two, quickly conveyed their news.

"Dresden just called, all passion and thrills, again. Sounded as though he fancied us under attack and promised to drive straight to the White House. It wasn't easy to talk over him, so we had to repeat more than once that the only worry we had was that you forgot your hat when you walked out here." And so saying he handed her a wide-brimmed article of indeterminate color. "Once he was convinced of our safety, he went through his usual rant about how simple everything was, how everything falls into place. We endured a few minutes of that before he came round to saying he got the votes we needed. It goes to the floor tonight, so tomorrow all of this nonsense surrounding us now should not matter."

Alicia showed no emotion over this news. She did put on the hat, but otherwise her gaze never left her struggling husband. He was still leaning on his cane and staring at the ground, his uneven breath now coming in wheezing spasms. Mrs. Monroe was only able to say "Jackson" once before the chuk-chuk pounding of copter blades distracted them all. The two transports had risen upward and started south back to Silas. Alicia showed some surprise, and Monica closed her eyes for a moment and breathed a sigh of gratitude, but when she opened them again she was startled to see the two ships tilt to their right, and suddenly arc back in a hard turn and head straight toward them. In a moment they were directly overhead, where they hovered momentarily, a louring iron growl that blocked the sun and stirred uneasy, intruding winds. A few helmets and goggles stared down at them, and then the vessels shot off again, their whirling silhouettes bobbing like dragonflies as they rapidly shrank out of sight.

"They grant us permission to be here, it seems," Alicia said in a monotone. "Well, Paul Morgan, we will see what stays and what does not."

"Nothing," came from behind them. The soldiers' rude display had everyone momentarily forget the old man and his cane. And so each of them – mother, sons, acquaintance – was startled as they turned about in unison and saw him suddenly radiant and clear-eyed. The cane was still in his hand, but, upright and buoyant, he wagged it at them merrily. He looked from one to the other and smiled in a way that Monica concluded was his characteristic demeanor.

Alicia went to him and took his arm. "Jackson," she said quietly, "this is Monica, from Silas. She is a very open-minded young lady, so if there is any message you think we should send back to the General, I am sure she will deliver it reliably."

Jackson looked at the lady from Silas briefly, and then at his sons, who were still standing next to her. He began to speak almost at once, but in a way that gave the impression he either had not heard, or was not interested in, what his wife had just told him. His voice was low and deep, and he spoke in a tone that Monica described to herself as confidential. "How delightful it was to see your faces just now. It has been one of the greatest pleasures of my life, watching that look of surprise in people when something unexpected happens. Yes, 'unexpected.' I know what you all had been thinking. I have, you could say, made a study of this over the years, since I am so fond of being the perpetrator of unlooked-for delight upon others. It is my true solace, my skeleton key that over and over again unlocks a door for me through the hard wall of the ordinary, be it only for moments at a time. This morning James here brought me my coffee, and I asked him to hand me the newspaper on the table behind him. In the moment he reached for it, I dropped one of my effervescent tablets in the coffee cup, and when he turned back around the liquid was bubbling like an infernal potion. He is used to me and my ways, but still, those few seconds of startled light in his eyes were precious – so innocuous seeming, but so profound. I can tell you, despite the reliability of their occurrence, given the right stimulus the soul of the unexpected dances to life like a genie momentarily out of its bottle. And in that infinitesimal window of nothing and everything, in that one tiny instant, anything can and does happen. As I say, I have made a study of this circumstance, and its tiny increments of change that pass before the eyes. Let me describe it to you. This is something I have often wanted to do, but have never done. So it should be now, shouldn't it? Who knows when else." And he moved a step closer to them.

"At once something curious happens in that tiny instant, which is much easier to experience, and see experienced, than it is to explain.

The first moment of surprise is the most important, like when James turned around, newspaper in hand, and saw voodoo in my saucer. What happened there was a brief acknowledgement of the impression – the fizzy noise, the numerous bubbles – without knowing how or why. Does the 'not knowing' matter? Maybe, but the more important experience was *seeing the impression*" – he used a hand gesture to emphasize this – "just seeing it. Ha! You are confused. We always see things, right? No, no we don't. What we usually see is what happened to James the next moment. In no more than a breath he realized what was happening and how it happened, and he looked at me and we shared a little laugh. But you see, people, the world had changed. The laugh, as gentle and loving as it was, had erased everything. Now James was back to seeing the way we always do, looking at something, hearing something, and knowing what it is. He was no longer naked before an impression he could not assimilate. In fact, it went by so quickly, he did not have enough time to register nakedness, or any other form of vulnerability. He saw without knowing… then he saw what he knew.

"I said it is hard to explain what happens in that tiny instant, and I am still finding it hard, because I haven't explained it yet. So far I think you all know what I mean. But something else happens right then, right alongside that open, vulnerable regard of the external world that is 'not me,' is only now, and will never be again. And that something – that happens right alongside it – is the feeling, the awareness, of what you were the moment before it happened. I recognized it in James, and he confirmed it for me afterward. When that light of raw awareness flashed in him, he saw, felt, both a sense of 'nowness' and a sense of not having been in this nowness the moment previous. He saw what he is, and he saw what he was. Put another way, he saw for an instant the unusualness of reaching for a newspaper, which, had I not had a spare tablet in my pants pocket, he never would have noticed at all. Don't you think that's strange?"

He paused. No one spoke, or moved, or looked about. Monica suddenly remembered where she was and the two crowds that made up the wide circle in which they stood, and she realized that every-one on the perimeter was as motionless and silent as when she first arrived. She then felt that even though no one out there could pos-sibly hear a word of what Monroe was saying, it looked as though he was declaiming a speech to the entire throng of men, women, and children, who by accident or circumstance were gathered together at the foot of this little range of hills in the southwestern desert.

Perhaps reading her thoughts the old man looked about, making almost a complete rotation on the axis of the huge circle, and then turned to his family and Monica once again. He gazed at them for several moments before continuing. "I am tired. Physically, yes, but also something else. I am not sure I have felt this kind of tiredness before. My friends and loved ones assure me I have many years be-fore me yet. Well-meaning words no doubt, but such a prospect is not a reassurance to me. Curious, is it not, how people tend to be optimistic about prolonging life, but not optimistic about being alive. Put those two things together, and maybe many years before you is not as much of a consolation as one joyous day.

"A few moments ago I tried to explain something that I have seen and felt and thought about for a long time, but now that it is said, a piece of me is gone. And I am not really sure I explained it either. A common futility, no doubt, when dealing with things that occur only between, in front of, one's eyes. And there is still some-thing I have not explained, and I am not sure I can, even though it is simple enough, obvious in fact. What I described to you was my son's experience. But I was there too. When his light went on, so did mine. It is the most curious of intimacies, when our expe-rience resonates with another's in silent accord. That is what the streaks give us, saturate us with, if we're lucky to see them. You've seen them, Miss Monica? But never mind the caprice of the skies, you don't need to wait for them to have these experiences; they are there any time or place. If you ask, 'How do you know this?' – well, don't ask. In this case, I saw how I had been the moment before the tablet slipped off my fingers and into the cup. Before, and after. Like now. Before… and now…" He murmured these last three words with a rising inflection that seemed to indicate he would say more. He raised his cane to the sky and pointed it at the sun, almost directly overhead. And then he looked into it. With eyes wide and unflickering, he stared into its noonday blaze and continued, "And when that happens, you know, there is not really an 'after'…" He remained staring upwards for several moments, following the fixed line of his heavenward cane, a motionless enigma that had them all in fascination. His presence and pose were so dynamic, so statuesque, that it took some moments for the women to notice that he was not breathing, and before Monica or Alicia could move toward him, Jackson Monroe tottered and, cane still in hand, collapsed to the hard ground.

The eruption from the crowd was instantaneous. The perimeter came to life, and movement and frenzy fell over each other in response. Men shouted, women screamed, children cried, several car engines started up at once, a few police sirens went off, and a horde of citizens and soldiers from both sides of the circle charged toward the center, armies of dust billowing forward, converging upon the helpless foursome and the lifeless figure they would attempt to revive. The women and boys had all rushed to the fallen figure immediately. Alicia put Jackson's head in her lap, Monica tried to feel for a pulse, and the twins, after a few futile attempts to rub his arms and legs, stood up and turned to face the approaching melee. A jeep lurched crazily ahead of the oncoming brigade of soldiers and state troopers, and as it drew up Monica saw Captain Gray standing in the rear with two orderlies. The vehicle screeched to halt, the men leapt out, and the two women abruptly drew away to let them work. Magically the oncoming storm of chaos diminished in an instant to a cautious step upon forward step. A few policemen actively formed a barrier between crowd and victim, creating a now much smaller circle around Monica and the Monroes, as an air of concern, curiosity, even solemnity pervaded the massive huddle of citizens and soldiers as they continued to inch closer on all sides.

While the medical attendants worked in silence, Alicia got up and moved away, and, arms at her side, as unmoving as the Pale Moon range behind her, fixed her gaze southward toward Silas in Sphinx-like intensity. Monica went over and stood facing her. The older woman remained impassive, but her eyes softened a bit.

"I have no illusions, Ms. Dearborne. It allows me to think more clearly about what to do next. You can tell the General I would like to see him tomorrow, at his convenience. No need to fight now. The fight is over, and there have been no casualties."

"You are brave, madam."

"I am a realist. Which to me means that I know how paltry everything is. This dirt we stand upon is nothing in itself. The standoff was amusing, everyone involved had to go through the motions of defending something, but we all knew there was nothing to defend. My husband had no particular desire to develop this land. That was my vision, and James' and John's. He used the freedom his wealth gave him to explore everyday life. That is how he put it anyway. This often meant unorthodox ways of meeting people and engaging them socially. I can't say I ever understood that side of him, but he was devoted to us, and he never let an injustice go by unchallenged."

"Some will think his death out here unjust."

Alicia brightened a bit without smiling. In a low voice she said, "Thank you for saying the obvious thing. Everyone else around here, given the chance, would tell me he's going to be fine. And maybe he is, but not in that body."

As she said this the attendants rose and turned to her. Mrs. Monroe stepped forward and spoke in their place. "Thank you, gentlemen. It was good of you both to rush out here. I am sure you did what you could. It is time now to think of his soul, and what it may need." The men, in spite of her words, said they did what they could, and then explained briefly the likely symptoms that led to his collapse. Alicia only half-listened, as she looked out into the crowd for someone and, finding him, gestured for a car to be driven into the circle. Amid this and other busyness Monica threaded her way through the many bystanders and began the long walk back to the helicopter. In a few moments she heard a vehicle approaching and knew who it was. Captain Gray helped her inside and they drove on in silence.

During the flight back to the base she watched only sky. The fascination with life at a distance had faded along with all the anxiety and confusion left behind on the desert plain. She felt empty, but it was a satisfying emptiness. Her mission as spokesperson had been a non-issue. She had done nothing. All eyes had been upon her and Alicia, then upon the ladies and the men, and then something happened that everyone understood. In an instant, the entire multitude was united – but in what? Sympathy with death? Fear of it? She thought of Jackson, and the ineffable privilege of the dying. That entry into no-existence. To be here, and not.

And Alicia. A woman perhaps more in love with words than she cared to admit, but one who managed to keep words in abeyance whenever her silence was more eloquent. That was a realism Monica could admire. Just then a vision of that face appeared to her mind's eye, and she fancied it hovering and running alongside her from the other side of the cabin window. The blonde-white hair simply pulled back, the firm mouth, the many lines along her cheeks and forehead that nicely enhanced her handsome appearance, and most of all those eyes, their amber gaze burning with the watchfulness of a tigress. And then another, unexpected vision appeared. A story, that in one elastic instant flashed inside her its beginning, middle, end. It was a sequel to *The Lady, or the Tiger?* She recalled the elementary school exercise of finishing the story, and deciding whether the princess would let her lover go, or have him killed. She smiled at how all the girls, including herself, yielded to love and another's happiness, while the boys, probably not caring one way or the other, went for a jolly good feast. But the episode that appeared before her now was something different, with a conclusion that Alicia Monroe herself embodied, and taught her, Monica, about what lies beyond a simple puzzle. She hoped she would remember the sudden inspiration of this moment, and find time to jot down the outline of her tale. And then she got lost for several minutes in deciding whether to have the story illustrated, and then whether Jack would be willing to draw the pictures for her. He was such a wonderful artist. Maybe it would excite him. But, would he help me? Why, why should he?

Soon the copter's descent erased all of this, and she all but leapt from the craft as soon as the ground crew opened the door. She knew that Gray wanted a report, which she promised to send him the next day, but she was anxious to get down to the Action Room and review the current progress. The political battle was lost, the citizens were reclaiming the land, so unless the General planned a full disclosure to Washington, which she doubted, the only hope was to silence that beast. Forever.

She took the long ride down the elevator alone this time, and never did that tiny space seem so large and inviting. The cool confines of concrete and metal were now a welcome embrace. Her assistant had thoughtfully left a sandwich and water on her desk, and this she consumed in rapid gulps so as to get to the latest printouts and error reports. Once up to date, she convened a meeting with her immediate staff, and they worked into the evening developing a schedule for the final uploads, and outlining scenarios for monitoring and verifying success after the monster was sent its last lullaby. These productive hours went uninterrupted, except for one brief interlude that had everyone smiling. For weeks Jack's makeshift solution to keeping Cyclops aglow meant that everyone had had to step around the desk lamp whenever they needed to work at the Bang Board. As time passed it was placed on stools, on swivel chairs, or just shuffled constantly across the floor. And someone was always responsible for dutifully replacing the sixty watt bulb every week so as not to risk another false alarm. Because of the importance the General had given it, the lamp was always treated with a certain gingerly reverence, no matter how annoying it sometimes became. But this day the new, custom-made light bulb arrived, and with a certain degree of ceremony, one of the engineers disconnected the lamp wires and inserted the blood-red sphere into its socket. There was a gentle ripple of applause, a few laughs, and everyone went back to work. The desk lamp disappeared and was seen no more.

Someone in the team spoke up. "What about Cyclops then? When the final code does its work, will he go out or stay alight? And if the latter, will we keep it that way? Because, after all, lights out was supposed to mean an explosion." This clearly stumped the panel, and soon the chorus of inconclusive murmurs and mumbles led back to the task at hand.

It was near midnight when Monica arrived home. An unexpected surprise was sitting in her mailbox. Jack, as promised, had transferred the cassette recordings containing the dinner conversation with Colonel Andrews to one spool of tape for her to listen to on her reel-to-reel unit. Her eyes became wet over his thoughtfulness, and despite her fatigue, when she had settled in for the night, she threaded the reel into place and prepared to listen for a while. Glass of wine in hand, she drew the curtains and turned off all the lights in the living room, settled herself on the floor amid a canopy of pillows, and, once comfortable, reached out and pressed the Play button. The tape whirred into life, and almost the very next second the Colonel's sonorous voice sounded clearly over a background of crowded chatter and tinkling plates and glasses: "Like witnessing a sweet kiss. That's real beauty."

She pressed the Pause button. She set her wine glass on the floor and groped about in the dark until her hand found the telephone handset. Maybe it was late, but she was pretty sure he was still at that number in Los Angeles. She tapped it in.

"Robson Andrews."

"Jack sent me the recording. I've just started listening to it."

"I hope a second hearing won't disappoint you."

"You said I gave a sweet kiss."

"Yes, I suppose I did."

"How would you know it was sweet?"

No reply. She said it again. "How would you know?"

"What else could it be."

She was silent a moment, and then, "Good night."

"Good night."

She lay on her back and smiled. She tossed the handset into the air and waited for the bang and clatter. She held her breath. Nothing. A lucky cushion somewhere, which made her smile. She looked into the darkness, and the darkness looked back. Then she turned on her side and nestled further into the pillows, felt for the panel of buttons, and released the Pause.

····· **6** ·····

I GUESS SO...SIR. I was about to say – 'Shall we start' – but since
I'm not sure what that starting point is, please feel free to lead us
where you will."

"Looks like Miriam is in for some particular attention tonight."

"She's too fond of him to get embarrassed. I would rather say her
real challenge tonight is keeping her delight to herself. Okay then, a
preamble of a story is in order, although along the way I am probably
going to feel as much led as anyone else. But before the preamble,
another preamble – which is, my friends, to explain to you how we
overlook an obvious deception. What I mean is this: there is a built-
in deception to any personal story. Relating something after it happens leaves with it the inevitable taste of understanding and closure.
Things make sense during recitation that they never do during a lived
experience. While an episode in our life is taking place, we are veiled
from its ending, even from the next heartbeat. So as I relate to you
what happened to me, how will I convey the confusion, the absence
of certainty, the feeling of no end and no resolution? Well, I will not.
But please try somewhere to keep this in mind."

"A thoughtful start, colonel. I hope Jack has lots of cassettes."

"I'm sure Rob's story will run out before the cassettes do."

"Most likely, corporal, most like. The preamble of a story comes
from my father, an 'adventure' he had in his teens. He had just bought
his first car, and was of course eager to wind it out whenever he had
the chance. Now in the suburban community where he lived, there

was a sheriff's patrol car parked at a busy intersection, all day every day. Its presence alone kept traffic in check, including the locals, even though they all knew the big secret about that vehicle."

"The officer behind the wheel was a dummy?"

"You both got it! That's right. Everyone in town knew it, and one early morning my father and a friend of his staked out the area and watched a few patrolmen arrive and set it up for the day. But even so, he couldn't help but notice how the presence of that patrol car continued to make him reduce his speed, even when traffic was light or almost non-existent. He couldn't shake the feeling of that symbol of authority influencing his behavior, empty symbol though it was. So one day as he approached the intersection, with no other traffic in sight, he decided to accelerate just a bit, only a few miles per hour over the limit. As expected, nothing happened. He circled back around and drove by at an even higher speed. No response again. Now a grand feeling of freedom began to fill him with new daring, and, fully realizing what a chimera it was he had been struggling against, he circled back around, put the pedal to the floor, and soared past at something approaching eighty. The phantom figurehead of justice was shattered. He was free…"

"Wait a moment. It looks like Jack's blonde waitress is coming to take our order. What a funny limp she has."

"My w – That's not a limp. What – ?"

"You watch her everywhere she goes."

"Hi. Have you all decided?"

"My, how pretty you are. I think we have. The men probably want the fresh fish, but just the large garden salad for me. And a mineral water."

"Well, yes, I think Robson and I will have two of those nice trout. And a bottle of this special chardonnay."

"That's no problem. Enjoy the streaks."

"Sure, I'm still doing that – and remembering how they started. We never forget them. How can we?"

"What else is there to do but 'enjoy the streaks'? Doesn't she know that?"

"Sarcasm aside, Monica, I'm sure she does know that. So colonel, I felt a little note of suspense at the end of the story there."

"Quite right. In brief, the phantom was no phantom. No sooner had my dad soared past the intersection – reveling in his liberation from the shackles of an imaginary prison – when that patrol car roared into life, the siren howled like a banshee, and my dad was overtaken and run to the side of the road."

"How cute. Cop as mime artist."

"Well, my dear, dad didn't think it was cute. And the officer didn't find his antics cute either. He was convinced that my father had been deliberately taunting him at that intersection, and so he was going to teach him a lesson. Nothing my dad could say had any effect. He tried explaining what I just told you, that it was all a game with himself, struggling against his own attitude, but this only prompted the officer to search the car for drugs. Then my dad tried congratulating him over the cleverness of the switch from dummy to human. This was met with the retort that a symbol of the law is the law. So my dad got cited for reckless driving, and an unpleasant court appearance loomed. But then –"

"Wait. Drinks coming."

"Here's your water. Shall I open the wine now, or do you want to wait?"

"We'll wait, thanks."

"Yes, Jack likes to open the wine himself."

"Oh, Jack is it? I'm Esther. Here, I'll leave you my opener."

"I'm Monica. You've been working here a while, haven't you?"

"Hello Monica. Only three months. Bye for now."

"I can't get over that funny walk. Why didn't she know your name, Jack?"

"Why would she?"

"But! – ladies and gentlemen. Surely you want to hear the outcome."

"He got off?"

"He did, but that was because the day of the hearing the officer didn't appear, and the judge was impatient to leave. So he just paid a reduced fine. But that was not the point of the story. The officer had finished filling out the ticket and handed it to my dad to sign. My father looked up at him, and the man looked back. My dad said once more, 'It wasn't defiance of the law; it was defiance of an illusion.' The officer showed no emotion as he replied, 'If we all defied our illusions, there would be no law.' My dad froze. He looked into the man's eyes to see if he was serious or joking, and after a few moments he realized that it was neither. The man was just being contrary, determined not to validate anything this reckless adolescent had to say. My dad signed the ticket and drove away. He thought about those last words of the officer for a long time. Eventually he concluded that, whether the man knew it or not, he was right. No illusion, no law. And then he realized that, after all, it had worked – the speeding back and forth did free him from a false spectre of authority, even though that spectre came to life and chased him down. He had succeeded, and it cost him only thirty dollars."

"Wait, how did he succeed? I'm not sure I followed that. What do you boys know about this that I don't?"

"Don't worry. I don't get it either."

"I'm with you both. That was my reaction too. It was only after what happened in North Dakota that it became an understanding and not just an anecdote. Let's open that wine now."

"Jack's very good at this. See… I guess I'll have a little too. Thank you."

"Thanks, Jack. Hey, did you hear that? The unmistakable roar of the General. This is a signature day for him. Miriam must be ecstatic."

"We all are, colonel, believe me."

"Very round taste. Good choice. You both know what my job was up there, so I am simply going to plant myself before a firing console one winter evening. Even a renegade like me needs to keep a few

EL TAJIN, NEW MEXICO

secrets though. I cannot tell you where the base is, or much about what goes on there. What I can say is that a launching station – where you sit and monitor the status of your missiles and their warheads, and await the order to send one of those flaming horrors out of its lair – looks like a slice of the Action Room on a garden swing. A launching station is basically an oblong box, not much bigger than about eight or ten of those long tables over there put together, that hangs suspended over a viewless bottom inside a concrete cylinder about two football fields wide and a quarter mile below the surface. A pair of monstrous steel cables hold the station in place. The box is glass and metal, but no one ever 'looks out the window,' because all you ever see is grey murk. Your world is just the lights and screens and readouts before you that glow and blink perpetually. Your only contact with the outside world is a teleprinter, and that is usually printing out blocks of characters that require your code book to decipher. No diversions are allowed. No reading material, no music."

"Why the swinging cables?"

"A gruesome reminder of why you are there, something you civilians don't even have to fantasize about. The workstation is suspended in that way so you can fire and be fired upon. You sway with the launches you send and the poundings you receive. Not that that has ever happened."

"To you?"

"To anyone. The military's ingenuity of anticipating 'what might be' is a hallmark of our time."

"Oh, I have grown into an understanding of that, quite unwillingly of course. I have been working in the Action Room now for, what, a month? Is that right, Jack? Maybe six weeks. The day of my first descent into that concrete tank, my civilian sensibilities wanted to push the elevator button and shoot right back up again, and tear out the front door and escape. But somehow I adapted. Mainly by forgetting where I am and what I am doing. That must be what hell is like – toil away in your little corner and don't stop until you stop."

"Then hell is here."

"Paradise too, Jack. Let me bring my story to a necessary halt for a few moments. Just look out there. The bands in the sky are so luminous, so magical. The atmosphere around us makes you almost giddy with desire to cradle every little second that we live and breathe. Every sound, glint of light, aroma of another's psyche and comportment, movement and vibrancy of one's own body, all turning round the still point of Now with no duration. I am never overfull of these prolonged evenings of rapture, of a present that never becomes a future. Some moments seem to almost kill you with their abundance, other times they go right through you, as though you were so transparent you barely exist for the joy. And always, in the end, their existence eludes description. All of the highest and most sublime moments elude, in fact. Such is the privilege of partaking of them, that we can never say, never equal what they are."

"That is so beautiful. Thank you, Robson."

"Yes, thank you, colonel. Though I must confess that words 'elude me' right now for a very different reason. What I mean is, this whole get together, and this recording, was motivated by my assumption that the streaks did not affect you. That is what I came away with after our surprise dinner the other night. You seemed in a place untouchable and remote – not cold, not oblivious certainly, but, well yeah, 'transparent' if you like. Now I have to laugh. Looks like this was all for nothing. But we do appreciate another evening with you."

"We certainly do."

"Let me add my appreciation for you both. It is difficult enough to nurture our internal experiences and not dismiss them out of hand, much less convey them to others. I was prompted to speak about what the streaks are doing to us right now only because we are here together in an intimate setting. I would never have articulated it otherwise. Nothing is a waste, Jack, especially now. Not affected? Hardly. I have been overly affected by things lately, which brings me to a silence I often don't know what to do with. I suppose it was that silence you were reacting to, which probably comes across as indifference."

"Overly affected? Do you mean too much emotion? I saw that you didn't laugh at the General's anecdotes on our way here."

"No, I couldn't laugh. I was happy for him, because he finally let the streaks into his life. I enjoyed his stories. As far as the streaks themselves are concerned, I simply try to remember that they will depart at some point – the state does not persist indefinitely. So a more receptive attitude seems to be in order."

"We can't always resist the giddiness."

"No, we can't. I only felt a little more secure in this intention during our dinner the other night. As things turned out, none of us spoke very much, and when the sun set and the night emerged, I, for some reason, continued to see a trail of departing light long after it seemed I should have. Then came a curious moment – as long as I watched the light, it was still there, but once I took note of the night and darkness, then the luminous trace disappeared. I then thought I had been imagining the light, but with some persistent gazing I managed to retrieve it, until it had dissipated undeniably. I believe I had tried to convey something of this to you both, but I suppose it was not clear. After we parted ways, I drove out into the desert and watched the night for a few hours more."

"A few hours? You could see sunlight for that long? Come on."

"No, no, Monica, it was not the sun at that point. I had had a special experience looking out into the desert a year or so ago, and wanted to recapture some of that magic."

"And did you?"

"Ha! Yes, I did. Back then the stars and heavenly bodies lectured me with their still points of presence; and their teeming counterparts in the desert – the unseen life that no doubt glows upward – left me reassured by invisible things. But excuse my incongruous laugh. The laugh was a gesture to another unexpected event that night. At a certain moment I thought I saw stars dancing on Pale Moon range.

I had become so absorbed and impressionable that at first I actually believed it."

"One of our choppers then."

"So it seemed. But I listened intently for the telltale sound of the blades, and nothing came. All the while the lights moved horizontally, close together and near the ground. Then they disappeared. I decided to think no more about it, but this morning, when you talked about 'journalistic instincts,' it inspired me to test out a theory. So I drove out to Pale Moon this morning, and sure enough found traces of tire tracks. And as I began to climb along one of the foot trails, I saw clear signs of human life – garbage. People have been spending time out there – no doubt the Monroes and their associates – and apparently right under the General's nose."

"Have you told him? I can at least hint at it during our next briefing…"

"Well, I had the chance myself. One of his patrols caught me out there and flew me to Silas in handcuffs."

"Oh, Robson! I never would have guessed, with the way you and the General were chumming it in the parking lot. Did Miriam convince him to let you go?"

"She probably would have, if it had come to that. But Paul was unconcerned, much to the annoyance of the arresting officers. As for saying something to him, Jack, I guess I would hold off. He has enough going to light his fuse. Oh, here is our dinner."

"But what are the Monroes doing out there? This is dangerous, don't you think? Outrageous really. As you just implied, those copter guys take intrusions seriously."

"Sorry, everyone, as always I am obliged to say these plates are hot. I never understand why they serve fish on hot plates. It just makes it dry out faster."

"This looks splendid. Is everyone good? I guess that is all for now, Esther."

"Enjoy, and don't hesitate to wave or shout out if you need anything."

"Oh we will, sweetie. And I'm sure we'll see you soon enough."

"Monica, really…"

"Yes, Jack, it is dangerous. My feeling is that Silas should try a political solution, persuade Pondhurst to give the people up there the same deal somewhere else. There must be land somewhere in the state that the military can do without. The General is going to let me and Feldon feel the congressman out about such a change."

"He built his coalition, you remember, around taking back Brandonville. Can you really see him allowing the military to dictate his policy? That is how it would look. And that is how he beat our poor Feldon, by railing against the puppet strings."

"It depends on what people know. This whole saga is about 'not knowing,' wouldn't you say? Less people knowing the least."

"How absurd that sounds, colonel. Another one of our modern one-act farces. Are you two boys enjoying your trout?"

"It's very good. Here, have a taste. Once you've had a few bites, colonel, I'm hoping we can get back to that rectangular perch, swinging over its concrete chasm."

"My swivel chair was a nuisance, and worse. You can imagine how tight the space was. And the way the desk and consoles were arranged, I needed to keep rolling back and forth in order to check my readings, type in commands, and set and reset the numerous switches and buttons. One of the wheels had a curious bend in the socket that I could never figure out. For long periods it gave me no trouble, but then it would decide to freeze up completely, so that I had to virtually drag the chair across the floor; other times, as I slid along, it would snarl around in an awkward turn and almost tip me over. I probably cannot convey the absurdity of this very well. I would arrive for my shift, listen to the updates from the officer going off duty, and then, hammer in hand, I would go to work on that chair wheel. But I never got very far, because the time-sensitive nature of our tasks had me plop into the offending seat and type like mad after only a few minutes had passed. Day after day, night after night was like this. In the end, the chair won. And No, requisitioning a new one was not to be thought of. Then in a final coup, it ratcheted up the torture by having the backrest abruptly snap out of place. I leaned back one evening to give closer scrutiny to one of the readouts, and the whole thing gave way on me. I wanted to throw the thing against the glass, but instead I challenged it to a wrestling match. I yanked and pulled and jiggled and hammered the shaft and back support until I was sure it was firmly in place. For the next two hours, only the wheel gave me trouble, but then another naïve attempt at the leisurely scrutiny of a report had me almost on the floor again. The thing was alive. What could I do. I called a truce and we decided to live together in an uneasy alliance, since the testing periods were so intense. There are always tests. It is what you do for the entire shift. Everything is a test for what may be. I was told the day would come when tests would cease, when you would sit and sit until your retirement as the horror of war never came; though others would say the assurance of tests only being tests would be taken from you, and then the dreaded call to launch a retaliatory strike would, before you knew what was happening, have two, three silos thundering into life because it was not the key you turned that set them off, but some earlier step in the protocol that you did not know and never would know. But for now I just waited for the next test, waited in my busyness. There is a fiendish genius in how they manage to keep you off guard about them. Even though you know they are coming, each new alert of an incoming missile attack feels unexpected and disorienting. The announcement of a simulation arrives, you are given either offensive or defensive coordinates, and then you have about eight to ten minutes to verify authorization codes, unlock the daily firing sequence, and carry out the maneuver. At each step something can go wrong. You can misread a code, or reverse the pressing of a few buttons, or omit a detail altogether. Only one hundred percent accuracy is acceptable, and there are no rewards. I was never told I did a good job, because something other than a good job did not exist. Either it was correct or you were placed before a firing squad. Figuratively. But sometimes the figurative is death enough. I always knew when I

124   EL TAJIN, NEW MEXICO

made a mistake. It made it easier for me to reassign men, very sincere men, who made mistakes without knowing they had done so. You have to know error. If you plough through your moments without pause or glitch, you cannot resist a feeling of control. Nobody can. And there is the trap, the real mistake if you will. Flawless repetition separates you from the world, and from yourself. I now consider it comical what we call control. Often it is just the body getting through its day. It cannot even stand as control of yourself; habits take over, they get imperious, they make you do their bidding. Luckily we are periodically rescued from this villain, and the 'hero' is Error. Error is whatever we are not. It is the world entering, intruding into our life. You thought you knew something; you thought you could do something. It goes wrong; it stumbles, it hesitates just for a moment, or it disappears in midstream. Or it never appears at all. True, isn't it? Sometimes the world just never shows up for our parade. Misery or indifference often follow – I speak only for myself – but then in that bunker the plethora of little mistakes squeezed another conclusion out of me. Correcting a mistake was, became, a participation. A deeper participation in the world outside of my own little head. From one point of view, everything we do and say is a mistake, followed, one would hope, by a lesson learned. The question becomes then, not whether we do things correctly or understand things on our own – we don't – but on how much intrusion from the outside world a person can take. What is the limit? The simulation begins with an unsettling alarm: a sharp onerous beep and glowing amber light on the wall above you. But your work shift begins with something else – something innocuous, like a report to complete or a set of diagnostics to run. That way the alarm startles you out of your pattern. You still have that task to do before your day is done, so you need to quickly set it aside and reach for the printout that begins humming and clicking moments after the alarm goes off. That night I was actually in the middle of completing a questionnaire that Washington had sent to all military personnel. Everyone. It was a simple list of likes and dislikes about the job, the workplace, where you saw yourself in five years. It was beyond incongruous. I could not decide whether it was a joke or a very clever profiling technique, but I amused myself with it all the same, especially as regards my future. 'I have no future,' I wrote in bold capitals. For the rest, I began the following exercise, which was a variation on a habit I used to engage in while stargazing late at night at Silas, of trying to break psychological patterns: I decided on my answer and then in light pencil I marked down the exact opposite. Then I read question and answer again, and considered whether I now agreed with the opposite point of view. After maybe a half hour of this it brought me into an odd state of 'clear confusion.' I found myself often agreeing with both sides of an answer; my first impulse met its contrary and both rose up in sensible union before my mind. It was not a tug of war, it was crystalline coexistence of what was mine and what was not. Soon the questionnaire started turning into other things: my truth and another truth; then the loss of 'mine,' and so two truths; then not really 'truths' but relative points of view; and so on until it became what it started out as, several sheets of paper with strange markings on them. Internally I came to a halt. I stared at the sheets under my desk lamp. Words, boxes, circles, pencil marks. All notion of choosing answers, taking sides, melted before the solitary reality of holding these sheets, sitting in this chair, enclosed in this steel box hanging over this concrete abyss. I looked up at the console. Two steady lights burned. The digital clock burbled along. The dials and markers kept steady readings. Only briefly would an arrow waver from increment to increment. The printer clicked a brief staccato every minute or so. The mute electronic emblems spoke a language that I now knew nothing of. A third amber light joined the other two. Nothing else changed. Then the printer started tapping madly, sliding back and forth from line to line. I stared over at it. What was it doing? Is that for me? Then a horrific shudder shot through my heart as the tapping noise roused me suddenly to the wailing pulse of the attack alarm that had probably erupted moments before. How had I not heard it? The world I had studied and practiced so hard to partake of rushed into me like boiling lava. I was shocked, yet shocked such that I still did not move. My mentations had ruthlessly removed the yes-and-no of decision-making. Helplessly I looked about me, trying to recall the first step. The printer. The readout, and its command codes. I pressed my feet to the floor and shoved off sideways toward the still clacking messenger. But the chair wheel stubbornly froze up, the backrest snapped almost in unison, and I clumsily crashed to the floor. I shot up and threw the mindless beast up against the glass wall. I tore out the first section of readings as the printer ball continued lurching and pounding against the streams of ink ribbon and paper that dutifully scrolled at the reliable pace of all machinery, marks and more marks left in its wake. But where was the pace of my replies, the practice of many months of repetition? It was all lost. I knelt before the console and waved my arms, as though to conjure back my habits. Find the sequence. Reach for the right button. The key. There is a key. I yanked open a drawer with each hand. Not the drawers. A box. Find the box, snap up the lid, get out the big floppy disk. The printer stopped. I leapt at it, tore out the long sheet with the remaining instructions. There was no time to decipher them on a scratch pad. I stuck the disk cleanly in the drive (got one thing right), I placed the one sheet on top of the other, I spread open the code book and stuck it under the monitor, and began the maneuver. It was an attack protocol. We were to launch an ICBM. First press the two large black buttons to wake up the silo. Type in the first set of firing commands, and wait the many infernal seconds it takes for the drive to read and upload responses from the disk. My eyes moved rapidly from printout to code book to keyboard to monitor. Pour it in like lightning, but get it right. It had to be right. Murmurs of doubt began to circle and swarm. Was I really transcribing this correctly? Should I not take a moment to look it over line by line? My hands disregarded all of this. They flew about the keys. There was no time. There was no time. I finished typing and regarded the block of luminous green characters leering at me from the monitor. That was a mistake. I should have started reading from top to bottom. I should have engaged my thought process with the familiar practice of code-by-code comparison. Instead the spell of my mind game with the questionnaire persisted. I saw only an impenetrable gleam of characters, numbers, brackets, dashes. My heart wanted to despair but my finger pressed the Submit key instead. It all vanished and left a glassy opaque cataract staring at me in lifeless expectation, the tiny blip of the cursor in one corner winking its insensible duty. Even now I am not sure but that despair would have been better. I began the second tier of procedures. An arm reached without thought across the table and yielded up the box. The key, two keys in fact, extracted and inserted in their slots. Turn one ninety degrees clockwise. Thumb through the book for the command line. Type it in and submit. Turn the same key another ninety degrees. Type in the second command. Turn the second key – No! – the phone. Use the special phone. Call for final authorization, and for the final command pattern that complements my own. I reached for the handle, but it rang instead. It rang! It never rang. I grabbed the receiver and stood up. My knees had grown stiff and lifeless from kneeling before the console. I staggered from sudden pain and spoke into the mouthpiece while stumbling to my feet. A hard voice replied: 'Andrews…'. Then no more. I answered in the affirmative. Nothing. I recited the password request and waited for the keyword. Then the final code exchange would follow. Still no one spoke. I grew anxious, slammed the phone down, picked it up again, tapped in the four-digit number. The purr of one ring, then the reply. 'Station Aptos.' I gave the request again and received the keyword followed by the missing steps to the full firing pattern. The receiver was no sooner down than the second key was turned, the final command lines entered and sent, the two keys turned at once to their final position, and the plastic guard plate popped open to press the final red button. A more difficult button you will never find. You must put the heel of your hand on it and throw your full weight straight down. It yields slowly, stubbornly, you must keep exerting full pressure, then the final hydraulic click and lock. Done. As always, a brief silence ensued. That is to be expected, and is usually followed by either a phone call or a message sent to the printer. No doubt, in either case, it was going to be a stream of reprimands for my crazy tardiness. In that brief pause – how elongated and yet how miniscule it was – I conjured up excuses for what happened, but they disappeared as soon as they came for they were even more absurd than the truth, and the truth in this case would not do. In the next second truth and excuses vanished together. The power went out. Everything went dark. Everything. I strained everywhere for a glimmer, a spark, a glow, but the straining seemed to drain all sensation from my eyes. Darkness seemed to enter them, and saturate me with emptiness. Eyelids open or closed made no difference. The complete absence of light took away all contour, all sense of proportion and distance. With open palms I touched my torso, thighs, head, face. I listened. I strained and strained with my aural sense, seeking a tick, a hum, a distant thud. Nothing. Silence invaded me, every breath drawing it deeper and deeper into each pocket and crevice of my body. Silence and emptiness. My thoughts droned on, awaiting the return to normalcy and its humming and buzzing regimen, but before long those thoughts whispered, faltered, faded to blinks of fear, flashes of humor, fits and starts of reason, and finally all died away, leaving only the solitary rise and fall of 'I' with every breath. I obeyed the moment. I did not move. I did not try to change anything. My sense of self reduced to a still point in the dark, a point that did not exist but felt and knew the steady pulse of its not-existing. So does Atlas shoulder the world, staring at a fathomless void, empty of future and story, his burden his only anchor against oblivion. Our burden the body. I am visiting this part of the country now because the desert, especially at night, returns me to that moment. The special place of time stopping, in the sense that even if something happens next it is not happening, because there is no time even though things keep happening. Such is the paradox that Prometheus's brother bears aloft, the birth, death, foment of a billion billion souls, while he to eternity bows. To be what does not move before what moves. And what remains of an existence stripped of itself? Breath. We have to breathe; everything else is optional. The breath continued. That reflex, so often a symbol of more than itself. Was I alive? Could I exist like this forever? Hover no more than a pinpoint in a void which was filled only by its own endlessness? With the next intake of air came an infinitesimal renewal of persistence in time, the brief sensation that something was about to come next... until it perished to naught with the same exhale. Through lack of any other stimulus, I focused, was compelled to focus, on this rhythm, this pulse: every possibility followed at once by its finality. Never before did I see so clearly the beginning and the end, and, through the brevity of each breath, feel that all activities, experiences, lives, ultimately end just as briefly. The darkness was still there; my breath was still there, in it. Suddenly a thought flashed, 'Where is time?' And just as instantly another thought answered, 'I am time.' My body is time – there is no time apart from the continued breath, growth, exhalation, change of my own organism. The lights came on. The metal hum of computers and switches flooded the room, the printer started tack-tacking at once, the air ducts blew a light draft across my face. I did not move. My eyes saw arrows waver, lights blink, lines of green code race across the monitor, but I persisted in my ritual of observing inhale and exhale. My conclusion in pitch black affirmed itself in the blare of luminous activity: what I know of time is my own time. Not the time on the clock, not the work shifts of employment, not the cycle of day and night. All of these and more move in their own spirals and progressions, but they are not my time. I tucked in my trousers. This was my time. I walked over to the small refrigerator, took out a bottle of water, and drank a long cool draught. This was my time. As was my walk back to that rogue of a swivel chair, the setting of it before the console, the settling in and typing of responses to the diagnostic results that just arrived. And, as always, the next inhale and exhale, that which knows no master in the world of our own cosmos. All of this was the only time I knew, the only one that mattered. I continued with the duties of my routine, and wondered how long this awareness would stay with me. Would it be mine to keep, or would the villain

Habit take it away, as it takes so much else. Here I need not have worried. I could give you more details as to why this was so, but maybe the simple answer is best: the light was still darkness. It was the mute insensibility of it all. Of the computers, devices, air conditioning, even my rehearsed regimen. Still the pendulum sway of my own life, still the uncoiling hairspring balance that I knew so well and knew not at all. There was nowhere I could go, nothing I could be, where I would be without myself. Darkness is not the absence of external light. It is the absence of yourself and your own time amid the motion of so many other mortal cycles around you. Whatever you are, you are not anything else. I did become intrigued by the diagnostic and error reports. The curious thing about them was their normalcy. Everything was within the usual tolerances. My struggles with confusion and chaos, it seemed, left no marks and had no witness. Had I really completed the exercise without error? Flushes of pride passed through me momentarily, but lingering doubts soon swallowed any self-congratulation. I completed the post-firing exercise reviews. As my shift still had some way to go, I returned to the questionnaire and finished it unceremoniously. Then the elevator doors opened and out walked a major to replace me, a newcomer, someone I had not only not interviewed but had never seen nor heard of. He betrayed little emotion beyond a stark efficiency and crisp respect for the formalities of office. In the end there was little out of the ordinary to tell him, and as the elevator doors closed I was amused to watch him sit down and immediately fumble awkwardly in the chair. The long ride upward was magical in its uneventfulness. Never did I appreciate so much merely existing, without the weight of expectation or intent. As a result, probably, my surprise was the greater when the doors opened and General Malik and five other officers were standing in a row, apparently waiting for me. Not expecting a surprise visit from such a notorious hard-ass, my curiosity got the better of habit, and so I neglected to proffer the obligatory salute. Instead I walked over to him with an air that came across as too casual, for Malik barked out, 'On your way to dinner, colonel? We need some of your time, I'm afraid.' Unable to resist the bait, and not really knowing what he meant, I said, 'Let's talk it out over cocktails, general. Looks like you could use a little lubricating.' His face reddened and he barked again, 'My daddy told me never to suffer a fool, and I'm not about to start with you, you jackass.' The same arm that several minutes earlier unthinkingly reached for the box with the trigger keys now unthinkingly rammed a fist in the General's face and knocked him to the floor. He leapt up at once – I was surprised and impressed at that – but then he rocked uneasily on his feet and crumpled to the floor again unconscious. Three of the officers had me pinned down in the next instant, as two small crowds quickly gathered either to attend to Malik or to stare down at me, their commanding officer, in disbelief. I could do nothing at this point, so the next several hours went by without my resisting or saying anything. The upshot was that the day's attack exercise was intended as a demonstration for Malik, who was touring missile silos unannounced. His team was observing and evaluating procedures and efficiency levels. The simulation I was meant to engineer contained additional alert sequences that were supposed to be sent out to specific attack centers around the world. But once they received the code stream – the delayed code stream – I had sent from my monitor, with an astounding number of errors, they realized that something was not right below, so they pulled the plug on the whole operation and, at Malik's insistence, to prevent any unwanted ramifications somewhere up the command chain, shut down the power in the workstation until they could stop the entire simulation sequence in the mainframe. It could not have gone more wrong if it had been an act of sabotage. In fact, that was their first conclusion, absurd as it seems, so Malik sent one of his own men down to replace me and comb through the hard drives and my personal notes. Well, at least he found a thoughtfully completed questionnaire. What ended up being my final testament. Two weeks later I gathered with the team at the control center for a little champagne and a few heartfelt goodbyes. Then, as I was leaving, there was a curious moment as I handed in my badge to the head of security. I noticed his wristwatch and commented that I had one just like it, and added something about its quality. He did not reply to that, but as I turned to leave he asked me, 'Do you have any last words, colonel?' I laughed, 'Where's the noose?' Unemotionally he replied, 'I only mean, sir, if there is a final statement that you want to leave us with.' Perhaps it was the incongruity of the request that led me to say, 'Until now, my last words were about that watch. If you never saw me again, that would have been my final statement to you. What is wrong with an innocent exchange like that serving as final farewell?' He said, with a little emotion this time, 'It seems to me, sir, that the intentional word means more than the inconsequential word.' I said without thinking, 'The inconsequential refers only to itself; it is usually about what is not said. Maybe more of our lives should be like that.' I did not intend that to be a fulfillment of his request, but as I drove home I concluded that he would probably take it as such. Then another curious moment sounded the real note of finality to this whole affair. My mailbox was full to overflowing with chaos forwarded from the Pentagon, most of it official business, and hordes of printed matter. But there was one small blue envelope with my address written in ink by a fragile hand. I opened it carefully and took out and unfolded a single sheet of paper. As I did so, a smaller slip of paper fluttered to the floor. Across the sheet reeled and staggered one ink-scrawled question that I could only just make out: 'Why didn't you speak to me?' I stared at it without moving for I know not how long. Then I went to the phone and called the front desk at the command center. The same officer was still on duty. I said to him, 'This is Colonel Andrews. You wanted a final statement, so here it is: If we all defied our illusions, there would be no law.' I hung up without waiting for a reaction. That was it, you see. In that moment, that eternity of darkness, there were no illusions, and no laws, except the need to breathe. That officer who gave my daddy a ticket was right. After I placed the receiver down I spent another several minutes just standing there. I had become an outlaw. A metaphysical outlaw. I could turn right or turn left. I could call someone on the phone or read a book. I could go through all of my mail or hurl it into the garbage. I could do any-thing, and any thing would all be the same – the next use of the next breath in the next moment of my personal time. I had no illusion that there was anything else, and I followed no law that forced me in one or another direction. I was, I am, a pinprick of awareness floating in a universe where everyone and everything pursues its own tail, as I had pursued mine. It was deliciously nice to stop. As for how I was going to survive the rest of my life, well, I stood there still holding a piece of good advice in my hand: 'Why didn't you speak to me?' Why not speak? Speak back to the world, to those I meet in it. Does it matter what we say? Yes, sometimes, and No, sometimes. A long learning curve was in order. The silences too: now that is a language I need to know more about."

"The streaks have gone, Robson, Jack. A gentle quiet lingers, though, doesn't it? Strange how luminous the shadows are. And look at the street. Where did everyone go?"

"I watched them begin, while I was waiting for you both."

"You watched the crowd gathering outside? Did something happen?"

"Not the crowd, the streaks themselves. They appeared just at the start of sunset, like the horizon giving birth. I was impressed by how quickly the colors shifted."

"I've never heard of anyone seeing them begin. Are you sure?"

"Esther didn't believe me either. Perhaps witnessing unheralded magic is part of the language of silence the colonel was just referring to."

"Women often don't believe in beginnings. Either something is there or it is not. Here she comes, you can ask her."

"Hello. Sorry not to clear your plates sooner. I didn't want to bother you during your taping session, and then you were all so in-tensely quiet for so long I didn't want to break the spell. Can I get you anything else?"

"Coffee for me. Colonel?"

"Yes."

"I'll have another mineral water, Esther. Thank you."

"So Jack, did you see the streaks end tonight?"

"Not end. But I didn't want them to. Never do. Oh, almost forgot, here is your wine opener."

"Thanks. Yeah, we have to find a way for things not to end. I'll be right back."

"She's right, boys. I don't want this evening to end. Sometimes you feel that everything is perfect, and you just want to dwell in it. You cannot make the streaks come back, and you cannot carry them around inside you either. You just have to taste and taste as much of the moment as possible, as it all passes away."

"Funny how when you want an experience to linger you feel it passing away. You feel its mortality. Well, colonel, seems we're now spouting some of your wisdom, unearned though it may be. You gave far more tonight than I expected."

"Not sure but I should be the one expressing gratitude, Jack. I never expected to tell this story to anyone, and now that it's happened I can't but feel embarrassed by my reticence..."

"Oh, look out, gang, this moment we're sharing is not going to have a gentle passing. Shh! I think I'll keep the tape rolling... General – great to see you here. The proprietor giving you the grand tour?"

"I could say, 'At ease, corporal,' but you certainly look at ease enough already. Yes, we just had a peek in the kitchen. I wanted to offer the chef a job. Best steak I've had in years. And Miriam's burrito dish had more flavors in one bite than an entire menu of tastes somewhere else. But what about the colonel over there. He looks a bit of a mope."

"So I'm a bit of a mope."

"Ha ha! Suits you, Rob. And you, Ms. Dearborne? Something ailing you? You look a little pale."

"I'm all right, general, thanks. I was just a bit short of breath earlier this evening."

"Don't drink too much. We need you."

"So is the canteen getting a new chef?"

"He had already gone home. But I'll get him. I want to jazz things up at the base a bit. We're going to paint the offices. I put Miriam in charge of picking colors. She's overjoyed. I see that I need her to be more happy. Heck, we all need that, right? Makes me think about early retirement."

"Retirement… the death knell. What do we do when we have nothing to do."

"Nuts, colonel. Life goes on and on. I got an ocean full of marlin–"

The hard snap shocked her eyes open. Somehow she was flat on her back staring at the ceiling. The ceiling must have been there, but she could not see it in the darkness. She closed her eyes and breathed deeply a few times. The fog of sleep shrouded her senses. She reached for the tissue box she kept on the vanity by the bed. With eyes still closed she stretched her arm out and down – but instead she hit something solid. She gasped. She opened her eyes again. All was dark. Not a sound. Where was she? Where was her bed, her bedroom? She became frightened. Distant murmurs of thought peeped about the crevices of her mind, then slinked away with wily smirks. She forgot how she got here, wherever this was. She did not know where she was. A few more sneaky glimpses from the gremlins of some memory somewhere slithered by…and now she did not know who she was. Who was this person, breathing and blinking at darkness? She spread out both arms. She was on a floor somewhere. Was she imprisoned? Rendered unconscious and kidnapped? Did anyone know where she was, or care? She shuddered and flailed out a leg, but otherwise could not move. Was she in some kind of box? With a supreme effort she sprang up and shouted, "Open me!" and the quiet darkness did not reply. A few tears streamed down her face, and then it all rushed back and the world made sense again. She laughed and cried at the same time as she reached around for a few pillows and sank back down into soft comfort. She fell asleep at once.

····· **7** ·····

S UCH A clean look, Miriam. I'm so glad I came, though I am
 disappointed the General is not here. I hope you don't mind if
I consider this visit a distraction – I need some way to step out of
my grief, though I trust it does not rule me. Explain your vision to
me as we walk down to his office. And," Alicia's brow crinkled with
bemusement, "tell me how you ever persuaded him to let you change
everything."

They were standing in the foyer of the administration building
admiring the freshly painted walls. Despite the familiar tone of military grey, the expert finish revealed not the slightest trace of a brush
mark, and the white trim mixed with a hint of the wall color framed
the entire reception area in crisp unassuming clarity.

"Over dinner – with the streaks," Miriam laughed. "Despite his
determination never ever to fall under their spell, he was thoroughly
bewitched by them that night at the Summit. I'm sure Colonel Andrews was behind it all. He's a clever one, that colonel. It was so nice
to see him."

"Clever, yes, though I never understood the man's reserve, exces-
sive when it didn't need to be. He and Jackson could never agree on
much."

"Jackson and all of Silas could never agree on much. But now you
can make everything better, don't you think?"

Alicia held back a sardonic, "At a price," and in the next breath
substituted the more diplomatic, "We all will. What else can we do?"

Recognizing a growing uneasiness in her companion she added, "I have accepted his passing. Please, do go on, I want to hear about your design."

Miriam blushed and sighed. "Well, you are too kind to let me speak so much. Okay, so here, we are tame and keeping good manners, which is supposed to tell everybody the serious mission of the Army. But you will see, things get pretty daring on the other side of those doors. This was really my only chance to change something. And I confess to you, I feel a bit nervous about so many layers of color. I never do this at home. Mario, my husband, reminds me how I stubbornly refuse change, and color extravaganzas, wherever we have lived. Our house now is stucco in pale yellow, and inside all the walls are white, pure, pure white. We redo it every three years. We have these dark wooden beams, you see, and a big stone wall in the living room. I just love rock; I wash it all the time. And clay tile flooring everywhere. Oh, but I go on –"

"I'm not sure I would call all of that being stubborn, Miriam," Alicia forced a smile. "It sounds to me like a firm decision, from a clear vision of what feeds your life. I often remind James and John of this. When you find something you love, no matter how innocuous it seems, don't turn your back on it, because it is part of your soul."

"Oh yes, that is so true. White, you know, it has like an inner brightness. It's both cool and warm. And my rugs and paintings and native masks, they hang so neatly all along the corridors. I can see them, concentrate on them when I want to, without the color competition…"

Unable to contain her curiosity, and feeling rather sated with design tips, Mrs. Monroe walked ahead and pushed open the swinging doors into the long hallway leading down to the General's corner, but stopped after only a single step. "My God, Miriam! What have you done! The streaks, practically wrapping their arms around you!"

The modest little secretary clutched her breast and smiled, by turns proud and embarrassed. "I didn't expect such emotion from you, Alicia. I hope – "

"Well, after everything you just said to prepare me for it – Oh, how otherworldly this feels. The main foyer back here has you in a disciplined attitude, like you said, but just a step through these doors and – this hallway! It's overwhelming. Here we see the desert air under that twilight spell, with an enveloping atmosphere and mysterious tones of light."

Miriam took a few modest steps forward. "It's so strange how it happened, Alicia, and I don't know how the painters did it. On a whim, we were talking about this strange evening phenomenon we have all grown up with, and so I asked them to try to create it, to vary their palette of color as it radiates toward the viewer. Pale violet was to predominate, as it must, but if it was just that then it would not be much different from anything else around here. So I said to them, Think of the window there at the far end as the sun just coming to the western horizon; sunset is starting, and the light emanating from that far end begins in gold – that orangey golden aura – that by subtle degrees moves to amber, dark pink, and then the surreal bands of violet they managed to create, looking like, as you said, they are coming right toward you. Isn't it special? You can see the gradations quite clearly from here, but if you put your nose up against the wall, you can hardly see where the changes occur." And she walked over to the wall and acted out her comment. After a pause Alicia joined her, and they both regarded the wall in silence for a few moments.

Alicia said finally, "It's always fair to ask how an artisan achieves his effects, though my own answer is always the same – I don't want to know. Too much knowledge of the process would spoil it all. And that is after all what the artists want. An impression intended to create mystery and awe should be allowed the space to work on us in just that way. Unless you plan to pick up a paintbrush, let yourself be affected, even overwhelmed. That is also difficult, artistic work. Jackson taught me so much about that. I used to look at a painting or a sculpture for a few moments and then head for the next object, but invariably he would call me back. 'It's like enjoying a fine Bordeaux, darling. You take a number of short sniffs to saturate the olfactory nerves with the aromas and tinctures in the glass. So let us look at this one a little longer, and sniff with your eyes. Let it bit by bit wash over your gaze. And then let it wash over your heart.' I am such a doer, you know, that for the longest time I needed him standing next to me to keep me in one place. Eventually he changed me entirely. Changed what I see, which was changing what I am."

"Sniffing with the eyes. Oh, that is so sweet. And in your case, Alicia, a cute accent to those strange peepers of yours."

She smiled in agreement, and the two women began walking down the hallway toward the General's office.

"Jackson used to call me his Sphinx," Alicia said. "He was always charmed by the first sight of dawn, which that ancient monument represents. He often rose in the night to await the sunrise, and he did this with the conviction that if he relaxed his gaze and looked calmly and steadily into the eastern darkness, he would recognize the first hints of light sooner and sooner each morning. It was no use trying to convince him that an objective measure of distance and movement of the earth would keep this within certain limits. He would say that light was a law unto itself. And that is why, most of all, twelve o'clock noon had a special meaning for Jackson. 'The Glory of the Witness' he called it. I know he tried a few times to write a song with that title, but he always tossed his attempts away without sharing them. He was so embarrassed by half measures."

"That is why the funeral is at noon tomorrow?"

"Yes. Here's the General's door. Can we go in?"

His secretary gingerly touched the door knob. "Please. Let me... No, it is not locked." She stood aside and let Alicia enter first. "What do you think?'

The smell of fresh paint greeted their nostrils. Alicia switched on the light. "You surprise me again, Miriam. Yes, very clever of you. He would no doubt have scowled at anything other than blue, but this hue is so deep, so interesting, like the clearest desert afternoon. This big space can handle it. I feel as though I could find the hint of a star if I looked into its depths long enough. But, what is all this? Oh, I see, his souvenirs, waiting to be rehung."

All of the General's framed photos, certificates, and mementos were laid out on the floor in neat rows, in the order in which they were to go back up on the long wall opposite his desk. Picture after picture of celebrities, government officials, and family nestled alongside the occasional letter or document. The trophies and display cabinets were piled in a far corner of the room.

"The painters did that," Miriam said. "They set them out last night, intending to put it all up this morning. But since the General's plans changed, I suppose they are in no hurry."

"You don't know why he's delayed?"

"I'm really sorry, Alicia. He was very sincere in his regret that he would miss Jackson's funeral. His delay in Washington was completely unexpected. I suppose he is getting money for something. That is usually what it is about. Or plans for some new war games. The Action Room people are always excited about that."

"Curious what excites us." Alicia grew silent. She walked around the General's desk and stood at the window. "Such a beautiful garden he has. Of course, I would have preferred that he attend the ceremony. But at the very least I was hoping to speak with him, to feel that we could achieve some level of closure and of understanding between us after all of these hard unpleasant months that ended so abruptly in Jackson's heart attack. I still cannot fathom it all." She turned back to Miriam. "Can I not call him?"

"Our talk yesterday was so brief. He would only assure me that he would be here by the middle of next week, but that he needed to be out of all communication until then."

"Strange. And you say Ms. Dearborne went away this morning?"

"I did not speak to her. She left me a message that she had to go to Los Angeles. It is a bit unlike her, but she was due the time off."

"Well, I will do my best not to take all of this personally. I hope I will see you there?"

"Certainly. Captain Gray and two of his officers will drive up with me. I believe the captain is going to say a few words."

Alicia forced a grim smile. "I could say that complete silence is more honest and more meaningful, but experience does not bear that out, at least not in the realm of our rituals. Something always needs to be said, however much speech fails to converge with the circumstance it honors. I suppose we sometimes grasp an episode in our lives more clearly by means of everything others are unable to say about it." She walked slowly toward the door and cast one more glance at the General's collection. "How odd they seem, lying there on the floor, don't you think? So vulnerable to the casual misstep or some other such accident. On the wall they arouse interest, even a sense of dignity and achievement. Here they are just, things. The difference, I suppose, between looking down and looking up." Suddenly her general regard roused itself to a focused interest. She leaned over and peered into the sea of frames. "That is Jackson and Paul. And strangely enough, it was taken up at Pale Moon. Help me get it. I don't want to risk stepping on anything."

She gripped Miriam's hand and stretched her other arm out and down almost to the geometric center of the grouping. "I'm going to need a bit more support. Better place your foot against mine. Wouldn't want to stumble." Her arm and shoulder trembled as she gradually worked her fingers under the small picture and managed to slip it into her grasp. She hopped back up and gently collided with her companion. "Oh! Sorry. Look at this. A funny little square mounting, even though the content is a five-by-eight snapshot. Jackson, and the General for that matter, so much slimmer. It was our land then. And is now." She held the picture to her heart and took a long, trembling intake of breath. Miriam could see that she was suppressing the urge to cry.

"Let's go over to my office, Alicia. I have some wonderful teas that you can choose from. And now I think about it, instead of you writing a note and putting it here on his desk, let's try calling him at his Pentagon office and his house both. We might get lucky."

Alicia gave her a grateful look and made a move toward the door, but then hesitated and looked back at the floor. "Do you think the workmen will leave that empty square space when they put everything back up on the wall, or will they close it in with the other hangings?" She looked at Miriam and laughed. "I guess I'm not sure what the more sensible thing to do is."

Miriam shrugged her tiny shoulders. "A problem for another day – I get used to that, there are so many of them. And hopefully it will be someone else's problem."

They went out and locked the door behind them. After settling in with tea and biscuits, Miriam did try once again to reach General Morgan, first at his home, and then at the Pentagon, but after almost a half hour wait with the second movement of Mozart's Piano Concerto Number 20 looping through the speakerphone she had to surrender the attempt. The ladies parted without a good-bye, knowing they would see each other the next day.

No one at Silas, or at any other base in North America, would have been able to reach Paul Morgan that day, because he was disinterestedly watching yet another baseball game at his condominium in Northern Virginia with no telephone hookup to disturb him. Not that he would have minded that or any other disturbance. He did not care for baseball, but being under house arrest there was little else to do while the intense, confidential negotiations were taking place outside the scrutiny of all but a handful of officers to save him from a prison sentence. Many involved in the case expected, even feared, the outdoorsman in him, the restless giant that would soon rage against his confines, confines the more oppressive because the most familiar, and so two agents were on duty day and night to at least remind him that opposition existed, whether or not he paid it any heed. But for now the General was all silence and composure. He was not going to sulk over recent misadventures, as he had done after Whiting lost to Pondhurst, and he was not going to imagine that what suddenly became out of reach remained a star in his future. A hard reality sat next to him on the couch, a reality more formidable than the sentinels who wandered through his rooms and sat on his balcony. Stahlbergen was in the hospital, and he had put him there. No one had witnessed the altercation, and the General's refusal to tell anyone, including his lawyer, why this had happened left a dumb-founded division of the Army in search of legal justifications, friendly politicians, and a line of credit to fund the potential battles ahead.

One curious expertise had flourished around the persona of Paul Morgan over the past year or so (to be precise, from the moment Cyclops opened his brooding, blood-red orb) and that was the adroitness with which the corridors of power confined the crises under his aegis to few eyes and even fewer ears. The menace he had franken-steined into precarious near-life under rock and sand induced such a cold terror in those who knew of it that they allowed their own hearts and minds to be thoroughly entranced by the black magic spell that human psychology knows as "doing something else" and "thinking about something else." You do not speak of your final heartbeat, to be fair, because you will never know its arrival, and to be unfair, because you imagine it never will arrive. The officials and officers who were regularly informed of the cyber-wrestling between code and colossus read their briefings but briefly and then found ever novel and creative means of filling the next second with an important issue or amusing pastime as far removed from the Silas Testing Grounds as their tangential interests could take them.

This new crisis was therefore addressed with the same careful calculation, that is to say, seal tight the rumor lid, keep the TV remote in the General's hand, and convince the doctor from Switzerland to take home some extra cash after his bones knitted. And for the moment the strategy was working, as far as to acknowledge that charges against Morgan were teased out in conversation, but not yet acted upon. Stahlbergen himself was also passing many hours with a remote in his hand, for he was once again indulged to a fault in the private wing of a military hospital, every idle request or wince of pain assuaged within minutes of its manifestation. His physical healing did not require this extreme attentiveness, but, as the theory went, if a man for a period of time always gets what he wants perhaps he will eventually believe that whatever takes place is what he wants. So the orchestration of pulse-takings, x-rays, reassurances, and three-course meals persisted, and every evening the officer in charge of negotiations made a new offer. The doctor for now said "No," or nothing, but that he continued to confine his complaining to creature comforts reassured the strategists that the patient's only concerns were indulging his appetites and prolonging the torturous apprehension of his caregivers.

Had he allowed himself to follow a wispy trail of speculation about his current predicament to its most petrified conclusion, the General could only have seen his career and current identity at an end, and a new and formless death-in-life awaiting him on the other side of a gavel and sentence. At moments such fears did creep about him, an impassive future pressing its enigmatic nose up against the glass pane of his present, leaving that present a crystalline emptiness that held no movement or variation, no hope or diversion. Fortunately, the dawn knows no fixture, and light finds its way through crannies unexplored by resignation and despair.

Thus it was that in the same moment that the ladies were having their tea and biscuits, and both the General and Stahlbergen were each in their respective corners of comfort watching the same listless pitcher's duel of no hits but sundry walks and errors, a curious turning point blossomed forth into the ether right between Morgan and a high fastball over the catcher's head (which brought home what proved to be the only run of the game). He could not explain it to himself just then, and a few months later he could only say to his secretary in passing – during an afternoon when the two of them were going through a stack of personnel folders – as she was tucking away one folder of documents and taking out another, "What we are doing, Miriam, is the most ordinary of the ordinary. But what makes it ordinary? Not that it is tedious and unimportant, but that it is the most important thing of all." Confused, and a little nervous over her boss's state of mind these same past few months, Miriam's fingers trembled a little as she reopened the folder and started going through the papers thinking she had overlooked this "most important thing." The General reached across the desk and took her hand. "I only mean that no one notices. No one cares about the mundane things that people do, or that they themselves do. That is why I am now staying as mundane as possible. Hiding under the folds of normality, fading to invisible, right in front of everyone." As his secretary still seemed a trifle uneasy, the General found it necessary to lighten the mood, "You must admit, an ordinary Paul Morgan is not such an ogre to be around, wouldn't you say?" And here she laughed, and soon they were out the door and over to the Summit for an early dinner.

The birth of that ordinary Paul Morgan occurred that moment on his couch while the catcher scrambled for the ball and the runner from third kicked up a triumphant cloud of red dust, and the travail went unnoticed by his captors.

"Sounds like the crowd finally came to life," the officer called out from the kitchen. "Someone get a hit?"

There it was. Morgan saw his moment. He rose from the couch and joined his interlocutor at the coffee maker, who was tidying up a mess of water and grounds from the counter.

"Someone finally made a mistake he can only chase after with futility," the General said. "Which, I suppose, sums up many a day of many a man and woman."

"Like me and these filters. Am I doing this right, general? I should have asked you."

"No need to fold it like that. That will inhibit the flow of water. I would just throw it out and start over."

"Right. Sorry for the waste."

"Oh hell, I wish such things bothered me. My sense of purpose used to allow me to get annoyed at whatever stood in its way. Without it, everything stands still, or falls as it falls."

"Sounds like some good advice in there, general."

"If I leave the misery out. Everything seems to get neutral, too neutral if that were possible."

"You mean no attraction?"

"No dreams. No color. Nothing that wants to exist only for whimsy's sake, or an unexplainable intent. Just hard, intractable reality. Nothing budges, or even thinks of doing what it is not."

The officer placed the filter in the coffee maker, correctly this time. "Well, you have to see what is going on around you. But, yeah, dreams are important. You live the usual, and you dream the magic. Gives you something to hope for."

Morgan shrugged. "Depends. Dreams come true. Daydreams do not. A false hope is despair with a fur lining. You'll excuse me while I use the head."

The General heard the officer fumble with the coffee canister as he quietly walked past the bathroom door and downstairs into the garage. He reached into the cupboard for the keys and bundle of cash that he always kept handy. Then he got into his car, pressed the garage door button, started the engine and backed out into the street, and drove away. He reasoned, correctly, that they would try to head him off both northeast toward Philadelphia and south toward Florida, so instead he took back roads through Maryland and Pennsylvania, and made his way to Cleveland. From there he took the highway up to Buffalo and towards evening slipped across the border into Canada, where he paid cash for a modest motel room. After he settled in before yet another television and turned on the news, he was amused to discover that indeed no other run had scored in that inconsequential contest that had occupied him hours earlier. And, as he expected, there was no mention of his escape or what he had escaped from. This lack of reporting on this current episode of his life was to be expected, but the sheer silence of it all, the absolute absence of recognition by the conspicuous theater of human life as to what he was experiencing and feeling and noticing around him, served to underscore the truth that pierced him that afternoon as sharply as the knife thrust near his heart that he had suffered in a Vietnamese jungle those many years ago. Here was his chance to disappear, maybe forever. Live and breathe the normalcy of today.

Leave the maelstroms alone, and if others wanted to stand in their way and get swept into unneeded chaos, at least he would keep to the shelter of his simple life. There were a few critical tasks to complete at Silas, and once he completed them he would melt away forever, unless of course the legal fingerwaggers insisted on their pound of flesh. But blood they would not get.

The next morning he began the long drive across Canada, with the intention of eventually crossing the border at some point to continue on US back roads as best he could until he arrived at Silas. Urgency to conclude the saga that began with tunneling up to Pale Moon only to build a nest for a thermonuclear Argus whose eyelids still drooped, stared, and winked in unpredictable terror rustled in his heart alongside his innocent desire to just look before him and think of nothing else. He smiled at the curious experience of going nowhere and somewhere at the same time.

The days were spent driving and drinking in the views that passed before his eyes. He only ate an early breakfast and a late dinner, and as such his journey became an unimpeded passage through light in all its forms: the milky whisper of dawn fluttering away shadow and dream; the golden rays that set life ablaze with early industry and promise; noontide's majesty, inflaming forest, mountain, hillock, and town; the clarity that shone back from every object and form, each itself revealed for whatever it humbly was, as all things before the fixed star are humbled; the gradual strengthening of shadow and tone throughout the afternoon, this interval when darkness served its master to vary moment by curious moment the rich palette of color, depth, and contour enrobed in nature; then the final joyous heave of pale blue and pink, silent splashes bidding adieu with miniscule resignations each second toward grey, and grey again, dispersing at a pace that could never quite be seen. Each evening when he stopped for dinner and rest, this silent communion with the aureole world left him with motives only to see, taste, touch what was around him, and the noises that life made lifted and died like the desert wind. The televisions were not used, the newspapers were never unfolded. His greatest distractions were the juices of his own organism and electric flashes of his own mind. They never ceased, though he was able for long moments to cease regarding them.

So it went for many days. But this contemplative run came to an end somewhere in Montana when he could not find a motel that accepted cash and was forced to sleep in his car. The discomfort did not matter; he was certainly used to cramped and drafty quarters. But the change to his daily routine could no longer hold back a reliving of the memory, the scenario, of what led to the end of his former life, of what he saw his life to be. He curled along the back seat under two blankets, with knees bent, spine curved, and a bright full moon intruding its silver wash about the car interior, under his eyelids and, it seemed, even into his thoughts. At once the event replayed itself, and the wheel turned again and again until dawn without reprieve.

When he had received the news of the protests at Pale Moon and Jackson's heart attack, he flew to Washington at once. He had one aim only – confront Stahlbergen. He found him by chance in a Pentagon corridor, and with a restraint he was barely able to maintain for the thirty seconds they spoke, he asked to meet the scientist for an early private dinner. A charming restaurant was chosen, both men were decidedly punctual, but in the end all that was consumed was half a martini and volumes of bile.

"I suppose, doctor, you understand I am here to talk about what happened at Pale Moon."

Stahlbergen's eyes seemed to narrow in imitation of his narrow face. "Sure, general. What could be worse. Chaos is certainly the last thing we need right now."

"When do we need chaos?"

The professor started up in his seat and gave a nervous cough, not expecting a confrontational tone from Morgan. He took a sip of his drink and looked up at the ceiling for a moment. Then he put his arms on the table and did his best to exhibit his reliable mask of patience and scholarly learning. "General, the Monroes were trying to force a conclusion to this land issue only because they were sure of their legal – and political – standing. The response of the Army bewildered both them and Congressman Pondhurst. Helicopters and armed troops to stop a picnic? Gentle diplomacy is a tougher adversary, don't you think? Let them have their party, make their noise, and once they all rolled home we could have settled on a transfer date."

"A transfer date."

"Yes, but it's too late now. They plan to pitch a few tents out there, maintain a vigil until the funeral."

"The funeral. A transfer date."

"We've already been staring at a hard reality, general. Now it's adamantine. The Monroes are taking back their land. We cannot undo this. Everything has shifted away from our control. Maybe it was never under our control anyway."

"A philosophy of helplessness is not going to save us, doctor. But you forget the obvious – we can just tell the truth. Then everyone will run for their lives."

Stahlbergen let slip a rare guffaw of sarcasm. "We both know that enough officials already know the 'truth.' And what is the result? An ever tightening circle of silence and secrecy. That is what a truth like this does. A worldwide announcement would weaken this nation immediately, terribly, even if an incident never occurred. People would speak of nothing else."

"You seem to find time for plenty else, sir. You and Pondhurst. I, of course, read his absurd brief. You should tell your pal that there are many other ways to convey important news. What kind of perverse alliance have you formed with that character? You and he had been scheming for some time before the Monroes made their move. I was naïve enough to think that you were quelling his curiosity on our behalf, to prevent a nuisance congressional visit that would have forced us to conceal our shutdown operations."

"And that I did."

"By helping him endanger an entire population?"

"By feeding what he starved for. He wanted to meddle in your affairs at Silas, but as a private citizen, an outsider. He is proud of his ignorance of military ways, and he has no interest in learning them, or in befriending you or your staff. He went after that land arrangement you and Whiting had come up with because it was, after all, extremely fragile."

"So the congressman can break a toothpick. You admire that?"

"Fortunately he asked my advice on what he saw as a simple verification. Was there danger of fallout from the tests down south that occurred twenty years ago. I checked a few figures and told him no."

"Nothing like lying with a fact. South, as you may recall, is not north."

"Well, any further curiosity about our programs vanished. His 'supermarket' constituents saw his vision quickly enacted, and they and the Monroes forgot all about us."

Now Morgan sat upright in his seat, and rocked his shoulders in a way that should have been a warning to the thin man sitting across from him. "Please, doctor. Jackson got him elected. He had no choice. We were not forgotten, just disrespected that much more. I am only sorry that I underestimated everyone's interest in that, yeah, in that rattlesnake turf. But this pseudo-diplomacy of yours omits mention of the snow-white hands you have managed to scrub clean of any culpability in our little problem. I can smell the perfume from here."

"We must be confident, general. We will defuse it."

"Yet I've seen how terrified you are."

"When I think about it. I—"

"Why are you not always thinking about it? How could you possibly think, breathe, live anything else?"

It was almost a shout. The General still managed to keep his voice within the range of acceptable table talk and not cause an undue flutter among the other diners, but his anger was rising and he could only grip the sides of his chair for so long. A waiter started to walk toward them, but Morgan waved him off and shifted in his place as though to stand up. He paused, paused for what seemed to him a very long time. Then he shifted back and put his large hands and arms on the table. He leaned forward and spoke as quietly and intimately as he could manage.

"Two days ago, doctor, my son and I organized a marlin fishing party. We were three boats altogether, and our trip out, I am embarrassed to say, was nothing less than a loud and raucous old boys' affair, with a lot of drinking, laughing, shouting across our bows to the next boat over, and at one point, even a volley of fruit missiles with our starboard neighbor. Brad, my son, who is bigger than me – 'Bull' we call him – managed to bounce an orange off someone's head, which finally put an end to the silliness. When we reached our target area, the three of us fanned out to form a large triangular space between us, with each boat barely visible to the others. Then came the cutting of engines, dropping of anchors, and the arrangement of our lines and rods. And then the wait. I was already so tired from all that useless banter that I was happy just to sit and stare into the sea. A favorite pastime of mine anyway. You wait for all that agitation to settle down, to fade into a static buzz that you can tolerate without it upsetting the mellow place you try to find and hold inside yourself. You know what I mean? I sat and gazed at the water, appreciating the undisturbed surface, a complete lack of ripples, swirls, eddies. It was, for a long, long moment, a perfect sheet of glass, a sheer blue triangle – as I kept my gaze within the outline of our party – no different from the clear heaven it reflected. I was calm. The water was calm. The sky was calm. We were the same. No ripples in my mind, no movement overhead. Blue, and nothing. Only the sticky sweat around my collar reminded me that I was sitting in a lounge chair on a boat, or I might have melted away completely. As it was, I felt like I was disappearing and reappearing in the same instant. Can you understand that, doctor? To not know if you exist or not? That smoothness, it just stayed and stayed. But then – a thought started to nag at me, a thought about when it would all end, when the wind would pick up and the surface start to wrinkle, or some streaks of cloud quietly appear, or beyond all that, the moment everybody was waiting for, when someone's rod would bow sharply and start shaking like crazy, and soon that perfect sheen would explode into froth and tempest as a wild, angry creature burst aloft and threw himself about in defiance of our hook and line. It was not happening, you know, the pure calm was still there, but I couldn't get it out of my mind that soon the thrashing and chaos would be back. And then I thought of Pale Moon, and before it that immutable plain of cactus and shrub, calm in its way, and innocent of the monster who could so easily be roused by one successful code loop. Then white hot annihilation, an instant so quick you could not manage a startled intake of air, nor even raise an eyebrow fast enough to react to the horror. That is our life, doctor, yours and mine. The apparent serenity of desert wilderness a gloze to immanent nothingness. Nothing happened that afternoon. No fish, no wind either. When we got back at sunset the news of Jackson's death was waiting for me. Which just confirmed what I had to do."

Stahlbergen sat back in his chair and placed his hands in his lap. The General watched a curious smug expression materialize on the scientist's face. "So we don't exist, huh? Your philosophy of helplessness is no better than mine. But let us just draw a clear line, shall we? Leave the word games to reporters and elected officials. I built the device, well, managed its construction, and I can dismantle it. You dug the tunnel, and you accepted the depth your team arrived at. And you approved this software monitor-cum-ignition project, a contrivance so convoluted no one seems to know what it is doing or how to find out what it is doing. I will take the thing apart – unscrew every bolt and cart off every metal plate. And of course the radioactive core. But I cannot, and will not, go near this 'monster,' as you call it, until those code loops or lines or whatever are stopped. Stopped permanently."

"What about Alicia's crowd?"

"Talk to her. You have more charm than I."

The General winced at the dig. "Pondhurst is encouraging this settlement, right there at the foot of Pale Moon. You must have sway with him. People need to wait, stay away, Jackson Monroe's memory notwithstanding. It is a simple equation."

The scientist dared to entertain a leer. "Simple equation? It should have been simple enough to heed Colonel Andrews' warning in the first place. Where was one-plus-one-equals-two when it mattered?"

Morgan stood up. Maybe if he had not stood up it would have been different. But he stood up. He stared down at Stahlbergen, and continued to make a valiant effort to keep his voice even and subdued.

"It won't work, doctor. That clear line only exists inside your head. You knew, we all knew the facts from the start. Together we established—"

"What facts? I know how to assemble a nuclear test device. That is my only fact. I don't have other facts and I don't need them."

The General took in a long breath and let it out slowly. He looked around the dining room, a tasteful understated arrangement of dark wood chairs and tables, fine linen cloths, silverware and crystal, walnut paneling, large French porcelain vases with young orange trees, a quiet and efficient staff modestly observing and attending their discreet clientele. "That first debrief with Andrews, you insisted upon revisiting every ridge and rook of that firing sequence. You cannot claim to be ignorant of these other facts."

Stahlbergen smiled his last smile for several days to come. "I don't recall that. Was there such a meeting? Never saw a transcript... but of course, there was none, since, as *you* insisted, nothing was recorded."

One meaty hand gathered around the tie and shirt front of the hapless scientist and yanked him up to meet Morgan's ferocious gaze. "Perfume has a way of washing off, doctor."

"Not if the right people like the smell, general."

Fingers of iron snarled into a fist, a single jab of rock-hard knuckles into the scientist's rib cage. He had only wanted to inflict a sharp rejoinder, but forgetting both his own strength and the frailty of the other man, he felt the bones give way and Stahlbergen scream in what seemed more like surprise than pain. The Imp of the Perverse, with the impeccable timing he is famous for, chose in that moment to have the General ram a second jab into the same spot before dropping the man to the floor. Now the scientist was howling and writhing, but Morgan calmly and intentionally put on his hat and coat, and quietly strolled out into the street. He knew what tomorrow would bring, and he made no effort to conjure up excuse or escape. In fact, he realized he was rather hungry, and so drove to his favorite Chinese for a takeout.

As dawn began to emerge the sound of passing vehicles grew from the occasional rush and rattle to a steady rumble and surge, gradually breaking through his murky attempts at rest. The drama of his encounter with Stahlbergen faded back into the phantom world of the past, and the loud and louder morning imposed daylight and clamor on his restless thoughts. Despite the lack of sleep and comfort, he stepped out of the car, folded the blankets and placed them in the trunk, got behind the wheel and joined the stream of traffic southward. He drove until midday, stopping in Idaho for a meal and quick wash, then continued on with only one other stop for gas through afternoon and evening and into the night, crossing into New Mexico after midnight and continuing south toward Silas. He winced as he passed a sign for Brandonville, and did not venture to stare into the blackness where beneath the arid terrain his Iron Serpent lay coiled in a hollow cul-de-sac, eternally at rest or milliseconds from rage only Fate could tell. He had hoped to steal onto the base in the dead of night, but after straying off the road for the third time he yielded to the need for rest and stopped at the next neon-lit outpost he encountered. How strange it seemed that a person was sitting at a desk at this hour, ready to take his money and hand him a key without question. The row of pale green doors was only partially lit, such that he had to walk the entire length and back again to find his room number. Once inside he was on the bed and probably asleep even before his head hit the mattress.

One eye opened momentarily when dawn came, and closed again for several hours more. When he finally sat up it was already well into the afternoon, and he laughed to himself at the feeling that he was on vacation and could do whatever he wanted. After a bath and fresh change of clothes he was ready for the final few miles to his office and the myriad challenges that awaited him. The long drive across country had helped him clarify the steps he needed to take, and the entire plan that he had charted out in his mind was ready to be implemented, each action numbered and poised for its ticking off. Since it was now day he could not expect to enter the gates unseen, so inevitably he began to doubt whether his arrival would pass unheralded, or a posse of MPs were waiting to escort him to a holding cell. He had calculated that the latter was unlikely, given all the secrecy that had been engineered back in Washington, but prudence won out over hunches and he called Miriam on her private line. Her familiar musical voice was such a welcome note that he had to brush away a few tears before he could say hello.

"Such timing, general. I received two calls for you this morning. Do you want the messages? Are you still in DC? The offices are finished. I'm very excited to see what you think."

"Two calls today, you say? And how many others since I've been away?"

"Why, none. You need not worry. We've managed all of the routine inquiries, and everything seems to be humming along just fine. Monica is back, and she told me yesterday that some changes have taken place in the Action Room. She is keen to tell you about them."

"She's back? Where had she gone? Never mind. Yes, I would like to have the messages. And yes, I am looking forward to seeing the new paint job. I'm nearby, and should be arriving in an hour or so. But you need not wait for me."

"As you wish, general sir. You sound quite perky. I'm sure the base will soon be jumping at your pace once again."

"I couldn't do anything without you, Miriam. Those messages…"

"Oh yes. Someone from the Pentagon called to say that Doctor Stahlbergen left for Geneva two days ago, and that he accepted the offer. And Colonel Andrews called."

"What did he have to say?"

"He only left a number." She read it to him, and they said good-bye to each other.

He knew the silence surrounding his "escape" from the condo did not mean that no one had been looking for him. But with Stahlbergen back home counting his money, the military's only concern would probably be whether he had driven himself off a cliff somewhere. With these and other such images in mind, he called Miriam back and asked her to inform the necessary authorities in Washington that he would be at his desk later today, in case someone wanted to reach him. He then called the number for Robson Andrews.

At the first ring it was answered, and surprisingly the familiar voice said at once, "Let me guess, the escaped convict decides to make contact."

Morgan laughed. "Let me guess, the bounty hunter tasked with bringing back my head on a pike."

"A platter would be more poetic, don't you think?"

"You, kissing my dead lips. The mind boggles."

"Are you back at the base?"

"Just north, in a motel called the Rise and Shine. Ordinary, but clean."

"Yes, I know it. I stayed there when you last saw me."

"I'll put up a plaque. What did they tell you?"

"Generalities, and that I was the most likely person to hear from you. I asked if you were in trouble, and the officer replied, 'We only want this to be an incident. So help us keep it an incident.' So what was this incident that has had you incommunicado for almost two weeks?"

Morgan sat back on the bed and painted a long and colorful narrative, from his arrival in Washington to his phone call to Miriam moments ago. He included all the minutiae of his thoughts and inner impressions, and ended with an outline of the plan he intended to enact in the coming months.

Andrews responded to the General's intentions with some surprise. "The Pentagon will appreciate the chance to save money...and spend it somewhere else. But you should speak to Monica first, before shifting the pawns too drastically. Once you're done, the world we had created will decompose before our eyes."

"Is the world decomposing, or are we? Events are shifting past us already, Rob. I'm just trying to keep up. Yes, Ms. Dearborne has already requested a meeting. It cannot be good news, but like I say, I am determined to make bad good." Morgan paused for a few moments until he was quite sure of his confusion. Then he asked, "But why is she in touch with you about this? Have they hired you as a consultant now? Desperation knows no shame."

"I won't argue that," Andrews chuckled, "but the truth is I continue to savor the bliss of ignorance concerning this torturous battle with our own creation. I only refer to general gossip, which I hear about because Monica is now my wife."

"Well. You must have stolen her heart that night at the Summit. You weren't such a mope after all. What about Stephson?"

"Friends all around. No trouble there. And yes, I have to agree that events are spinning off into orbits we could not have foreseen. First the Monroe's land grab, then Jackson, then your disappearance – and what I now see was an embarrassing few days for the Army – and then yesterday I learned about poor Feldon."

"Whiting? What about him?"

"No one seems able to diagnose his condition, though I believe the cause is obvious enough to us. They found him in a hotel room in downtown Washington, sitting on the floor babbling nonsense. It was the day he went to see Pondhurst on our behalf. Apparently he stole some pictures from the congressman's office, took them right off the wall, and tore them apart back in the hotel. A complete breakdown. I have to sympathize. He well sees the precipice we teeter upon, and probably could not pull his gaze back from the abyss. He's at home now in Cape Cod with Ethel, probably for good."

Morgan grunted, "Until she leaves him."

"He's earned our sympathy, Paul. Mine anyway. I may pay him a visit soon."

"Not until that wife of yours saves my ass!" And they both laughed. Then Morgan abruptly shifted his tone. "You told me once that life without death is shallow. Keeps you from seeing things. You didn't use those words, but the gist was something like that. I thought you were just talking about losing someone close to you, which I've had my share of. But after all of this running and driving and hiding, I feel, you know, partly dead, or empty. And I can tell you, I don't mind. It's like being a ghost, merging into things, even though everybody still sees you and talks to you. Not sure whether I'm describing this right."

"You say it better than I could."

The General waited for more, but Andrews remained silent. Then he realized he had been gripping the phone receiver hard, and relaxed his arm and shoulders. He wanted to keep talking, but the feeling suddenly overwhelmed him that nothing more would come of talk, at least not now. "Okay, Rob, I should get down there. We'll talk again soon?"

"I will probably be out in a week or so anyway."

"I'll do my best to not have you arrested this time."

In under an hour General Morgan was passing through the main entrance. The near vacant parking lot indicated that most of the staff had gone for the day, and a quick scan of the vehicles that remained told him that neither Monica nor Miriam were inside. He considered turning back around and heading straight to his apartment, but he felt it best to see if any other messages were waiting for him.

As he walked toward the main building, he noticed with some surprise a circular depression of earth in among one of the flower beds. A slight irritation began to smolder as he went toward it for a closer look. Indeed it was an incongruous sight – a hole about six feet wide, neatly trimmed around the rim with a carefully arranged border of earth. But what was this corner of vacancy doing here amid the shrubbery and rose bushes? He looked along the entire length of plantings that adorned the grey façade of the building, searching for a clue to this anomaly, or worse, more holes. Then it came to him, and he laughed out loud in spite of himself. This was the scar from the flagpole debacle that took out a few vehicles, including that damned fool Osbourne's. He still hates me for it, the General mused, but no matter. Accidents occur without malice, and either they teach us something or they don't. He walked on a few steps, then stopped and looked back one more time. Just a hole. Inconspicuous emptiness. Curious how many months had gone by without his noticing it. He supposed the gardeners expected another flagpole to be erected in its place. And maybe there would be.

He passed through the foyer and saluted the lone sentry on duty. Then he pushed open the door into the long, dimly-lit corridor that led down to his offices. He flicked on the light switch and continued walking in stride as the cascade of overhead lamps came on one by one from the swinging doors to the large picture window at the far end.

And then he stopped. And stared in disbelief.

In the distance a halo of gold seemed to surround that picture window, such that the window itself seemed buoyed aloft by pillowed light. From there the walls glowed with a twilight radiance of amber and pale pink, then gradual shimmers of soft prismatic tints appeared, undulating in just seen ripples along the edges of discrete bands of violet that seemed extraordinarily to materialize, stretch toward him, and surround him in their mystic embrace. He gazed along the wall, his eye caressing the subtle gradations of color back to the sunlit "source." A giddy lightness began to pervade his senses, and, as he started walking again, this time in slow measured steps, he felt a sweet trembling pressure accrue in his heart, a gap of feeling that wanted to, and could, do anything, go anywhere, make love to anyone; and in that freedom he decided, desired really, out of the million possible things that could happen next, simply to put one foot deliciously in front of the other. He fixed his gaze now on the painted light he walked toward, and soon began to feel a similar illumined glow within his own breast; and then, in unheralded surprise, as a reflection of sky and trees reveals its inevitable outlines when troubled waters recede to smoothness, he now saw the beefy frame of General Morgan, that stocky muscular body, like a figure cut out of this empty corridor and pasted back into it, walking in calm silence, the heart of his attention curled into a disembodied sprite floating inside of, and now suddenly above, that body, like an unheralded gossamer anchor watching only this simple inconsequential walk down a corridor, as though nothing needed doing except to take in his next breath and listen to the sound of leather soles on linoleum, the rich click and slight echo, fall, press, rise, and fall.

He was before the door to his office. A phone began to ring, the muffled sound coming from behind him, in Miriam's office across the hall. He waited for a moment, and a moment more, feeling about inside himself for that floating sprite. Then he walked over and let himself into her room to answer the call.

As he suspected, it was one of the Army lawyers, hoping to go over the details of the agreement with Stahlbergen. He settled behind Miriam's desk and spent the next hour absorbing both the legal ramifications and the budget adjustments that were needed to pay off all the bills. The lawyer faxed him a number of documents to sign, which he did and faxed back. After he hung up, he was surprised to find a physical calm overwhelm him, which led to renewed feelings of fatigue and hunger. The entire episode had pressured him more than he had been willing to acknowledge. Now it was over, but now new challenges awaited him. But that was for another day. Tomorrow, to be precise.

He straightened up his secretary's desk, locked the door, and strode briskly out into the evening desert air. Only when he was almost at his car did he realize that he had not looked into his own office. He was fairly sure its new paint job would not please him as much as the hallway, but for the moment at least this day and its conclusion did please him.

At dawn Silas growled awake and into life as it had not for many weeks. The General ordered a full review of troops for eight o'clock sharp, to be followed by tours of all buildings and offices, right down to the last custodial closet. Miriam had been called in early to coordinate the inspections, and the pace of the morning was such that she could say little else to her boss other than, "Yes, sir," and "Here it is, general." The font of her feelings was thus restrained such that she could not give him even one moment of lingering eye contact to acknowledge her gratitude for his energy and return. Once he had paperwork in hand, off he went in his private car, and as the day progressed she now and then glimpsed him driving by as he passed from one corner of the base to the next. She was confident that the food service inspections would surpass his expectations, but she remained in suspense throughout the exercise as to what he would say about the office colors. Beyond that she could only trust that Silas had kept its disciplines intact. It also amused her no end that Captain Gray had called all morning long – at one point three times in less than five minutes – demanding to know when the tour was scheduled for the Action Room; and when the General finally radioed in Gray's instructions, the Captain's disappointment was palpable when he was told to assemble a team and scour down all the underground service tunnels.

The General intentionally omitted the Action Room from his review. He did not doubt the cleanliness and industry of the staff down there, and the peril of their task obviated any concern over negligence or trivial pastime. Monica's request to meet had kept him ill at ease ever since Miriam conveyed the message, and it gnawed at him all day long, despite his satisfaction with the troop review and general state of things on the base, and the superb lunch of grilled trout and fresh vegetables. So toward late afternoon, once the inspections were done and the follow-up orders given, he sent word that he wanted to see Captain Gray and Monica.

He entered the building through a side entrance and walked directly to his office door. He had yet to see the new look that the workmen had given it, and he wanted to get behind his desk and review a few documents without interruption before the important meeting. He saw that Miriam's door was closed, and he paused just before inserting the key to listen for her voice. And soon it came, that familiar musical timbre that so often interrupted itself with half giggles and sighs, as she was no doubt in the middle of one of the many calls he had asked her to make. He smiled to himself as he pushed open the door, switched on the lights, and closed the door behind him. The familiar taste of fresh paint saturated the atmosphere. He went straight to the window behind his desk, pulled up blinds and sash, and leaned out over the sill. A rush of warm dry air cleansed his nose and palate, and just in that moment the irrigation sprang to life, the rapid synchronized pulses obediently sending froths of cool spray about the garden. Flecks of soft damp air lightly teased his face and arms, and the rich earth soon began to impart its deep pungent aroma. The distant hills sat mute and omniscient against the clear sky, their lines and silhouettes razor-sharp in the afternoon light. He felt himself relax against the window frame, content to drink in this simple array of sensations that nature offered, perhaps indifferently, perhaps for him alone.

From the far end of the corridor he heard the swinging doors bang open and shut, and this was punctuated by a howling cackle. An internal spurt of annoyance began undoing his tranquil moment, as he assumed that the meeting attendees were already here, with Gray thoughtless and unheeding of his female company, as usual. The voices quickly grew louder and more boisterous, everyone seeming to speak at once, and he soon realized that the two, no three, people raising this cacophony were all men. A rapid knock at the door soon followed, and before he even finished closing the window Captain Gray popped his head in. "Sorry, general, but I'm sure glad you had me go over those tunnels. I felt it couldn't wait for a written report."

"Come in, then," Morgan said, keeping his voice low and even as he sat down and placed all the folders and papers on his desk onto the floor.

Gray was closely followed by two privates, who were smiling to themselves in a curious manner, no doubt the residue of some foolish banter they had carried with them on the jaunt over. The General decided to let them plash about in their own discomfort, and said nothing while the visitors awkwardly looked around for chairs and settled themselves in a line facing their leader. In those few moments the General made a quick appraisal of the room. All of his furniture and paraphernalia seemed to be in their proper places, which pleased him a great deal. Other than that, here they were, floating in midair – or so it felt, surrounded, even somewhat pressed in, by this unusual sky-like color that would not let you ignore its presence. He stared at the wall close to the right of his desk. A mysterious blue, with a tone as variable as a high altitude flight on a bright afternoon. Now it seemed open and pure, bathed in clear sunlight; another look, and a dark hue emerged, as though he was moving toward the edge of the atmospheric envelope. Could he almost see a smattering of stars? He disallowed such conjecture and looked again. Bright, and dark; a veil of murk behind the purity of day, now intruding itself, now receding, but never receding so that you ever forgot it was there. He looked again, and now he saw just a flat wall, the same flat wall. How were the painters able to do such a thing? Or did they do anything at all? Maybe it was all his own conjuring.

"...loosened in a way that showed someone tried to break in. Looks like they used a crowbar. My recommendation, sir, is to plug it with concrete. At least the exit hatch, if not the entire passage. Not sure we need that bunker anyway."

"We never needed the bunker, captain," Morgan said, only catching the last sentence of Gray's exposition. "Colonel Andrews had asked for it. But filling it with concrete is overkill. Just weld the hatch shut."

"But...!" For once Captain Gray's infernal habit served him well, as he chomped down on his lower lip in time to spare himself a potentially serious drubbing. A bit red in the face, he shuffled his papers about on his lap and murmured, "I was thinking, general, that we will want to apprehend this vandal. And then there are the cracks all along the tunnels."

"Such a moron will find his way into our clutches without our industry, if it is meant to be. But somehow I think it was a one-off attack. Now, what about these cracks?"

All three men started speaking at once. The two privates had obviously been involved in the discovery, and were eager to make their mark. Amid the polite jostling for attention Gray managed to prevail, and he introduced Private Nix and Private Shanklin and permitted them each in turn to present their findings. Loose-leaf binders were opened (Shanklin's papers spilling onto the floor), diagrams on graph paper were unceremoniously dropped on Morgan's desk – soon followed by a checkerboard of Polaroids charting the entire trajectory of the cracked walls and floors – and a non-stop shower of anecdote, observation, demonstration, and opinion maintained a steady downpour for the better part of an hour. Well into the height of this storm the office door opened quietly and Monica walked in. Neither Gray nor the privates noticed her, but Morgan watched as she looked about and unfolded a chair as though she were in the room by herself. She sat behind the three men and opened a notebook in her lap, which she began perusing and thumbing through without once looking up. Despite himself the General gazed at her for several moments. Her dark curly hair was charmingly pulled back in a way he had not seen before, and the composure of her eyes and mouth indicated an internal calm that emanated both intelligence and repose. His eye followed the soft contours of her brow and cheeks, the slight moisture on her pink lips, the clearness of her complexion, and suddenly she lifted her brown eyes and met his gaze. She instantly smiled and looked down again, and the General, now himself a bit red in the face, summarily pressed the button on his intercom. "Miriam, please bring water for the three of us," he said and stood up without ceremony. The three men shot up at once and snapped to attention. He continued, "Excellent work, men. Now get those cracks fixed."

Gray inevitably hesitated. "How about the idea of filling the tunnels completely, sir. We probably have enough–"

"We'll need that concrete elsewhere, captain." He addressed the two privates: "Let's get this done by end of month, gentlemen, shall we. Dismissed." Shanklin and Nix gathered up their paperwork and made their exit, and the General followed them out into the hallway to greet Miriam, who was just approaching with a tray with pitcher and glasses. Morgan took it from her, and they greeted each other with silent looks. Before he turned to go back into the office, he glanced along the corridor and back again, and with a wink of one eye said, "You rascal, bringing the streaks in here." Miriam flushed with delight and scurried back into her office. The General brought in the tray and set in on his desk, and took the time to pour out three full glasses of water. Monica and the Captain rearranged their chairs.

When all three were settled in, everyone drank from their glasses in silence, which seemed to amuse Gray, as he set his glass down and, still with water in his mouth, struggled to suppress a spasm of laughter. To avert a possible shower, Morgan's stentorian blare of a question reset the tone of the atmosphere at once, "Only one thing matters – is it over, or not?"

"No, general," Monica replied with quiet firmness. Gray at the same time shook his head, and after a hard swallow, added, "Well, almost."

"Almost may as well be not at all," Monica insisted. "Until something can never happen, it can happen."

"I think we should try to be positive," Gray retorted with an impetuousness that was at once undone by a quiet burp and hiccup.

The General reached down and picked out a note pad from the heap on the floor. He slapped it on the desk and took a pen from his shirt pocket. "Captain, Ms. – Mrs. Andrews, pardon me – I am going to write out the lyrics of a lullaby that my granddaughter taught me while I was in Florida, before I forget them. While I am doing that, I want you to tell me what the issues are. Don't look for a reaction from me. Don't worry about whether or not I am listening. Just talk."

Gray wanted to speak first but another untimely hiccup interrupted him. Monica, obviously prepared, opened her notebook and began, "We did manage to isolate the pollings between mainframe and trigger. Though I will need to clarify what I mean here by 'polling,' because more than one type is involved. The difficulty in trapping every incident had been the random pattern used. I suppose whoever devised the original software ignition was trying to make it tamper-proof…which worked well, by the way. But we managed to outwit that programmer's cleverness with enough of a delay, whenever an exchange took place, to send out our dummy code. Two unexpected anomalies followed, or I guess I have to say, one anomaly with two results. The first was that the device kept talking to us. The dummy code was supposed to stand in for the mainframe reply, but although these fake replies were accepted, the device kept sending out a signal request. Only this time it became –"

The Captain interrupted, "But keep in mind there are two kinds of polling –"

"She already said that, Gray," the General barked without looking up or lifting his pen from paper.

Monica hesitated for a moment. Gray hiccupped again, and she continued, "The polling became regular. Every hour on the hour, to be precise. We watched it for a couple of weeks to make sure that it was not an accident. Once we were sure the pattern was now predictable, we were encouraged to prepare an acknowledgement string that we sent off a few milliseconds prior to the hour, in the hopes that the instantaneous 'meet and greet' would stop these last twenty-four requests. We missed the first few tries, but eventually we got the timing just right."

Another hiccup punctuated the brief silence that followed. Morgan put down his pen, filled a tumbler to the brim, and held it out to the Captain. "Drink it in one gulp. Swallow hard." Gray did as he was told. He set down the glass and panted for several moments, gasping for breath and stifling a few burps.

The General looked at Monica. Her face remained calm and relaxed, but he could see an unresolved emotion in her eyes. "All optimistic so far," he said, "but you said there were two unexpected results."

"We erased all the pollings, general, all but two of them. There are still two calls from the device every day, and there seems no apparent way to stop them."

"When do they occur?"

"Midnight and noon, precisely."

"Does it matter?"

Gray spoke up. "This is where the other polling comes in, sir." He interrupted himself with a cough, glanced over at Monica, and looked at the General for permission to continue.

"Go on, captain."

"If you recall, when the request to initialize finally appeared ten months after the planned detonation, this was only the first stage in the firing sequence. There are…"

"Eleven stages. I remember."

"All the while that Monica's team was trying to close down the signals from the device, we were waiting to see how long it would take for the next stage to complete. And not just waiting. We developed a program that went in and spied on the detonator's computer as it analyzed each request line by line. Like watching a beast ruminate from the inside. The logs were curious. They revealed that it seemed to pause at the end of a line for hours, days even, as though it were thinking over whether or not to agree with each call as it was presented in turn."

"We both know, captain, that that is not possible. Something 'presented,' something 'decided.' These are just analogies – a fairy tale that science weaves around its machinations. Were there electrical surges perhaps? Or more likely the code itself is flawed, which I suppose means someone's carelessness is our good fortune."

Gray had been ready to continue, but the General's final comment stopped him, stopped him with his lips parted, pale lips growing paler, as the General now noticed. The Captain turned to Monica, but she only lifted one thin eyebrow by way of reply. He looked back at the General, looked into his lap, looked about the floor. Silence murmured, lifted to a chatter, and was soon screaming its unknown message across the desk, as Captain Ghost appeared ready to get up and walk through the freshly painted wall. Morgan stared at them both, the two people he trusted most to guide him into the heart of this tangled labyrinth that he had hoped would soon end with the Minotaur's severed head dripping firmly in his triumphant grasp. Another fairy tale, apparently, that science had no doubt despoiled. He crumpled up the sheet of paper he had been writing on and threw it at the office door. He stood up and again opened the window to the garden. The sprinklers had ceased, and a damp haze permeated the near ground. He breathed in the moist air and gazed into the distance. The sky had grown pale and milky, the sun a mere white disk above the hills, and the approaching evening seemed only to remove light rather than impart a luster of its own. He turned about and sat on the windowsill. Gray was still visibly unsettled. Monica was expressionless, which began to unsettle the General, so he picked up the thread of the Captain's narrative, "You had, then, these week-long pauses between lines of code. Does that mean we are still waiting for stage two to complete?"

Gray was quick this time, "There are no more stages."

"What do you mean? Ten more. You are in the middle of the second."

"They all completed, sir."

"You just said –"

"– how it had been. What we were observing. But then, well, I asked for a probe."

"A probe."

"Yes, sir. To see if – I thought, general, sir, that if we poked the routine just when it was pausing at the end of the line, we might find out why it was pausing. And finding that – replicate it, and insert it as a permanent stop. Or at least know what –"

"Had you consulted Mrs. Andrews about this idea?"

Gray wiped his forehead. "Our teams were working in parallel –"

"You did not."

"No, sir."

"And so you – 'poked' – it …"

"Yes."

"And …"

"It all unraveled, all shot through, all at once. In a minute or so – all ten stages had completed."

A pale light filtered through the window, and the room began to darken almost imperceptibly. The blue walls seemed to emanate their own nuance of twilight and dusk, and the murk pressed forward. Morgan looked at Monica and Gray, and they looked back at him. In their simple unaffected faces he saw mirrored his own empty helplessness. Neither fear, nor depression, nor agitation enshrouded their mutual gaze. Three pairs of eyes, open doors with nothing inside, stared into each other, stared down a highway that vanished into an infinity in either direction with no hope or promise. For several moments his mind was so blank he could not conjure up any association or meaningful comment, and in the next moment he almost forgot what they had all been talking about, until Gray's reliable habit of squirming his lips in and out his teeth resurrected the horror that would not go away. He had walked onto a freeway at rush hour, and an automobile hurtled toward him so suddenly no reflex could save him. And it kept coming, and his reaction was always too late, and there was no escape anyway in this violent river of metal, for any leap to safety would hurl him under the next barreling hulk of steel. It never quite happened, but it would happen, and he would, after all, see the end just before the end. Was that the real horror of oblivion, that you remained aware of it? Knowing that you did not exist, or existed only in pieces that never added up to anything? A final eternal sleep was too easy – life was not easy, so there was no reason to think death would be. And anyway, sleep is always troubled.

He did not move from the windowsill. He had nothing to say, but out of this nothing he managed the one competent statement that presented itself. "Let me sum this up: the bomb is ready to go off, basically wants to go off, and the only thing stopping it is a final signal from the Bang Board. And twice a day the bomb asks for this final signal."

Monica sighed and reached back to undo her hair. "If only it were so, general. The truth is, that final signal was sent over a year ago, the morning of the test. This polling at twelve hundred hours and zero hours is not a request, not a command, not a process message. We do not know what it is. As such, we do not know whether to stop it, speak to it, or just do nothing. We, of course, do the last, but it is not a choice."

Morgan realized from Monica's movements that the room was becoming a bit cool. He stood up and closed the window. He looked at them again, and still could find no meaningful words. He did not want them to leave. There should be a plan from them, an order from him. Something had to happen. He pushed his chair under the desk. "Let us stop here. I would like to say, 'Tomorrow is another day,' though I am not sure but it will be the same day. The whole stark business, in fact, has been one long day, wouldn't you say?"

They stood up to leave. Gray gave a brisk salute and went to the door first. He was doing his best to conceal his desire to make his exit, but with his hand on the knob he turned back and said, "We will have a new plan for you tomorrow, sir."

"Thank you, captain. Make sure this is one team now. You and Mrs. Andrews. Run it all as one operation."

"Yes, sir." And he left.

Monica started after the Captain, but she stooped to pick up the crumpled piece of paper the General had tossed away. With her one free hand she unrumpled the sheet and scanned what he had written. A quiet smile played over her beautiful face as she read. She handed the sheet to Morgan. "One stanza, looks like. A good start, general. Can I have a copy of the whole song?"

Morgan laughed. "If I can get it all down. I promised the little girl I would remember every word she taught me, so I don't want to disappoint her by asking for help just yet. Give me a few days. If we have a few days."

She laughed. "Chin up, sir." She started out into the corridor, and Morgan followed her to the threshold. She only took a few steps when he called to her, "Monica."

She looked back. "Yes, general?"

He had to ask. He had tossed it around for days, deciding whether or not it mattered. He concluded that it did not matter, and so he was able to speak. "What were you and Jackson arguing about that day?"

"Arguing?" Suddenly she seemed far away, and continued to recede further and further from him without moving. "We were not arguing, sir. Who told you that?"

"It was the general impression of the crowd. That he got worked up over something. Was shaking his cane at you, something like that. Alicia apparently will not speak about his last—"

"And neither will I." She turned and strode away down the corridor without looking back, and in an instant disappeared through the swinging doors.

One last failure to punctuate this day of revelation and uncertainty. With slow steps he went back to sit behind his desk again. Miriam seemed to have left already. He looked down at his papers and notebooks on the floor, and decided to leave them there. There was nothing for him to latch onto, nothing really for him to do. The long day's work was over, and everyone had their assignments. The interminable saga in the Action Room was out of his hands. He turned over the substance of what had just transpired, and as he replayed in his mind all that had been said, a new concern welled up in his heart. The dilemma they faced was clear enough. He could find no omission or misrepresentation in what either of them had told him. No, it was not the words. What revealed itself to him now with more clarity than he cared to admit was the unstated attitude they each carried with them, attitudes perhaps only partially visible to they themselves. Monica was reliable, smart, and incapable of deviation from a stated goal. But Monica was not wedded to this quagmire, and her skills in oversight and long-term thinking told him how distant she was able to keep at bay the more morbid details. She was a civilian after all, obliged to keep secrets and to do her job, but the day would soon come when she would collect her last paycheck. Could she be held accountable? With a whisper of guilt he dangled this possibility before his mind for a few brief moments, and concluded that a lawsuit from her (with Robson's help) would dwarf anything Stahlbergen had ever fantasized about. Anyway, he could not betray her. And – now felt more deeply than ever – how could he deny it: he was the one. He did this. Why should anyone help him at all? The answer to that question was encapsulated in the ever present Captain Gray. The man had risen from his chair and marched out the door as he no doubt would do, no matter how many times failure begged for success. This is who he is – a man who would dutifully reach for the next weapon he could find ("We will have a new plan for you tomorrow") and charge back into the fray. And so he would continue, who knows, perhaps stumbling upon a probably nonexistent solution, and more probably unwittingly poking us all to kingdom come.

He sighed. He could do with a little solace. He sat back in his chair and, for the first time since his return, settled in to enjoy anew his elaborate display of prints, photos, letters, and awards, apparent chaos to the casual observer, but each item carefully arranged in an emotional order known to him alone, and, he quickly noted, faithfully rehung by these impressive craftsmen Miriam had hired. He had wanted to relax and delight in reliving the stories that attended some of these pieces, but only moments into a reverie that he thought would go on indefinitely, he was forced out of his chair and stared hard at the wall.

A picture was gone. An empty space, forming the outline of a blue square, stared back at him, just as hard, a silent gap in his historical menagerie. He walked right up to the blank space and looked at the pictures surrounding it. Yes, that funny little snapshot of him and Jackson was not there. He glanced around the room, and then went down on hands and knees to look under the desk and couch. Nothing. He went back to the desk and dialed Miriam's number from an outside line, so as to leave her a message about it on her external answering machine that she would have to pick up the first thing tomorrow. Then he sat back down and stared at the wall again, and at that empty square. Reminiscence was now impossible. This innocent little void, which no doubt meant nothing to anyone else, unsettled not only his idle time, but suddenly transformed the entire wall display before his eyes. They were all just things hanging up there, so many shapes of wood, metal, and glass, wiped clean from the recent paint job for another round of multi-year dust collecting. And the trophies and medals just the same. Objects. Dead objects. The memories were in his head, not on the wall. And what was a memory? What was his life, and what was just a dream?

But he knew the answer to these things. Yes, he knew what mattered most. It was shown to him in silent blazing detail just twenty-four hours ago. He sprang up and went out into the hallway. He turned on the corridor lights and strode down toward the swinging doors, trying to take in the magical wall color as he walked, trying again to grasp that translucent violet aura with its occasional rainbow glints. And most of all, trying to lift out that silent happy sprite and his delicious bouncing float of here and him, himself in this only place, not thought, not dreamt, but simply, delightfully, seen. Before he realized it he arrived at the doors leading to the foyer. He stopped. "I am the same," he thought. He turned back around and saw the soft yellow radiance surrounding the picture window in the distance. Ah yes, this is what I need, this is the secret that Miriam inserted under our very noses. He walked back on down the corridor, as he had done what now seemed like moments ago, fixing his eyes on that artistic light while expanding his peripheral gaze to absorb the beckoning halos. Slowly, but not too slowly, breathe and look. Feel yourself. See yourself.

He arrived back at his office door. He looked at the window. He turned around and stared back down the corridor. He felt like a piece of cardboard. This was absurd. You could not replicate the streaks. What he experienced yesterday must have been an accident, or worse, just his own fantasy. These purple walls, that yellow wall. The truth is, they were rather silly looking. They belonged in a kindergarten, not a military installation.

But the streaks. You could not deny their reality, though for many months he had tried, until that evening in his office with Andrews and the stirring crazy dinner that followed at the Summit. He looked out the window and saw dusk beginning to settle around the base. Could they still come tonight? He rushed out the side door and into his garden. The sun had just set, and its pale glow cast hills and landscape in a greyish silhouette. Phantom shapes, of cars, people, swam in the far distance through dim and dimmer light. How heartbreaking the inevitable passing of day seemed to him now! Where was that divine lift the streaks infused into the moment? Why not this moment too? If the grace of Nature's caprice refused to visit, perhaps he could push himself into Her sweet ether by forcing his body out of its stolid rigor.

He looked along the ground until he found the valve box. He popped off the cover and opened the sprinklers. The cold shock of gushing water shuddered through him, as he returned to his vantage point and stared at the fleeting horizon. A hard splash hit him on the right side of his body, followed by a freezing tickle at the back of his neck. The line of light diminished, he stared and stared, looked for soft tints of something, felt for some uprising in his heart, perhaps some glinty dust bobbing about the atmosphere. Another hard splash to his side, another faint tickle teasing his neck. He began to shiver. Soon it was dark and the forms dispersed, and the grunt of traffic moaned a steady tremor in the night.

···· **8** ····

H E WAS avoiding it. He knew it, so it did not matter how much praise he was receiving from the casual passersby. For many weeks he had not noticed the gentle downward slope of the land away from the monument and toward the foot of Pale Moon; this was both because it was so gradual and because the crisp mountain shadow constantly interrupted the eye with its abrupt shift from darkness to bright light as the day progressed. Once he discovered this, it took him several days longer to find the right vantage point from which to fashion a drawing at once dramatic and mysterious. But here he was, and as it emerged now from under his charcoal and steady hand, he was more and more pleased with the happy meeting of intent and result. He accentuated the distance, so that the three-sided structure appeared to be higher and further away, in order to make room for surrounding details that he would sketch in later. A rare straggle of cloud spread a curious brush stroke across the arid afternoon sky, and it was this he was just now bringing to life on the page before it vanished like an unspoken platitude. Three of the men lingered for a few moments, boxes in hand, and when he glanced up one of them said, "Impressive work, sir." He nodded appreciatively, and they passed on. So had a few others given him similar compliments, and the welcome incentive kept him quietly at work while his squad finished loading the last palette before the airlift was to begin.

Still, he was avoiding it. What he was succeeding at rendering here in landscape, only underscored what he was unable to achieve in portrait.

Moments later a soft brush of hair against his cheek, followed by a welcome pair of hands upon his shoulders, brought his private industry to a relaxing halt. He leaned back to greet her smiling eyes, and kissed her face. She giggled and kissed him back, then sprang up and started walking off toward the group of women who were sewing the banners and bunting. As he watched the carefree retreat of her lilting step, he realized that something had to change, and now was the moment to change it.

He stood up and clapped the chalk off his hands and the dust off his trousers, then started walking toward her. "Esther, wait."

She stopped and turned. He reached her in a few moments and took her hand. "Let's go look at the monument up close again. I need some fresh inspiration."

"Oh? Is that from me, or him?" They smiled at each other and walked on in silence. Another of her guileless comments, that always so charmed him. As often happened lately, her manner prompted him into remembering how right Monica had been about her, about them. That evening of the streaks (his deepest experience of them, ever) and Robson's story had changed all of them, changed them in time, place, and heart. His surprise promotion by the General the very next day from Corporal to Sergeant Stephson took him out of the Action Room and in charge of both the stores and the helicopter patrols. He was not even debriefed over the status of the mainframe hardware, which he at first attributed to Morgan's perennial impatience over such details, though recent events made him suspect other motives. Monica had kept her distance from him, even after her traumatic encounter with the Monroes (he had assumed it was traumatic), and then she went away to California for several days, and he knew what that meant. And so he began to frequent the Summit night after night, and as he and Esther now approached Jackson Monroe's tomb and memorial, erected on the very spot where the dignified gentleman had suddenly departed from this earth, he was again flooded with gratitude for the minor turmoil and unrest that led him to this tender companion, one who understood him so well and anticipated so many of his concerns and needs.

And he realized that there was one other detail of those tumultuous days that he needed to be sure about. They stopped before the single shallow step that led up into the tiled area of the shrine proper. He turned to her and asked, "Am I imagining this? I don't think the streaks have ever come again since that night of my interview with Robson Andrews. Am I wrong? It's been the better part of a year."

Esther smiled up at him. "You're always wrong. But it's true. They've never come since. I don't remember such a long hiatus. That captain of yours, the one who grew up in Brandonville, he had this theory that some zodiac shift was coming, that we may never see them again."

"When did you talk to him?"

"He used to come in for strange late lunches by himself. After Morgan retired. The poor guy seemed constantly depressed. Unlike many people, though, it made him talkative. He would go on in this low monotone about how the universe was changing and we could not do anything about it. My attitude is that that's nothing new, and I told him so."

Jack laughed. "What did he say to that?"

"That unfortunate things were the norm, in this case, that I was 'unfortunately too too right.'"

"Captain Gray said someone else was right. Now there you achieved something."

"Don't be unfair. Whatever happened to him?"

"He was reassigned to Antarctica. I actually believe he is happy down there."

"Happy? How is that possible?"

Yes, how. Jack knew very well how, and here was the one aching concern that created a quiet rift between them. Because he could not tell her. Not yet anyway. "He's away from here. That's enough. And, I suppose, the bonus of as many solitary meals as he could desire."

She frowned. He knew she was not convinced, but he also knew that she trusted him enough not to probe further when a silence needed to be respected.

A different silence enveloped them now as the blonde couple stepped up in unison into the monument to Jackson Monroe. Before and either side of them eight-foot high solid black granite walls framed an open space about forty feet square. The large floor tiles were of black marble flecked with gold, and the entire paved area reflected a flawless sheen of sunlight and open sky. The smooth high polish of the walls bore the gold-leafed inscriptions of the deceased's favorite sayings from antiquity, two on each wall. Here the eye was compelled to linger over the beveled precision of characters that seemed to glow even in daylight. They took a few minutes to wander separately about the memorial and spend some time with each of the quotations. After a while they met at the center of the far wall and gazed again with admiration at the centerpiece of this unusual structure, dedicated to the memory of one man by his one and only belovéd.

The bronze bust was set in a niche at eye level. The smooth inner surface of the niche was not gilded or distressed in any way, such that the portrait seemed to hover in and then emerge from the surrounding black to challenge you with its presence. And that presence. The face, though modeled by a sculptor, was basically a death mask, with solemn features set in the mortal repose of finality just moments after his final breath. Unlike a death mask the entire crown, ears, temples, back of the head, and neck were all rendered in full detail. And unlike a death mask the eyes were open, as though while lying in state Mr. Monroe quietly raised up his eyelids to regard for one last time whichever visitor happened to be standing over his corpse trying to pay their last respects. For Jack, no number of repeated viewings diminished the feeling of casual equanimity the portrait emanated, the feeling of someone, who has just departed this life, taking a muted appraisal of you and your many concerns and ambitions with merciful indifference. He had tossed away many an attempt at recreating this understated, piercing gaze from eternity, and since his last failure he could not help but consider all his current industry as so much avoidance of a task beyond his abilities.

"What does he know that we do not?" Jack asked.

"Who he is." Her voice was barely above a whisper. "However complete or incomplete his life was, he sees it all."

Jack put his arm around her. "I have tried and tried to sketch this bust, to capture the surprise of him catching us out. It's like that, isn't it? He catches you napping, and you are never quite ready for him."

"That feeling is not in the bust, darling, that is in you. The sculptor did this. You want to create something else entirely, not the drawing of a drawing."

"What I want is to see what Jackson sees."

"Then you will have to die, or step out of yourself somehow. Of course, if that happens, you won't want to draw anything."

"His look does that to me already. Everything seems inadequate in the face of this gaze."

Esther nudged him. "Don't think so hard. Draw it again and again if you like. Just don't throw them away. How silly of you."

Jack grunted. "I should probably finish the drawing of the town center first. I want Alicia to be impressed."

He looked about him and took in the entire volume of space of the monument. How improbable was its sudden coming into being. As he considered it now, he could only say to himself that it was there because Alicia Monroe willed it to be there. After the funeral service Jack had approached her just as she stepped into her limousine. He expressed his condolences and apologized for General Morgan's absence, even though he assumed Captain Gray had already done this. He then asked, on behalf of the staff at Silas, if there was anything he could do for her. Those amber eyes gazed up at him unblinking, and after several disconcerting seconds she said, "Yes, sergeant, there is. Have your helicopter patrols ignore the trucks and workmen who will be coming and going over the next several weeks while they erect the monument." Not knowing what this meant, but not taking it seriously, he replied mechanically, "Yes, Mrs. Monroe, as you wish."

When a few days later he started receiving reports of those trucks and men arriving, and a backhoe starting to gouge out the land, and a tractor scraping away what proved to be the beginnings of the long avenue, it jolted him into realizing that he could never take those amber eyes, and what might lie behind them, for granted. True to his word, he gave orders that no helicopter was to fly within a mile of Pale Moon from any direction, reasoning to his staff that continued provocations could only complicate what had passed well beyond a minor border dispute, and that their superiors in Washington were in better stead if no further accident or violence marred whatever negotiations were about to occur; and reasoning to himself that the still-dreaded murderous flash of incinerating horror, which would obliterate in seconds all reverence and future vision embodied in the industry newly set in motion, would not move a tick closer to being silenced by tampering with the daily toil of life and lives unconnected to the dilemma he shared with his reluctant compeers. Death crept in everywhere; death was only the next breath away, each exhale standing apart from any assurance the next inhale would follow. And where was the General at that time? No word, no guidance. Jack could not move what he could not move. He could only react, and wait.

And now a village was coming into being, germinating and spreading outward from this dot of desert where an old man's death sparked both momentary chaos and a committed visionary purpose.

He looked again at that enigmatic head, then turned around and looked east, with Jackson. It was working. Against all odds, the large architectural plans that Alicia Monroe had spread out for him on her living room floor six months ago was starting to reveal itself in this flat, wild landscape, and week by week the pace was accelerating such that her guarantee to him that the first anniversary of her husband's passing would be celebrated with children frolicking on a large green in the town center, shopkeepers barely able to keep pace with lines and crowds of customers, a covered hexagonal bandstand large enough for a modest-sized musical ensemble, and a tree-lined avenue stretching a quarter mile to the horizon, was realizing itself in startling detail. The cypress trees had all been planted along the entire length of either side of the avenue. The square itself encompassed the monument at the western end, the bandstand at the south facing Pale Moon, the avenue entrance at the eastern end, which Alicia said would eventually be demarcated by pillars or an archway, and the municipal building and its clock tower at the north, set back slightly under the range's shadow. The building itself was a modest two stories, but the tower soared upward from the center another four stories, the large white clock face and black Roman numeral lettering crowned by a shingled pyramid, creating an awkward but undeniably eye-catching impression. Jack watched the painters quietly applying gold to the trim work, a perfect complement to the three tones of blue already completed. At the top of the tower two other workmen were tinkering with the half-open mechanism. Apparently an ingenious little computer was being installed to reliably trigger the sounding of every hour. When they ran the first manual tests on the bell yesterday afternoon, he and Alicia had been walking up the avenue to take in the newly planted trees and the lawn in the center of the square. The solemn tones that emerged from the shadows interrupted their lively conversation about the final steps of the full handover of the land from the Army to the residents of this new community that had so suddenly materialized out of naked barrenness. Jack had halted in mid-sentence while the bell rang out four times, a silence lingered on the air for several seconds, and then rang out four times again. After a brief pause they continued walking, and Jack had to resist the silly impulse to say that it was not four o'clock, or eight o'clock. Instead he asked, "Why is the clock tower isolated in that way? The ringing seems to come from nowhere, and no quick glance around would confirm for the listener its origin, unless you were standing right under it." Alicia was looking down as they walked and smiled to herself, and for a moment Jack thought she had not heard him. Then she said, "About a month before my husband died, we hosted a dinner party for Congressman Pondhurst and a few state politicians. From hors d'oeuvres to digestifs the entire conversation was about the future of our state and our community. The ideas and plans and strategies were endless. At the end of the evening we were out on the veranda, all very quiet and contemplative, no doubt because we had talked ourselves silly. Then, apropos of nothing, Jackson spoke up, saying to everyone assembled, 'People look to and think they know about what will happen in the future – next week, next month, next year. It's all about guess and approximation, and funnily enough it is often as accurate as it needs to be, within its own vague limits. And so we imagine that we master the future. But there is one future that no one knows about, no one can master, and no one can ever guess what will happen. Do you know what that is? Any of you?' After an unblinking silence he said, 'It is the very next second.' Pondhurst immediately made some contradictory noise about the importance of knowing what you're doing, but Jackson interrupted him, 'Hold up, Dresden. Just look at me. Are you looking? Okay. Now, what will I say next? What will you think next? What will *you* say next?' 'That you're crazy.' 'There you go. A moment ago you didn't know you were going to say that. Why is it different now? We are all standing on the edge of the Grand Canyon, ladies and gentlemen, all our life, with our next step forward extended over nothingness. The next moment keeps coming and we never know what is in it.' Someone else grumbled that everything is always the same, but Jackson would not respond. Later on, after all the goodbyes were said and done, and everyone had departed, he smiled at me mischievously and asked if I had been embarrassed. 'For them, darling, not you,' I said, 'because they never know what to do around you.' He laughed at this and said, 'A reminder of time passing never goes amiss. Who among us does not need this every day of his or her life.' And so, Sergeant Stephson, it is from that event that I decided to make the tolling of the bell a perpetual surprise. Out of the unseen sky, the notes of now and no return."

EL TAJIN, NEW MEXICO

Jack rubbed his eyes and squinted in the hard sunlight. Too much reminiscence, about what was right here in front of him. Memory always the laggard, making more of what was than is, no matter how recently Chronos has wiped his lips. The monument was done, and not infrequently visited. Fresh groups of tourists came every week. Soon they would come, in large and larger numbers, to see the town as well, and some would no doubt purchase a plot of land and start to build their dream home. How ordinary it was, and therefore all the more crazy, considering the foundation of molten lava this new world naïvely rested upon. The craziness he now simply acknowledged; it no longer frightened him. The taste of uncertain certainty that brooded under his feet was too deeply steeped in his psyche. Was it, after all, different anywhere else? Could he fly anywhere in the world tomorrow, get off the plane, settle in a hotel room, throw open the windows onto beach, mountain or bay view, and not feel that the next second his sense of who he was could vanish forever? How often the vision of Cyclops stared back at him – a mechanism seemingly awake, unmoving, unperturbed, but a mechanism whose very existence was to signal, by its final good night, the end of existence. "The quiet close to a successful mission," was how the General had originally christened it. Now, so many light bulbs later, he could only hope that that mission would never see success.

Somewhere amid his private musings Esther had walked off back to the bandstand. That he had not noticed her leave bothered him for a few moments, but soon he settled into enjoying the sight of her helping two other women unroll and carefully spread out a large piece of red cloth on the lawn, then take up scissors and kneel on the ground to cut it into unrecognizable shapes. Their work intrigued him the more because he could not fathom what was to come of this quiet labor, and so he intended to continue watching them until he experienced that curious transition from formless unknowing to obvious comprehension, when a series of strange, high-pitched warbling sounds from somewhere in the distance behind him interrupted his meditation. He turned around, certain of the cause of this annoyance, and though he could not see him, he knew it to be the one who was, unfortunately, his second in command.

About a hundred yards behind the monument was a large transport helicopter surrounded by a number of palettes stacked with boxes, equipment, and miscellaneous cargo. Jack strode over and took a quick appraisal of the operation. The men were all hard at work, either strapping down the palettes, preparing the copter's interior, or maneuvering the two forklifts in place to begin loading. He glanced at his watch and decided to devote a half hour to examining each load, and assessing with a few of the men how it was all to fit in the available space. The time went by quickly, and once he was satisfied with the details, he could see an interval was in order, both to give the squad a rest and to deal with the nuisance that continued to chirrup foolishly in the distance. He climbed up on one of the palettes and clapped his hands to get everyone's attention. He announced a half-hour break for leisure and refreshment, and suggested that everyone find a few moments to visit Jackson Monroe's monument.

As the men dispersed, Jack clambered down from his perch and peered into the shadows that the creeping outline of Pale Moon was gradually deepening as the afternoon progressed. Beyond the loading area and abutting the foot of the mountain range, the people of this new community had constructed a series of pens for livestock, and a large enclosure containing several chicken coops. It was from the latter that he could hear, and now see, Spooner cackling and running up and down chasing the chickens by flapping the sides of his large raincoat like some manic bird of prey. Droves of tiny chicks scurried about in startled unison, while their hens raced around squawking in terror, now and then leaping into the air as far away from this madman as their futile wings would take them.

Jack sighed and reluctantly walked toward the pen. When he was sure he would be heard, he called out, "Okay, Spooner, time to organize the load."

The warbling stopped instantly, but otherwise Spooner showed no acknowledgement of his superior's command. He continued running about silently, arms flapping, body oscillating. After several irritating moments went by, he gradually slowed to a saunter and made his way out of the pen without closing the gate behind him.

"Get the latch, will you," Jack said.

The private abruptly halted and stood stock-still, head titled slightly upward as though watching chicks and hens fly past his line of vision. Moments went by and he did not move. Jack was used to this sort of behavior, so after waiting a few moments more he walked over and put his face up close to his immobile adversary.

"You only have to pretend, Spooner. I don't care what you really think. I'm the first officer, you're the second. One comes before two, so two does what one says. It's a rule that's only as real as duty requires. Got it?"

The only satisfaction Jack received from this confrontation was that the private did not blink. Whenever that happened, he knew he had penetrated at least a few layers of this man's rhinoceros hide of a psychology.

They continued to stare at each other without moving. Jack looked him over – the tall wiry frame, the oversized hands, awkwardly long neck, and that defiant, hardened gaze – and considered for a moment whether it was time to settle their differences and mutual dislike according to the old-fashioned rule of the street. He knew Spooner, like himself, had wrestled in college, but he also knew that, although Jack was the more muscular and more experienced, there nestled deep within this strange character an unyielding kernel of iron that would not succumb to a final defeat of any kind, no matter what the cost to his own body or dignity. And so, after a few more eternal seconds went by, Jack concluded that in this moment, and perhaps at any moment, he could not afford to come away only a little less defeated than his opponent.

Spooner caught the look in his eye and recognized what was going through Jack's mind. A smirk formed across his thin lips, and he relaxed his shoulders and moved his left leg back a half-step, as though readying for combat. Something else needed to happen, and quickly.

"Let's not get Mrs. Monroe complaining to the base, Spooner. Not now. Close that gate and get the men back in fifteen. Looks like most of them are at the monument. You'll be in charge of both the loading here and the unloading at the base. I have to assess the damage our target practice caused over the years. Mrs. Monroe wants us to repair it all before the anniversary. Which I'm not sure we can do."

A moment's hesitation. Would lashes and chaos follow anyway? Then Spooner gave an exaggerated salute and said, "Yes, sir, sergeant, sir. Private First Class Spooner ready to take charge, sir. Madame Monroe must always have her way, sir." He turned about and walked back toward the pen. Then he stopped and said, "And l'amour must have her way, too, sir, as she always does, sir. We like your new lady friend, sir, with her bouncy blonde curls and funny little limp – but we will all miss the lovely ass of Ms. Door Burn pumpy-pumping down the hallways. Sir."

Jack winced and balled his right hand into a fist, but walked away without replying. He held his breath for a few paces without looking back until he heard the squeak of the gate being closed shut. A few paces further and he heard Spooner begin singing "l'amour, l'amour, l'amour" in high-pitched silliness. He glanced back at him momentarily. At least the man now had something to occupy himself for the rest of the day.

Private First Class. Why had the General done that? It had happened the same day as his own promotion, and all the congratulations given to Jack back then were immediately crowded out by even louder complaints as to why such an undeserving character was elevated above his station.

It appeared that most of the men were indeed visiting the monument, though it was a bit incongruous to see many of them wandering around the back side of the edifice, examining the stonework and crouching down to check the solidity of the foundation.

As he walked past them he shouted, "Don't forget the front, guys," gave a few vague salutes, and wandered over to and then stopped at the perimeter of the square, so as take in the activity without being noticed. Esther and the other ladies were still on the lawn intently working the red cloth. They had cut it into a few separate sections and were now busy shaping them into wavy patterns that Jack still could not recognize. He smiled to himself at the incongruity of their attentiveness to a work that he could not fathom, and did not really want to. He resolved not to go over and ask what they were doing, and instead watched the people still busying themselves around the bandstand. The carpenters were sanding the floor boards and thick support poles in preparation for paint, or varnish more likely, while a group of men and women were working the new flower beds around the entire perimeter. Some were turning over the fresh black soil, while others began removing young plants from flats and setting them out in a delightful array of random colors. Jack glanced over at the municipal building. No trace of the workmen remained. The scaffolding was gone, and the clock face, with its elegantly formed black Roman numerals, was set to the proper time. He admired for a few moments the restraint of the building's color scheme, and then smiled to himself at the curious disproportion of the modest two-story structure and its elongated tower, as unnecessary, and amusing, as it was striking. Such anomalies begged for explanation, but Jack decided that even if he asked for one, the answer was likely to come in the form of another "Jackson special," so he decided not to bother.

A movement in the far distance caught his eye. Two figures were walking along the avenue conversing, one of them talking and gesticulating with great fervor. He found himself drawn to watching them for a few moments until, to his great surprise, he saw, only about twenty yards away from where he stood, Alicia Monroe sitting quietly in a folding chair on the lawn watching the busy labor around the bandstand. There was no one else near her, and yet he had not noticed her at all until this moment, as though she had just materialized out of nowhere.

She sat perfectly still, her hands in her lap, her gaze steady. She was dressed in her characteristic white, but uncharacteristically her long straight hair lay ungathered down and about her shoulders and breasts. Even from where he stood he could see the glow in those eyes. That, together with her inconspicuous stillness, began to absorb him to the exclusion of all else. Curious, he thought, how unassuming a body at rest is. Like he himself just a few moments ago, any of the other people at work around the bandstand, or the men behind him at the monument, could have glanced over at her for the two or three seconds it took to register her existence and then wheeled back to whatever preoccupied them. To not move, but with attentive open eyes – here was true invisibility. If she had been fast asleep then no doubt one or another mischievous character would have been tempted to steal over and tease her awake. He looked at her eyes again, and dwelt for a few moments on their gentle motionlessness. What happens to a person in these still, quiet moments? Here was a woman alive to what was in her immediate awareness: perhaps what was happening in front of her, perhaps what filled her heart and mind. He realized how often significant images or connections came to him in such moments; how they filled him so solidly, how he felt that here indeed was a major event in his personal life, a quiet understanding that no one could ever take from him. He continued to watch her, and marveled at what goes unnoticed and unheralded. It would be impossible to stand up after experiencing some profound or satisfying revelation and announce it to the crowd. The crowd cares not for your understanding, and surely it had to be that way. To declaim the whisper of an angel would be to lose it forever. Or worse. And what was worse than forever? Maintaining an imaginary belief that, any day now, that quiet understanding that you had let slip away would come back to you.

He suddenly remembered Monica's request to him from a few days ago. He dropped his reveries and strode over to the figure that had been so absorbing him. As he approached, she looked up at him with a vague smile on her face.

"Sergeant."

"Excuse me, Alicia. Looks like I have a bit of an interval while the men load the chopper. Do you mind if I do a sketch?"

She furrowed her brow. "Of the bandstand?"

"Of you."

She gave him a wry look. "I don't mind, but you might have had a better result if you had not asked permission."

"No doubt. But thanks."

Jack hurried over to where he had left his pad and folding chair and hurried back to the same spot where he had been standing. After clipping a clean sheet to the board and readying the chalk in his hand, he looked up only to find Alicia no longer sitting down. She was over at the bandstand pointing something out to the workmen. He leaned back and smiled to himself. Then he caught Esther's eye. She was sitting on her heels with a piece of that strange red cloth in her hand. She smiled and waved, and he waved back. He considered drawing his belovéd instead, but mercifully Alicia quietly strolled back over to her seat and sat down again, resuming the same relaxed pose as before.

Jack worked quickly. It was not ideal, but this was probably the best he could manage for what Monica had asked of him. He had actually forgotten all about their conversation the other evening and her insistence on keeping to the deadline for this weekend, so he considered this opportunity a happy accident that was not likely ever to repeat itself. He took a little more time with the eyes and mouth. He wanted that quiet attentive gaze, the relaxed sentinel vision distracted neither by movement and sound nor her own internal broodings. The unwavering pupils as still and unfathomable as the dark gap between two stars. The lips gently at rest, servants to that gaze, at this moment more guardians of her silence than bard to her reflections.

He was nearly finished when a sudden boisterous roar of laughter from behind him disrupted his labor. He stood up and turned around to behold a sight that flared him instantly into anger. All of his men, all twenty of them, were crowded into the monument and boyishly tussling about, no doubt amusing themselves at the feat of cramming into that modest space. The ones standing on the open edge of the entrance had their arms spread out pushing everyone else inside, and soon the waves of laughter and shouting began to escalate into near chaos. Jack at once assumed that Spooner was behind this, but to his surprise the gawky figure came sprinting toward the monument from the direction of the copter, still wearing that foolish raincoat, and loudly clapped his hands and shouted at the men to get back to work. To his further surprise, they heeded the private's command without a sound, and in moments the men had dispersed and hurried back to their posts. Spooner looked over at Jack and gave a proper salute, and Jack saluted back and gave an appreciative nod to acknowledge the quick work he had made of this minor embarrassment. He watched a few moments more as Spooner walked away behind the last of them, then turned and looked over at Alicia. She was still seated in her chair, but it was clear that the disturbance had caught her attention, though she showed no signs of an immediate reaction.

A litany of apologies began playing through Jack's mind as he went over to speak with her. Alicia stood up as he approached and extended both of her hands toward him.

"Only moments after its completion. Not a little daring of you, sergeant. Many an artist would want to massage and tinker for weeks and months before showing something to his subject."

"Ma'am? Oh yes, please, have a look. I'm obliged to show you anyway, because there are special plans for it. With your permission, of course." And he explained in brief Monica's project.

She smiled. "As long as I have an early copy, with both your auto-graphs." She took the board from him and held it straight out in front of her. Those eyes silently drank in her own portrait for several long seconds. Jack in turn grew fascinated by their luminous gaze, and he had to resist the urge to take back the drawing and add a few further touches to pupils and eyelids. Once again he confronted art as ap-proximation. No matter how much we catch the spirit of someone else, it pales beside that person's living, breathing actuality. So, what was the conclusion? If not intentionally looking in order to render a subject artistically, then just – looking? Could you live your life just looking at what is in front of you?

He dismissed his unanswerable self-interrogation and addressed why he had really come over to her. "I must apologize for my men, Alicia. I don't understand what antics they were up to, but you have my word it will be dealt with."

"Seems to me it was dealt with, sergeant. By that private of yours. No need to be punitive on my account. It more surprises me that such things have not happened in abundance already. The monument has evoked far more reverence than I could have hoped for."

"Which it well deserves. I will just want to make sure there has been no damage."

"Not likely, but do what you have to do. Sometimes the vaguest possibilities nagging at our consciousness need to be checked off in order to have them leave us alone." She handed him back the drawing. "I am now keener than ever to see your rendering of our new square. Will it be ready for the anniversary celebrations?"

"It's what, seven weeks away? Yes, I can do that. But please set your expectations low."

Alicia raised her eyebrows in surprise. "I shall do no such thing. Set higher expectations for yourself, sergeant. What else is there to do with one's life?"

Jack did not reply. He looked about and saw that the women working the cloth had begun to put away their belongings and go their separate ways. Esther waved and walked over to join them. The enigmatic pile of red cloth was left behind on the grass.

"So it was not me after all," Esther said. "Was it because you thought I would be too self-conscious?" She reached out a hand and Jack gave her the drawing. With one quick glance she gasped in delight. "Oh, Alicia, it's not you, it's more than you."

"How fortunate," Alicia said. "I always wanted to be more than myself. And all I had to do was sit still."

"I'm not sure why you say that," Jack said.

"Because, my darling," Esther said, "here she reposes without any preoccupation. Nothing sticks to her, and she seeks nothing that would stick. I'm proud of your clear eye." She handed him back the drawing and gave him a kiss. "Maybe now you are ready for Jackson's head."

"Jackson's head?" Alicia asked.

Esther described their visit to the shrine earlier and Jack's concern over his futile efforts to do the bust justice.

"The sculptor himself would probably agree with you," Alicia said. "I was watching him work the clay model that first day. For the better part of an hour it was little more than a wet lump. But gradually, and then suddenly, miraculously – in a transition I could not detect – there was Jackson's face starting to come into being. I did not question what was happening. I just kept watching my husband emerge again from nothing. At a certain point I could not contain myself, and I started to effuse feelings of gratitude for what he was doing. But the man quickly said, without looking at me, 'I can only get this once.' And that was an ultimatum between him and his order-from-chaos that I had to respect."

"Sounds like he got it, once," Jack said. "Which means, I guess, that it cannot be done again."

Esther tossed about her golden hair in gentle Nays. "I still say you think about this too much."

"Or just draw it too much."

Alicia spoke up. "My conclusion from that day was this: that the sculptor molds the material, but we, the viewer, mold the ether nestled in the empty spaces the artist drew away. When you look into the eyes of that bust, you do not look at the metallic bumps and scoring. You look at Jackson and he looks back at you. And that 'looking and looking back' is our communion with the suggestive, holy space circulating round the portrait. You see, the viewer recreates the experience each time he or she looks anew." She paused and placed her open palms lightly over Esther's face. "Maybe some things are not to be created a second time."

Esther relaxed under her touch and said, "I see what you mean. The seeing is the creation. We rechisel the ether each time we look at the bust. Really look. In that sense, the science fiction story is true – the world is reconstructed wherever we go, and torn down again when we depart."

"You connoisseurs begin to convince me that appreciating a work of art is superior to fashioning one," Jack said. "Although I now understand something a degree or two better than before, which is that the artist also draws that ether, looking and looking again moments innumerable to unfold the indefinable identity that dwells in every person or object. And as you say, the viewer must do the same work – plow through their own dreams, through what they think they see, to engage the particular disclosing an artist was able to reveal. It is always partial, though in a sense the partial is also whole. So, ladies, why don't we tear apart this lawn, dismantle the bandstand, and go rebuild the shrine once again. Shall we pay another visit to the founder of this land?" He started walking toward the monument. In silent agreement Alicia and Esther started to follow him.

But they had only gone a few paces when Jack stopped and pointed to the pile of cloth. "What is that? Unlike your sculptor's magic, I can't see anything emerging."

"It's for the banner," Alicia said. "We will sew those red letters onto large white squares of cloth that will hang on both sides of the avenue entrance, just there." And she pointed to a framework of horizontal metal poles already in place high above.

"Quite a dramatic way to say welcome," Jack said.

"It will say 'Welcome to El Tajín.' Our new town's name."

"Oh, not 'Jacksonville.' "

"You're allowed to be a smartass this one time only, sergeant," Alicia scoffed at him. "Savor it."

"I do like the name. Settles nicely into the landscape, if you see what I mean."

Mrs. Monroe continued with her mock indignation. "I don't want to see what you mean. Let's say goodbye to Jackson for the day."

She strode off ahead of them. Jack continued looking at the stack of cloth letters.

"How did you ladies cut them out in equal proportion? I'm very impressed."

Esther laughed. "The obvious. It was already drawn in outline on the material. We just had to follow the lines. Carefully, of course."

"Well, the obvious never ceases to amaze." Jack looked again at the bandstand and tried to picture it filled with guest speakers, as it would be on the upcoming anniversary, and then imagined the new square filled with men, women, and children. Soon he was thinking about the dreadful cleanup job that his men would no doubt be saddled with. Some justice there…

Alicia screamed.

Startled out of their reveries, Jack and Esther ran to her as quickly as possible.

Alicia was standing in the middle of the shrine, her hands to her face, staring at the back wall. Visions of red spray paint or pock marks in the granite flitted through Jack's mind as he got nearer to the monument. It was not until they were nearly abreast of her that they saw what had happened.

The bust was gone.

The marble floor tiles were lightly smeared with dirt and dust left behind by the men's boots, but otherwise the shrine was perfectly intact. The granite walls gleamed in the afternoon sun, and the golden characters of the six aphorisms shone their messages in high relief. Yet despite this beauty and precision, the empty cavity in the middle of the wall sounded a jarring, vacuous note that undid an otherwise sacred silence.

Jack walked up to the niche. He felt all along its inside surface and examined the ledge where the bust had rested. He turned to Alicia.

"It was not fastened in any way. Why is that?"

"We could never decide the best way to do it," she replied. "We ruled out welding it in place, and the bracket and hook ideas that we looked at never seemed right. My mistake."

Esther stepped over and took her arm. "There is no mistake, Alicia. Why must a thief be thought of ahead of anything else in creating such a space?"

"Why would a thief come at all?" Alicia whispered.

Jack walked back over to them. "Obviously I need to go see the men," he said. "Why don't you both go on home and let me figure this out."

"I want to stay for a while, thank you," Alicia said. She looked around the monument interior. "I suppose, Esther, that we'll have to sit on the floor. How strange that it never occurred to me to have benches installed. We will need to work on that." She and Esther walked over to one of the side walls and slid down into lotus positions.

Jack looked at them for one long moment, and looked again at the empty niche. Then he headed over to the helicopter, all the while scanning the ground for signs of errant footprints going off in an unexpected direction. But the confused trail left by the men's comings and goings told no tale.

As he approached the site, he could see some of the men preparing to load the one remaining palette. The forklift was maneuvering in place, the hook and ropes were being secured. Many of the men were already inside the chopper, settling in for the ride back to the base. He could see Spooner in the cockpit, headphones on, talking to the pilot in strange distorted grimaces and gesticulating in a way that suggested a bawdy story.

He trotted over to the forklift operator and signaled for him to stop. Then he climbed up onto the palette and gestured to the others to swing the hook away. The men stared momentarily but then did in haste what he asked. Once he was sure he had their attention, Jack clapped his hands and called out, "Everything stops. You there, call everyone out of the cabin and have them line up just in front of the palette here." As two of the men scurried off into the hold, he looked over at the cockpit again. The pilot had turned to see what was occurring outside, while Spooner continued to banter on seemingly oblivious to anything but his own words. Jack pointed to the pilot and indicated that they were both to debark and join the others.

In a few minutes the entire squad was standing at attention. Jack jumped down off the palette and walked in silence along the single line of men, eyeing each of them closely. Then he stepped back a few yards and addressed them all together.

"Gentlemen, no one would call what has just happened here a crime, and I will not try to persuade you that it is. Trivial deeds hide evil in their seeming smallness, and if they stay small perhaps their buzzing may after all only annoy. But I've always had a problem with things that don't seem to matter. What to one man is a mere speck of feeling may be the heart of someone else's fire. Inconsequence is no standard of truth: worse, inconsequence does not exist. A turn of the head, a dismissive mutter, a too-oft repeated indulgence that chooses, just this one more time, 'not to bother' – such are the dire handfuls of earth we drop upon our spirit. I have no idea what any of you are thinking right now, and I will never know. Not even if you tell me. Because the same inner brush stroke never shapes both words and fancies. What we rue upon and what we utter flow in separate channels, and know each other more as echo and reflection than as issue from a single wellspring. It is easy not to say what we feel and what we want, which has to make you wonder all the more why we all talk so much." Here a few men snickered. Someone coughed. "Yeah, me too. I only mean that our own idle amusements may do far worse than amuse someone else. So to the point – something precious, precious to probably very few but no less important for that, has disappeared, and I want you all to know that it matters. Matters to the point where we are going to pry open and empty out the contents of every crate on this palette here, and if we don't find what I expect to find, then we will pull the other palettes out of the chopper one by one and give them all the same treatment. Before we start, then, does anyone want to save us all a lot of trouble?"

No one spoke, or moved. The only ripple in the crowd came from Spooner's characteristic blinking. Jack took the time to walk along the row of men once again and look into each impassive face that stood before him. He then had to admit that there were no signs of guilt, or anger, or even curiosity from anyone as to why this assembly was called or why their commanding officer had decided to pontificate the way he did. If anything, the men showed only a resolve to do what he had just asked of them, and find whatever it was they were supposed to be looking for.

"All right, let's get to work." In unison the team broke formation and quickly surrounded the palette. Jack spoke up again, "I don't know why none of you asked what we're looking for. But you shouldn't have to ask if you find it." More blank looks met his gaze for another moment, then to the ropes and crates they went.

As the search commenced, Jack called aside members of the team in twos and threes and asked them to recount their movements since he had last been there to examine the loads. With little variation everyone told the same simple story, that they all went over to the monument, and after some time Spooner called them back, and the loading continued and went uninterrupted until Jack himself had returned.

To the repeated question, "What were you all trying to prove there in the monument?" he received one of two answers: either "You told us to go, sir" or "Just a little fun, sir."

The men went about it. Some lids were pried off slowly and intentionally, others ripped away from their stubborn bindings. In one instance an earnest private hammered a packing case almost to splinters. Jack could not but call out to him, "I hope you didn't find what you weren't looking for." Because a few of the keenest members of his team had been the first ones up onto the palette, they were the last to be interrogated. Jack had to shout a few times to get them down and around him in a tight circle. He asked again for a recap of what had transpired over the past couple of hours, but again he was disappointed as even with these few who he prized the most, the same mundane narrative unfolded. They had been at the monument, most of them anyway, and then Spooner came and called them back. Jack dismissed them all, and as they walked back to the palette he stared into the empty sky uncertain what to do next. Was it really the best idea to pull out every other palette already in the helicopter, and undo all of the hard work his men had put in since dawn? They had dismantled sheds and fencing, emptied out two long office barracks and packed up myriad cartons of files, searched out every stray rifle, ammunition round, tool, spare tire, light bulb, wing nut. Nothing was overlooked. The realization of these efforts now began to overwhelm him. He could not undo all of that sincere labor, reduce it to the inconsequence he had just railed against. The obvious solution intruded with its thud of blatant common sense. Just fly back to the base and examine each load as it came off the chopper. The momentum of his indignation bucked at this compromise with simplicity, but after several moments of angry silence enough smoke cleared inside his breast to give the men the order to stop. The confused mess of broken boxes, metal straps, and clumps of straw they had already created was unceremoniously tossed back onto the palette or into the cabin, and in a quarter hour the moorings were back in place, the hook was lowered, and the forklift driver started up the engine once again.

Jack wandered away from the copter. He took out his small note pad and wrote out the search procedure he wanted the men to follow when they arrived at the base. As he worked he began to realize that this extra demand on his men was going to require some compensation, and so he also wrote himself a reminder to contact his secretary in the morning.

He was nearly finished when he heard footsteps behind him. He turned to see the young private who had demolished the crate approaching him, hammer humorously enough still in hand. He saluted his superior and, in an awkward moment of self-conscious-ness, dropped the hammer on the ground.

"Permission to speak freely, sergeant?"

"Of course. What's on your mind?"

"A bit of confusion, I guess. I can't help but wonder, sir, if we gave you the right impression."

"I understand, private, that this whole thing should not be hap-pening. It's often like that, isn't it, that what happens is what should not happen. Maybe most of the time. You've all been very patient and I have no complaints."

"Thank you, sir, that is much appreciated, sir." The private paused, and remained where he was. "And just to let you know, that box was empty, sir. Nothing but straw. Kind of strange."

"It met an appropriate end."

The private chuckled but still did not move. Jack knew this young man to have a character of simple earnestness and honesty, so his uneasy lingering was clearly not for gain or pretense. He said, "Looks like you're still trying to get to your point, private. So why don't we go there together."

"Okay, sir. Very simple, really, and I hesitate because, well, maybe I am pointing out the obvious. So if you understood this already, my apologies in advance. I just think it wasn't clearly stated that what happened, happened twice."

"Twice? What happened twice?"

"Going to the monument. When you had told us to take a break we all paid a visit, as you had suggested. After I guess about twenty minutes PFC Spooner came round and ordered us back to the chop-per to continue the loading. Then maybe fifteen minutes or so after that he rounded us up again and suggested that scheme – well, prank I guess you'd have to call it – of everybody cramming all together into the monument. Some of us balked at what Mrs. Monroe's reaction might be, but he said she probably wasn't around. So we all trundled over there and did it. It felt really silly, I can tell you. And I guess we got a bit too rowdy, because Spooner soon ran over and made us all hurry back again."

As the private unfolded his little tale, a fire spurted to life in Jack's heart and soon enveloped his breast in a smolder of rage and confusion. He strove to retain his composure, and the flame rose and sharpened to a single jet that seemed to lick at the inner cavity of his skull. He kept his eyes fixed for several moments on an empty corner of nothing in the sky. When he finally looked at the private again, he could not tell how much time might have passed. His reply, when it came, was barely above a whisper.

"Thank you, private. Dismissed."

The wide-eyed private saluted and scooped up his hammer, and hurried back to the others. Dismissing any desire to make sense of details, Jack trotted over to the cockpit and rapped on the passenger door, then without waiting for a reaction he pulled the door open and addressed the pilot first, "I guess you'll be ready to go in about fifteen. But first, Spooner and I need to get some of those nice plump chickens. Mrs. Monroe's treat. Come on, Spooner, let's chase 'em down."

Spooner laughed. "Roosters too? Why not."

"Sure, why not."

They trotted in unison toward the chicken coop, Spooner breathlessly chortling over Alicia's generosity. "She sees me, now. Now she understands," and as they neared the poultry complex he was almost laughing out loud. He got to the gate first, undid the latch, went through and jumped up and landed with a loud flourish, sending hens and chicks scrambling away in squawking fear. "Here we are, oh dinner mine!"

Jack was quick. He thrust a leg between Spooner's, threw a forearm around his neck, and placed his free hand against his back and shoved him to the ground. The private's muscular limbs writhed wildly, and his first lurch of strength almost tossed Jack away. A large calloused hand tried to wrap itself around Jack's forearm, but he was ready for this and, keeping his leg wrapped around Spooner's thigh, he brought the other forearm up against the back of his neck and pressed hard against his windpipe.

"Where is it!" he shouted in his victim's ear. The man snarled and continued thrashing his arms, trying to find some leverage to push his assailant away. Jack brought up a knee into the small of his back and tightened the grip on his throat. He was now clearly cutting off his breath. "Where is it, Spooner. I will press harder. Don't try me."

The private gurgled angrily and tried one more desperate thrust, and then went prone and lifeless on the dirt. Jack was not fooled, and did not release his hold or even ease up on the pressure. Another futile thrust followed, and then Spooner truly seemed to give up the fight. A few moments passed. Jack relaxed his grip slightly, but since there was still no answer he began to press on the throat once again. Then Spooner threw up a trembling arm and pointed to the nearest chicken coop.

"It's there? No joke?"

He spat out a gurgle of assent. Jack let go and jumped to his feet. Spooner likewise scrambled up and turned to face his sergeant. He was all wild rage and indignation. His breathing came hard and labored. He opened and closed his large hands as though readying for combat.

Well, then, Jack thought, if we go all the way, so be it. "Come on, private. We're due, wouldn't you say?"

Flushes of anger, confusion, even fear and hurt, rippled in crowded succession across Spooner's face. Then he dropped his arms and looked about him. A few hens were innocently pecking in the dust nearby. With a single swoop he snatched up one in each hand by the neck. He glowered at Jack for a moment, then rushed into the brood and snatched up two more. With a bluster of juvenile pride he held up his prizes in an incongruous display of triumph, then stormed out of the pen, the hens flapping and shrieking helplessly in his powerful fingers.

The dust settled and a quiet soon pervaded the enclosure. The hens and chicks went back to pecking about in silent innocence. A shift from afternoon sunlight to shade winked into place, and a slight chill tinged the greying air. Jack walked over to the coop and opened wide the wooden panel. He stuck head and shoulders into the enclosure and looked about.

There he was. He lay in the straw on his right cheek, ever still the master. No dignity lacking, his simple open gaze stared out unperturbed as though he had been patiently expecting his rescuer. Jack reached in and tugged at the bed of straw, dragging it close enough to gather the bust into his arms. He stepped out again and looked down at his prize.

"I owe you a debt of thanks, Mr. Monroe," he said out loud. "It's not every day I get to cast out a demon once and for all."

Jackson replied with wide-eyed silence.

Together they headed back to the monument, Jack every now and then glancing down at his elder. He always expected to see that same unwavering look, and yet each time he took in the frank contentment of a face that knew no existence but the present, he was curiously jarred out of every thought or impulse that strayed from the simple motion of his legs and the muscular tension in arms and back needed to hold close his precious burden. And so it was a slow joyous trek of silent awareness, until they were once again before the glinting pile of polished black stone.

The women were not there. Jack looked around and saw them in the distance walking slowly down the avenue just beyond the green. Esther happened to turn around and he happily signaled to her. He watched her throw her arms around Alicia, and then he turned and walked up into the shrine and across to the niche.

He set the bust in place and made sure it was properly centered. In a moment of abandon he rested his hands gently over the face of the bust as Alicia had done with Esther. Then he took his hands away and backed up a few paces.

"I'm home," Jackson said. "Are you?"

"I'm not sure. I suppose not. What must I do?"

"Just look at me. Then look again. No, don't move. Keep looking."

"Harder than it seems."

"It's impossible. But so what. The possible is uninteresting, right?"

"Right."

He heard the ladies' footsteps behind him. He turned and Esther was in his arms. He held her a long moment. Mrs. Monroe passed by them and walked up close to the bust. The couple soon joined her and they stood for several minutes in silence with Jackson.

A gradual envelope of blue light seeped through the late afternoon ambience and softened the shrine's mood. Twilight had come, and with it a gentle pull of resignation among the three of them toward reflection and rest. They turned to depart, only to pause once more. Unheralded, but unmistakable, the diaphanous atmosphere suddenly seemed to hold them in a crystalline stillness, as though they dwelt inside an ethereal jewel cut and mounted for the present instant, an instant begun before it was recognized. A molecular giddiness began to rise within each of their hearts. Eternity graced the air, secrets always latent, what whispered just beyond the senses now emerged in joyous familiar chords of surrender. Loss was love, pulse was stillness, what came next never had to be next and so the clock tick was no more. An unspoken acknowledgement of their mutual absorption in this bath of timelessness lifted them into quiet suspension for an elastic, elongated second.

They had only taken a few deliciously brief steps more when they were in unison surprised to see a tall dark silhouette at the other end of the shrine facing them in silence. The next instant a bristle of fear and anger rose up Jack's spine. It was Spooner.

He quelled the impulse to rush ahead of the women and challenge him, and instead took Esther's hand as the three continued walking in measured silence. When they were but paces away from him, Spooner took one step up into the shrine and stopped. They stopped with him.

Through the haze his face and features soon came into relief. To Jack's surprise, the private had changed into a clean shirt and trousers. His face was clean-shaven, his hands newly washed, and his hair combed and neatly parted. There was a slight citrus waft of cologne. The man stood relaxed and composed, his hands held together before him in quiet attention, his head still reliably tilted upward as though not quite seeing they were there before him.

Confusion blurred Jack's finer senses, and the elusive taste of timelessness fumbled into fact-and-figure normalcy. Where could Spooner have changed and groomed himself? And how do it so quickly? The light had shifted. It was no longer day. The bizarre impression began to gnaw at Jack's mind that maybe hours had passed, or even weeks, or maybe he had been in a coma and this was an entirely different month and year. Where had his life gone to? Why didn't Esther tell him?

"A beautiful evening, ladies and gentleman," Spooner said. "I am glad to catch you all before we head back to Silas."

Jack sighed, the whirligig fled. He took a deep breath and formulated a polite sentence or two to thank the private and send him on his way. But before he could begin, Spooner spoke up again:

"I was never one to admire art, and I don't really understand it. This I consider an area of consistency in myself, because you cannot admire what you do not understand. Inevitably I had to ask myself at some point – well, truth be told, at this point, right now – if that is something that I want to do. To understand, and so admire. My conclusion is that, No, I don't want to understand – but not because I don't want to admire. I don't mind if something is better than me. Many things are, like Pale Moon here. Been around such a long time, has seen so much. Not that a mountain can see and hear. Probably not. But you've got to admire longevity, because that particular quality is just not on our side. Not in our corner. We're the flare and spiral of a lonesome firework exploding across a black sky. The golden propulsion stream holds such promise as it soars aloft. The flickers of color catch a few onlookers. The bang of the explosion is heard only after a delay. That's us. Only recognized after a delay. Then gone anyway. And a lot of fireworks just fizzle. Like a lot of lives. Whoosh, zip, pop. Dead. The black sky is the only constant. That never moves, never changes.

"So, no, it's not because I don't want to admire, though like I say there isn't much to admire, except sky and dirt. No, it's because I don't want to understand. Understanding is just too painful. Some of the pain comes from all the trouble you get into studying something and trying to figure it out. And once you do, the morsel of certainty, of pure knowledge, is so small you feel only slightly less of an idiot... and only about one thing. That's a real big trap that it took me a long time to find out about. Once you're smart, you're dumb. To know a bit more, you have to put in that much more sweat and work, and then you only get another tiny nugget. We don't live long enough to really get anywhere. And so the conclusion? Just stick with the one little bit you know. Translation: stay dumb.

"That's part of the pain. But most of the pain is the emptiness. You look out over your life, you look at someone else's life, and if you're honest, all you really see is nothing. Four things happen: we get up, work, eat, sleep. Between those four we insert a few variations of entertainment – or mostly more work. It's a flat crawl from proneness to proneness. And eventually we don't get up. Pronated. We were told this from the start since that is where we always end up. But we always believe we're going to fly away somewhere. Or we believe we're all flying together, all at about the same speed, and that's why we can't see anyone far ahead or below us. Well, I have to say, 'So be it.' Accept your fantasy, and enjoy the show you've conjured up. But how empty that acceptance is. Mere surrender. You just give up everything to nothing. Heck, truer to say, nothing to nothing.

"What does art add to this? Does art teach you that everything is nothing? No, art creates things, fills the world with stuff. Then we get so used to all this stuff being around that we forget that it was not there in a natural way – we put it there. So what art really teaches is that you are nothing unless you have something, some of this stuff. Of course, stuff is beautiful. Some stuff is. But how long can you look at something? You look, you say, 'That's beautiful,' and that's it.

You can look again and have the reaction all over again, but it always comes to an end. You don't stare at a painting all day long, not even if you could and didn't have to work. Nobody does that. Don't you see? You look at something for a minute, maybe five, okay let's say even ten or fifteen. But that's only a quarter hour out of a whole day. And all you did was look. Looking doesn't do anything.

"Connoisseur types say they get some kind of taste of harmony or intangibleness out of art. I feel that way when I have a nice old-fashioned daydream. I'll probably have one on the way back to the base. I have the time for it. Meaning, everyone has the right to their private feelings, but private feelings go no further than that. They're just inside you and they have no effect on anything else.

"And that too is pain. To understand that all you have in the end is your own little dreams. I've learned to live with that. Now I just want everybody else to let me live with that."

This maundering diatribe was uttered in an even-toned, unbroken stream of bland intensity. As Spooner went on, with no sign of let-up, the ache in Jack's heart grew from patient reserve to impatient grating to an anger that smoldered in silence against his every wish to tear the man and his outrages apart. But the women were wiser.

When the private finally came to a lingering pause in his speech, Esther quickly interposed, "That's what I want too. To be allowed to live with my dreams. I want to start living them, without explanation, so that what I wish for comes to pass. No one else has to know what they are."

"Not sure you can make a dream real, miss," Spooner said. "Dreams aren't real."

Unfazed, Esther said, "If you use daydreams for entertainment, private, then you can allow that others use them as milestones or aspirations, no?"

"We all need to have our prejudices, even our loves, reduced to naught sometimes," Alicia added. "I live with emptiness every day. It hurts. But it has taught me so much…"

"Taught?" Spooner interrupted. "Taught what?"

"That I do not matter. The world matters. Other people matter. I appreciate every day what I am now able to see, to let into myself."

"That's female, ma'am. Letting things in. Men don't do that."

"Maybe you all should," Esther said. She looked at Jack, and then made a face at his glaring dislike of this entire proceeding.

"Still, like I said ladies," Spooner went on, "it's all emptiness. But I don't see a reason to let it in. I can just see it and know it, and know that there's nothing to be done about it." He paused and stared at them, mouth slightly open. Then a new thought seemed to turn before his eyes, and he cleared his throat as though to start speaking again.

"Everyone has their own relationship to nothingness," Alicia interposed, now a little irritated. "You are right about that. But here you are trying to fill every gap in our talk with another burst of verbiage. Opinion should enlighten, private, and if not, then best to leave it out. Leaving things out gives room for new thoughts to appear, which otherwise would never come if we always spin the same wheel of rumination. My experience has been that a man who has never had the feeling that he has nothing to say, has nothing to say."

Spooner was clearly unsettled by this last remark, and he started to shift uneasily in place. For a moment the upper part of his body made a half-turn as though to leave, when he suddenly seemed to gather himself into a different, more aggressive momentum. He locked himself into an erect position, looked directly at Alicia and said, "Mrs. Monroe, I might be executed for saying this, but in the name of God and country, over the past three years General Morgan, Colonel Andrews, and their staff have been working on a secret hydrogen bomb and firing mechanism project. Sergeant Stephson too. Not many in Washington know or care much about it, so no one bothered to stop it, or even look at what they were doing. Now I figured out from the excavation work they did in the beginning that the tunnel and installation point went north instead of south, like all the other tunnels had done. In fact, I can say with certainty that the bomb is right here under us, right before Pale Moon. And that weird firing system that they set up, with all those computers and printouts and monitors, well the whole thing has backfired and has a life of its own. In the end they never wanted to set the thing off, but now they can't undo the countdown. It's been counting down all this time, and it's all the way to 'one.' And when it blows, it won't be a deep underground tremor. No, ma'am. They dug too high. So when it goes, this little town of yours will go with it. It's going to be a surface blast, a mushroom cloud."

In a wink he turned and walked off, and in another wink he was around the corner of the monument and gone.

The soft blue light began to succumb to the grey of dusk. Without another word the three of them walked across the green and the full length of the avenue to their vehicles. Alicia turned and looked at the couple as a gesture of good night, a trace of her amber eyes seeming to glow through the gloaming, then got in her car and drove off.

Jack and Esther watched momentarily as the taillights disappeared into the distance, then climbed up into the jeep for the ride back to the Monroe ranch, where Alicia had loaned them a private apartment for the duration of the handover. Jack put his hand to the ignition, but before he could engage, a hollow roaring sound filled the air behind them. They turned to see the transport helicopter rise a black monolith against a pale yellow western sky. It rocked slightly until reaching altitude, then leaned slowly southward almost as though a stiff exertion was needed to push home its burden. The sound of thudding blades softened from roar to pulse to muffled throb as the object shrank to a dark lozenge, red and white signal lights blinking in silent diminution.

These departures left them quiet and immobile for several moments. The evening still held the slightest hint of blue as a pale sunset aura released its final meager glory along the horizon. Jack reached for the ignition once more.

"Is what Spooner said true?"

"Yes."

The jeep rattled into life and pulled away. As they rode home Jack continued to watch, to look into, the blue-black darkness. The final spectre of light gradually enfolded itself in shadow, and as it did so he watched his own thoughts and apprehensions fade in similar fashion. The labors of the morning, the moments stolen from duty to render a few precious images in chalk, the silent dialogues with and about the bust, the antics of his PFC, all passed before the black screen of coming night and flashed their final pulse before departing. And curiously a new light began to emerge. In place of these fixations of memory and their confused messages, he saw with clarity how small they were, compared with holding the steering wheel just now, the warm desert air on his face, Esther quietly beside him. As troubling, as unresolved, as circumstances were, no past regret, or future, well, regret in fact, would bring him nearer to solutions he did not even know existed. Instead, this was the solution, letting fall away all that clamored within him for urgency and reassurance. As night came and the headlights painted a feeble rectangle of illumination over the mute wilderness, he saw only this, himself and the minimal light before him. All else scattered and melted as air. For a few moments a stranger held the wheel – Who was he, and where out of eons of time and space did he come from? Not quite a question, and not an answer. It just was this, an unfathomable fact of breathing, being somewhere. Here. He smiled. Now he understood Robson's "epiphany," as he could not fathom it that night at the Summit, looking into the dark at Pale Moon, and what he related of that moment in the missile silo control room. For an infinitesimal eternity all was taken away, and he knew what he was not. It was like the streaks in reverse. Not flooding him with inspired subtleties, but stripping his whims and ardor, leaving him suspended in nothing but himself – himself also a nothing, suspended.

"He did make one interesting point," he said out loud. "Captain Gray. At the eulogy last year."

"What do you mean?"

"He said that Jackson Monroe would live on in New Mexico. He was more right than he knew."

"Everybody says that at funerals. They have to."

"Well, after today it just means more to me. That bust helps him live on in a special way."

"You and that bust," she said and curled up further into her seat.

When they arrived at the apartment, Esther passed along into the bedroom and closed the door. But Jack had a lot of work before him. First he called the base and left word that his men should leave the helicopter on the pad without unloading it, and for everyone to take two days off. They had earned that and more, and he knew the aircraft would not be needed for other missions in the near term. Then he sat at the typewriter and drafted a message to General Morgan. It ran:

"Hope you are enjoying the calm Florida waters, sir. Waters a bit troubled here. Turns out PFC Spooner knows about the project, and today he actually told Mrs. Monroe. In stark detail. Not sure how this oversight occurred, but recommend having him join Capt Gray down south. Awaiting your blessing to set this in motion. Warm regards, Sgt Stephson."

He faxed the message through, then opened the folder with the large sheaf of inventory documents from the office barracks. A lot of detail to pore over, but it was better to work than to pretend fatigue would save him from his agitated state.

He thought over his message again, and smiled to himself at the term "the project." Such was the phrase the General coined when he returned to Silas after Jackson's passing. The man exhibited, to Jack's perception, an inner fire he had not seen prior to that time. Some kind of restless urgency came back with him from Washington, that had him bounding out of his office each morning just after dawn and scouring every corner of every building and boundary line. He cleaned up the base, reorganized his staff, and initiated a new round of secret meetings and brainstorming sessions to search out the elusive key that would turn the ignition routines off forever. Because he was no longer an Action Room regular, Jack was not privy to the details, but the General had wanted him to know it was happening. Which he did, in a curious way.

One afternoon Jack took a shortcut around the side of the main building, and suddenly came upon Morgan on his knees in his private rose garden. In spite of himself, he blurted out, "Practicing for retirement, general," and then immediately wished he could take those words back. But Morgan just looked up and smiled, "Have a look at this, sergeant. Go ahead, just hop the fence." Jack was by his side in a moment, and peered down into the soil. There lying in the damp earth was a golden-colored bullet. He knew it was for a rifle, though the type was unfamiliar to him. The General poked at it with his hand hoe, as though it were a special prize that one dare not disturb too far. "I came across this critter while checking the irrigation pop-ups. I noticed the other night that some of them were not working properly. But you know something, sergeant," and here his voice became low and intimate, "I don't want to speculate how it got here. I just take it as a sign. This is what we're looking for. Our final push. Find the golden bullet that we can fire right between the eyes of that beast ticking away at the end of that tunnel, and put him out of his, and our, misery." Jack looked into his face while he said this. Buried deep inside that wide brow and flushed cheeks and black eyes a restless, ephemeral embryo of determination kicked and floated with life. Was it only for the sake of that mechanical prey? It seemed not. The man had his sights on something else, something he seemed prepared to seize upon whatever instant it might appear. This impression passed in seconds as the General then gave him a summary of what they were trying to accomplish this time around. Jack's discretion was assumed, and nothing more was said at that juncture.

Monica more than ever was at the center of this kill switch effort. He had heard that she was in the General's office almost every day. A few times he passed her in the hallways or out in the parking lot. He could only gauge the success or failure of these new operations by his former partner's demeanor. She often seemed alternately happy and distressed, no doubt because of the two important dimensions of her life at this time. He was happy for her happiness, but it was clear that her distress level remained unabated, the unfound solution to their collective dilemma still hovering a phantom in an unknown future. If indeed the phantom existed at all, though the unknown future certainly did.

A few weeks went by, and then "the project" took an unexpected turn, or rather, an unexpected addition. Jack was called into the General's office late one afternoon after all the clerical staff had gone home. Morgan sat at his desk behind a mountain of beige personnel folders. He held a half-full tumbler of water in his hand.

"I only drink water now, sergeant," he said and took a sip. "Have a seat."

Jack was no sooner in his chair then the General put down the tumbler and folded his arms on the desk. "It's time for naked bluntness, sergeant. We don't have a solution. I won't say there is none. The staff are working tirelessly. I could not ask more of them. But several weeks ago, as I made my way back here across the country, I decided to myself that our complicated folly needs a bit of simplification, and now is the time to get that done. I am going to start pruning our tangled vine, sergeant, and I want you to take the lead. In front of you are the files of everyone here on the base who I believe has ever participated in the project, or knows something about it. Miriam and I have been working hard on this for a few weeks now, and we just finished putting it all together this morning. I think we were pretty thorough. I want all of these people transferred somewhere else. Overseas if we can pull it off. Look over each person's history, skill set and qualifications, and come up with suggestions as to where we can relocate them. I want these all to be promotions, or at least to look like promotions. No abrupt changes of situation if we can avoid it. Suit each candidate to a new mission or a new opportunity. No need for people's lives to lurch sideways because of our burden." He paused, and the gentle sadness that enshrouded those last few words lingered on in the silence. The General cleared his throat as though about to continue, but then seemed unsure of what to say next.

"I'll give it my full attention, sir," Jack said. "And if I remember anyone else who should be on this list I'll let you know."

The General laughed. "You won't find me there, though I should be. And will be. I'm taking early retirement. Another one, maybe two months, that's all, just to get this done."

"Is there a successor yet?"

"An unlucky soul, whoever he will be."

Naked bluntness, all right. Though it never extended as far as to bluntly state the obvious reason for these transfers. As the days and weeks passed – and he worked through the folders, and the lives, of the men and women he was reassigning – it sometimes felt like a curious logic at work, suffused with the charm of rarified hope. Pare it all down, take away everything surrounding this monstrosity. As all its protective layers disappeared, perhaps it too will dwindle to the naught everyone prayed it really was.

Such wishful thinking never took him so far as to forget the real motive behind this purging of the Silas ranks. Captain Gray underlined this for them both as they stood together on the tarmac waiting for the transport that would take him on the first leg of his long journey to the bottom of the world. Jack had handed him a brief that the General had put together before his own retirement with a list of duties and goals for the Captain to address during the first six-month interval of his stay. It included a call for a thorough examination of the arctic base with a view to itemizing all defects and deficiencies, and then preparing a cost analysis of repairs and upgrades.

"Since you recently managed this exercise here," Jack said, "I suppose the General felt your experience with all of our upgrades will help you uncover what others would not see."

Gray stared at him with a frankness he had never before seen in the man. "My recent experience," he said in a hard, measured cadence, "has been to cover our dire incendiary mechanism with as much busyness as possible, so that no one would see or know what they should not see or know. And now," he sighed and stared into the sky, "my disappearance completes the task."

A few empty protests began to coalesce in Jack's mind by way of reply, but Gray mercifully spared him the hypocrisy by continuing, "Covering something, forgetting something, not knowing about something. Rather the way life works, wouldn't you say, sergeant? We have gone from unstated obfuscation to direct confrontation to magnificent error – most of it mine, I don't deny – to an intentionally orchestrated rubbing out. So here we are, basically running away, hands over ears, while the fuse burns its last unknowable length. I sometimes feel that what we want to pretend is not there, is the only real being that exists. We, instead, are not there."

"But Monica's team fights on," Jack protested. "I know her. She won't stop. She has every reason not to."

Captain Gray stared at him again for several long seconds. "She is very brave," he said.

The General had departed several weeks before Gray, and did so without the least ceremony. It was abrupt and unexpected. Jack entered Morgan's office for the usual 10 a.m. review, but instead of sitting behind his desk, pitcher of water by his side, the General was standing in the middle of the room looking at the mementoes on the wall. He did not at first react when Jack came in, so he simply took a seat and waited.

After a full minute Morgan turned to him. "I was trying to figure out what it would take to pack up all of this stuff. And then, you know, the simple alternative of throwing it all out came to me. Now I can't seem to shake it. Ironic, isn't it? That complete destruction now seems to me like such a good idea."

"You still have the memories, sir. Losing those would be the real destruction."

Morgan grunted. "True enough, sergeant. Though some memories I can do without. As for the plaques and trophies, I no longer remember what they mean to me. The event is not the brass. Anyway, it all may as well get boxed up. I'll just need to find a new wall before it can come out again."

"Or build one."

The General smiled and walked over to sit behind his desk. He looked up at his wall hangings once more, then looked directly at Jack. "I won't force you to read between the lines, sergeant. I am leaving for good. By the end of the week, in fact. I had prepared my retirement papers soon after I got back from Washington, and all the approvals and signatures have come through already. I know I gave you the impression that it would all drag out a bit longer. But that's the point. Why drag out what, in a way, has already happened? Better to yield to circumstances when all the pawns have aligned themselves. But I am not abandoning our project. We will stay in contact, and if something unexpected arises later on you are welcome to apprise me of the details. I plan to maintain the leverage I have here at Silas and in Washington, especially for what concerns us most."

They spent an hour over the usual status updates on the relocation project. At the end of it the General told Jack that this would be the last such meeting. "You don't need anything more from me for these final transfers but my signature. And we can do that long distance."

Jack stood up to depart, but Morgan stopped him. "There is one last item, and it is all in this envelope." He handed across a slim package that contained probably no more than two or three pages. "Final instructions are in there. When the time comes."

Miriam was not allowed to arrange a farewell lunch, or even open a bottle of something in the office. She and Jack were the only ones to see him off, if it could be called that, standing in the parking lot while Morgan loaded his car and then took each of them by the hand to say goodbye. Miriam cried through it all, and continued crying all the way back into the building. As they passed through the swinging doors and into the hallway, they paused for a moment and stared at the yellow patch of painted sunlight in the far distance, and its violet multi-tones radiating along the walls toward them. All was empty and silent.

"You put so much work into this, Miriam. I'm curious – did anyone ever recognize this as the streaks?"

"Only Alicia and Monica…Oh, and the General. He in fact was the most animated about it. I guess he wanted to be nice to me when he came back from Washington. And he must have remembered our special dinner, when I convinced him to let it happen." She smiled at the memory.

"It's a striking symbol of how nature invades our sensibilities – and more than a symbol, I would call it a testament to the enigma, the enigma of experiencing something, living within something, without knowing what it is."

"But isn't all of life that way, sergeant? I don't know what I'm doing here. Do you?"

"No, no, of course. Only to say, the testament is not the thing itself. These painted hues serve to recall, but they cannot give a direct experience."

"Well, he wants this all painted white again. His last request. The offices too."

"Funny that he cares about changing it back."

Miriam looked up at him with her soft wet eyes. "I don't think it's a change, sergeant. It's a shutting of the doors. He said that it served its purpose, and now it should go."

"Do you agree?"

She smiled in spite of herself. "I like white. But after it's done, I'm going too, into my retirement and garden. And I take my colors with me. But you and me, Mr. Jack, we will have our champagne."

And they did. The reassignments continued as far as they needed to go, and with Gray's departure, of all those who knew of the unconscious life that stubbornly refused to stop pulsating its immanent horror, only Jack himself, and Monica and her small team of programmers, then remained.

And, as he now knew, there was Spooner.

The narrative of his reflections flicked away as the fax machine suddenly hummed into life. A sheet of paper slid into place, and the printer tapped out a few rapid clacking lines of black ink and slipped the sheet across the desk and before his eyes.

It was from Morgan: "Concur in full with your proposal. Prepare the paperwork and I will sign it and personally see that it is carried out. My oversight is your blessing. M."

A pleasant surprise, to know the General was up and about at this late hour and so quickly approved his recommendation. He smiled at the last line. Another small burden lifted, even though the greatest burden remained.

And the silent few left behind were to bear witness in quick succession to the final nails in the coffin of their discontent.

Within days of the General's departure a staff circular contained a memo from the desk of Congressman Pondhurst announcing the completion of the contract that handed the lands around Pale Moon "back into the bosom of its rightful heart." Bottles were opened in the canteen, courtesy of Major O'Connell from the Information Center, the interim head of Silas. Someone handed Jack a glass, but he could only watch in silence the absurdity of smiles and toasts that clinked and lauded God knows what. Presumably everyone was gratified by the end of the helicopter patrols, the protesting crowds, the heckling billboards, and the pomposity of Pondhurst and his guarantees to "drive out the invaders." Well, congressman, welcome to the curse of success…

Almost every day the local papers carried articles charting the progress of Alicia's ambitious vision. ("The City From Nowhere Appears" one headline ran.) She herself tactfully declined to be interviewed or even to allow herself to be quoted, but she could not stop the press from printing photos of her overseeing excavations, foundation pourings, and construction framings. A general air of merriment pervaded the base, as though Morgan's retirement and the Monroe reclamation and regeneration had shifted the military's mandate from vigilance in preservation of life to celebration in praise of it. Not that this attitude ever prevailed in practice. But a peaceful rhythm in the daily mechanics of duty allowed a charmed passivity to settle over the people of Silas, and dreams often surpassed drudgery.

Jack himself succumbed to this spell, mainly because his own role had diminished in scope. The patrols were grounded, the purging done. Major O'Connell seemed unaware of his existence, or of the existence of many other departments supposedly under his command, an all-too-fitting addendum to the man's acute nearsightedness. Instead he increased his Information Center budget and ordered the production of a new line of promotional brochures, articles, and flyers touting the "new vision of civilian and military cooperation." There was even a booklet devoted exclusively to: *Dresden Pondhurst, from Supermarket to Senate.* ("Such is human nature," Jack mused when he saw the banner, "always living one step ahead of itself.") O'Connell clearly knew nothing about the Action Room or the tunnel. This army base soon looked and acted like any other ordinary army base, and turned its gears from day to day in the ordinary fashion that everyone expected of it. As the weeks passed, invisible walls of disregard grew up around each realm of responsibility, and soon the private world each person at Silas lived in glowed with the reflected happiness of their own preoccupations.

No one's reflected happiness was disturbed the day Monica walked unannounced into Jack's office. He was grateful for the interruption of nothing in particular, and when she unceremoniously looked about for a chair and sat herself down, her determined air caused a wellspring of hope to rise in his heart. Have they done it? Has the insentient beast ticked away its final remorseless second?

Her smile was sweet and familiar. She said, "I understand you have some sealed instructions from the General. I have some too, and item number one on my list was to come and see you. Can we look them over?"

That envelope was always the first thing he saw whenever he pulled open the middle drawer of his desk. He did so now, and handed it across. "Open it, please."

Her long slender fingers soon had the two spare sheets unfolded before her. She smiled again. "You're number one is the same as mine. I guess he wanted to make sure we talk to each other before we go our separate ways."

"Go our separate ways? Surely we've done that already," Jack said. "No amount of talking changes emotional distance."

Monica closed and opened her eyes. "I'm surprised. Why are you resentful?"

"I'm not. I love you. And Robson. I just think Morgan had other motives. He knows we cannot lie to each other. That's really why we're here. Actually, that's why I'm here. I was always expendable. You're not."

She was tired. Her dark curls hung about her face in uncharacteristic abandon. Her eyes lacked their usual curious intensity, and her posture was a bit too casual. But after a few quiet seconds she sat upright and leaned forward onto his desk. "You are not expendable. Only you can carry out these final operations. The most important element in all of this is stealth. We must, as far as we are able, wind this down without O'Connell or the others asking questions. You see here, the General has set up this private budget that we have exclusive access to. Our expenditures will pass through no one's scrutiny. And as for the physical work involved, I'm sure your men will follow your orders without question. The only tricky part I can see is hauling in all of that concrete. Maybe Alicia can lend you a mixer truck, hopefully without asking any questions."

And indeed Alicia did lend him a truck. Two, in fact…without asking any questions. The tunnel was flooded with concrete, per Morgan's instructions. Jack was also tasked with reassigning the military personnel that were members of Monica's team, and with offering the four civilian members contracts at bases in the Far East. To his surprise they all accepted, which made other provisions for maintaining secrecy unnecessary. When Jack faxed Morgan that news, he felt the sigh of relief all the way from Miami Beach.

The Action Room was methodically dismantled. Monitors, printers, terminals, firmware, furniture, and reams and reams of printouts, reports, and meeting minutes were removed in inconspicuous increments night after night and placed either in storage or scrap. The large mainframe remained, as did the Bang Board and the cooling system necessary to keep it all functioning safely. No one questioned this, and Jack himself assumed that after the final shutdown took place he could begin shopping the equipment around to his peers across the country.

But then Sergeant Stephson and Cyclops had a staring contest.

Another midnight removal operation had just concluded. His three-member team had packed up the elevator and climbed on top of the boxes. They held the door for Jack but he waved them on ahead. The doors closed with a quiet hush, and the cool silence of electric mentation clicked and hummed its indifferent business.

Jack wandered along the glass partition that separated the cubicles from the mainframe, and found himself in front of the Bang Board. Cyclops glowered a crimson hello, then kept on glowering. He smiled at the mischief this simplest of nineteenth century inventions had caused, a burnt out bulb flaring up momentary terror and confusion, then causing months of oddball inconvenience as workers shifted and stepped around his patchwork lamplight solution until the silly replacements, one centimeter larger than standard issue, had arrived. ("There has to be only one of these in existence," the General had insisted.)

His gaze lingered over the steady red light. Around it a host of miniature green and yellow and white lights blinked and flickered in response to unknown processes buried in the caverns of circuitry. Alone this sentinel of stillness paused and paused, and paused again, ahead of its ultimate promise to wink away into the finality of naught. Up until now, until this very second, that final dropping of its lid embodied all the horror of hell's indifferent ferocity, shivering to atoms what was at first an empty wasteland that now cradled the nascent pulse of an enigmatic death and its visionary rebirth. But now the hope of closure, of that final line of code writing itself away on the cyber-wind, nevermore to loop its stubborn recurrence, stirred him to fancy a serene moment of triumph as he watched that fiery filament dim and dwindle to darkness, and the long silence that followed expand in ether joy. So when ye see the shaggy beastie at last hath closed his eyen, shall we all weep or sleep at last?

In the distance he heard the elevator doors whisk open, and a sure step tap briskly on the hard concrete. Assuming it was one of his men, Jack called out, "Over here," but a startled gasp from the yet unseen visitor then startled him. It was Monica.

She appeared from around the corner and walked slowly toward him. She stopped a little more than arm's length away.

"If I could disappear right now, I would," Jack said and smiled.

"Never mind," came her flat reply. She clearly had expected to be alone. Not wanting to challenge her privacy, he tried to make light of the moment.

"I was just looking at Cyclops here, and wondering when the best moment would be to put him to sleep at last. It would be a shame to let it be just another step in the final dismantling, don't you think? Seems like a little ritual is in order. We could have a ceremony with a few members of the team, and you can do the honors of disengaging him yourself."

Monica remained impassive. Jack was not unused to that, so he carried the jest forward another step. "No, that sort of thing was never your style. And it's true, we've managed to keep all of this such a secret up until now, that ceremony might raise an unnecessary blip of awareness. And besides, the beast doesn't deserve it. So instead, here in the presence of one adorable witness, I shall personally say farewell to this one-eyed nuisance and his vacuous staring contest. Colonel Andrews' bent folding chair should do nicely." And so saying he picked up the folding chair, swung it back and walked briskly toward the glowing red target of his contempt. Another instant and he would be looking for a broom and dustpan...

"Jack, no. You cannot."

He stopped and looked back at her. She walked over to him and touched his shoulder. "Please, put it down."

He put it down, without taking his eyes off her. They stood close together. He allowed his gaze to caress that face he knew so well, her dark mass of curls through which his fingers had so often played and rested, her clear warm cheeks and soft pink lips that he had kissed and endlessly kissed, her thin arching eyebrows that framed those dark brown eyes.

It was this that intrigued him. He looked into those eyes, for what was probably no more than a heartbeat but felt like an age, and what he now saw was not her usual confidence, not fatigue, not indifference, nor any trace of fancy or amusement. It was fear. Naked fear, hidden perhaps from anyone but himself, at the black center of her pupils.

This perception began to assemble itself into a line of words that was about to stream forth as why and wherefore, but her continued silence withered that line before he could give it breath. He put his arms around her and held her for a few moments. As he let her go, she touched his cheek and then stepped away from him. Jack walked to the elevator without looking back.

She could not say it, and he would not compel her to. But he need not. The beast was still alive. Buried, muted, reduced to a single electric pulse they were obliged in secrecy to keep humming via some walled-up cable. But still it lived...

That startling moment, that he had lived and relived so often, suddenly dispersed before the humming and clicking of the fax machine once again. Counter-instructions from the General? Or new orders entirely? He watched as a blank sheet of paper slipped into place. But the typing ball did not move, and the next moment the sheet was discharged without a single character imprinted and slid across the desk to arrive just in front of him.

He stared at the empty sheet. Then in the distance he could hear the faint tolling of the bell of El Tajín. From across the clear desert air he counted out twelve distinct rings. How old was this custom, to ring the hour, every hour, all night long? It must at least date to medieval times. But how could that be? Someone sitting on a bench, or lying in a bale of hay, fighting off sleep throughout the night, just to pull on a bell rope the proper succession of hours? And how would the fellow know the correct time? Turn over an hourglass after every set of pulls? Seemed ludicrous.

He looked at the empty sheet of paper again. Another face suddenly emerged in his mind, one newly familiar, practically a friend. He took up a pencil and started to draw. First a deft oval, from which he decided to make it a three-quarter view, head turned slightly to the left. The all-important eyes were next – if they were rendered well, then all else would follow. In a few quick minutes they were there, looking slightly to the right and therefore directly out of the page, and those eyes continued to watch him in mute appraisal as he completed nose, mouth, ear, hairline, and the characteristic creases of age and its burdens. He paused a moment, and decided only to hint at the neck and throat. He wanted to be sure that the viewer always returned to that steady gaze of eternity, a gaze stronger than the glare of Cyclops, more sensitive than the secret terror from deep within Monica's breast.

He sat back in his chair and closed his eyes. Then he looked at the picture again, to assure himself that the face was real, and not just a projection of his wishful thinking.

"So you finally got there – drawing me and not the bust. Nothing like the obvious, eh? And yes, I am real."

"Not sure about that. Lines on paper, real? And my lines, no less?"

"Yours? What's yours? Not this face. What's real is what we're both looking at."

"Yes. The gap. I should have known. I had been looking in the wrong place. A place that did not exist."

"So, you got it?"

"Got it," he said out loud, his voice startling him back to seeing papers, pens, fax machine in the pool of light before him.

He smiled. This was for Esther. He needed to bring her a new gift, especially one that she would understand better than himself.

He got up from the desk, turned off all the lights, and passed into the bedroom. He disrobed quietly and slid under the sheets. He reached out and placed his hand on her warm back. A gentle welcome sigh responded, and she turned and crawled over and on top of him. Her soft breasts and belly pressed against him, her arms surrounded him, gentle kisses pecked his face and neck, and the nighttime melted into love.

····· **9** ·····

A SHARP HINT of salt air itched her nostrils and brought her out of her reverie. She had been staring at the pavement as they walked, and had drifted into an aimless daydream. She glanced up at him and clutched his arm tighter. He seemed oddly taller in this moment, his chiseled features as quiet and impassive as when they had stepped out of the car. She was about to ask her question a second time, but stopped herself with a low breath. No, there was no need. Questions can be answered, or not. It did not matter that much.

She tried again to look up into the bright blue sky, but the hot blaze overhead again forced her to look back down at the ground.

"This light is so clear, and so awful. I've never seen it like this around here before. You never had to squint like this out west, not even in the Arizona and New Mexico deserts. How do people live in such glare?"

He smiled down at her and reached for the shopping bag. "I should take that. It must be getting heavy by now."

She handed it to him, and in doing so laid her head on his chest for a moment. She looked up at him again. "Let's walk down to the water for a bit. I need to get closer to that cool breeze. And we are early anyway."

Robson gave an amused grunt. "Yes, a half hour late is acceptable, if not preferred. To be on time…well, one is pitied. But to be early is an affront to the world's sensibilities. What can ever be done with those extra minutes?"

"Your sarcasm, my darling, is a secret safe with me," Monica said. "The world shall ever believe that your aloof regard dispenses no judgment."

"Just as the world still believes I am a colonel," he said with the shade of a grin. "I judge, and command not."

"Whatever that means."

The residential street they had been walking along now bore to the right and ran parallel to the shoreline as far as they could see. All of the homes opposite the ocean were set well back behind trees and shrubbery, so that one could see only the anonymity of greenery, asphalt, and sand. In the far distance the street seemed to bear to the right again, leaving the eye a vanishing point of mere sky and horizon. They slipped off their shoes, stepped off the pavement into the pliant earth, and wandered down toward the water, stopping about ten yards from the gently cresting waves. No other person could be seen. The mild wind caressed them with only slight relief from the heat. The sheen of azure sea betrayed but occasional lilts of foam here and there on its surface. The low hush of the breakers continued its steady pulse.

She looked at him without expression, and, recognizing her thought, he put his arm around her and held her close.

"You're right – what you asked me when we got out of the car. I have never spoken about those two weeks…after I flattened Malik." He chuckled at the memory. "I was relieved when neither you nor Jack brought it up during the recording at the Summit. If you had asked, I guess I would have said something, but I was grateful not to dredge up those memories that night. So, my love, I'm impressed that you had noticed all along."

"I always notice what you don't say."

"Then am I that much more fortunate." Robson glanced up at the sky and winced. "It's this sunlight that evokes it for me now. Not a memory. An atmosphere. An atmosphere that still envelops me, that I still live in, that has somehow become the guardian of my sensibility.

EL TAJIN, NEW MEXICO

The causes have receded, as pain and uncertainty must always yield and be transmuted by newer comprehensions. I say that now, realizing that to 'transmute' is often to change garb. I was stripped naked, and donned the filmy vesture of acceptance." He paused, then smiled. "Not the Emperor's New Clothes. The Peasant's."

Monica had grown a bit alarmed listening to this confused monologue. "Sweetheart, you don't need to undo a locked room on my behalf. I'm not curious, in fact. You had given us so much that night, but I could feel that there was a silence in you where another story no doubt lay. Perhaps that silence should lead its own private existence."

"Words will not kill it. I don't feel invaded; I want you to know. The truth is, the whole inconspicuous farce would never have taken place but for a faulty light switch."

She frowned at him and snickered. "Of course not."

He laughed. "Never, never believe me. I so much prefer your doubts and disbelief. How did I ever live without them." Like her, he glanced out to sea for a long moment. "I was arrested, and as you know there was a trial. The espionage accusation played itself out quickly enough, largely because of the dubious reassurance that I must have been incompetent that day rather than cunningly devious. 'Willfully incompetent' was the official branding, recalling how I had closed down the underground test at Silas the year before. Which, as we know, is not what happened – not what is happening. Would that I were guilty of that! The wheel of unknowable and unstoppable events collected around and ascribed to the decisions and activity of a single person – thus is blame engendered, and ever thus the simple fix to the most complex of crises: 'He did it!' And this I now embrace. Yes, let it turn on me; if you call me responsible, then maybe I am. I am at least responsible for being the target."

"No, not even that," Monica said. "You only become a target because someone wants to fire arrows in your direction."

Robson looked at her and closed his eyes. He kept them closed as he said,

"Tell me again the status of the firing mechanism."

"I wish it were a 'status,' something that we could quantify," she said. "It should have gone off. It is going off. Every twelve hours, at twelve and twelve, midnight and noon, the bomb polls the master for the final ignition signal to detonate. But as you know, your team sent that signal that morning using the manual override. It's looking for something that is right in front of it."

He opened his eyes again. "How quintessentially human, not to see what is before you. Beasts usually know what is right in front of them. They live for that alone. So too mechanisms. So why is it not being recognized? Perhaps Gray's poking around, collapsing and deleting all of the firing stages in a few hysterical seconds, erased the ignition order along with everything else. In which case, the detonator is waiting for something that has already happened. Maybe there is no problem."

"Captain Gray our hero after all? Yes, I have wanted to believe this. But I dared not voice this theory to General Morgan, nor to anyone else in authority. They would have too readily believed it." She sighed. "I don't know, Robson. Maybe it is all over, and Alicia's new village can begin to thrive in all its earnest innocence. She certainly deserves the chance to complete her and Jackson's vision. But a hot, active signal waiting only for the right sequence of electrical pulses – only a few milliseconds worth of pulses – to unleash its flaming horrors? I cannot doze upon such a 'maybe.' I wish I could."

"No," Robson said, "we cannot fall asleep, not even to the next second, when it may bring oblivion. That is certainly true." He took her by the hand. "Let's walk along the beach until we see their house. I only gave you a partial answer anyway." They started walking through the sands, and he continued, "The trial itself was not so dramatic, or unsettling. I knew what was coming, and what the outcome would be. But it was those first few hours that followed the scuffle in front of the elevators that permanently turned the world upside down." He glanced up at the bright sun again. "There I was pinned to the floor by three of my men after Malik collapsed, with several other faces looking down at me in a curious mix of approval and fear. I relaxed at once, not because struggle was useless but because an extraordinary thing happened. The men looking down at me formed more or less a circle, which framed a bank of fluorescent lamps directly above us all. The illumination was soft and did not sting the eye, so my gaze lingered over them for several moments. But then, in just those few extended seconds of dwelling upon those rectangles of pale light, my sense of self suddenly reduced again to a still point – as it had in the workstation during the blackout – but this time in the full brilliance of movement and detail. It was literally a reduction, as though I had shrunk to the stature of a Lilliputian citizen sitting on the chest of this long body spread out on the floor. Powerful hands gripped my upper arms, my body was lifted up and shoved down the aisle toward the detainment area and I floated along for the ride, above my body. Yes, I don't know how else to describe it. I watched myself from above myself. I still wonder sometimes if I could have just sailed off out the top of my head and up through the roof into the sky and stars. I guess there is no choice, but for a brief second it felt like that. They escorted me along several corridors ablaze with the same fluorescent illumination, and pushed me into a small room with only a chair and a table. And here too light filled the room to every corner and crevice. An MP slammed and locked the door behind me, and through the small window in the door I caught a moment of petulant mischief pass through his mind, and he hit the outside light switch, intending to leave me in darkness. But the bulbs burned on. He clicked the switch on and off several times, but nothing happened and he walked away leaving only a grunt behind. And so I sat in full light for, I sup- pose, about half a day."

"That's torture."

"Not really. Everyone was more concerned with placating Malik. There was no hiding the test failure, but they didn't want the Pen- tagon coming down hard on our operation and gutting the entire staff just because two guys had a jawing match. Anyway, everyone's sympathy was with me. Somehow they convinced him to run the test operations himself, which, with his own personnel behind the consoles, passed without further incident. He was gone three days later, leaving a trail of wine-ings and dine-ings in his wake. He did not even testify at my hearing. Long live the full stomach."

"Life's little secret. You were sitting in this lighted room then…"

"Alone, with myself. And this floating feeling, which persisted. It was like two people. The one could not talk, the other had no reason to. I literally just sat. And breathed. The breathing mattered, like it did down in the silo. Only twice did someone pass by the door, but without looking in at me. At a certain point I slid off my watch and stuck it in my pocket. I decided not to know what time it was, or how much time was passing. Thoughts came and went. Nothing else moved. Soon my body gelled into just another object in the room. The table, the chair, me – or 'it.' What happened as those hours rolled by I can now only describe as some kind of leeching out, or purging. I felt almost invisible, almost 'not existing,' as every thought lived and died without mood or impact. I became like a paper cup, a tin can." He laughed at the images.

"That sounds awful," Monica said. "You said before that your uncertainty had changed into something more beautiful, but this sounds like the ultimate uncertainty. I've had that feeling of not knowing who you are, and it frightens me."

"Oh it is frightening, sweetheart, I stand with you there. The bright lights had me constantly aware of that tired body and the uniform enclosing it, a uniform that got sweatier and more rumpled as my energy waned. Eventually I fell asleep. A hoarse cough woke me up in what seemed like the next minute, though about two hours had passed as I found out later. It was the major who had taken my place at the workstation. A Major Dawkins. He was curiously new to interrogation. He read all of his questions from a typed script. I cannot tell you how much fun that was, the absolute absurdity of it all. He read a question, I answered, he went on to the next one, without once pressing me further on my replies. It was like rehearsing a high school play. The hardest part was not laughing out loud. I stifled more than a few chuckles, I can tell you that."

"If this ineptitude tickled your fancy so much, why do you refer to this experience as some kind of ordeal? Or did that come later?"

"It was the emptiness. I trembled with it. If I tried to latch onto something, to call something 'me' – like my shoes, or my arm – the incongruity of this set me off into momentary bursts of panic. Where was I? My heart would swell wild with fear, and the next moment subside back into a curious observance of the Q&A between me and Dawkins as it continued to putter along. Parallel dramas unfolding in that little, well-lit room. The interrogation peculiar but monotonous, the search for my reason and identity hopeless and chaotic. Eventually I gave up trying. And that resolution later saved me during the court martial, since the same weird feeling of a scripted, one-act farce pervaded those proceedings as well."

"Some kind of peace settled in at last."

"No. Nothing settled. Is settled. I just don't exist. I can now live with that."

Monica put her arms around him and held him close. "Then I'll be your Self, Mr. Anonymous Andrews, Esquire. How about that?"

He smiled at her and started to reply, but then he paused and turned to look over at the row of residences on the other side of the beach and roadway. Their walk had brought them parallel to a large, two-story grey house set back further and higher up than those around it. A stone stairway wended its way forth and back up a steeply graded front garden of green bushes and fan palms, dotted with new buds of color and an assortment of plants and flowers, making two wide curves to right and left as it ascended to a large portico and polished black front door.

Without another word they walked off the beach, cleaned their feet and put on their shoes, and crossed the quiet street and up the stairway. They climbed slowly, the better to admire the plantings on either side of them, and in this way the subtleties of the garden delightfully revealed themselves. Each step and turn presented varied tones of green from lime to deep forest, unexpected arrays of purple, red, yellow, blue nestled side by side among white gravel and black soil. Fragrant hints of rose and lilac, orange and lavender, whispered their delicate secrets and flitted away the moment they were tasted. Butterflies silently glided here and there among the bobbing tendrils. Monica paused at one point to absorb it all more completely, and then she turned to look back out to sea. Tufts of foam dotted its elastic shimmering surface, gentle coils of water rolled and hissed ashore quiet and unendingly. At the horizon a dark cobalt, and nearer to shore gradations of sapphire, turquoise and pale green.

"I can't decide what is more beautiful," she said, "the austere mystery of the ocean – always different and always the same – or these intentional creations at our feet that feed all sensations at once."

He smiled. "Me neither. So I won't decide."

She gave him a mock slap, and they continued up the stairs. When they reached the portico, Robson sat down on a bench and took off his shoes again to clean out some still lingering sand. Monica glanced through the window to the left of the doorway, which looked into an open kitchen, the sink just in front of the window and a large surround of black granite countertops, with plates, wine glasses, a decanter, and platters of food all laid out in even symmetry. Beyond the kitchen was a large open area, the end of which that she could see taken up with a long table holding an elaborate cardboard model of what looked to be the design for a three-story private residence.

The next moment Monica noticed the back of Ethel's head just visible above the other side of the kitchen counter, her light brown hair gathered up in casual folds. She was apparently kneeling down examining the model from the edge of the table at ground level. In another moment she slowly stood up, and into Monica's view gradually appeared Ethel's bare neck, bare shoulders and arms, bare back, bare bottom (rather an attractive one, she had to admit), and bare legs.

Robson rang the doorbell.

Ethel shrieked and scurried out of sight. Monica started laughing, and her attempts to cover her mouth and calm herself only had her cheeks flushed and her eyes red with merry tears that much more.

Robson stared at her. "What did I do?"

"You rang the bell," she managed to gasp out.

All the while they could hear Ethel's shrill voice in the distance, but it was several moments more before they recognized the equally high-pitched tones of their host, responding to each of his wife's epithets with the same, "All right now, dear," which grew audibly more distinct as he approached the door, each of his footsteps punctuated by the thump of what sounded like a cane. Soon came the single clack and metal scratch of a latch undone, and the next instant the smiling face of Feldon Whiting greeted them.

His wide-open hazel eyes and rosy cheeks shone with welcome. His dark blonde hair was perfectly groomed and parted, and his restrained dress of pale yellow shirt, camel cardigan, and chocolate slacks were all crisp and perfectly arranged. His soft hand lightly grasped the handle of his mahogany cane, a brass lion head that seemed to eye them with indifferent vigilance.

"Pardon the ruckus. Trying to decide between a cascading series of steps or gently sloping pathways. I like the steps myself. More stately – almost demands a slow lingering approach to the building. But Ethel seems to want to go with pathways. 'These days people don't climb, they meander,' as she claims. But look at the model and see what you think. Of course, a straight set of steps did not suit us here. Much too steep, as you could imagine. Oh, but please come in, come in. I bore you right at my threshold. How silly of me."

"Not at all, Feldon, not at all," Monica said and gave him a warm hug and kiss. "You're garden has already inspired us, and I'm sure Ethel's project will as well." She reached over and took up the shopping bag. "We've brought along a few gifts for you both. But please, don't open them until we are gone."

She placed the bag just inside the doorway and went off to find Ethel. Feldon turned and looked up at Robson. He set his cane aside and extended both his hands, and for several moments the two men kept a firm grip as they exchanged a long silent look.

"The cloud has not passed. How can it? But much of the light that pierces through it I owe to you," said the former congressman.

"That cloud hangs over many of us. So we should all be grateful for any glimmer of light, however brief," said the former colonel.

"How will this end?"

"I don't know."

Robson closed the door and they walked together into the house, which felt remarkably cool despite the summer heat. To the right a corridor led away to private quarters and a staircase to the upper floor.

"Ethel will be with us momentarily," Feldon said. "Come and sit. It is my great practice these days, my first of hobbies, to sit. To sit and sit."

He and Robson stepped down into the sunken living area, and wandered over to the large stone fireplace dominating the opposite wall, an arrangement of leather chairs, love seats, and ottomans surrounding a large Persian carpet in green and blue tones placed over the tiled flooring. They chose places side by side in adjoining chairs with a view of the residential cardboard model.

"Where is the building site?" Robson asked, taking in the elaborate structure that rested on what appeared to be the dining table. Beyond the table and model, a wall of glass and sliding doors looked out onto a patio adorned with a few potted trees, matching metal chairs and circular glass table, and an enclosure of more shrubbery and flowers.

"Not far from here, just the next town over. Her real achievement with this design is that the owners have still not seen it. She won't let them have even a glimpse until every detail is settled to her liking. It seems now to come down, as I said, to the walkways and the approach."

"But then after the unveiling, the clients are sure to want changes and refinements. Not everything gets decided before…"

Feldon laughed. "Never hire my darling wife, old boy. One does not 'change or refine' what Madam has in finality decreed."

Robson laughed as well. "She's not all that popular, then, I suppose. Appeals only to those with the most passive of desires."

"No, no, you would be surprised, my friend. In our experience, people seem to love tyranny. The tyranny of taste. How many there are who have convinced themselves they know nothing."

"And do they know nothing?"

"If we don't know – and if they think they don't know – then…?"

The ladies quietly appeared exchanging whispers. Ethel, her hair still pinned up but now wearing a light wool olive dress, stepped down and walked toward them with open arms. Robson stood up and embraced her.

"Colonel Robson, darling, it has been too long. How is our favorite warrior? You're still as strong as ever, I see."

"Maybe in some ways," he replied. "I see strength rather differently these days."

She squinted in mild confusion. "How so?"

"Difficult to explain. Sometimes just the air and sunlight toss me about inside. And I don't mind that. I now conclude that being influenced is more interesting than exerting one's own influence."

Ethel stared at him a bit incredulous. "Either you're becoming a poet, colonel, or you've gone batty. Either way, it makes you more loveable." She patted him on the chest. "But don't go flabby on me. Now for some drinks, everyone."

She turned and walked over to an elaborate bar area just beyond the open kitchen. Monica lingered a moment to make merry eye contact with her beau, then wandered over to help Ethel.

Robson looked down at Feldon and said as he eased back into his chair, "So you sit, do you? I like it. I bet it's hard work."

"I'll assume that's not a joke. Yes, it is hard work. One needs to let so many things just be what they are, and happen as they do. I felt so deeply during the height of the debacle at Silas the illusion of influence. We certainly set things in motion, in the manner of kicking a boulder over a precipice, but that is not influence. We watch people dodge the boulder and self-congratulate; and then, to our horror, the boulder turns about and hurtles back upward to mow us down." He turned and looked directly into the eyes of his friend. "I sit here, you know, seemingly at peace, but Robson it feels like clinging to a freight train. And not clinging all that securely. Time is cruel. It relentlessly hurtles along, yet convinces so many of us of a slow-motion luxury tour that may never come to an end. We don't think about ends, do we? I tried. That's true, I really did. Tried to conceive of it, of my ultimate finality, but I can't do it. So now I no longer try to think or imagine such a thing. I sit here and live it."

"Is that an erudite way of saying that you've given up on yourself? The passage of time, the accidental happenings, the miniscule dot that constitutes our impact on the world – these things were always true. Rather a relief to finally recognize it."

"Maybe. But what follows from that recognition?" He paused. "You call relief what I call…well, I won't say 'despair,' but all dreams have come to an end. I no longer brim with stories and options. It is one long single line into a distance that may or may not be far away."

Andrews raised an eyebrow. "So a finality, after all, that you experience."

Feldon smiled in spite of the pensive mood that was starting to overtake him. "Touché, officer. Would that we could cross swords more often."

"Whatever pact you two have concluded, you can now drink to it," Ethel said approaching them with long cool glasses filled with orange-red liquid. She handed them over and sat on an ottoman with her back to the fireplace. Monica followed close behind with two more drinks and gave one to her hostess. She sat on the love seat facing the two men.

"In my political life I proposed many a toast," Feldon said, brightening up a little, "but they were all out of obligation. I never really meant it – not a single one."

"Is that a confession, darling?" his wife said.

"To you, no. To our friends here – no. To myself, also no. Call it rather the wish to experience something that I have acted out countless times, without ever experiencing it. So now," he leaned forward a little, raising his glass in one hand and keeping a firm grip on his cane with the other, "let us toast to the end of a life, or, in deference to the shunning of all things morbid, of a phase of life. The end so final that we have forgotten of what it was constituted; the beginning so fresh and unknown that we know not even its first steps."

Robson quickly flicked out his arm and tapped Feldon's glass. The women looked at each other blankly for a moment, then politely clinked round. They all sipped their drinks for a few moments in silence.

"How delicious, sweetheart. Magic it is. Delicious magic." And their guests murmured assent.

Ethel smiled, and then said, "If you won't confess to anything, I will. Though I call this a positive confession. You say you did something repeatedly without experiencing it. Well, I experienced something repeatedly without doing it. And that was being a congressman's wife." Feldon's face furrowed into an amusing mass of puzzlement, and everyone could not help but chuckle. "Relax, darling, momentary confusion will soon evaporate as though it never was. On your arm walking through the crowds during the first campaign. By your side at the reception dinners greeting and shaking hands – and sometimes the horrible wet kisses from the wealthy lechers. Sitting on the stages behind the podiums while you made your speeches. How doubly strange it all was. Sometimes an interviewer would stop and ask my opinion about water pollution or poor school children. I always answered with something you had just said – I memorized his speeches, you see – and the lad or girl would scribble away as dutifully as if I were president. And my clothes. How they scrutinized every blouse and shoe, and asked me about color and fabric and favorite stores. I dared not wear much jewelry at that time. The crowd admires the drapery but hates your gems and metal. Then my walk, my tone of voice, how the fork came to my mouth, the wisps of hair against my cheek that had me searching for the first reflection to right my appearance. I developed a self-preoccupation as though my body were a mannequin that I constantly pursued to tweak into place its perfect look."

"That constant attention from everyone must have been maddening," Monica said. "I always hated meetings, when all eyes and ears were on me rather than the results of my labors."

"Well, Mrs. Colonel darling, that is what I mean by doubly strange. Constant attention, yes, but not on me. I doubt that I was noticed the entire period of Feldon's tenure. I was looked through, not at. They saw the dresses, eyed the lipstick, jotted down the sound bite. They watched the mannequin till their eyes were sore. But I was not seen. I moved as a ghost among the curious and the self-interested. My own feeling of who I was, was ignored. I wanted to be offended, but then I realized how safe I was. I could stay inwardly naked. Pity it was only inward." And here everyone paused to share a laugh once more.

"A very positive confession, Ethel," Robson said. "I will presume to say that it helped you clarify how you felt about yourself as a personal identity."

She nodded. "A moment arrived – uneventful to anyone but me – when the congressman's wife walked on ahead of me down the sidewalk toward a local coffee shop. I watched her move, and smile, and extend her manicured hand. And I was free."

"Who are you then sitting here?" said Feldon, tilting his head to one side.

"Don't be superficial, darling."

"I want to feel solid about myself," Monica said. "I guess I'm a bit logical that way. I want to know that when I'm sitting in a chair, I am really there doing it. But love is different. I love with abandon. Everything I am should belong to the one I love. I don't want to possess something he does not."

"There I agree," Feldon said. "How I used to clutch at things, surround myself with them, nail down my boundaries like an iron fence. Then the horror, when I discovered I was inside that fence, and couldn't get out. My possessions possessed me. They just held me in…" His voice dropped, and he began to mutter to himself about being "held in," such that Ethel started to lean across to him, when he said out loud, "I didn't really know how to give them away. I couldn't do it."

"It happened anyway, darling. We are grateful, are we not?"

"Yes, we are. And grateful to have our friends here with us. Robson, Monica, you grace our home."

"That is a toast I understand, Feldon," Monica said and clinked glasses with him again.

"Will you mind then playing that role one last time, Ethel?" Robson asked. "I mean, at the commemoration ceremony next week for the first anniversary of Jackson Monroe's passing."

"And the christening of El Tajín," his wife added.

"Ell what? Yes, we're going, and I suppose the role will play itself out well enough. Though I may have a bit more to do during my final performance, since our former congressman here is determined to lay to rest the archetypal former self. He will give them not a whiff of the one-time politician, not a sliver of nostalgia for the antic representative who, despite his masterful anonymity in deflecting credit for anything, more than once had the House floor rolling in the aisles as he successfully passed yet another piece of legislation for his state and district. Though I don't see how he will resist once he sets eyes on Pondhurst again."

Feldon sat back in his chair and looked at her. "I have paid a great price to be a normal person. I now want to live out my purchase."

"Pondhurst won't be coming," Monica said. "He will be on some Asian tour. More than coincidental, no doubt. As for the name, Alicia said that it was Jackson's idea. He took a fancy to its namesake, the ancient site in Mexico. Apparently it means something like 'place of invisible beings,' a phrase that rather absorbed him in his last months."

"Did it really," Robson said. "So he believed invisible beings dwell among the plains and hollows of Pale Moon?"

"Invisible beings are likely to live anywhere, sweetheart. Maybe even on the end of your nose. Anyway, that was what drew him to it. Another tradition says the name means 'land of thunder and lightning,' which fired Alicia's imagination. She told me that she plans to make something of this in the new town square, though probably not for next week's ceremony."

"Thunder and lightning," Feldon moaned, half to himself. "O God." He glanced over at Andrews, whose eyes twinkled briefly with acknowledgement while his face maintained its impassive demeanor.

"Darling, please," Ethel said, "leave the ancient peoples and their names in peace."

"I am willing to leave the whole world in peace, my love, but the world seldom cooperates."

"You're becoming silly." Ethel stood up and motioned toward the dining area. "Leave your glasses here. Before we sit down at the table, we need to move Portsmouth Lodge onto the floor. If we each grab a corner, we can settle it nicely in that empty space over there. Don't worry, it's a fraction of the weight it appears to be."

They all stood up and walked over to the table. Robson said, "I like that name. Did you select it?

"Oh no, they're from Portsmouth. That's all. Unlike this El Tajín thing, most names people give to their properties are rather elementary. If I don't like what they choose, and I usually don't, I just cringe in quiet. That's my professionalism. All right, careful now, just keep it level."

It was indeed light of weight and lifted into their hands with ease. A momentary wobble had them all giggling as Feldon shifted his balance on his cane while keeping one hand under the model. They walked it across and set it down on an area of parquet flooring, which had looked to Robson like a small alcove adjacent to the dining area. But to his surprise the wooden flooring continued into another room on the other side of the wall. It was a library, just as long as the living room but slightly narrower. He stood for a moment and marveled at the sundry Persian carpets that graced the flooring, and the massive surround of bookcases that enclosed it on three sides, with a second stone fireplace that bookended the one in the living room, and complemented by an inviting arrangement of chairs, sofas, and reading lamps.

"My domain," Feldon said, noticing his admiration. "It's my notion of what heaven must be like. I will never be able to read all that these shelves contain, and thus there will always be secrets up there hovering over me like uncharted galaxies. You can't, you know, fight that. You have to accept what you can comprehend along with what is uncomprehendable, if I may put it that way."

"The philosopher muses," Ethel said. "But I would have thought that heaven was an infinite number of naked girls, darling. You would never know all of their secrets either."

"Oh no, that's purgatory, darling. At best."

Ethel gave an ironic shriek and walked over to the kitchen. Monica followed her and helped lay the table with placemats, cutlery, glasses, and bottles of water and wine, while their hostess filled each plate from the array of foods on the counter. Soon an ample portion of meat, fish, vegetables, and garnishes sat before each place setting, with the remaining platters set in the middle of the table.

Robson stood before his chair and looked at it all with eyebrows raised. "This is more than I could possibly put away."

Ethel frowned at him. "That is the great virtue of 'more,' Mr. Colonel. Eat."

And so they ate, and drank, and talked. A silent electric understanding between the two guests, ignited without the need for eye contact, led them to steer the conversation into the conventional channels of recent plans and projects. They talked about the property they recently purchased in Malibu, and their search for an apartment or townhouse in the Boston area, Monica wanting to be near her elderly parents from time to time.

"And us," Feldon added.

"Yes, of course," she said, leaning across and giving him a kiss on the cheek.

Robson had wanted to rent a car and drive to New Mexico for the ceremony, and he described the route through the South and West that he had hoped to take. But they now agreed that there was not enough time not to worry about time, and that a leisurely cross-country vacation was further off on their horizon.

"Nice to have horizons," Feldon said. "No point in considering the future if it holds no promises of delight."

"Pardon us, friends," Ethel said. "Morbidity is my husband's newest hobbyhorse."

"Only to say that the present restricts the future. You can't plan what can't happen."

"Things happen, darling, that we never imagine. That is the charm of tomorrow."

"No," Feldon said, "that is the charm of today. Tomorrow is a hoodwink. But the unexpected seldom happens."

"I don't know that our vacation plans are a real future," Monica said. "We talk about so many trips and cruises. All the while we just eat and spend money." She laughed. "Sometimes I think all future is an illusion."

"Living devoid of all illusion is no fun," the former congressman said, persisting with his theme. "The nakedness of bed to bathroom to kitchen to chair, and back again in reverse, doesn't promise anything other than itself. It's the truth, without the freedom."

"Then it's not the truth, Feldon," Monica said. She gave him her most beautiful smile, in hopes of brightening his mood, then reached over and took his hand. "We shouldn't recite our bodily functions as though they were a credo. Such things don't have any special meaning, that's true. So why expect more of them?"

He looked at her for a long moment, and then seemed to acquiesce. "Maybe I just need something else to do," he said finally.

Everyone laughed except Ethel, who arose and started to clear away the plates. Over her shoulder she said, "Coffee and fruit in the library."

Robson got up to help her, and Monica and Feldon passed along into the library to sit before the fireplace. Once they were out of sight, Ethel turned around and threw her arms around Robson and held him close. "Sometimes we need something different," she whispered. She pressed her cheek against his and nibbled at his ear.

"We love you both," he said. He rocked her gently from side to side, and they shared a warm kiss. They separated and stood apart in silence. He looked into her eyes for a few moments, but could not fathom the cluster of tenderness, solitude, intelligence, even amusement, that looked back at him.

He said, "I guess this is the moment when I ask you where the coffee filters are."

She squeezed her face into a smiling frown and gesticulated toward the cupboards around the kitchen sink, then turned to arrange the fruit. In a short while they were carrying flask, cups, plates, and platter into the library. Feldon was lying well back in a large leather armchair and staring up at the top shelves of the bookcases, while Monica sat before him on an ottoman massaging his bare feet.

"I'm next," Robson said.

"Mañana, old boy, mañana. Don't covet another's ecstasy. We were just talking about the Big Bang. Got a whole shelf of books up there on it. Your wife has just stumped the panel, so to speak, on this subject. The panel of one."

"I didn't know there was anything to stump," Andrews said. "The matter in the universe used to be more compressed and now it has expanded, after some primordial shock." Ethel began pouring out coffee into the cups, and as he passed them around he continued, "Maybe all shocks are primordial. Every shock is the beginning of something – well, usually the end of something. Something inconsequential most of the time. Whether a beginning follows from that depends on luck, or spiritedness."

"But why would the universe get a shock?" Monica asked. "Who would have given it?"

Robson smiled. "So this how you stumped the panel? Well, I agree, I have no idea, and really it makes no sense."

"It would make sense if that is how the world began," Feldon said. "So it's not a question of one force shocking another – or an outside, or inside, force exploding the material world into a billion light-year fragments. It is the actual beginning of everything."

"Why does a beginning have to be an explosion?" Ethel asked. She had curled up on the edge of a long sofa near the fireplace opposite the other three. "So many beginnings are anything but. More often they are the most inconspicuous of whispers, and the true beginning is invisible to us, only realized in retrospect. If at all."

"Come sit by me, dearest. You can get a massage too. Right, Monica?"

"I am always by you, darling. I'm just doing a bit of an orbit around the outer reaches of our socializing. Like Neptune."

"Oh, I love Neptune," Monica said. "It's so beautiful and mysterious."

"Come now, Madame Scientist," Feldon said with eyebrows raised. "It's a little dot in the sky. Anything can be beautiful and mysterious if it stays far enough away from you."

"I'm not really a scientist. But never mind, I like my mysteries to stay that way. I don't need them to come any closer."

"The Big Bang isn't really about the first moment of creation, you know," Feldon continued to everyone. "Or about how matter came into existence. It just tries to understand why the universe is moving and expanding. Not a theory really – more of an attempt to 'catch up' to what the evidence suggests is going on."

"How positively existential," his wife murmured. "Even the theory doesn't exist."

"I would say that Ethel really nailed it," Robson said. "We assume that the universe had a beginning. But where in our experience do we ever see a pure beginning, unrelated to anything that went before it? There is not a single life-form, object, or event that we can point to and say, 'This came from naught.' If you trace back any of these things, you come upon other versions of it, never its pure nascence. There probably is no such thing."

"But she didn't say that," Monica said without looking up from her pinching of Feldon's toes. "She said that we don't recognize a beginning when it happens. Though I would have to disagree with you, my love. From the point of view of our personal experience, many things come from naught. Most things, really. Even clouds and rain appear and envelop us, and when they leave, they leave. We can mentally ascribe this to the meteorological template that we've all heard about, but a mental construct is not personal experience."

"Don't you just love her," Robson said after a brief silence. Feldon and Monica chuckled their approval, but Ethel remained silent, staring into the empty hearth.

"Well that notion rather plunks us down onto our royal bottoms," said their host, becoming more animated. "The conclusion being that what comes and goes around us is all that we really know. If that is true – and I don't know if it is – then beginnings come out of nowhere and endings pass into nowhere. In which case, what really matters is to see it and feel it as much as you can. Otherwise, you yourself are nowhere."

"Sounds like another mental construct to me," his wife said without looking up.

"True, true, the mind can replace any experience," Feldon continued undaunted. "Yet the simple things we see and feel are undeniable, when we pay attention to them. And what else is there really? It stings me to say that I've spent so much of my life following my own thought-wheels and fervors, never noticing that I was the only one along for the ride. If instead I just look around, listen, smell, look again, listen again, then that is a beginning that perpetuates itself. A beginning that re-begins, over and over. Maybe this is how God creates the universe. He perpetually renews what he sees, what he is."

Ethel suddenly shuffled to the edge of the couch to face her three companions, and raised her eyebrows. "Bang!" she shouted with a laugh. She reached up behind her, pulled the pins out of her hair, and tossed them on the floor. She shook her head gently and let her brown tresses fall around her in casual ease.

Robson stared at her for a moment, struck by the fiery beauty that suddenly enlivened her appearance. She smiled at him, almost a little shyly. He suddenly felt that his indulgent stare had exposed his feelings to everyone, so he got out of his chair and knelt on the floor behind Monica, his back to Ethel, and started massaging his wife's shoulders. He heard a rustling behind him and the next moment a pair of warm fingers were firmly wrapped about the back of his neck kneading a steady ripple of soft caresses.

Feldon was delighted. "A train of bliss. You see, old chap, instead of coveting, you gave. And then you got. A life lesson, right here on my library floor."

"Heed the lesson yourself, darling," Ethel said, gently digging her fingernails into Robson's flesh.

"I shall, I shall. You all realize, I suppose, that we have touched upon every origin story possible in these past several minutes. The absolute beginning, out of nothing. The continuum of everything, that when followed backwards leads to other things, and so on, such that the beginning is never found, not only not the beginning of all, but not of any particular phenomenon either – implying there is no beginning. Then the…"

"Followed backward or forward," Robson said.

"Ah, well we never discussed that part, but I suppose if you go one way you needs must go the other too. We always think in these terms, but I'm not sure why. Must be all our science fiction hypnotizing us. The future is less known than the past. Not a fair comparison. We don't really go forward, you know, any faster than the pace of our next breath. Anything else is a daydream…"

"But gentlemen, really," Ethel now interrupted him, "we don't go backwards either. Never. Not one milliliter, or millisecond, whatever it is. We can't. Many of us certainly live much of our lives in the past, but talk about daydreams. If you walked back into the kitchen, or out the front door and down the stairs again, that is the future. You could never recapture what was…"

"The future becoming the present, darling…:

"Whatever," she was now a bit irritated. "We have to be normal about these things. If something is new to us, then it's a beginning, for us, even if everyone we know has had our experience already. You talked about perpetually recreating the universe. Well there it is. I experience what another may have experienced, in my own way. Past, present, and future of it. That is my universe."

No one spoke. Her husband screwed up his face as though about to make sport of her words, but the contortions of his mouth as quickly relaxed, and he nestled in his chair and closed his eyes. The massagings continued for several minutes. The silence that grew around them became so complete that gradually the distant hush of the waves invaded the room and sighed a gentle lullaby. Eventually Monica applied a few final rubbings to her host's feet and leaned back into Robson's arms, while Ethel kept her warm hands lingering against his back. Feldon opened his eyes and regarded the three of them. He stared in silence for several moments.

"A harem would suit you, my friend," he said without emotion. "You're a natural. If I may risk everyone's ire for a few more interminable minutes, I do want to let you know that asking about the first primordial shock is not how your beloved stumped the panel. Why don't you say it to all of us again, Monica, and then we're done with metaphysics, hopefully forever."

She smiled and eased up out of her husband's arms. "I didn't see anything special in it. I just asked, 'What's the matter?'" She turned to look at Robson's puzzled expression and laughed. "The matter of the universe. All this talk about matter exploding and forming into planets and stars. But what about feelings, ideas, thoughts? Are they matter too? If so, how did they form out of all that cosmic dust? If not, then where do they come from? Did they have their own Big Bang? Or Big Whisper." She leaned over and smiled at Ethel. "This vision of congealing matter stops at what the sense of touch and sight perceive. But so many experiences, so much of our life, stand outside these senses. If we can come up with a model whereby the start of everything were both a Bang and a Whisper – the Bang the matter, the Whisper the soul – then we might get somewhere with our first creation…"

"Oh, my God!" Ethel exclaimed. "Of course, of course. We have been saying it all this time."

She sprang up and tripped over to her Portsmouth Lodge sitting mutely on the floor by the glass doors. She laid down flat on her stomach, her chin under her hands, and stared at the model. The others got up severally and made their way over to her. She paid them no heed, and her unperturbed focus held them all in a respectful silence. Eventually Robson got down on the floor and stretched out next to her. Monica slipped off her shoes and stepped up onto the small of his back, then slowly began walking up and down his spine.

"Obvious, really, when you stop insisting on something," Ethel said without looking up. "Feldon and I were arguing over steps versus pathways. But the model should be both – as Monica was just saying. You see how this central incline leading up to the patio needs a grand stairway? Paths can loop around up to the patio from the sides – we need some shrubbery to soften the angles – and then, just as the paths approach the paving blocks, we add a three-step touch. Delightful, don't you think?"

Feldon saw at once what she had in mind. "A perfect melding. It will be seen as a single vision all its own, and not a combination of different pieces. Well, done, my love."

She glanced up at him and smiled appreciatively. "The stairway, you see, is needed not so much for practical circulation as display and leisure. We will set large planter vases here and there on some of the steps. Guests can linger about, admiring the landscape, and the distant wood. And the house, we hope." She paused. "Then, you see, we follow the same idea downward into the little vale below. Pathways loop in curves that mirror the upward approach, and again a series of steps lead down the center. But less grand. And we should have them not so much end at the bottom, but seem to merge with the grass and undergrowth. Oh, we will have so much fun with all of this."

Feldon was obviously happy for her. He knew she would want to turn over the ideas for a day or so before adding the details to the model, so he looked down at Robson and said, "How about some air? I will show you our private path to the shore."

Monica, still standing on his back, folded her arms in mock defiance. "Yes, darling, off you go." She jostled him playfully, then stepped off and poked his ribs with her toe. He quickly sprang up, and she just as quickly settled down into his place and stretched out on her side. Robson arched his back and moaned with pleasure. "Oh, that was perfect," he said.

Ethel gave a luxurious sigh and turned over on her back. She dropped her arms about her head, and looked up at the two men with some curiosity. "Are you sure you want to leave?" Monica also turned onto her back and let her arms sprawl, and their tender faces, surrounded by casual halos of soft hair, settled into dreamy half-smiles and slightly lidded gazes. Their breath came quietly, and their soft bodies, relaxed into nonchalant abandon, exuded a delightful languor that held the two men entranced for longer than they themselves noticed.

At length Ethel went wide-eyed and broke the silence. "Begone, boys, the moment has passed." And the ladies turned in toward each other, and were soon giggling uncontrollably.

"Let's go," Robson said and started toward the sliding glass doors.

"No, this way," Feldon said. He walked back into the library, hopping and thumping along at a surprisingly quick pace. Robson followed with hesitation until he noticed a door at the far end of the room set back amid the crowded bookcases. This led to a small anteroom containing a minor chaos of coats, boots, benches, and tools. Feldon strode across the room and with some exertion pushed open a thick wooden door. They stepped out onto slate tiling that extended in both directions along and around both sides of the back of the house. A brick and stainless steel barbecue area, with a long trestle table and several wooden chairs and chaise lounges, dominated the back patio. A large expanse of lawn was bordered by a high wooden fence on all three sides, with beds of flowers and shrubbery beneath, and a line of oaks and cedars along the far end of the yard.

Feldon continued straight ahead and unlatched a flimsy wooden gate that seemed at first to open onto but a small patch of gravel surrounded by enormous hedges. But he plunged right into the thick of them, and in so doing revealed a long gravel trail that descended like a tunnel through the shadows and greenery. The bushes were so close about that only slight glimpses of homes and fencing revealed themselves on either side all the way down to another wooden gate, this one substantially larger and set within a frame of thick beams and boards. He pulled a key out of his pocket, and unlocked the gate and let them through.

They found themselves on an expanse of parkland with a mingling of turf and sand, and a thin wood of scrub pine that led to the beach. Just to the left the asphalt road ended in a barrier of logs and concrete blocks. A stiff breeze trembled through the branches and kicked up small tufts of dust. The sea hissed and surged with more frequent dashes to the shore, and massive white clouds now bunched against the sky, here and there blocking the sunlight with arcs of black shadow.

"Eerie change in the weather," Robson said. "We were wilting all the way to your door. Is this common?"

"I'm used to drama queens," Feldon said and winked. "Nature's the greatest of them all. Let's go this way."

He set a more leisurely pace through the trees, and they eventually arrived at a small bluff overlooking the sand and surf. They absorbed the fresh wind and raw sounds for several minutes in silence.

"Do you believe in a collective consciousness, Robson?"

"No."

"In the days following my breakdown I felt so penetrated by everything. It rained needles all around and through me. I beheld strange puppet shows almost without end – nurses and visitors and doctors who talked and nodded in a manner at odds with what they were really feeling and thinking. They did not seem to notice this, and I truly did not want to see it. What can you do when you see what you don't want to see? Immobility became a blessing, enforced muteness was my savior, or I surely would have thrashed out at the world. Not that the world would have cared. I saw – saw by means of feeling, since I never left the room – the world as jungle, as bestiary, the thinnest veneer of politesse preventing all of us from tearing each other to pieces. How strong that veneer is. Or is it? Who can say. The forked tongues lick and spew in perpetuity, the film of 'good boys and girls' holding them invisibly at bay. Despite this horror, I existed, and though it was but a groat of nothing, this single pinprick – 'exist' – kept me sane and accepting. You see, I don't exist alone, and I am certainly not the center of anything. You are here, my wife, neighbors, nature. I guess this is what I mean by a collective awareness. Not a herd, a world." He paused. "Though I don't claim to get inside another's self."

"Have you ever experienced the streaks?"

"No. Ethel has, several times. She would berate my habit of napping at twilight, saying I was 'sleeping through the supernatural.' Never has she been so quiet as in the wake of those experiences. I did not really yearn for it, you see, because I enjoyed their effects so much in her. Don't snicker. No, I don't mean a character change. I would not want that from her. She would glow like a little star sitting in her perch on the window seat. How I loved to sit by her as darkness fell after the streaks' departure and chat about nothing. I would mete out question after incidental question just to keep her animated, watching that curious inner fire infuse everything she said with poetry and taste. She sat there religiously in the late afternoons when we lived in New Mexico, waiting for them. But they were so unpredictable, as you know, and the gaps in their appearance so many days and weeks apart that she often passed an unhappy evening. A curious sort of addiction I could do nothing about."

"They tell a secret tale, the streaks, though I could not tell you what it is. I would describe it more as a detachment than a connectedness, but as you say, it is a detachment that exists, and nothing exists alone. I just can't say I have ever felt a 'consciousness' of the every. Or, not to play God, of the some."

"During my last campaign the lack of response from the crowds was to me a turmoil of surprise, intimidation, just plain bafflement. They were not hostile, certainly not supportive. They were just silent. The team all wondered of course why the huge turnouts, just to voice a collective voicelessness, and everyone concluded it was the free burgers and chicken. Maybe so. I could not fathom the 'crowd,' you see, so I stopped looking at it, and instead looked at a woman in a pink blouse and a young man with sunglasses in his shirt pocket, and started talking to each of them. I talked to persons. Not people, persons. Looking back on that experience, I am prompted to conclude that there is no crowd, there is rather individuals standing in close proximity to each other now and then, either by accident or out of instinctive need or wish. So the thread of consciousness is through each individual, not a mass of bodies. Bodies can be seen, what lights someone up inside cannot, at least not from a wooden podium."

"You felt reduced to simple existence lying there on your hospital bed, feeling very solitary, I'm sure. Each of us has burned in that way from time to time, and perhaps it is that that we all ironically share in. Our solitude."

"As I said, it kept me sane: a slender wire out into the world that said, 'I am here,' and nothing more. I felt none of the inspiration or exuberance that seemed to inflame Ethel. It was just a simple compass point, keeping my sense of self in one place – in front of my nose, if that doesn't sound too preposterous."

"It doesn't, and by different means I came to the same conclusion: that we need a simple, non-egoistical attitude about how life comes to us. The Peasant's New Clothes, I call it. A nothing that knows it is nothing."

They made momentary eye contact, as though to confirm by sight that such an exchange had just taken place between them. The wind was gradually increasing in intensity such that they were forced to turn their backs to it for a moment, and wider and higher waves crashed in haste upon each other. Feldon tamped the earth with his cane a few times and shifted his feet in place. He looked far out to sea and breathed deeply. Then he said, "You need to know what they're doing at Silas. It's O'Connell. He's been made a colonel, and a rather irritating one."

Robson stiffened at his ominous tone, and also appealed to the distant horizon to anchor a sudden concern. "Tell me."

"He found the Action Room. What was left of it. The extra power the air conditioning system was drawing caught someone's attention. I suppose that was inevitable. What was not inevitable is how O'Connell reacted. You won't believe it."

"Probably not."

"My people in the Pentagon passed it on to me just last week. I'll show you the letter. He ferreted out the whereabouts of some of the members of your team and brought them back. The whole project was explained to him, and he redeployed a few workstations with the aim of doing what you could never do."

"Dangerous perhaps. We all know his lack of qualifications for running such an enterprise, but maybe his blundering about will surprise us."

Feldon shook his head. "No, it won't. The programmers did a lot of tinkering at first, with a lot of downloadings and uploadings. Not something I understand really, but I do know all of those experiments were not changing anything. So one day O'Connell abruptly concluded that the computer and its terminals are a dead end. 'Technology can't save itself,' he proclaimed. And so he made the decision to burrow through the concrete tunnel and dismantle the device by hand."

"Everyone knows that won't work."

"He had a one-liner for that too: 'In the end what cannot work is the very thing that will work.'"

"Such is the wisdom of one who has written too many brochures. Have they started yet?"

Feldon tamped the ground again and bowed his head in resignation. "It's well underway. They've been at it for weeks already down there, all the time Alicia's town has been coming to life up above them."

"We will have to contact Stahlbergen and have him fly out there to explain it all. I suppose you can get travel money somewhere."

"Stahlbergen's dead. He took his own life."

Andrews abruptly walked off down the slope and onto the beach. He paced back and forth against the angry breeze for several minutes, holding his hands to his head and kicking at the tiny dunes. The wind was whipping up the sands into dry, wispy spirals that whirled and vanished, reformed again into momentary clouds of grit, then flashed apart like silent fireworks against the now teeming background of surf and sky. Robson eventually made his way back up the slope, muttering to himself and still kicking at the ground as he came.

"Sorry about that," he said. "I had to walk off a few fantasies about breaking into O'Connell's office and pummeling him into the linoleum."

"Almost sounds worth a year in jail, old boy. I guess we'll have to use diplomacy instead."

"Does Morgan know about this?"

"I don't think so. After I received the letter from my contacts, I made a few discreet calls to them to get as much detail as I could. Since I knew you were coming, I waited to tell you alone. Strange that O'Connell has such a free hand. It has to stand as one of the perverse legacies of this whole operation, the extent to which 'not wanting to know' has been its ruling principle. 'Ruling principle' is an absurd way of putting it, but I guess I have the right to say it because it is an absurdity of my own creation. How can I ever forgive myself, Robson, for being so dismissive of your warnings when this whole thing started?"

"We all take lightly what we think never touches us. As we were saying just a few minutes ago, eventually you have to conclude that there is nothing – no person, no experience – that does not touch us."

Feldon stared up at him with a mixture of desperation and respect. "I sometimes wish I had never been put back together. Easier to face yourself in shards than the world in one piece."

"Nonsense. You've been a busy man after all, Congressman Whiting, for all your sitting and sitting. We need to push against this dilemma as we find it now. Our hopings and prayings didn't make it disappear – we disappeared, in a false hope. I will call Paul tonight. We need to stop this. The vibrations of the jackhammers and drills alone are a terrible risk, not to mention the dismantling itself."

"After the ceremony perhaps we can all go down there in force as a delegation from the new world of El Tajín. The irony is artful. I'm sure we will be well received, probably given new glossy maps and flyers." Feldon continued to poke the earth with his cane. "Can't we go back to what we were talking about earlier? Don't you prefer personal examination to political maneuvering?"

"I have no sweater or jacket. This wind is getting to me. Let's go back to the ladies." They turned and started walking toward the gate. "Sure I prefer it, but we have to digest our thoughts, don't you think? Doors turn back into walls when you play with the knobs for too long. And philosophy is not going to save us from this."

"Oh? And what will?"

They reached the gate and passed through and back up the path in silence. In the anteroom they took a few moments to clean the sand off their shoes and trousers. Feldon handed Robson a worn, somewhat musty plaid blanket, the squares of faded green, red, and yellow randomly decorated with many a hole and pulled thread. "I guess you should shake it out, but it will help take the chill away. I suppose I'll start a fire. Strange thing to do in the middle of summer, but Nature has the right to ignore her creation when she wishes."

Robson shook out the blanket and wrapped it around himself. He put his hand on the door to the library and paused. "Does Ethel know about any of this?"

"No. Maybe it's selfish of me. I still want to enjoy a feeling of innocence, a feeling that the world breathes pleasure and sweet promise, offers us industry and rewards its completion – and is not simply ready to snuff you out the next instant. Through her I can. Without her naïve open door to life, I would have shriveled into a troll long ago."

"I wish you luck with that. Innocence needs to be tested too, you know. And we may underestimate what an open heart can endure."

"Then maybe I'm the one who can't endure."

They stepped into the library and were greeted by a welcome bath of warm enveloping air. Their wives were nestled on the couch by a now blazing hearth, wrapped in thick shawls and gazing dreamily at the men's arrival. A pot of hot cocoa and cups stood on the side table. A powdery staccato of sandy wind beat against the glass doors in the distance.

"What were you two mumbling about in there?" Ethel asked. "I think I'll set up a hidden microphone in that room, darling, to spy on all your machinations."

"It's time I machinated in public then," Feldon said leaning over and giving her a kiss. Robson did the same with Monica, and then poured out the cocoa. The two men settled into armchairs opposite their beloveds and smiled at them with gratitude.

"Colonel Andrews, what are you doing wrapped in that horrid rag? Really, Feldon, how could you. I mop the floors with that thing."

"No, you don't," he snorted and shook his head.

"Well, I certainly shall. Give it here, Robson, you don't need it now." He pulled it off and handed it over to her, and she held it up to the hearth. "Maybe I should toss it into the fire, a sacrifice to the god of decorum. Or cut it up and make mittens and gloves."

"And ski masks, darling. Then we can go around robbing the neighborhood."

Ethel gave him a playful smirk and set the shawl aside. "We have been enjoying a long quiet stare into the flames. Monica was just saying how strange fire is. A powerful form of matter sometimes contained, but only controlled by extinguishing it – and it in turn always destroys what it settles upon. Yet it cannot exist on its own. It needs a hapless auxiliary on whom to rage and consume, and disappears when no one else will have it."

"The metaphors are unspeakable," Feldon said through a grin. "I shall refrain."

"You'd better."

"Yes, Monica and I have had this discussion before," Robson said. "I agree that empirically it is the only conclusion. But it might hold a different message. Anything brighter, more powerful, more encompassing, only manifests episodically. Lightning, volcanoes, inspiration, ideas..."

"Orgasms," Ethel said.

Robson smiled. "And we can't say that their departure is mere destruction. Or that these experiences can't exist without 'victims.' Would we were so victimized more often. If a higher matter consumes a lower matter, it only means that its nature can only exist in our world for brief periods of time. But it may exist longer, forever, somewhere else."

"Everything important is always somewhere else," Ethel scoffed. "But Mr. Colonel, darling, we can't deny the fact of annihilation. You can't tell an islander he was visited by a higher power after his village is buried under molten rock."

"I can't, but he may think so. Does science always know more than superstition? Of course the body cannot bear high temperatures and the like, but our psychology can. Don't forget, falling in love and being in love – that which is the most precious to us all – destroys, and destroys most thoroughly. My darling wife obliterated and remade my life. Something that needed doing, though I could never have done it on my own."

Monica blushed a little and turned to her hostess. "We were saying earlier how unbearable the truth is. She is so frank with everyone, and you noticed, didn't you Ethel, during your years in political society how people either cringed behind their shields when around you, or learned to relax naked and disarmed."

"I see two kinds of truth," she replied. "What people are and what people think they are. The latter is more a fact than a truth, and at times – well, many times – facts be damned. Everyone thought it was my fiendish pleasure to hold converse with someone's representation of who he or she was, and then tease out the way for the hot air to escape somewhere other than through their mouths. It wasn't long before the puff pastry collapsed into goo. Feldon became the master of apologia, but people really loved me for it. Why? Because what is obvious to me is obvious to everyone else. So what is that, that lightning bolt, if we must, which only appears when you say out loud what is right in front of you? Why is silence so one-dimensional? So dead."

"It isn't all bolts and flashes," Monica said. "The slightest comment can make any of us twinge, and it feels unfair when there's no love in it. We feel that no one else knows our entire story, a sliver of ourselves on trial for all we see to be our life and experience."

"I agree with your distinction, Ethel," Robson said. "I'm just not sure that it's a bad thing. We are whoever we think we are. True enough. And what lies behind that? Nothing. Let's not deny it. If we could just settle into that, we could make and remake ourselves according to what life demands of us."

"You're starting to sound like a self-help manual, Mr. Colonel. I say you both are what I think you are, two lovely darlings. Isn't that right, Feldon?"

She smiled at her husband, and he at her. But Feldon did not reply. Instead he let his gaze linger over her clear and tranquil face. Her cheeks were flushed with a tender porcelain delicacy, as though about to weep for a silent joy just now uplifting her heart to secret unshareable wisdom. Her soft eyes relaxed into quiet dalliance, like two mature roses inviting close and closer appreciation and wonder. Her lips were moist and slightly parted, the hint of a possible word suspended on an instant forever, reminding Feldon of the lined portrait of some antique maiden lost in a frescoed corner. Robson too rested a silent gaze on his beloved. Her dark curls cuddled about chin, cheeks and lips, framing an oval portrait at once demure, loving, and worldly wise. Her bright, fully open lids mirrored a multitude of heartfelt shimmers, the flaming hearth of her vibrant soul: vulnerable with wonder but no trace of naïveté, expectant of kisses without insistence or lust, resigned to mortal needs yet infused with ethereal confidence. Her quiet upturned mouth invited by its closed lips the one and only she knew and wanted.

A sweet elastic atmosphere soon enwrapped the four of them in delicious repose, each even unnoted breath keeping them enchanted by the Other who was their sun to flower, flower to sun. The tearing wind continued to rage and shudder window frames and shrubbery, and suddenly a howling gust rattled and tumbled about the patio furniture, knocking over the table and sending the glass top rolling on its edge. The four lovers were unperturbed and continued to melt and unmelt in and out their loving spell. With mild curiosity Robson glanced over at the window and watched the glass top roll to a halt and fall towards its center, spinning in tighter circles until it shuddered to the ground like a giant coin. The next moment the wind and its grainy peltings as suddenly subsided, and in a few more breaths Nature wafted calm, and warm shimmers of light began to reemerge.

A tender silence reigned. Nothing was heard, and all that mattered most was seen. Each of them felt deeply the unnecessity of living even a millisecond into something elsewhere. The waning hearth glowed without flame, but the ether torch in each of their eyes continued to blaze eternal.

Out the window Robson watched one tiny leaf drift in lullaby descent from branch to air to pavement.

As soon as it landed, he arose and Monica rose up with him. They held each other a lingering while, then sauntered arm in arm over to the windows and sliding glass doors. Robson peered out to examine the tabletop and turned back to Feldon.

"Not a crack or scratch. Just a shiny disc reflecting sunlight." He then stooped down and lifted up one end of Portsmouth Lodge, Monica following suit and taking up the other end. In an instant it was back on the dining table, and the couple disappeared from view.

Ethel slowly drew up off the couch and walked over to Feldon. She leaned over him and brushed her lips against his cheek.

"Tell me if I've been crying," she said.

"No, my love, you have not."

"Kiss the tear that is not there." And he kissed her under each eyelid. Then he stood up, and they walked out hand in hand to bid their guests farewell.

They were standing by the open door looking out on Nature's latest caprice. The wind had abated and the clouds receded to the horizon in hazy blue-grey billows. The sea was still choppy, but the gentle hush of the breakers bespoke a return to serenity.

"Looks like the beach has staked a claim on your garden," Monica said. And indeed dustings of sand had settled here and there on branches, flowers, walkways, and stairs.

"It will no doubt conquer eventually," Feldon said, "but mercifully at a pace that we can live out our days withal."

"As you've said before darling," Ethel added. " 'Time will tell, but probably not us.' "

"Sometimes time doesn't have to tell," Robson said. "This impression right here tells enough of a story."

"Really, Colonel Robson, you must save some of these solemn pronouncements for your generals and senators."

He laughed. "Yes, you're right," he replied. "I apologize for yet another lead balloon."

Ethel walked up to him and gave him a hug. "Until next week, then." She walked over to Monica and hugged her a long, long moment.

EL TAJIN, NEW MEXICO

Feldon grasped Robson's hand. "I'll send that letter over to your hotel tomorrow."

"Very good. And I will call you in a day or two after I've spoken with Paul and Alicia. Let's hope this is the final act in this dramedy."

"Final act? You do realize there is more than one way for the curtain to come down."

Robson patted his arm and smiled. He turned to Monica, and they began walking down the steps. Then she stopped and dashed back up to embrace Feldon. "Oh, how could I! Thank you, thank you so much." She gave him and Ethel a final loving look, and soon the Andrews were down the stairs and out of sight.

Their hosts stepped back inside and in so doing Feldon noticed the shopping bag on the floor.

"They left us these gifts. I had forgotten." He picked up the bag and was greeted with the clink of bottles.

"Wine, no doubt," Ethel said. "From California, I hope."

He set the bag on the counter and pulled out three bottles of chardonnay. "Yes, indeed. How generous of them. But there are a few other things in here."

"Let's get back to the fire and see what they are. Here, darling, unzip me." She held up her hair as he unhooked the back of her dress and let down the zipper. She pulled the dress off over her head and tossed it on the floor, kicked off her shoes, bra and panties quickly followed, and she wandered naked back around to the library. They resumed their places opposite each other in front of the hearth. Feldon set the bag next to her, and poked the fire and added a few small cuts of wood. Soon welcome waves of bright heat helped them relax and settle into comfort.

Ethel pulled out the contents of the bag and placed them in her lap. "Some lovely cards. See? All of them floral designs. Oh, and look at this engraving. A charming wooded landscape. That lady has exquisite taste." She handed it across to him and then held up the final gift. "But this is a surprise. Did you know she was an authoress?"

"News to me," Feldon said. "Looks like a children's book."

The large thin volume indeed had a laminate cover, all in white with dark blue lettering and a dark blue filigree border on both sides. She began thumbing through the pages and soon let out a soft gasp. "Oh, what remarkable drawings! Who is this Stephson?"

"One of Monica's former lovers, I believe. He worked at the base."

Ethel raised her eyebrows and laughed. "I'm sure Madame has many a former on her emotional payroll. But he is very good. These renderings of an ancient Middle Eastern bazaar, the narrow crowded streets, this mosque, all have extraordinary atmosphere. Look Feldon." She turned pages and held each of the images up for him to see. "These leathery faces are curious. I wonder where he found the models. But these buildings are special – he has a real eye for mass and proportion. I might consider hiring him myself." She reached the end of the book and stared a full minute in silence at the last page. "Why, this is Alicia! I could say it is a remarkable likeness, but I've never been good at understatement. How these eyes speak. Look at that."

She held the book up again for him to see. The full-page drawing faced what appeared to be the final page of text. Even at the distance he was looking, the portrait's quiet, luminous gaze unsettled him. Not only were the features of her countenance – brow, cheeks, mouth – in total relaxation, her eyes were as well, pupils dark with the plummet of eternity, as though the meditative figure both saw and absorbed everything he ever knew and experienced, and found him still too green for her continued interest. So does a galaxy ignore the mite that squints in its direction.

"Can you read the story out loud? It doesn't seem to be very long. It must be simple enough."

Ethel turned to the front and began reading to herself. "It's not really a children's story after all," she said. "Though this approach of a large typeface coupled with these marvelous drawings is very interesting. The lady has concocted a modern fairy tale. I wonder what motivates her." She glanced up at Feldon and gave him her sly look again. "Yes, my love, I will read it to you. Then you can tell me what it is I don't know."

She drew a couple of pillows behind her and settled back into the couch. Then she propped the book up on a small pillow that rested on her naked thigh, and read the entire piece in a steady, musical tone, without comment or undue emphasis or drama. When the story was finished, she set the book down gently on the floor and stared into the hearth. Feldon did the same, and for nearly a quarter hour neither of them spoke or moved.

THE LADY, THE TIGER, AND THE PRINCESS
by Monica Andrews
Illustrations by J. David Stephson

Gratitude is often misdirected. Let me qualify that a little. I mean, gratitude, as a spur to action, often ends up pointing us in the wrong place. Not infrequently I hear friends and family members, peace be upon them, appeal to this word, this "concept," as though it were the mainspring of their life. "I am grateful for what I have, and I want to share it"; "How grateful I am – what can I do?"; "I must express my gratitude." Must we? Why? Who needs to know that we are grateful? And when we feel gratitude, what are we experiencing?

I ask too many questions. As a young girl, my father was always after me about my chatter and my questioning. "My Little Swallow," he would call me. I know he loved this in me, but I also know he did not want me to love this in myself. He said many things about talk and discourse that I no longer recall. But I do remember one thing he said, seemingly in passing (but who knows?), that a clever mind asks questions, an intelligent mind answers questions, but a wise mind treats the one as the other. And so I do. If someone asks me something, I attend first of all to the answer in his or her heart – what they have just told me by their question about what they already know or understand. And if I ask for help or advice and receive a reply, I remark in the certainty of my friend what remains uncertain, what he or she also does not know about what I have asked. And so life's mystery deepens. To live there, to remain there, is now more than ever the resolve of my final years. Because of my journey.

Both my father and mother had impressed upon my young mind with vivid immediacy what they only knew by hearsay at several removes when they themselves were young: that the city and neighboring environs of a semi-barbaric kingdom, two weeks journey from our own peaceful land, had been under the rule of a tyrannical king for many years. The term "semi-barbaric" always puzzled me, because no one could ever tell me what the non-barbaric part consisted of. In any case, the stories frightened everyone in our village, such that all were content to listen to details both real and, no doubt, exaggerated from traders and pilgrims who passed through our lands, without ever having the urge to venture anywhere near that ungodly kingdom themselves.

What filled everyone with terror most of all was, of course, the king's notorious method of meting out justice to his subjects. When either apprehended in the act or otherwise suspected of being complicit in a crime, the accused was cast into an arena and forced to choose one of two doors set side by side at one end of the stadium circus. Behind one door was a wild, half-starved tiger ready to unleash its fury on whichever unfortunate unbolted its chamber, while behind the other stood a beautiful young woman or handsome young man ready to bestow a lifetime of love and favor on the fortunate one who opened their portal. For the many who silently condemned this form of tribunal as the rule of chaos, there were just as many who felt that Fate, the Great One, the Unknowable, was the true and final judge of each single life, however unfair the apparent injustice seemed to be. What the king himself felt about this was never known, and those who considered the matter in any depth usually concluded that the king thought neither of chance nor destiny, but merely reveled in the simple animal thrill of the moment.

The stories of these trials were never without their fascination, first of all, because the greatest of joys was as likely to reward the accused as the greatest of horrors was to tear asunder his or her untasted days and hours. And secondly, and perhaps more importantly, because for those of us who heard these stories, the most famous trial of them all continued to fascinate with an unending allure, for no one ever knew the final outcome. After that particular trial had ended, so ruthless had the king been with regard to maintaining the secrecy of its conclusion, that many another poor soul found themselves walking across that dusty arena trembling with fear, the attentive hush of the onlookers terrifying the victim all the more, as they approached those two massive wooden doors.

That famous trial was, of course, the story of the secret lover of the king's own daughter. The king was especially enraged that his daughter would consort with a commoner, and it said something about his own principles, such as they were, that he cast the young man into the same arena as all his other prisoners rather than make an exception, which would have been his right, and have the fellow tortured and killed in private. It was assumed that the king took pleasure in the fact that even if the young man selected the door that concealed the blushing young maiden, his daughter would still learn the lesson of obedience, and realize anew her place in society and seek among her own for the father of her children to come.

As we all know, the story was equally famous for the extra layer of suspense that surrounded the heart of the princess herself. She knew which door concealed the maiden and which the tiger, she knew who the maiden was (and detested her as a rival for the hand of her beloved), and at the crucial moment, as the victim faced king and daughter for the last time, she had signaled to him with the slightest flick of her hand which door to choose. He in turn bowed to his royalty, turned about and walked with slow modest steps across the arena, and without hesitation opened the door the princess had indicated.

Did his trust in her kill him, or exile him from her heart forever? Did he choose the lady, or the tiger? No one knew.

And no one knew what became of the princess. That she married and raised children of her own was certain, but her secluded life within the labyrinthine walls of the palace and its grounds kept her forever concealed from prying eyes and overcurious tongues. She no longer attended the trials of the arena, since her father forbade her ever to be seen again by the common folk. And she herself had no doubt found the memories of that day too painful to willingly resurrect them.

I still marvel at the curious tricks the passage of time can play on one's mind. For, what had arrived in our village as news, quickly became anecdote, gossip, wild speculation, and, a generation later, legend. By the time I had become a young woman, the tales of this king and his brutal ways were told and retold as though the dust of centuries had long ago buried both him and all over whom he had ever held sway.

But I knew my arithmetic, and a simple calculation brought with it a simple conclusion: the princess herself might still be alive. Because my father was a successful merchant, I came to know many of the traders and, to be honest, smugglers, who included our village in their seasonal rounds from importer to exporter to marketplace. One old rogue in particular, Four-Fingered Abdul (he had lost a pinkie in a sword fight), had always been fond of me, so early one morning before dawn I stole out of our home and caught up with his caravan as it was about to head eastward into the desert. I had with me a near-bursting wineskin that I knew would not be missed, and after passing it into his hands, I took him aside and unfolded my strange request. I reminded him of the legend of the lady and the tiger, and told him of my suspicions that the princess was passing her final days within the walls of the ancient city. Could he inquire after her? And if indeed she lived, could he discover a way for me to pay her a visit?

"Little Swallow," he said, "this task does not inconvenience me, your request, strange as it is, does not surprise me, and the possible dangers to my person do not frighten me. But I am a bit offended that you thought it necessary to persuade me with a bribe."

"Now I am offended," I replied. "A gift is not a bribe," and I kissed his grizzled cheek.

He shook his head and laughed. "I prophesy, no man shall ever triumph over you," and I watched the train of camels, men, and wagons depart into the dawning light until they disappeared on the horizon.

I could say I thought of nothing else until Abdul's return, but it was not true. My young adult life and its myriad responsibilities, and amusements, were a whirlwind from rising to setting sun. So when the flaps of my father's tent parted one quiet afternoon three months later while I was sitting on the floor mending old garments for resale the next day, the smiling old rogue entered with bolts of colored silk in his arms, and the joy of a half-forgotten anticipation realized flooded my innocent heart.

"You are here!" I cried and threw my arms about his neck. The lovely gift was spread out on a rug, and tea brewed and served. He began with variations on the usual stories and descriptions of his travels, but soon his vivid narrative led me through the gates and down the central artery of that mysterious city. The dread king had been dead for many years, and no one had ascended the throne in his place. Instead, a group of nobles and wealthy merchants formed what was at first an uneasy alliance, but as time went by and the people accepted this new and more benign leadership, the group evolved into the official governing body of the kingdom. Through its membership all the people had a voice and a vote, and in less than a generation the "non-barbaric" spirit pacified and civilized the land. Buildings, squares, and streets were cleaned and repaired; new markets, farms, and workshops hummed into life; and the arena and its outbuildings were razed and replaced with a grand park and gardens. Some of the more resentful townspeople also wanted to tear down the palace and drive the king's family out into the desert, but the wisdom of the governing alliance prevailed. The royals were allowed to keep their home and maintain it at their own expense, but family members were each obliged to serve the community according to their capacity, the men as soldiers, builders, and administrators, the women as caregivers, matrons, and artisans. The princess, a widow for some years now, because of her station and special history, was permitted to find her own way to engage the people...

"Oh!" I interrupted him with a cry. "So it is true! She is alive!"

"Yes, she is," Abdul replied. "I did not see her myself, but I spoke with a few who have spent an afternoon with her. She receives visitors four times a month." And he explained the procedure. All women (men were not permitted in her presence) who wanted an audience with the princess assembled before a side entrance to the palace on one of the appointed days. The commissar in charge of the audiences selected from among the hopefuls a cross-section of the classes of people who resided in the kingdom, as well as a few visitors from other villages and lands. The fortunate group was then led into a comfortable room adorned with tapestries and colorful tiles, and invited to sit upon an array of couches and divans arranged in a square, the murmuring trickle from a low marble fountain in the center the only accompaniment to silence. The visitors sat on three sides, with the fourth side reserved for the princess and her train, which usually consisted of one or more of her children and grandchildren. Tea and sweetmeats were served to the guests, and frankincense burned from large brass censors standing in the corners of the room. The princess always entered without ceremony, refusing to have her guests stand up or otherwise proffer gestures of obeisance. She joined the ladies in their refreshment and engaged them at once in conversation, which she led and sustained with the ease of one who has mastered all the delicacies of social interaction. The talk usually ranged over the news of the day, the current public works projects under construction, and even a tease or two of local gossip, which was always greeted with amused titters. In this way a pleasant hour soon passed, and as the visitors departed they were each permitted to take the extended hand of the princess and share with her a personal moment before passing out of the room and down the corridor to the appointed exit. An orderly stood at the doorway with an armful of roses denuded of thorns, and handed one to each guest as she passed back outside.

I had to go. Stealth was out of the question. I arranged a meeting that evening with my father and my betrothed, and with Abdul by my side stated in plain terms what I intended to do. I was firm, but not defiant. I was actually close to tears but somehow managed to restrain them as I spoke. I assured them, the two men in the world most dear to me, that the journey was safe, the mission benign but necessary to me, and in any case, Abdul would be with me at all times. My beloved at first took it all as a joke, but the silence of my father soon convinced him that my mission was a serious one. They both gave the journey their blessings, more out of resignation than eagerness, but my father at least, so it seemed, saw how my heart would never be at peace until I braved this encounter, an encounter that I already tasted at a distance without understanding what it would disclose.

We left at dawn the next day. Any lingering farewells or fusses over luggage would have been inappropriate, and an insult to my father's and fiancé's good will. We made only the briefest of stops at the oases and way-stations to take a simple meal and rest the camels and horses, then on we would go. When we came over a ridge and saw the walled and turreted city before us, Abdul remarked that he had never traveled this far this quickly, and probably never would do so again.

We passed the day at one of the large bazaars and slept on the ground wrapped in our blankets and skins. To my good fortune the next day was one of the four appointed for visitations, and I was among the first group of women to arrive at the designated portal. Abdul sat on a crate on the other side of the road, motionless as a carved sentinel god before a mausoleum. I waved to him and smiled, and he nodded his head slightly with reassurance.

EL TAJIN, NEW MEXICO

When the wooden door creaked open and the commissar appeared, I was underneath his inquisitive gaze in an instant and explained to him from where I had come and how brief was my one and only stay in his famous city. The man furrowed his brow and eyed me even more inquisitively, but to my relief he as quickly relaxed into a smile, and gestured for me to enter. Down the dark cool corridors we went, small barred windows set high above us at regular intervals letting in small patches of light. The audience chamber was even more elegant and colorful than I had imagined. A veiled woman was passing from corner to corner lighting the incense, and she nodded a friendly greeting as we found our places on the couches.

I set myself directly opposite the place reserved for the princess. I looked around me, gazed far up at the carved geometric patterns burnished in gold leaf on the ceiling, mumbled a few pleasantries with the other ladies. Tea was poured, platters of candy and cake were passed around, servants fluffed up the pillows and straightened the cushions on the royal divan. Suddenly I was terrified. How rash was my impetuous curiosity! Why did I come here? How could I ask the princess, herself a stranger to me, in the company of so many other strangers, about the most personal, the most traumatic experience of her life? Was this why my father silently agreed to this journey, that I might at last learn the lesson of leaving the mysteries of the world alone?

So lost was I in my agitation that I did not even see the princess arrive. The happy giggles of two young girls startled me out of myself as they fussed about climbing up and over the couches. They were accompanied by a woman of middle years, and so I took them to be daughter and grand-children. Another pretty girl in her teens glided in and sat demurely in one corner of the square. The princess was dressed in modest homespun materials of grey and blue. Her loosely worn headscarf revealed whitish-blonde hair that was combed straight down and parted in the middle. She eased into her place, took a sip of tea, and held out the platter for her little granddaughters to take from. She passed it along without taking anything for herself, and took a moment to survey her guests. Then she began to speak, in a haunting mellow tone that captured us all at once. Her talk was easy and congenial, and it felt as though we had all been reunited after a brief interval to deepen an acquaintance already established. I marveled at this quality in her, and all notion of asking questions or offering comment melted to naught. Now and then she would ask one of the guests their name and origins, and I could see that she was tactful enough to choose a lady capable of engaging her in talk without embarrassment or bravado. I sat and stared. I neither ate nor drank. I decided to let go of my curiosity and return home to my new life and start a family. This, after all, is what life should be.

The hour flew away, and the guests rose and passed before her for a final farewell. Once again I was oblivious to the change until the last visitor was sharing a few words with our hostess. The lady departed, and the princess's daughters and children scurried away out of the room. I did not move. I did not know what to do. The princess pulled off her headscarf and ran her fingers through her long hair, letting the mass of it lie flat along her shoulders and breasts. Then she looked at me, and the frankness of her gaze showed that she had been aware of me all along.

"I know why you have come," she said. Even though she was on the far side of the room, the intimacy of her voice could just as well have been at my cheek.

"I hope you will forgive my intrusion, princess. I shall be on my way."

"I do not forgive you. And you should not apologize for your boldness. You will undo your own character. Please, come sit by me."

I stood up and walked around the fountain, and sat beside her on the divan. "What is your name?" she asked. I told her, and added a few details about my family and my home.

"I know of your land," she said. "Your village has had the great gift of simplicity and anonymity bestowed upon it. I hope you are aware of your good fortune."

I said that I had not considered it in those terms before, and I thanked her for the thoughtful insight.

She carried on talking in an impersonal manner, and it quickly dawned on me that unless I put my question to her she would continue her stream of incidental chat without cease. She had presented the opportunity, brought me to the portal, but it was for me to knock on the door. And since her talk continued unabated, it meant interrupting her.

"What became of your lover? Did you send him to death or to another? Did he choose the lady or the tiger?" I paused, and then added, "And what of yourself?"

She stopped. She looked at me, and the trace of a grin appeared. She then looked across the room for a few moments, seeming to gather her thoughts, and in that brief interval my gaze lingered over her face. At first it struck me as homely and rather ordinary, but as I continued to look at her I saw the ravishing beauty that had once hypnotized all men and intimidated all women. Her complexion was smooth and unlined, with but a crease or two at the corners of her eyes. And those eyes. They did not pierce, nor evade, nor dream. They absorbed her surroundings with a calm unconcern, myself an equal but perhaps not exceptional part of her tableau of the moment. And in that brief interval a new realization blossomed within me, that I was a part of my own tableau.

She began to speak. She did not look at me because she was looking at her story. Her voice rose and fell with the cadence of her narrative, by turns reflective, happy, pensive, even angry. The drama of that day passed before and into me, where it shall forever remain.

"I knew you would come. I could say, 'I knew someone would come,' but it is not 'someone' – it is you. And it would be unfair of me to generalize over the personal trials and efforts you no doubt suffered to arrive here now.

"A certain amount of time has had to pass for me to tell this story. A lot of time, as it happens, which liberates all concerned, since no consequence can follow from its telling.

"I indicated the door with the lady, but not out of any artificial sense of generosity or self-sacrifice. I indicated that door because the lady was me. As soon as he turned and started walking across the arena, I rose out of my seat and whispered to my father that I would not allow him to subject me to the horror or humiliation of my lover's choice. I hurried out of the royal box and down the stairway, accompanied by my serving woman and most faithful bodyguard, and ran underneath one of the service tunnels to the other end of the stadium ahead of him. As I ran I threw off the cloak that had been covering my marriage garb and, with my lady's help, put over me a different cloak and thick veil that covered my head and face right to the eyebrows. My woman was even clever enough to quickly clean and change the painting around my eyelids. I arrived at the door no more than a heartbeat before it opened, and there I stood before him. I was the happiest woman in the world. The crowd gasped in unison and rose to their feet as one body, not suspecting for whom they were about to witness a wedding. The side door opened and the procession and musicians emerged as previously arranged should the lady be the victim's choice. My beloved took me by the hand, despondent and reluctant, unable to look at me, unaware of his prize, which pleased me all the more, and led me to the center of the arena, where the high priest awaited us. The vows were exchanged, the union consecrated, and I placed my hand to my breast and bowed my head to all and sundry, my heart filled to the brim with love for my one and only, and with sublime relief at soon being able to escape the tyranny of my father and his brutal ways. We passed out of the arena and back into the underground passages. My bodyguard led us down a narrow corridor toward an unused portal where fresh horses and servants awaited us for escape into the desert and beyond to a new life and home. My beloved was only half-aware of what was happening, and it was not until we approached the portal and the horses that I pulled down my veil, and amid his startled joy and tear-filled gasps we embraced each other for a long ecstatic moment. Then we mounted the horses, and I turned to bid a final farewell to my two faithful friends, who had risked their all to set us free.

"A figure filled the doorway behind them, a giant of a man, who I did not recognize, with a scimitar in his sash. He strode toward us, and soon a second, third, and fourth man of similar height and proportions followed and surrounded our small party. They drew their blades in unison and stared hard at us. There was nothing to be done. We dismounted and followed them back into the arena. The men separated myself and my love from the others, and led the two of us down a tunnel unknown to me. It descended an additional story underground, eventually opening into a wide chamber lined with solid granite on all sides. Torches burned from sockets high above us, and a group of four more men surrounded the person I of course knew would be awaiting our arrival.

"A peculiar feeling of relief passed through me when I saw that my father was not gloating. At least we would confront each other without his foolish pride obscuring the proceedings. In a few ruthless words he explained how the lady who was to have been the prize in today's trial had come to him with my secret the night before. I had bestowed upon her so many of my possessions in order to trade places with her: jewelry, clothing, perfumes, even a gold bar. I had arranged for her the hand of another handsome one that she favored, and according to our stratagem I had assumed

EL TAJIN, NEW MEXICO

that she was already leagues away with him and my wealth, of which I had had no desire or need.

"'But her gifts easily won, and undeserved, only led her to desire a greater gift, not easily won and also undeserved,' the king said. 'She wanted me.'

"'Where is she then?' I asked.

"'Dead, of course.'

"He motioned to his men, and two of them seized my beloved and shoved him past the group and over to the edge of a large pit that had previously been hidden from my view. This pit was about ten cubits wide and extended from the center of the room to the far wall, where it abutted a narrow ledge. I wrapped my cloak about myself and walked gingerly toward the edge. Two of the guards started, as though they would lay hands on me, but my icy stares kept them at bay. But oh! what horror! At the bottom of the pit roiled a seething mass of cobras, their slimy bodies oozing and slithering over and about each other and emitting a dank stench that nearly suffocated me. I shuddered at this reptilian indifference, knowing full well how the sudden dash of a body among them would arouse the darting heads and dripping fangs. My lover, nay, my husband, engaged my eyes with his, terror for his life mingled with his love for me, and a world of desires, affections, and resignations flew between us in seconds. Then my father spoke again.

"'I expect no lesson to be learned from this. Death does not instruct. It simply has the final say. And I wield that final say. I don't create law, I am law...'

"He was obviously going to go on like this for some time, and, who knows, perhaps it was only that that prodded me forward. I threw off my cloak and ran toward the far wall. The guards shouted and fumbled after me, but I was too quick. Without a flinch I leapt out across the pit and landed on the ledge. I flattened my face and arms against the stone until I had a sure footing, and shuffled my way to the center. Then I turned around and pressed my back against the wall. I kicked off my slippers to give my bare feet a firmer grip on the ledge. They fell and hit that clump of damp flesh, which instantly shot up in venomous indignation, fangs agape and hisses terrible. Their reaction rippled through the entire mass, and in a few moments all those horrible triangular heads flashed erect, a tight coiled sea of ruthless attention bobbing and swaying, keen to strike at the barest flicker of a yet unseen prey.

"From across the pit I felt my father's two black eyes bore into me. I locked gazes with him and stared back in defiance. I did not need to voice what my bold move had just accomplished, but I wanted my words to carry forth my deed: 'If this is the final say, as you call it, then it shall be so for us both. You believe you can take his life as your right. Then you shall also take mine, as your curse. May it hound you for eternity.'

"His pupils widened in confused anger, unaccustomed as he was to any hint of opposition. The next moment his eyes, wild with rage, became the bars of a cage, against which his inner tiger crashed and snarled, furious for revenge and frustrated by what restrained his untrammeled bloodlust. And seeing this, there shot forth from the base of my spine my own inner tiger, which bashed against the iron of my fixed stare, eager to thrash and assert its hardened stance. Thus did these tigers growl and spit at each other for several moments across that pit of slimy focused horror beneath us. How long we held aloft this fiery standoff I cannot say, for after what seemed a lifetime I shuddered to find my tiger had disappeared. The phantom that he was deserted me, and I was left on that narrow ledge all alone, a soft help- less girl incapable of battling the hard fingers and arms of these soldiers, and certainly not the needle fangs and acid poison of the serpents below. Suddenly I was a fragile wisp trembling in tornadoes, and yet I dared not, I could not, betray my purpose. I continued to stare at the tiger within my fa- ther's gaze with the same show of anger, even though naught but feather and tremor stood behind it. Then gradually, and subtly, as the minutes passed and passed, my helplessness became my strength. Yes, I would die, yes, the animals of this world would triumph yet again, as they always do, but I would never undo the gossamer thread of my love and my dignity.

"All throughout this trial no one else in that dark subterranean room dared speak or even move so much as a hair. How my husband looked and behaved through all of this I cannot say, for I could not allow my eye to wan- der even for a second. Eventually my father's face collapsed into a broken smile and, his tiger still alert and ready to pounce, he laughed and said, 'You will yield soon enough. How can you not. Your character is ill suited to these stratagems.'

" 'My character!' I shouted at him. 'I am your daughter! Forget not that!'

"This startled him. The tiger retreated a step. And contrary to his own manner the king himself glanced about for an instant, unsure of what to do next.

"This was my moment. I realized I could not force him to surrender entirely before those of his innermost circle. He had to be seen to have made a final decision that maintained his credibility among them. And just in that instant I saw how I could put the elements of that decision before him.

"'All right,' I said. 'I will come back to you. But on this condition: Either you give me my husband in lawful wedlock, or you send him away safely from our kingdom forever. Choose one of these, and I will return to your good graces. Though, I swear to you, before all here present, that if you agree in word only and have him killed later, I will find my own way down to the netherworld, and in a fashion that shall humiliate and disgrace you forever, and send your name down into future ages with the blackest of curses upon it. Say that you understand me!'"

With a gasp the princess broke off her narrative. She covered her face in her hands and wept quietly for some time. I reached out and touched her arm, but felt at once the weak unneed of such a gesture. Though vulnerable with sorrow, she remained anchored in herself and was in no wise lost in this momentary surrender to her feelings.

Eventually she gathered herself and dried her eyes with one of her kerchiefs. She looked at me and smiled. "How it cut through me to speak in such a savage way to my father. Even though he deserved that, and more. Where I received the strength to avoid the tears I now have shed I know not. Those words were bitter to the taste the moment they left my lips, but a beast only understands its own tongue. And so he understood, and relented. His heart clutched tight its reluctance for one final second, then the tiger grunted, flashed a final leer at me, and turned and shuffled away back into his soul. The king made his choice and vowed before all present to honor it, and he did so honor it. I sidled back along the ledge and was gently lifted to safety by the powerful hands of two of the guards. We all walked together a silent procession up the ramps and through the corridors, and stepped back out into the beautiful light of day."

Faint traces of incense lingered on the quiet air. I listened for distant sounds of incidental domestic life, but all was still and serene. A quiet joy glowed like a young flame in my breast. In the end the princess had received her heart's desire. She had defied her father and won the man she felt to be hers for the remainder of this life. I was happy for her happiness, and my thoughts turned toward my departure and my parting words to this most remarkable of women.

And then all stopped. Her happiness…?

"Princess!" I gasped. She turned her face toward me. My gaze met hers, and there it ever stayed.

I beheld those amber eyes, flecked with delicate sparkles like the pinpoint fires of an opal. Their beauty, now revealed to me for the first time, held me suspended on a ductile thread of tender firmness mingled with a curious disinterest. This was but the threshold, and so I entered. I now looked into those eyes, searching, seeking, wanting to find her happiness and to know that it had blossomed to fullness throughout her long years. And yes, such happiness I saw, perhaps beyond anything I myself would ever know, but with many another companion alongside this. Long deep sorrow, solitude hardly to be borne, pleasures enjoyed in the sweetness of secrecy, frustrate shivers that only patience resolves, spells of indifference, riles of confusion, precarious gambles taken and achieved, and a galaxy of gleaming facets that were the many, many moments of her life that she shared with eternity.

My question was futile, but my outbreath could not hold it back: "Which did your father choose? Did he let you live with your beloved, or did he send him away?"

I continued to sail through that galaxy, my question but a waft of air that she registered without a flinch. In one trailing flash I saw her living with her new husband, the two of them arranging their apartments in the palace, enjoying days of idleness followed by months of happy industry, receiving with joy their children into the world, she burying her father and, after many happy years together, burying her dear friend, and valiantly accepting what the demands of her position made upon her. The next instant the opposite comet-like story streaked across her pupils, where she stood on the parapet the day after the terrible confrontation with her father and death, and watched her husband ride away into the desert forever, relief for his safety mingled with the pallor of loneliness that gripped her heart, months of solitude following that almost wasted her frame, until another young man managed to reopen her affection for everything she had wanted to forgo.

Love, happiness, success, hatred, failure, unrest. I found neither height nor bottom within the majestic world of this woman, and all my desire to know the answer to this or that riddle melted in the understanding that any joy must live alongside its companion heartache, and whatever we can live and keep and burn into our heart is what will make us who we are.

We were soon standing and in each other's arms. She kissed my forehead and asked that I send her love to my family. I bowed and turned and found my way back to the exit. To my surprise the orderly was standing there patiently with one last rose in his hand. He proffered it gracefully, and opened the door to let me pass out into the afternoon light. Across the road I saw Abdul stand up, pick up the crate he was sitting on, and walk toward me. I looked at the full delicious blossom in my hand, and slid my index finger up the smooth stem to press the soft petals against my nose and lips.

"Oh!" I cried. A sharp pinch pierced my fingertip and oozed a spot of blood. A thorn hidden just under the blossom had remained undetected. My finger in my mouth, I inhaled repeatedly the sweet fragrance of this final gift. In a moment Abdul was by my side and I followed him to the carriage awaiting us for the journey home. I joined him and the driver on the front board, the horses were prodded forth, and as we pulled away I grasped his four fingers and leaned against his shoulder. I thought not of anyone nor anything, for the sure flame of gratitude consumed me in its stillness. And for many leagues there lingered in my breast this certitude of wanting naught but what each moment places before my eyes and heart. To this day I remain grateful for what the princess had shown me, and shall hope to greet each new pulse of my life with the gesture of truth it deserves. God be praised.

She stood up and walked the few nimble steps into his lap. She pressed her firm breasts against his face, and he kissed and kissed them repeatedly. Then she laced her fingers through his hair, and tilted his head upward.

"So, my darling, what is it that I don't know?"

Feldon rose out of a mild confusion. "I don't understand."

"When you two came in from your walk, the door opened a crack and I heard Robson ask you if I knew about 'this.' Then the door closed again and your talk was too muffled to catch out. I looked over at Monica, and her attempt at a blank stare told me that she also knows all about 'this,' whatever 'this' is. Don't leave me in a corner, all of you. Out with it."

He looked at her breasts and began to relax into kissing them again. He placed his lips over one of her nipples, but suddenly she thrust herself backwards and stared at him, a tinder of wildness starting to ignite in the distance of her gaze.

"Tell me!"

"All right, all right," he murmured. He reached around and placed his hands against her soft back and held her close. He pressed his cheek against hers, an affection he knew she particularly enjoyed, and began to whisper in her ear.

···· **10** ····

CURIOUS, SHE thought, what light can do. Moreso than clay, plastic, water, even air, can light mold itself into shapes obscure, divine, fantastic, and figures unexpected. Just now a square of orange-yellow sunlight shone against the center of the floor-to-ceiling bookcase on the far wall, as though from a phantom slide projector, illuminating the spines and lettering of Plato, Goethe, and the other volumes within its frame, while the rest of the library receded into the pale shadows of pre-sunset. She stood before it in silence for several moments, wanting to accept and absorb the phenomenon without tracing its origin, when suddenly, almost in opposition to this simple resolve, her body, on its own it seemed, leaned over and looked about for a crack or crevice through which this impish play of form originated. She just as abruptly stood back up and smiled to herself at the antics of her willful flesh. Then she remembered why she had come into the room, and walked over to the large pencil and pen drawing spread out on the long pine table.

"Do you want some light, ma'am?" A tiny click and it flooded the room before she could reply.

"Oh!" She turned about to say, No, please turn it off, but instead came, "Yes. Thank you, Mal." She turned back around and looked down at the drawing once again, but the next moment she stopped herself and walked over to the doorway.

"Mal." Soft retreating footsteps. "Malvin. Can you come a moment?"

The steps paused and then just as softly resumed, with the sub-tlest increase in volume indicating his approach. He emerged from around the corner, and stood before her. "Yes, Mrs. Monroe?"

Alicia regarded his portly frame and large dignified head for a moment. She lingered over his large brown eyes, frank but unthreat-ening, and the sculpted contours of his nose and mouth. Altogether his face was not unlike the monumental head from a Mayan ruin, the semblance of his Mesoamerican ancestors passing intact to the faithful household manager that had arrived into her family's life so many years ago.

She clicked off the light again. "Come and see this." She stepped back into the library and stood aside for him to enter.

The square had already faded to a pale outline, as though the enigma sought to elude confirmation of itself by another. "Oh, how unfair," she said, gesturing toward it. "My special moment little more than anecdote…once again."

Malvin, quick to dispel her disappointment, smiled and said. "It is there. I see it, ma'am. You saw its body, I see its ghost. Very nice." And then he continued, "And you must know, ma'am, I see such glowing in your eyes all the time. My special moment, that you give but cannot see."

As always his even-tempered courtesy melted her idle trouble, and, as an instant testament to his reassurance, her grateful glance toward him set aglow those amber eyes, twin suns gently shining brighter in the darkness of the library than the square now faded almost to naught. And so her manservant beheld a special presence only he would know.

A moment more and the shadows of the room began to invade their sensibility. Understanding this Malvin switched on the light again, and Alicia returned to her appraisal of the drawing on the table.

"Shall I bring you dinner here, ma'am?"

"Yes, Mal, thank you. Out here on the terrace. With this clear sky the sunset colors should be a delight."

She listened once again to the soft retreat of his footsteps as she cast an admiring eye about the details of Jack Stephson's work. The "drawing" was actually four drawings taped together into a continuous narrative, as it were, of the town center. They were all done with the Pale Moon range behind the artist, and his subtle use of cross-hatching revealed the faint shadow of its peaks and vales throughout the composition, such that its massive but gentle presence loomed in silence over this New World in the desert. The leftmost drawing, beginning from the eastern end, depicted the tree-lined avenue, with impressive observation of the cypress foliage and the occasional pedestrian strolling unhurried here and there along the pathways. This led into the next drawing of the large public green and covered hexagonal bandstand, the long shadow of the clock tower stretching at a ten o'clock angle across the square. The third she admired the most, and here her gaze, that had deliciously wandered and circulated around each of the picture's careful renderings, rested for several moments on Jackson's monument. She drew in a fluttering breath, this her quiet approval of the artist setting the structure slightly off-center, allowing the viewer to enjoy the transition from the square to the array of fresh plantings that led up to the monument entrance, now flanked on either side by two majestic cypresses, taller than all of the others bordering the avenue. Because all of this landscaping occurred only two weeks ago, after Jack had given her the drawings, she was reluctant to ask him to include it in the finished work, and had quietly resigned herself to the irony of an "historical" drawing, already superseded by a little incremental progress. But without prompting Jack came back to retrieve this one sheet, and he artfully melded the trees and shrubbery into the whole, as though it had been there all along. Her eyes had filled with tears of gratitude then, as they did so now, as she recalled that instant when it was placed back into her hands.

Most of all, though, she admired the touch of the gentle wispy figure that hovered above the monument. Jackson's soul, lifting away from the corpse of life's indifferent confusions and floating toward a sphere that could only exist in hope, the hope of something more personal and more serene. She did not doubt that an existence beyond the flesh needed to be earned, and she also did not doubt that she knew nothing of this. Only the charm of the artist's pen remained, a charm that she was willing to accept into her heart and cradle softly as a wish eternal.

The last drawing was unasked for, and was Jack's initiative alone. Here at the western edge of the town the continuous narrative ended in emptiness and stillness. To the left of the composition was a partial view of the back end of the monument, for now undeveloped and unrefined. The heart of the picture was simply an empty expanse of plain and rock, dotted with the occasional cactus and desert sage. In the far distance, looking south, a burble of cloud cover on the horizon suggested perhaps a coming storm, perhaps a receding one, but almost certainly a reminder of the Silas Testing Grounds. Alicia had at first given this curious composition no more than a polite glance. She assumed that Jack had been whiling away an idle afternoon as he awaited the return of the transport helicopter. Not willing to argue over an addendum that did not detract from his principle efforts, she had silently decided to set it aside after a few weeks had passed.

But this unassuming image continued to invade her thoughts in quiet moments, and not infrequently she found herself getting up from her desk or leaving the dining table just to walk back into the library for a moment and stare at and into it. She decided that she had to be sure the sergeant was not concealing some clever pun or curiosity amid the rocky arid turf he had so artfully depicted. And this persistence was rewarded, for one evening her gaze retracted, seemingly by chance, to take in the picture in its entirety. In one instant she understood something – not something Jack Stephson had composed, but something her husband had said to her some two and more years ago on what, she now knew, was that fateful dawn when the man-made cavern beneath El Tajín blinked into life and set abroad the monster that still shrugged aside its own demise.

The soft steps and gentle tinkle of glass and plate told her that Malvin was arriving with her evening meal. A wave of relief swept over her. Now she could sit and dine, and relive that talk with Jackson outside at the round table where it had occurred. She slid open the large glass door to the terrace and stepped into the warm evening air. Once again, as so often, the contrast of the darkening room with the bright evening light tripped open her eyes in momentary surprise. Another of the many clever touches of their architect friend, who, at Mr. Monroe's request, had arranged for the angle of the sun to fill and persist around the outdoor living space until the final rays departed, while the library was allowed to settle into premature evenfall, a little pool of lamplight next to his worn leather easy chair being all her husband desired when the contemplative mood was on.

All the more curious, Alicia thought, as to how that square of light found its way into the room. Had it always been there? Why had she never seen it before? And then Jackson's voice was at her ear again, as she recalled him once saying, "Light, my darling, isn't really in a place. It is place. Some, well many, of these places are not meant for hands and feet and rear ends. They peep around corners of the larger Now; they let us through a door eternal for a moment or three; they imprint a timeless icon on the mundane and simple, such that later on the simple is all we ever crave." And so her square became another room in her mansion of memory, and yes, she wanted only this simple bath of meal and sunset and Now.

She nestled into her favorite wicker armchair. Malvin set the tray on a side table near the sliding doors and made several trips back and forth setting out placemat, napkin, cutlery, glasses, water pitcher, wine carafe, and her plate of chicken breast and rice, and side plate of greens. Each momentary arrival and departure of her servant and friend both tickled her with delight and instilled in her that extra delicious yearning to mark each second as it came and went. She watched each fluid movement of his thick, powerful hands and fingers, their evident strength at the service of the minutest touch of loving attentiveness. How this man instructed her with his silence. Yes, silence. Why speak? Why ever make a sound.

He filled both her water and wine glass and set each bottle down without a whisper. Alicia looked up and gazed with gratitude upon Malvin's noble burnished face. For once his lips smiled almost as much as his eyes, and after a lingering instant he turned and with another soft step or two he was gone, the glass door gently rolling shut behind him.

She held her wine glass aloft and toasted the settling day. At the far end of the terrace the wide western horizon was framed at the bottom by a low line of potted flowers set upon the ledge and on either side by two large banana trees arching in symmetry several feet high. The orange-pink sun disk was just a hair above the demarcation of earth and sky. "To you, to us," she mouthed without air and continued watching the sun as she took a long refreshing sip. The heavenly orb, seeming to oblige her awareness, nudged an inch back up away from the nether regions. An eyelash flicker passed, and suddenly the entire canopy of sky flushed a pale translucent pink. Thick rays of light spread out from that shining circle in all directions, up and around her, then separated into distinct bands, their edges begilded with golden fire, and over a seemingly ageless span of eons Alicia watched them shift their chromatic glow back and forth across the spectrum of rose, azure, mauve, emerald, russet, diamantine lemon, until at last a clear violet locked into place and the amber stillness of eternity held her gently in its ageless embrace.

She thought she would never breathe again. Her body continued to live though she could not fathom why. All else perished in her. Clarity of nothing, clarity of clarity, was all she beheld. She wanted to take another sip of wine. She kept wanting to. She wanted something else, but forgot what it was. Clarity. Yes, she wanted this. But she had what she already wanted. So that too must cease. Don't want. Don't know. How magnificently terrible, how pulverizing, was her unknowing. What is this world I am in? Why doesn't it just devour me? Why let me be? She did not recognize the fold in her index finger or the weave in the cotton placemat or the small pool of water on the glass table. The pool reflected violet. Pass and stay. Pass and stay. The flowers and banana leaves glowed unmoving in the amber half-light. They knew how to be obedient to eternity. They knew they could be torn up or hacked away in an instant. They knew what divine mercy was. She knew it now. She a plant, a flower, budded, blooming, blown: what step was she in? She didn't know this either. The bell sounded. The distant bell in the clock tower, in her new town center. Six tolls. How unlike a passage, a progression, it seemed. Separate but not one at a time. Six unsimultaneous sounds that yet were a single instant. Time in eternity was not time. The blossoming, fruition, and dying gloried and bedecked the light that will ever stay. Many bells in many places around the country were tolling. She knew this without hearing them. What happens next was. What happens. Next.

Jackson was beside her, in his favorite wicker chair. The memories of that beautiful talk in the evening twilight and the decisions they made in the early dawn those many, many months ago now unwound without effort. She would relive it all, suspended as she was in this timeless ether.

"There is no gradation – no gradual passing from civilization to wilderness," Jackson was saying. They were sitting with an after-dinner glass of wine and gazing into the gently darkening day. "I can see finished work, complete culture, right up to the border of the desert – then complete wasteland. The two side by side, like our own park and landscaping. You see, my love, it is always that way. There is no intermediary between the beautiful and the brute."

"You are a glorious pessimist, my darling."

He looked at her and laughed. "Pessimism is an attitude. Really seeing something is better, and worse. I don't always enjoy what is obvious to me. The clarity of truth more often leaves a shudder than an embrace. I suppose because we spend our days endlessly flattering ourselves. Do you ever wonder of what that flattery consists?"

" 'I am the greatest.' " She turned to face him. "And you are – to me."

Jackson took her hand. "As you are to me. But I don't think it's the superlatives that keep the ego afloat. It is more just that – staying afloat. Putting one's little head and nose above the infinite stream of oblivion. Insisting on a personhood more akin to a godhead than a stick figure."

"Please, sweetheart, stop being so hard. Our life has to matter to us. Why is that so illusory?"

"The positioning of it all. The claim of origin. The closed fingers around one's supposed share of matter. We must yield to accident and caprice now and then, but we seldom yield to the day, to relinquishing the ordinary cardboard cutout of habit. Even though just outside those habits, those cutouts, looms the crushing spot lamp of the World's indifference. And the World doesn't just ignore us like an absentminded prelate, it rolls over us, or it includes us in its own plans and we are not asked permission."

Alicia sighed and gave his hand a squeeze, then removed her grasp and nestled back in her chair.

They drank their wine in silence. Suddenly the black sprawling silhouette of a large owl shocked into view, flapping in unhurried jagged angles across the pale grey sky. Jackson grunted a chuckle. "You see how Nature makes the most of her necessities. Is he chasing down prey, or dancing for his mistress? The cause, the reason, almost always something elementary, elemental in fact. Yet for us his raw desires paint such peculiar beauty, such unspeakable delight. Nature plays, and laughs at our sweat, and she will conceal her concerns even as she lets us watch them."

"Is civilization sweat, then?" she asked. It amused her how her words started him out of his reverie. But she wanted to continue. "The Untamed rule the wasteland, adjacent, as you put it, to our canapés and topiary. Doubtless this magnificent creature cavorting above us would happily gouge out our silk-covered love seat to nest his brood. And yet his mere appearance haunts us with the unknown, and our wonders surpass our words. Since that is not civilization, are we then saying only the civilized can appreciate it? If the answer is

Yes, then distill that thought to its inevitable conclusion – a civilized person is one who sits and stares like a child upon the wilderness, upon what he thought he knew but now cannot fathom at all. Well, darling," – she raised her glass to him – "looks like we have finally achieved a cultured innocence."

Jackson looked at her, and Alicia noticed, once again, that his look took in something that she never could, even in a mirror: her own amber gaze. She repressed a mischievous impulse to close her eyes. But no, she would not do that. Everyone emanates something that only others see, in her case, this glow in her irises of which she had heard so much, but heard of as though it were a mystical palace hewn out of rock, or a strange configuration in the heavens, or a far away canyon in the humid jungles of the south seas, that travelers, after a long exhausting journey home, told her of in the hushed tones of awe and disbelief. How little belongs to us. Even our laugh and gesture, our spontaneous word or sober appraisal, our gait and frown and eyebrow arch and smile, were as much or more the property of those who beheld and absorbed it than it was our own. Departure and always departure. We are always at the threshold of today, saying farewell to what we are and were, even in our greetings.

"My Sphinx," he said, "always surprising me. I suppose if I defend my point of view too much I will be trodding upon my own ego objections. I will just say that toil is not purgation. A piano lesson, or a few hours before an empty sheet of paper or a stretched canvas, is not the predator's reek. These so-called creative activities have, I know, been analyzed into dishwater, and the lukewarm loss of understanding that follows prompts us to start over again. And that is the point, isn't it. To catch that elusive ether of inspiration, to let it abide without disturbance. All civilized work is therefore only a frame for the invisible, not the creation of her. Rather, the invisible creates us, though unfortunately her works seldom endure past the minute of their flourishing, while our frescos crack and fade a span of ages, pale witness to someone's private elations. We know so little of the other end of the paintbrush."

"Civilized work? You see, darling, that is what I question. I want to drown in wonder while stirring my tea. I want to comb out my hair and feel the gloss as though it were spun starlight that I dreamt into being–"

"I want to comb your hair too."

"Shush. In other words, I want to be able to know nothing and live that each second. And, well all right, my dresses and silverware and daily habits are indeed the frame that lets my Wonder habitate in safety, and sometimes with abandon. That is frame enough. I feel no need to carve or compose a secondhand experience."

"All true, and I love you for it," Jackson said with quiet emotion. "Too bad this is everything the barbarians hate, and hated. They know nothing of the power of delicacy, and they never tire of rending the gossamer webs whenever subtlety starts to confound their prejudice. Strange that a porcelain vase evokes the mallet as much as the pedestal. Rubble must be in love with itself."

"Pedantry is barbarism too, without the courage. We had been talking about Nature, and beheld the antics of that wondrous creature moments ago, and as you said, whatever he was about, it roused in us spontaneous echoes of a mystery we would rather taste than comprehend. Here the rarified instant enchanted us, and whether Nature does it as deliberate lesson or wayward insouciance, we were raised and silenced." She paused and drank in the warm dry air. Then she added, "Of course, we did keep talking." And they fell to laughing like children for a few moments.

Jackson leaned forward and folded his arms on the table. "Oh, Alicia, here we are, arrived at the border between culture and wasteland, only to find it is no border at all. There can be none such, because it is there the Unknown lives and thrives. Only such contradiction enables the pure silent awe of what can never be said, to burn about its unseen lantern. The truly tame region, so clarifying in its silence and incomprehension."

"Is the Unknown tame? That is naïve."

He gave another of his ironic grunts. "Probably. Then let me just say, the Unknown is definite. Unbearably definite. Most of us cannot take it most of the time, so in consequence we refuse to feel it, and therefore it either does not exist at all or it gapes before our heart a pothole nuisance awaiting the proper plug of 'problem solved.' How often can a man drive by himself? Probably his whole life." He stared out into the now black sky, and then continued. "If there are no laws, then either chaos or will inhere. Man cannot live in the wild without becoming a beast, but that is because the barbarian, who hides about our loins and breast, would slip its cultured shackles and preach a freedom answerable only to its self-interest, as meaningless as that is. But since Nature retains its allure without man or man's endeavors, the conclusion is that a divinity guides it all. I have probably asked more often than I should, Can we ever see it, this divinity? Now you, my darling, have provided the Yes, the Yes that shows it was, is, always there before our eyes. It just needs continual stripping away of…whatever we think important."

Alicia pushed back her chair and stood up. She laced her fingers through her hair and looked down at him. Then without another word she turned and walked into and through the library, and passed down the corridor toward their bedroom. Soon she heard his light footsteps approaching steadily behind her.

A warm rouse and tumble lasted a near delicious hour. She lay awake on her back long after Jackson's final endearments and gradual decline into repose, the midnight air caressing her naked body in gentle eddies of delight. She looked over at him and took in his motionless form and the sound of his gentle breathing. Her eyes closed and opened in languor, then she turned back and stared up at the ceiling once more. There appeared before her a vision of Jackson singing and dancing on an outdoor stage. What was the music? She listened and listened but could not hear a note, even though Jackson kept swinging his hips and belting out some unknown number probably improvised on the spot. She turned on her side and reached over to shake him awake and share with him this silliness, but her hand touched only air and sheets. She sprang up and gave a soft cry. He was gone. She looked out the window and saw the first touch of dawn filter through the grey air. She must have been asleep for several hours. In minutes she was up and in her robe and back down the hallways to the terrace. As she expected, he was sitting in his chair staring out into the distance. But as she did not expect, he was looking west instead of east.

As she walked toward him she said, "Did the world literally turn inside out, darling? The sunrise is peeping behind you. This time the 'Glory of the Witness' is him, witnessing you."

Her quip met with no response. He stared unwaveringly into the west without acknowledging her presence. Her idle humor vanished and a shudder of embarrassment overcame her. She kept looking at him but he remained unmoved. Then she slipped into her chair beside his, drew up her legs, and grew into his silence.

Several more moments passed. A buzz of questions went through her mind as to why he had reversed his habit of gazing toward the sunrise, but the buzzing eventually melted to murmurs of no intent. The gentle dawn seeped a rosy tincture through the pale morning air. Shape and contour and depth gradually emerged from the blank film of night. Yet a silence still reigned, and if earth's creatures had awakened they lingered over their dreams.

Jackson finally spoke up. "Last evening we floated for hours. How does it appear, that elevated clarity? Did it come from our talk, or did the clarity engender our talk?" He smiled. "The absurdity of opposites, which of course is no help at all. When we leave out ourselves – the selves that embrace an effect – only the effect remains. We are that. I would rather be such an experience than a wealthy landowner, but since I must be the one I will be the other as well. That is playing a part, is it not, to imbibe the manna invisible as we negotiate contracts and miss a quartet of easy putts on the first green?"

She smiled. "It helps that you never really try too hard."

He chuckled and seemed about to recount another of his fairway stories, but then his demeanor changed and he frowned at a thought unuttered. He shifted in his chair, and she, sensing the nascent germ of a new consequence, stood up, set her chair directly facing his, and sat back down, spine erect and hands in her lap.

He looked at her with some resignation. "We will need to support Dresden for congress. It is almost summer so we must move quickly. I have nothing against Whiting, but that looming void out there on the desert plains bothers me." He gestured toward the western sky. If he was waiting for a reaction from her it did not come. "Pale Moon sits a solitary, abandoned mistress in a wasteland of disregard. She looks out upon an emptiness that seems to devour the innocent life scampering and crawling and winging about her. Maybe I imagine things, but this deathly silence, after so many machinations by government and army, is unsettling."

She still did not reply.

"The world loves irony," he continued, "partly because it is often treated as the exception. Yet our daily life is one absurd reversal after another. Too bad we always clean up after ourselves by making sense of it all. Ironic, yes, that the military gave when they thought they were taking away. The innocence of a business transaction, buying up our wild acreage, followed by the innocence of a property tax. Nothing is more guilty than innocence. After all these artful manipulations – trucking Brandonville residents east of the valley, stopping and then destroying the Hacienda project, threatening to fence off land that has been in our veins for three generations, making us pay for it all – Morgan and Whiting breakfast, lunch, and dinner their way through private meetings while the distant chuk of rotor blades reminds us of what is no longer ours. I don't know why I was so passive to it all. I suppose I took it as a signature of mortality, and found the holding on too strenuous."

All of this was uttered in the quiet abstract tone of someone musing over the backyard turmoil of some foreign land. But she was confused by one of his conclusions. "What did you mean that Silas gave when they thought they were taking away?"

"Why are there helicopter patrols?" he asked back. "We are not at war with the ocelots. No one defends nothing...save their own vanity." He stopped himself. "I shouldn't be so logical. That was not what started me on all of this."

Alicia got out of her chair and crawled into his lap, laying her head on his chest. "So what did?"

Jackson put his arms around his wife and held her close. "It was too dark when I arose to await the dawn. But the stars, the stars were magnificent: multitudinous, brilliant gem clusters winking their quiet enigma. They were joined by the sudden streak of a shooting star, followed quickly by a second. I could not help but feel I had happened upon a conference of celestial beings, their omniscient discourse almost within spiritual earshot. I sat here looking west to mull over our dinner, thinking about, then trying to feel enthralled by, the unknown life we spoke of. The wind flushed in gentle pulses over my face from out along the desert channels. Soft tastes of cedar, moss, rock, and sand. Then warm clear plumes of odorless air. A few more shooting stars flashed their brief, mayfly arcs. I counted six in all. Amid this simple savoring of nothing, something shifted. The unknown appeared, sitting right here, in this chair. Total amnesia set in. More than just not knowing who I was, I did not know who he was. A body, pressed against the reed back and wicker bottom. Clearly a bit overweight. I started watching him to see if it would spark a remembrance. All he did was breathe. Reduced to this, in the black of night. Inhale and exhale. Even a blink of the eyes seemed an extravagance. Only a single dot of awareness hovered in the dark, like one of those distant dots above me, seeing but unseen, unable to do anything but try not to go out. And then, out of naught and nowhere, there appeared before my inner gaze the imprint of all these recent happenings and personal upheavals, all gathered together. Not as a movement of events, but rather as a rich, elaborately decorated tableau. Whiting, Andrews, Morgan, the pilots, the governor, the state

EL TAJIN, NEW MEXICO

senators, the residents in those trucks. Jackson. Yes, there he was, finally. And you. We talk of being moved about by our passions, or other gremlins or angels out of our control. Here, though, each one of us hovered in our appointed place, each figure, in his and her appropriate attitude and gesture, settling into this ether frieze, carved, perhaps, out of time by some whim from eternity. Dresden was there. Others I did not recognize. This picture taught me in an instant what has been and what must be. The consequence already exists."

Alicia wrinkled her nose. "So we are going to campaign for Dresden Pondhurst? Does absurdity ever lead to reason?" But she held back a flood of further sarcasm.

He raised his eyebrows at her with mock effrontery. "Don't look at me like that. There are many strains of respectable chaos. And yes, it does. When something precious is taken from one, the wisdom of deprivation inhales what is not itself, and wants it back." He sighed and relaxed further into the chair. "We will campaign for and with Dresden Pondhurst. So what. God decreed eons ago that we all must take out the garbage. The land that Silas, Morgan, took from us sleeps unchanged. A piece of paper says it is no longer ours, so another piece of paper, with Congressman Pondhurst's help, is going to say the reverse. We are coming home to our desert world. And more than that, darling," he looked down at her with affection, "we are going to erect your village, realize your dream. You asked what Silas gave us. It gave us back our resolve. And not only that – we will fulfill by our opposition to them what we could not fulfill by our wish alone. I am tired of dreams that only live in the idle drifts of hope unfollowed. The dream will take root, and thrive."

And then, until the sun was well into its morning blaze, he outlined what he intended to do. And he did it, despite the stroke just three weeks later that so ravaged his body.

This they were able to keep a secret, from everyone, including Dresden. Jackson never lost use of his limbs or his mental faculties, or his spirit, but the toll on his stamina was evident to her and, as the campaigning progressed, she eventually had to admit to herself that years of life had been taken from him, the hale squire in a single shiver of pain and unconsciousness forced to become the old man who bore every footfall as a stagger, perhaps as some unfathomable counterpoise to the inspired way in which he caught Whiting and the Pentagon off guard, and manned the peaceful "invasion" and reclaiming of their lands.

And that other, horrible secret, which Silas had kept from them, from everyone, and which concealed the strangest of ironies. The morning after that bizarre encounter at the monument with Private Spooner she waited outside the door to Jack Stephson's apartment and confronted him as soon as he appeared. She wanted to know the whole truth, right then, and immediately wanted not to know it as soon as he had given it to her. At first she would not believe that they had dared to tunnel north, in violation of all ordinances and sheer common sense, and she never really fathomed the absurdity of that decision. Then came Jack's detailed account of the early morning when they had tried to detonate the bomb: the mysterious failure, the arguments, the probing, the confusion and near despair, the tribunal that followed and all its attendant closing of ears and eyes and any and all reminders that such a thing ever happened.

And to know that that failed detonation had taken place the same early morning she lay in Jackson's arms while he softly recounted his plans to put Pondhurst in office and take back their property. How unbearably prescient of him. But what if the test had succeeded? What if a blazing fireball had thundered out of the dawn, sheets of fierce lightning flaring in seconds across miles of desert, flooding their eyes with radioactive madness? Blindness would have been certain, followed by clouds of contaminated death gushing up and forth in all directions...

"Open my eyes!" she shouted at the streaks, startling herself out of her now febrile reverie.

Open them she did. The streaks still blazed their amber magic in the heavens. As she watched and watched, the bands of violet deepened in color yet grew more translucent, like sky-mounted panes of glass steeping what lay behind them in a curiously sharper and more uniform tint. The air was saturated with stillness. Her fingertips trembled and she was surprised to find she was still holding the wine glass in her right hand. Had she never let go of it? How long had she dwelt in those memories? As she lingered over this question those memories flapped their loving wings and tripped away in quiet wisps. She took a deep breath and reached not for them. Neither did she reach for the mites of anger that wanted to complain about daydreaming through the streaks. But did she dream? That memory had mounted itself before her in a timeless instant, like one of Jackson's ether friezes, word and touch and posture a continuous past, present, future narrative of their discovery, their intention, their industry.

And their love. Her breast was aflame with love for him, like the orange-pink disk on the horizon that she stared into unflinchingly, gentle flickering blaze of selfless bliss. Each breath had to share the chambers of her heart with this joyful pain of loving both what stays and what never will. Only those memories had kept her aware of who she was; otherwise, her petal-soft feeling imbibed the darling light, a light alive in her, whoever she just now was.

It was soon over, the departure of the streaks always as abrupt and enigmatic as their arrival. The sun set, the sky greyed, the air chilled. She lifted the wine glass to her lips but set it down untasted. Lingering would now be failure. She stood up and walked back into the library. One last look at Stephson's drawing, and then to bed. Tomorrow was the ceremony and she had to be there at dawn.

The room enrobed her in its quiet darkness, the gentle smell of musty paper a welcome balm for the ecstasies that still shimmered in her breast. She turned on the table lamp standing at the center of the drawing. The public square and bandstand lit up before her eyes. So much of what she wanted for the present and the future would happen there in just a few hours…

The far edges of the drawing were still in shadow. She slid the table lamp along to the far right past Jackson's monument to gaze again upon the desert expanse that was, after all, most of El

Tajín. The swell of hope she harbored for the future of this land now crested against her reawakened memories moments ago of she and Jackson dallying over the meaning of civilization, or its lack. So what was her new village to be after all? A sprawl of order gradually consuming the wild with pavements and public restrooms, or a mere ornamental dot on the silent, untamable miles and miles of a nothingness that would never allow the fists of logic to subdue its unknowable majesty?

The soft footsteps at the library door dispelled her dialectic. "Oh, Malvin, I am glad you came. I would probably have left the meal for the crows. Thank you."

His large golden face spread into a momentary smile that settled back the next instant into his inscrutable enigma, not unlike the sunset she had just witnessed. "Or the bears, ma'am. Shall I bring you a tea?"

"No, thank you, Mal. I am for a short rest."

"So you always are, ma'am. All rest is short I suppose. We crave it because it is not. I will join you there when I can. James and John want to clean the driveways before we head over. When do the ceremonies begin?"

"Hopefully at ten." Without another word he stepped out onto the terrace to retrieve her meal. She looked down at the drawing again, but now saw only paper and chalk. The internal dramas of this evening would not allow her to take in any more magic from it tonight. She reached for the lamp to turn off the light, and lingered for one instant over Jackson's departing spirit hovering over his monument. Then she gasped with some embarrassment. It was a cloud. Stephson had simply drawn what was there.

Malvin entered the room. He set the overflowing tray on the floor and turned to lock the sliding door and draw the curtains.

"Come look at this, Mal." He was beside her in a moment. "What is that?"

"A bird."

"Really?"

"Why not." Before she could reply he was stooping to lift the tray. The next moment he was gone, his soft footsteps soon a distant whisper.

Alicia stood still in the desert of her opinion. "Yes," she said to herself, "why not." She touched the cloud with the tip of her finger. "Safe travels, my love."

Sleep was not rest. It was a shuffle of hours where she did not exist. She existed again in the shower just as dawn made pink the air. She dressed methodically and brought a piece of fruit with her to the car. As she started out, the arrow of road pointed to a western sky that seemed to yield begrudgingly its skirts of murk before the roseate sheen of day. She drove with the windows open, her mind as clear as the dry wind that rushed about her, and she resisted the habitual urge to turn on the radio. She traveled due west for several miles, then turned south off the main highway and west again for the final stretch to the foot of Pale Moon. As its modest peaks came into view, she was relieved to see that the dirt road that led down to the town border had been widened as she had requested, and ahead and to the left a large area had been leveled and graveled over to create a makeshift parking lot. Aside from the dump trucks and scraper still standing at the far perimeter, no other vehicles were in sight. She promised to remind herself to have plans drawn up for a proper asphalt area, with lighting and rest areas, and then almost laughed out loud at such a notion. "Get through today, Alicia," she said to herself, "and forget football stadium amenities."

She drove past the graveled area and slowed to a halt at the start of the cypress-lined avenue that led up to the town square. She realized a barrier would be needed to keep today's festivities for pedestrians only, so she maneuvered and parked across the mouth of the entrance. A brief look about her, and she spotted a few orange safety cones near the work vehicles that she retrieved and placed around the opening to augment the message.

Already she was tired. Alicia leaned against the car to catch her breath and gazed down the avenue. No other car was visible either nearby or in the far distance. She fought back a tinge of disappointment. The two lines of cypress, their early morning shadows crowded up against the trunks and foliage, converged to a trim open frame around the heart of the great square. At the top of that frame the broad white banner with its red letters, "Welcome to El Tajín," hung unmoving in the quiet air. She read those words over and over, mouthed them a few times, sighed with a flush of pain for all that had to happen to rise in one short year to this inflorescence of a dream realized. Ends teach beginnings. After his death she had no right to die; her dreams would have turned on her had she not bulldozed, hammered, and plastered them into existence. And here it was, and here she was before it all. She peered into the distance, beyond the trees, banner, square, and fixed her sights on the lustrous black cube that was Jackson's monument, anchoring the far end of their little town. She stood up straight and leveled her gaze with the entrance. Then she let the patient seconds relax her face and eyesight until she recognized through the clear morning light the ever-present witness, the tiny recognition of his bust, seeming to hover in its little niche against the back wall. Even at this distance she could feel his uncompromising regard upon her, neither approving nor disdaining, neither welcoming nor ignoring. Real existence was none of these things, neither was it many another attribute the centuries of philosophy and worship crowded us with. Shedding it away, living by removal, peeling back opinion, surmise, learning, even culture. Let them all shrivel and die, what she knew she knew, but only when the time called for it. Nothing called her now, therefore she nothing knew.

She started walking down the center of the avenue. Nothing moved, nothing sounded. Just beyond the trees bordering the avenue on either side she remarked the four or five concrete pads already poured, the prelude to a construction marathon scheduled to begin in late summer. On one of those pads sat a large open grill, ready to feed the many visitors after the morning ceremony. As she approached the square she paused a moment to linger over two structures near the clock tower already framed out. One was to be a general store and post office, the other a restaurant and inn. She turned and looked back down the avenue. Her car and its sentinel cones stood as she had left them. Beyond them, looking east, the sun was just above the horizon, a pale disk against a milk-white sky. All was silence. She continued on into the square and stopped at the center of the green. She faced north for a few moments and gazed upward along the rounded contours of Pale Moon, cool shadow and hard earth, with here and there a patch of green as yet unwithered by the blaze of day. She sought out the family's favorite picnic spot halfway up a nearby slope, a little alcove of rock cradling them from sight and extreme heat. She smiled at their success in thwarting Paul Morgan's copter patrols, now a fond memory rather than a battle won. She turned about and looked at the octagonal bandstand. Not much of a band for today's ceremony, only two horns and a drum (a bit embarrassing to be sure), but plenty of room for herself and her guest speakers. She dwelled a few minutes over who would be on the stage and where each would be seated. Somewhere in these musings she realized that the musical performance would have to finish, and the musicians step down, before everyone else could mount the stairs and take their places. She made a mental note of this...

The clock tower boomed a resounding hollow gong. She trembled in surprise, took in a sharp breath. Six more tolls followed. She stood motionless as they each sounded, her hand clutching her breast as the mournful tones hung in the air like a metal fog for several long moments. A wave of melancholy overwhelmed her. Her vision seemed to follow the waves of sound as they rippled beyond the borders of the town and dissipated into the wilderness of rock, underbrush, and grit, now emerging into firm outline in the hard light of day. In the next eyeblink she hovered above herself, her awareness a hundred feet in the air, taking in, in one long instant, Alicia Monroe standing on a miniature plot of grass situated within a silly array of road, buildings, and sundry construction collateral situated beneath the looming indifference of a range of rock situated in the endless miles and miles and miles of arid desert teeming with a hostile world of life that cared only for its own survival, the absurdity uselessness meaninglessness of all she had done for no reason but spurts of heart, what had she done, it was all nothing, worse than nothing, useless, comical even.

The last tinge of sound seeped into the distant sands. The silence silenced her. She started to cry. How naked she was, the dreams, aspirations, planning committees, building milestones, fundraising events, all melting away, and now she was here, a little breathing mass of barely credible identity begging for mercy she knew not why before she knew not who. She could only breathe, and resolved not to close her eyes. She turned again to the monument, sought out Jackson's still point of eternity. She was close enough to see those eyes, quiet, always diligent, equally reassuring and unmerciful. Her own skull could now be enbronzed – never had she felt so much like death, the sweating, trembling, self-aware death that never was and never would be anything, that barely had a right to exist. If only she could think it over for a while, feel her way to an understanding – but the blaze of emptiness in and around her burned unrelentingly. Another intake of breath, another look at her husband's visage.

Suddenly she was there. She strolled into view, her mass of dark curls teasing her neck, a tasteful blue dress complimenting her figure, a smart ivory handbag over one shoulder, and a white cashmere sweater draped over the other. She stopped before the bust and remained standing in relaxed attention, unaware that she was being watched from behind. Alicia realized she must have been sitting on one of the benches within the monument that were installed only days ago. In a moment she was walking toward her, telling herself as her pace increased that there was no need to run. And the next moment she called out in earnest, "Monica!"

Mrs. Andrews turned about with delight. The flash of a smile settled into happy stillness, and she stood in place to wait for her friend. Alicia tried not to hurry as forward she hurried, wanting to be with her but at the same time wanting to remember that fateful day exactly one year ago when she herself stood on that same spot, looking west, and watched as that trim, elegant creature, dressed in patterned blouse and white slacks, as though she had been called from a champagne brunch, emerge from an army helicopter and stride toward her bearing a message that, despite her alert mind and attentive looks, she never delivered. How evasive Monica was in that moment, how officious and business-like (attempting to be anyway), not only because of the secret she bore of that immolating monster droning all too near beneath them, but because she was so distractedly in love, so bounded in her feelings that every word she uttered was the sigh of his name, a name Alicia knew not but somehow guessed.

But now the figure in blue was all clarity and tender containment. How Alicia admired her bright composure, her still point of confidence, a confidence she herself was now in need of. Quickly across the green, past the soft new garden, up the single shallow step, across the black tiles, and into her warm embrace. In spite of herself, Alicia began to sob at once.

"I didn't see your car. I thought I was here before you. Then I thought you could not come. Or would not. But no, not that. It was so quiet, I really could not bear it for some reason. Jackson's ghost was troubling me worse than ever…"

"Alicia, Alicia, it's all right," Monica whispered and stroked her hair. "Come, let's sit down over here. I was savoring as much of this shade as I could, knowing how hot it will get later this morning."

They walked over and sat on one of the benches still nestled in the shadow of the high walls that surrounded them. There were four benches, built from the same black granite, two each against the opposite walls beneath the gold leaf inscriptions. Monica kept her arm around Alicia, who still trembled and sighed for several moments. They leaned back and rested their heads against the cool stone. The sky above was deepening into a clear blue. In the stillness they soon heard the merry chirrups of the cliff swallows no doubt dipping and winging about the peaks and hollows of Pale Moon. A few more moments passed, and the lightest of breezes passed about the shrine and washed over them with welcome coolness. Alicia relaxed and sat upright on the bench. Monica did the same and said, "The entrance garden is a lovely touch. Perhaps a few potted trees or flowering shrubs on either side of the bust over there would be a nice complement."

"A beautiful suggestion," Alicia said, now feeling a bit more connected to herself. "Let's work out the design together."

Monica looked at her and smiled. Her eyes seemed to caress Alicia's face for several moments with a quiet but loving scrutiny. "You're dressed in white again, like the day we first met. But this time, such a smart suit, and such a formal cut. Well, it's lovely. And I'm glad that you keep your hair long and straight. Nothing else will do."

Alicia blushed but did not reply. Monica looked up at the sky and said, "That bell is positively horrid. I had begun to doze off, when that first gong startled me almost into slipping off this bench." She laughed. "Any chance of toning it down?"

"I don't disagree with you," Alicia said. "It made me shudder as though I were the bell itself. But we would probably have to take it out and replace it entirely."

"What about pads?"

"Pads? What pads?" They looked at each other and laughed out loud until they were breathless.

Alicia pulled a handkerchief out of her purse and wiped her eyes. "Oh, I have certainly been in need of some silliness. The streaks were so overwhelming yesterday. I couldn't move, for so long I couldn't move. I had to find solace in one of my fonder moments with Jackson. Not that I want nostalgia to save my life…"

"Yes, they were overwhelming," Monica agreed. "We were sitting on the balcony outside our hotel room when the sky blazed forth in such color I thought I was hallucinating. I reached out and grabbed Robson's hand; we laced fingers and did not speak through until the violet faded into the gloaming. I was sure I was dead, a ghost that refused to leave her shell despite the meaningless prop it had become. We did not speak. When it became too dark and chilly, we got up and went downstairs to the dining room. We sat at a table, the waiter brought menus and recited the specials, and we said nothing and read nothing. He came back minutes later and we still said nothing. Either through understanding, or the complete lack of it, the young man went away again and returned with two bowls of soup and a bottle of wine. He went on to serve us three more courses, filled our glasses, brushed away the bread crumbs, presented the bill, and left a pot of coffee. We stood up when someone turned on the vacuum cleaner. The dining room was empty. We went back upstairs and to bed. At no time did we exchange a syllable, not even so much as a look. All evening long I begged for the feelings the streaks evoked to go away, and when they did, in the middle of my sleepless night, I begged them to return. How fickle we become with unknown energies."

Alicia sighed. "Maybe we never learn what should be left alone. But not to get too serious, I certainly admire that waiter, whoever he was." She paused and then asked. "Is Robson here? Or perhaps he's running errands for you," she finished with a smile.

"They dropped me off on the way to Silas, while it was still dark in fact. Robson, Paul, Jack, Feldon. They've all gone down there to confront O'Connell over the dismantling of the bomb."

"What!"

"Don't be angry. Please. I'm sorry to tell you this in what seems like an offhand way. They were going to wait until after the ceremony, but Feldon found out that O'Connell's team has already bored through the tunnel – Paul Morgan had plugged it all up with concrete – and are in the process, as we speak, of deciding how to take the device apart and prepare it for transport to a facility that eliminates nuclear waste."

Alicia scarcely dared to breathe while Monica spoke. But then she was confused. "Well, that's a good thing, isn't it? We will be free of the beast at last."

"I wish it were true, Alicia. But this is a strange beast, unlike any other the military has created to this point. It's linked to a software trigger that we've been unable to turn off. And the trigger has already been pulled. That was my job, you see, to turn it off forever. And I guess I failed. Shutting down the power, tearing out those cables… well, I dare not think about it. Such abrupt engineering was never supposed to happen, and once the trigger commands were activated any tampering with the casing, let alone the core, could set it off at once. That slender thread of code is all that has kept all of this beauty that you have created from annihilation."

"Jack Stephson told me about the failed test and the cover-ups. He only alluded briefly to the work that you were doing. I am no scientist, but I want to understand what I can, so please help me to see the dangers as you yourself see them."

Reluctantly Monica settled back against the wall again, stared up at the sky, and talked through the many plans, counter-plans, test scripts, blockages, intercepts, and other frustrating ploys she and her team had struggled through for those many unrewarding months. She recited everything in the monotone of one programmer speaking to another, making no concession to the untutored layperson sitting beside her. After more than a quarter hour of non-stop exposition she was out of breath, and she stopped to gather herself. Then she said, "Our logic, collectively and individually, was mangled. Plans that should have worked, well, did work, to a point…until they didn't. Then there were our larger risks, our capricious curves of chance, our castings of lots before the Pythia of wishful thinking – they didn't work either. As I say, we stripped everything down to the two pollings at midnight and noon…"

"I did not understand your vernacular, but it sounded to me like the 'stripping down' was just an accident. Captain Gray's accident."

"Not entirely, Alicia, but it is certainly not a hair worth splitting. That cascade through all the firing sequences shunted us straight to the precipice. We have been teetering there ever since, and I suppose in our despair we have become accustomed to living one inch away from oblivion."

"So you're saying, if the pollings are stopped, by pulling the plug – to use the most pedestrian of metaphors – either nothing happens or everything incinerates."

Monica's eyes filled with tears and she wiped her cheeks with the back of her hand. She seemed about to speak but did not.

In spite of herself Alicia went on. "And this red light, this Cyclops thing?"

"It's the devil, as far as I'm concerned. Paul Morgan's foolish symbol of satisfaction and 'Good night, gentles all' has become the electronic smirk that holds the secret, or perhaps holds no secret."

"If the devil dies…"

"That's what he would do – die, with us. The trick has always been for him to die, but we stay behind anyway."

"I don't know what that means."

"Neither do I."

They sat in silence a long while, listening to the birds and watching as wisps of cloud appeared and spread a feathery palette across the royal blue canvas above them, creating subtle shifts in light about the sparkling black stone and tiles.

"We may get some relief from the sun this morning," Monica said.

"Yes," Alicia murmured. "The weather report did promise a bit of coolness, maybe even a drizzle."

"Delightful. All of our speeches in the rain. I can't wait."

Monica stood up and walked over to the bust. She bent her knees slightly to put her face at eye level with it, then walked back to the center of the space and took in the entire wall. She looked around her and glanced up at Pale Moon.

She turned to Alicia and asked, "I guess I'm a bit disoriented. Is that where he fell, where the niche is now?"

"Yes, and the urn with his remains is set in the wall, just under the bu– …" and the iron gong of the bell sounded and shuddered them both back to silence. Monica bowed her head and folded her arms while the eight tolls rang out. The singing metal echo hummed and dimmed over several interminable seconds.

Alicia stood up and walked over to her companion. "The silence now is not unlike the silence of that wide circle of citizens and military that surrounded us that day, don't you think? I was so grateful that you had accepted without hesitation my request to meet me here this morning. I wanted this day to start with the two of us alone. Only we two really listened to and understood what Jackson said before he died – my boys, God bless them, were more concerned with the crowds. I remembered a lot of it and wrote it down in my journal that night. But I have refrained from going back and reading it again, lest his last understandings come to me through the written word rather than through the memory of what came from his own lips. In pain."

"And inspiration. His 'raw awareness' has stayed with me, has in fact become my new guiding light. During the flight back to Silas that day I tried just to sit and look out. It was not hard, since I was so drained by all the chaos. It seemed to work for a while, just me existing in an undisturbed corner of space and time. Then I saw you in the sky, my companion in flight. With those glowing eyes of yours." And she put her face up to Alicia's and gave her a playful nuzzle.

"You remind me that I never thanked you for the story," Alicia smiled. "You wrote in my copy that it all came from seeing my face in the clouds. I don't know how the one led to the other, but we should always be grateful for inspirations that seem to come out of nothing. That 'Nothing,' whatever it is, knows a lot more than we do."

Monica took her arm and said, "Let's say hello to him together." They walked up to the niche and stood before the image of the man whose death had led to this deathless bronze enigma and all that surrounded it.

"I heard that it went missing one day," Monica said. "Always a danger, especially at night when no one is here. Do you have guard patrols?"

"Yes, there is security. But after that incident Jack convinced me to have it attached, and I would say it is now virtually impossible to remove without destroying it."

"Really?" Monica said. "It looks like you could just lift it off that rod sticking out from the back." She walked up to the niche and looked in closely behind and above the bust. "Oh my goodness, how clever. You're right, this will never come out." She rejoined Alicia and they settled back into quiet admiration.

Eventually Monica said, "Other than our Jack, I'm not close to any true artisans. That simple fix holding the bust in place bespeaks, well, what to say – the silence of ingenuity. Something is invented, comes into existence, because it must."

"We learn to love enigmas, don't we," Alicia nodded. "We can ask and ask how it was done, which is not really the same as admiring it being done. And how it hides itself in its simplicity..."

"Yes. A clever person solved a problem that a hundred years hence will no doubt go unnoticed."

"Oh dear," Alicia laughed and clutched at her breast. "What confidence you have in our little corner of nowhere, Monica. Will any of this outlive even you and me?" She collected herself and said. "Funny how we need to abstract a point of view far into the future to appreciate what is before us now. So then – shall we do that? Let us travel that hundred years away and make of it our present."

They smiled together at her image, and once again returned to silence. But before long Alicia felt Monica struggling with some thought she seemed not to want to give voice to. She turned to her and said, "Out with it. What's bothering you?"

"A taint of guilt. Standing here with you, looking at him, I am reminded of a time when I accused you of merely mouthing Jackson's insights, as though you had no mind of your own. Even worse, that you had to speak him and his, in sacrifice of your own life. It is unfathomable sometimes how wrong one person can be about another."

Alicia shook her head. "Honestly, Monica, I have no memory of that. Anyway, I have come to feel the only original thing anyone ever does is look through their own eyes. Anything more – the merest utterance or brush stroke – is bound to be derivative of something."

"Some would call that nihilism, you know."

"And others reverence." She turned her amber gaze on her young friend and surrounded her in a warm embrace. "You will surpass me, you know," she whispered.

"No, no," came the whispered reply as all protests melted away.

Maybe they had been hearing the distant chatter without realizing it, but suddenly that chatter rose to a higher pitch, and a startled second later they both beheld with delight the two figures walking down the avenue, passing in and out the undulating cypress shadows that now slanted across the street and walkways. Esther bobbed along with her characteristic lilt laughing and talking without cease, while Ethel nodded and only interjected an occasional word. They each held the handle of a large sack that hung a dead weight between them.

Even at the distance they were watching, Ethel's pale demeanor and empty gaze was unmistakable, and Alicia remarked it at once. "Someone's happy and someone's not."

"So it seems," Monica agreed and then called out, "Here we are."

The walking figures both waved politely, as though already aware of them, but continued instead over to the bandstand. Eventually Ethel and then Esther each grasped the sack with both hands, an evident burden to them both, and with a bit of a hurried rush managed to swing the package up onto the steps and let it bang to rest. They both gasped and sighed and held each other for a moment, then Esther reached into the sack and pulled out a thin parcel wrapped in cloth, and soon they joined their friends at the monument entrance.

Hugs and kisses and pleasantries followed as they made their way to the center and stopped. The group of four stood in silence for a moment, then Ethel walked off to one of the side walls and gazed up at an inscription with what seemed like feigned interest. Despite the happy greetings, Monica and Alicia's perception was confirmed that Mrs. Whiting did not share Esther's bright enthusiasm and was evidently struggling to cap a bother, the pallor and flush of her cheeks bespeaking a heart suppressed.

Alicia turned to Esther. "What is that under your arm?"

She smiled and, with a little flourish, she placed it in her hand and undid the cloth to reveal a pencil sketch of Jackson Monroe in a simple wooden frame.

"Oh my!" Alicia was delighted. "This must be your sergeant, always surprising us." She took it into her hands and held it gently. "Jackson materialized anew on this little white sheet, the face so like and yet so unlike our sculpted head. Look at this. The same eternal, intimidating gaze, but with this interesting turn of the head, as though he glances sidelong at the viewer as he is about to step beyond the veil of mortal purview. Original, is it not, Monica?"

"Simple and of itself. Jack setting another of his personal challenges, and succeeding." And she and Esther exchanged a smile.

The latter turned to Alicia. "If you agree, we thought it could be set in the niche for the day. The man, and the man, bidding hail and farewell."

"Please do."

Esther bounced over and leaned in a bit to find the proper angle to insert the picture. She gave a little laugh. "Oh! What a curious fastening contraption up there. Not letting him run off any time soon, I see. Here, how does that look?" She managed to place the frame next to and slightly behind the bust, so that the two portraits almost seemed to touch. She stepped back a bit and turned to Alicia and Monica, who both nodded their approval.

"He fell, he was swallowed up, he almost drowned! But why – why did he fall? It was under his feet, he couldn't do anything about it. Like us! Like us. Like us."

All three turned round to the spectacle of Ethel walking with her back to them along the groove between the tiles as though on a tightrope, arms outstretched, continuing to utter "Like us" in shrill

CHAPTER 10

311

tones. Suddenly she whirled about and faced them. She let out a shrieking laugh and dropped to a crouch. "Walking on water, don't you see? He stumbled and walked out over the waves, he staggered and struggled in plashes toward the boat, toward that filmy glow of Light wavering through the cloud of rain and wind. The water heaved and tripped him up, slapped at him, sloshed his ankles cold, his sandals slipped away and gurgled down forever, his soles, toes, feet, calves, wet and always wet, and so so cold. It griped at him, the water of uncertainty, mortality. And he shuddered and sank to his ass, his wet ass, because his tunic billowed on the surface and drank in the water, and it grew so heavy, so heavy, and the drenched cloth was like a giant hand yanking and pulling him down – And then! And then, he was clutched aloft. Why clutched aloft? Why? He must have deserved it. Now here it is, under our feet, under this hard, adamantine, beauteous, perfectly crafted, lustrous, smooth, delicious black marble, this uncertainty, mortality, ready to puff us to naught. It will swallow us all, people. It was always, always going to swallow us all. And will we be clutched aloft? Eh? Do any of us deserve it!? Everything melts, everything drowns. We drown in air all the time, can't you see that!"

"Ethel, sweetheart, remember, you need to be careful. Why don't you go rest on the bench," Monica said and started to walk toward her.

"Don't make sense of this!" she sprang back up. "Not this time! How dare you! What greater, insaner madness is there than giving Death an amusement park! Look at all this! Smell the roses, and then fry! Read your Plato in big gold letters, then turn to ash! Take a stroll on the green, green grass and let it boil you like a chicken!"

Alicia stepped forward. "This is my argument, Monica, leave it alone." She took a few steps toward Ethel and said, "Shred my life, madam, but not my dream. Easy enough to stomp all over someone else's creation."

Ethel's eyes blazed wide apart. "Creation? A true creation should reveal, darling, tell a story, cast a beam, tingle the heart chords.

Yours, this, only veils us, veils us all – from death! Perfume in the crematory!'"

"The threat below us was assembled years ago, in the name of protecting life, as you, and your husband, know. The lie turned on itself, as it always is."

"Never mind my husband. Scoring points means nothing to the terminally ill, like we all are. This cardboard village of yours promises the nurturing and thriving of life, the hopes of a future life. Tell me that is not a lie."

"It is not a lie. What life has no death? We build for ourselves what…"

"You have no right to be philosophical! You are tucking in the blankets of everyone's permanent, unwitting sleep."

"It may never come. Not like this."

"Death always comes, Mrs. Diplomat. It is right here under our feet, as you have just admitted."

"Now who's philosophical. Shall we all sit still years and days, like good little boys and girls, until our turn to die shows up? I thought you had more heart than that."

"I demand you put up a neon sign pointing down at that ticking time bomb of horror that is surely going to turn this mountain here into a grotesque Hieronymus Bosch landscape. Surely you can afford it."

"Well, well. Wealth passes through people, darling Ethel, if that is your real complaint. It takes itself away. We ride and corral the beast of riches as it grows and thrashes, but tame it we shall not."

"Beasts. Always we blame the beasts. You let that beast build this tinker-toy world of yours. Who led who, I would like to know, not that it means anything. But why let hundreds of people die dreaming Nirvana stands as brick and mortar."

"Every vision realized lasts until it doesn't. I cannot turn people away from their own pursuit of happiness."

"You are impossibly stupid! We are standing on a goddamn incinerator! What is the matter with you!" And all three were reduced to shuddering at Ethel's wild brown eyes staring at them in unblinking defiance.

A naked unease began to pervade all four of them, but Alicia cut it short. "Okay, Okay – you're right!" she shouted back. She put her hands to her face and trembled through a few sighs. "Have your triumph. I renounce it all. I'll go back down the avenue and send them all away." She strode right up to Ethel until they were but a gasp apart, and in a steady voice she said, "But I, I am never leaving. From this moment forward this is my home. I will sleep on the bandstand, under the trees, among the rocks if I must. When you get back to Boston do please tell the world that I wished everyone a hearty 'Good Night,' won't you?"

Esther and Monica had been approaching them from either side, and in the stillness that followed Alicia's words they both watched Ethel's face melt from defiance and anger to timid fear to sorrow to a shivering burst of tears. "Oh, I missed them! I missed it all! How could I! I fell asleep! I hate sleep! I hate, hate, hate it!" And with that final shout she fell to the ground and wept loud forceful agonies. All the ladies rushed to her, and Esther, the most athletic of them, knelt down behind Ethel and raised her up and into her arms. She cradled the crying woman while the others knelt as well and waited until her sobbing dissipated to a breathy moan. Handkerchiefs were out everywhere and in her fingers and about her wet face. A few more minutes and Esther had her up and over to a bench, and all three stood around her.

Ethel continued to dab her face and breathe quietly. She glanced from one to the other of her companions several times without a word, though her eyes were filled with screeds of irony, confusion, even mischief. She coughed a few times and continued to dry her face and nose. She relaxed against the granite wall, her eyes fluttered closed, and she appeared to settle into a doze. Then she began to speak.

"Feldon wanted to stay up all day and all evening, since he was leaving around four in the morning to bring you here" – her lids parted for an instant and flashed at Monica, then closed again – "and go on to Silas. O'Connell be damned. I insisted that he lay down with me for a while in the late afternoon, just to get a little rest. A little rest. We always want a little rest. We're no better than worms, and the worms probably never sleep. So we lay down, I stroked his face and hair, he closed his eyes and fell asleep. I continued watching him and stroking him until it was dark. But that was the horror. It was dark. Why would it be dark? I sat up and saw that hours had gone by. And Feldon was not with me. I walked out of the bedroom and saw him sitting out on the balcony. I went out and sat next to him, and looked to make sure he was all right. But my husband was not there. It was another man. I almost screamed. He looked just like Feldon, exactly like him. And wearing Feldon's clothes too...wearing them even better. Ha, ha, ha, ha. Oh, I am such a bitch. He turned to me and quietly described how the streaks had come. He was so secure, you know, so rooted, in that chair, not a glint of distraction, no desire to get up and walk away, no desire to stay where he was. Do you know what I mean? He was there and would stay there...until he didn't. They killed him, the streaks killed him. So he said. He was dead. He described the colors, the Almighty blaze, the silent explosion flooding the sky, the oppressive weight of celestial majesty crushing him into a flea. He had never had the experience. It was his first time, and he helped me see it all. So beautiful. But I didn't. I didn't see it. I was asleep, lying in bed like a stupid rock, my animal body loving to be a rock. I hate it, but hate can't make it go away. What can we do? Can we become a streak, part of the streaks? Melt away with them into the dusk? Sometimes I thought, if we watched them enough times, their light would fill us up. Then, you know, we could shift from being us, being a body, to being that light. Do you see? Why can't it happen, because it does happen when they come, and stay. But they leave, they have to leave – well, they do leave – and it is grey and hazy here when the light goes with them. That always made me so sad. They left me behind sitting on a cushion watching them fade away. I always wanted them to take me along. How can I live with myself now?"

"It might have been worse for me, you know," Esther said. "I saw them out the window but I kept working. Jack needed me to type out his speech. I thought I could look at them while typing and get some kind of experience, but I didn't feel anything. I should have stopped. So I was kind of asleep, just like you."

Ethel gave her a half-lidded regard. "Hurray," she said with no emotion.

"I think you've got the streaks in you already," Monica said. "No need to doubt what…"

Ethel stood up. "I'm sure you are right, O Wise One." She walked over to Alicia and they embraced each other in silence.

Esther had been glancing over at the town square now and then for the past quarter hour, and suddenly she rushed to the mouth of the monument. "Oh goodness! If you really wanted to turn people away, Alicia, you are too late."

The others followed her to the entrance, and then could do nothing but stare. The silence of it all surprised them most. Already fifteen or more people were milling about the green. Some were setting out rows of chairs facing the bandstand, others were setting up tables on the perimeter of the square and laying out refreshments and reading material. A few men were up on ladders tightening the banner. In the distance they could see others moving about the grill area, laying down wood and setting out bins of food, plates, and cutlery for the lunch. Five women were working around the bandstand putting the finishing touches to an elaborate series of festoons, an intricate weave of tiny orange-red roses, baby's breath, and dark green foliage that wound like a continuous band of jewelry up each pillar and around the perimeter of the roofing. All four women lingered over the understated delicacy of this impression, the roses quietly nestled like fire opals in what looked like a setting of tiny white gemstones and emerald foil.

"Did you design that?" Esther turned to Alicia.

"No. I trusted someone and my trust has been rewarded."

And the avenue was soon teeming with more arrivals. They could now hear the distant sounds of car motors, crunching gravel, and thudding car doors. Groups of threes and fours sauntered along the walkway. Some stood and looked over the partially framed structures or out into the desert, others wandered over to the foot of Pale Moon and cast squinting gazes up along its rugged brows and wrinkles. A couple of families even came onto the green and laid out blankets and folding chairs. A quiet hum of converse and intent filled the heart of this new village-to-be with a drama of sobriety: a citizenry aware of itself and each other, modest pleasures and serious idleness, intelligent curiosity and insouciant attention, preparing for an event without waiting for anything, happy with now and what that now would become.

"It is a miracle," Monica murmured. "Like everyone is in a giant museum, or a library." She glanced over at Alicia as she said this, and her heart softened as she beheld those lamp-like orbs of the founder of this village filmy with tender emotion. A tear and two trickled down her cheek, and her lips began and unbegan several times to speak.

At last came forth a whisper of love: "It is all that Jackson had hoped for."

No one replied. Monica walked over and put her arm around Alicia. Together they continued to look around and into the distance.

"I did not expect so many," Alicia said wiping her eyes. "I do hope everyone will be able to hear. We only have the one amplifier for the microphone."

Monica looked over at the setup on the bandstand and nodded. "If everyone is as attentive as they are now, there should be no problem," she said. Then she turned to Esther and Ethel. "By the way, what is in that package you left on the steps?"

The two ladies looked at each other and smiled. "It's–" Ethel began and hesitated. She looked at Esther and they both suppressed a laugh. She cleared her throat. "It's Feldon's speech."

"His speech? It looks like a boxed ream of paper in that sack."

"That's exactly what it is," Esther said, and again the muffled smiles seemed to say much more.

"I will ask no further," Monica said and in the same breath uttered a soft cry as the clock tower sounded nine plangent peals out and over the sea of life and sunshine. Reverberations from the hammering steel gongs seemed to gather in billows and hover an aural nimbus for seconds, and seconds, and seconds more over the village entire. The crowd ceased to be a crowd, and however many individual lives had traced their path to this place at this moment in time, each of them now felt a tolling within, calling every man and woman in single private urgency to something only each of their silent hearts could follow.

The sound ceased, and the spell lingered one final second. Then to their lives everyone returned.

Or so it all seemed to Alicia. She looked into Monica's eyes, glanced over at the others. "That was so strange, wasn't it? Or did I imagine something?"

"Up to you, darling," Ethel said. "But it is very loud."

Esther was still suppressing grins. Alicia looked at her and said, "I am sure Feldon will start us off nicely. I have no worries about him."

"Oh, not that," Esther said. "You do realize, Alicia, that this strange tower here, thrusting upward out of the two-story structure like that, converging to a pyramid at the top, its silhouette even visible on the horizon from certain perspectives. People are already calling it the Big Dick of El Tajín."

"I think it's marvelous," Ethel said.

Monica frowned at them, but Alicia grew serious and stared at the building for several moments. Eventually she said, "Well, yes, I can't really unsee that, now can I? I suppose we can add two more stories at some point. We will hopefully need the extra space somewhere along the way."

"Oh, but don't do that, Alicia," Ethel said. "Then it would shrink down to the Limp Dick of El Tajín, and who wants that?" And in spite of themselves they all burst into a spate of cackles.

Ghosts emerged from behind the bandstand. Four of them, pale grey spectres, seeking or perhaps escaping their haunt. They moved slowly in baby-step unison, arms at their sides, gazes straight ahead. They took about five or six zombie paces until they were at the edge of the green. They stood motionless and stared out over the gentle busyness. They and the crowd about them proceeded to engage in a mutual non-acknowledgement, disregard for once, at least, a virtue.

"Oh, my God!" Ethel exclaimed. "What on earth! Feldon – Feldon, what has happened to you?"

The ghosts indeed transmogrified into Robson Andrews, Paul Morgan, Jack Stephson, and Feldon Whiting. The clothing of each of them, from shoe tops to trousers to jackets to shirt collars, even to their hair, was all covered in a fine, grey-white dust, which their collectively dazed demeanor ported with apparent resignation, for the paleness of their appearance paled before the mute non-appraisal they seemed to cast neither on the industry about them nor upon their own silent poverty.

The women were soon around them, Ethel leading the way, arms waving, shrieks and confusion, scoldings and tears. "A horror! What is this horror! Were you all tortured? Feldon, you're leaning. Stop cocking your head like that! Can't you stand straight? Where is your cane?"

"It did good service, ma'am," came quietly from Jack.

"Don't joke with me, you foolish boy! What is this powdery crap?" Ethel began slapping at Feldon's arms and shoulders, and cloudy puffs billowed up about them, causing them both to sneeze and cough.

Esther interrupted the chaos. "Come on, we need to take each of them into an open space and clean them off." She took Jack by the hand and led him out behind the bandstand onto the flat matting of wild grass. Silenced by this practical advice Ethel grabbed Feldon by the wrist and started to follow them, but he stumbled badly and she wrapped her arms around him. "Oh! Now we're both covered with this stuff. As it should be, darling. I'm sorry, I forgot your cane is gone – we'll walk as slow as you need." And together they stepped out gingerly into the empty field.

Monica could not bring herself to do the same. Instead she peered in and into Robson's vacant look, each flash of her eyes another attempt to pry away an obdurate mesmeric.

"You cannot do this to me," she said at last. "We will stand here forever if we have to."

"Despite how it looks, I, we all, are trying to bring ourselves back," he replied with a trace of emotion. "We needed you all – I need you. Now. Please keep looking at me."

"Robson, I can't, not like this. Where can we go?" She looked around, and her gaze inevitably alighted on the blue municipal building and clock tower. "Do you think we can go in there?"

Without a sound he began to walk across the green, and she caught up to him and took his hand. As they walked the preoccupied visitors, children and adults both, silently stepped out of their way.

Alicia and Morgan also had remained unmoved, and stared at each other for several moments. Then he said, "Your husband once told me that sometimes the only way to solve a personal dilemma was to let someone else solve it."

"Are you asking me for something, Paul?"

"I suppose I am."

"What?"

"Can you please help me."

Alicia winced at his appeal. Never had she seen, or imagined, he could be this vulnerable. She put her hand to her breast, and turned away for a moment. She watched Monica and Robson approach the municipal building.

"I wonder if the workmen unlocked it, as I had asked. Ah, yes, they've just gone inside. Probably the two first people to make use of it." She looked back at the General. "But I think we should leave them be. Come, let's go around behind the monument. There is a spigot and hose there." She took him by the hand, and the huge hard leather of his palm and fingers startled her. "Oh! You warriors. How many foes you must have rent and battled."

"Your softness has won far more, I'm sure."

Alicia gave him a wary look, but Morgan smiled and squeezed her hand. "Now, now. You know I'm a confirmed widower. Relax."

"Aren't we both," she said, and led him away to get him cleaned.

The bright brass handle clicked open with smart precision. Monica sighed with relief. "Oh, I am so glad. We can steal some privacy for a while," she said and locked the door behind them.

The quiet murmur of the crowd vanished. At once the fresh smells of completion – painted walls, sealed stone flooring, finished moldings, untouched cleanliness – drew them to look about with admiration at this new foyer and lounge area. Before them near the far wall stood a reception counter crafted from three types of wood in pleasing tones and overlays. To the left the promise of a modest sandwich bar and coffee shop, shelves and counters gleaming, stainless steel pots and fittings awaiting their first calls to service. To the right a tasteful arrangement of black leather sofas and chairs framed in chrome promised both the ambiance of social contact and the privacy of solitary reading and reflection. The cream-colored granite floor tiles were speckled with hints of gold and jet, and passageways led back to a few private offices, an elevator and staircase, and, they both quickly noted, a pair of restrooms.

Robson soon had his clothes off and began bathing himself in the sink, while Monica shook out his shirt and slacks in one of the toilet stalls. "The first casualty the drudge of life inflicts on this pristine creation," she said from inside. "Oh, this dust! I feel so guilty making a mess. Maybe I should volunteer to be one of the janitors. What do you think?"

"Hired."

"You too."

"Agreed. I am through with nuance. Things are either good or bad from now on."

"So dirty is bad?"

"Dirty is bad."

After he dressed and brushed back his hair with his fingers, she gave him a silent appraisal and wiped some dust smudges from his neck and temples. He yielded to her fuss without comment, and for a moment she was afraid he was receding into that strange hypnotic stare again. She looked close into his eyes, and this time a welcome softness yielded before her searches. She put her arms around his neck and they held each other a long relieving moment.

Robson kissed her and said, "Let's sit out there for a while."

Through the large window in the lounge area they could see the milling crowd ease its way more tightly into the green and the open spaces before the monument, arranging themselves in anticipation of the music and speeches. Monica and Robson lifted and turned around one of the couches to face the window, and settled in close to each other. Soon it was difficult to make out but the barest glimpses of the bandstand through the backs and backs of heads, and the waves of leisured movement and idle talk that passed before them.

"Is it Jackson who inspires all of this love and friendship?" Monica asked.

"His passing, and Alicia's determination, have certainly inspired this day. The love and friendship surely precedes it, though a contained world like this allows for its flourishing."

She glanced up at him. "Something you said the first night we met has always stayed with me: 'the unseen life that no doubt glows upward.' Is this what you meant?"

"I was expressing a belief, a belief in invisible beings, visiting and guiding us. Much of our real life – what we feel, think, perceive – is invisible. It must be an inhabited world, because we inhabit it… sometimes. I had fancied that I was chatting with those beings out in the desert darkness, that hour or so before The Blast That Never Was."

" 'Never was' is not 'never will be,' " she sighed. "Will this burden never leave us?"

"Oh sweetheart," Robson said – no, moaned, as Monica now detected it. She sat up and stared at him. "What is it? Tell me."

"Indeed I will tell you," he said. "But look there. The band is setting up."

Through a kaleidoscopic gap in the leanings and gestures of the crowd they could make out the group of middle-aged men in their smart blue uniforms, complete with red piping, gold epaulets, and bright brass buttons, opening their cases and taking out their instruments, two shiny trumpets and one trombone. A fourth man was struggling to arrange a kettle drum, which kept tilting to one side, the metal legs it stood upon apparently resisting all attempts at equilibrium.

"Four musicians after all," Monica said. "Only three had been found as of a few days ago. I do love those uniforms, and those caps with the polished black visors. A bit of Old World charm."

"Old is suddenly new again. I admire their willingness to suffer through this heat in those heavy coats. We must be sure to tell them to take them off once they're done performing."

"Hmmm. Remember now, you are not a colonel – 'Mr. Colonel.' You can let people draw their own conclusions about what they will suffer. As you did, apparently."

Robson raised his eyebrows. "The omens, so it seemed, after we dropped you off were not good. Jack had the notion to cut across the open terrain behind that parking area, but we hit a huge rock in the dark that destroyed one of the front tires. So after replacing it we had to go back and take the road and highway, but Jack shot along at such great speed to make up time that he was unable to avoid killing a coyote that dashed out of the underbrush. The animal was really mangled, run over by front and back wheels. Nothing to be done so we sped on. These incidents drained away what enthusiasm had been circulating when we first set off, and occasional matter-of-fact grunts was all anyone managed all the way to Silas."

Robson paused and shook his head. "Silas – how strange, how foreign it seemed. Even Paul called it 'soulless,' a curious derogation, I know, for a place that tests and perfects annihilation. But the emptiness was awful. The barest seepage of dawning light raised shadows and gloomy contours about the silent buildings as though a horde of spectres had arisen to spook us back to our beds. Things got worse. We arrived at the gate, the sentinel box was empty. Jack and I hopped out. I gave a few shouts into the nothingness, but it was clear no one was around, so Jack went up to the gate and with a few jiggles, lifts, and tugs he somehow managed to unhinge the thing and pull it open far enough for us to drive through."

Monica blushed. "That man. He's broken into my apartment more than once – always for the best of reasons, of course."

"What!? Don't tell me what I don't want to know. We left the car in the parking lot and walked toward that side door that has the quickest way to the Action Room elevators. I found myself looking over my shoulder several times to see how Feldon was keeping up, but he was always right there behind me. And always grinning at me when our eyes met. That last step before we reached the door I had been looking back, and as I turned around and reached for the knob a bullet struck the metal facing and sang away in shards, leaving behind an ugly black dent in the thin steel. We all froze, three of us in fear, but Paul in absolute rage. He barked out into the darkness for whoever fired that shot to show himself, and when there was no immediate reply he strode out several yards onto the asphalt and hurled a litany of off-color epithets about the shooter's mother and wife. Phrases that you will never hear me repeat. The 'strategy,' such as it was, worked, and out of the shadows a guard came toward us, his rifle cocked and ready, his finger on the trigger. Morgan marched straight toward him until his chest was inches from the gun barrel. And then we all noticed a curious carousel of expressions pass over the soldier's face, from startled recognition, to confusion, to fear, to anger, back to fear, but then – as though suddenly following a private instruction whispered in his ear – to a hard indifference, some inner determination taking him over that decided not to care or to feel.

"I am not sure how long we all stood there, but long enough for the pale morning to cast a bone-white pall over the proceedings. The three of us shared an unspoken concern for the General's temper and what it might lead to, but no one seemed able to make a decisive move. And then Feldon took off and hobbled with curious confidence over to the two men and placed his free hand right over the fellow's rifle scope. He leaned in and said something that Jack and I could not hear, and the next moment the weapon was lowered and the guard gestured toward the door, apparently yielding to our intentions. He walked away and without another word between us we went inside."

"What did Feldon say to him?"

"I don't know. I asked Paul later and he just said, 'He complimented his mother.' Probably not the case, but that congressman friend of ours has a way of creating opposite effects that all concerned go off pleased about. The disquiet we were experiencing from the messy drive down there, and then this muddle of a precarious entrance onto the base, made for an uncomfortable elevator ride, and when the doors slid open we stepped out into the hallway courting near despair. Again, complete silence, walls and corners washed in shadows, everything in darkness except one overhead fluorescent casting a meaningless glow on nothing. We did not know what to do. I suppose when we started out we had expected to be met, announced, even greeted at the main building or Information Center. Instead we were invaders, but invaders that bothered no one, due to an implacable shield of total indifference and disdain. We walked on into the Action Room.

"Oh! Monica, I will never forget turning that corner and seeing that glowering fiend again – Cyclops himself, burning like a dying red sun in the wilderness of outer space, as though he was expecting us and gloated over our melancholy. The mainframes stood in darkness like muted sarcophagi, which started to worry me, but after peering about I discovered one cluster of white and yellow lights still on, and recognized the just heard hush of the air-conditioning. So the total shutdown had not happened. We could have felt relieved, but instead we only became more anxious. We walked on past the computers and that monster eye, and Jack and I gave a few shout outs into the darkness. As we turned another corner, we abruptly inhaled the gritty smell of burned metal and stone. At the end of the final corridor, which always used to be a cul-de-sac of storage and cleaning supplies, we saw a huge gouge in the wall enveloped in a cloud of motionless white dust. Once we were before it, we saw that it was the entrance to a manmade tunnel that disappeared at a jagged angle into further darkness. Jack had a flashlight, and as he probed about he voiced a despairing incredulity that they could not possibly be boring all the way to the device from here. But after a few cautious steps we realized that this dig was following the line of comms cables (a number of them were exposed along the ground and wall) that joined the main passageway that led to the northern tunnel itself, which ran under the desert the few miles to the device. Of course, a good portion of the northern tunnel, near the device, had been blocked up with concrete, so when we came out of the makeshift tunnel and into the main passageway we were disappointed but not surprised to see…"

Robson abruptly stood up and walked to the window. He pressed his forehead against the glass and stared. A few moments passed. Monica was not sure whether he was staring out onto the crowd or in upon some feeling or awareness of his own. Perhaps reading her thoughts, his eyes turned toward her without moving his head and, with curious up-and-down oscillations, lingered upon her with an odd sort of appraisal. This she did not like.

"What are you doing? Stop it."

He stood up straight. "Sorry. I was deliberately trying to disorient myself. I can't narrate from continuous memory what happened next. But I don't want to forget it all either."

"So don't. And don't."

He sat down again and put his arm around her. Now and then he looked at her and now and then he looked away as he told in rambles and murmurs the rest of the story.

Out into the main passageway they came. Several men were either sitting on the ground or leaning against a chaos of equipment, hoses, and cabling drinking from thermoses and eating sandwiches. At the sight of their visitors several of them leapt forward and reached for weapons. The General shouted out his name and that of Colonel Andrews, but only a grim silence replied, and no one lowered his gun. What startled them most were all the unfamiliar faces. They knew not a single one of their adversaries. And the unfamiliarity quickly took another unfamiliar turn.

"You've got to be kidding, fellas," the General said. "I am Paul Morgan, and here with me are..."

"We know who you are," came the clipped reply of the captain who was apparently in charge. "Stand in a line."

"Is this a joke, Mr. Senior Officer."

"You're the joke. Now stand in a line."

The mists of despair that had begun to overwhelm them when they stepped off the elevator were now settled into the valleys of their hearts, and the cold oozings licked about their brains. Immobility was their only answer, along with the General's quiet, "We will not" – the feeble defiance that has already lost.

The men with guns were equally immobilized by their absolute power, and they also knew not what to do next. All freedom was no freedom, "all possibilities" replacing the choice of any definite action. Their baser instincts would no doubt have prevailed in due course, but Feldon stepped forward and asked with a deference that Robson knew to be ridicule to speak with your leader, Colonel O'Connell, "when he is able to give us some of his time."

For a moment the captain's mouth rippled with a nearly voiced refusal, the caprice of defiance almost eschewing common sense. He finally nodded to a compatriot who took up a walkie-talkie and stepped away to confer through a mush of static with a spurt of verbal crackles that Morgan and Robson knew to be the man. Guns were put away but the hard indifference was not. The men went back to their meals as though no one else were there.

During the wait Jack took in the equipment and murmured his observations to the others: an electric generator hooked up to an enormous compressor and blower; two large steel containers with hoses almost a foot in diameter running off the containers and down the passageway, one container full to overflowing with concrete dust, the other obviously intended for the same purpose; a pile of large drill bits and drill plates lying about, some bright and new, others worn and blackened; and a sprawl of power cords, hook lamps, and various hand tools. All of this obviously at the service of the effort to cut through the concrete plug. No sign of the special equipment needed to disarm the nuclear device, but Jack concluded that it was already at the other end of the tunnel ready and waiting.

The soft whirr of an electric cart could soon be heard, accompanied by the arc of a headlamp moving along the wall of the passageway, and O'Connell and one other officer drove out into the open space. His men stepped aside and O'Connell hopped out and strode over to his unwelcome visitors. He saluted General Morgan, gave a diplomatic nod of his head to Feldon, and then walked over to Jack Stephson, intentionally ignoring Robson.

"Why are you not on duty, sergeant?"

"I am on duty, sir. I am still on assignment to the Monroe properties, overseeing our remaining interests. My brief was until end of year, sir."

"I have seen no reports."

"I fax them in every evening, sir. And send the copies down with the weekly courier."

O'Connell grunted and looked him over with mock contempt, a mock exaggerated by his goggle-like horn-rims. In the brief silence that prevailed Morgan and Andrews took a long, close look at this curiosity of a colonel, and the incongruity of the thin, bespectacled ruler of the editor's chair, by virtue of his new title and position, posturing before them with tyrannical menace. Andrews well knew both sides of the label, how you were bowed and deferred to when everyone thought your title mattered, and how in an instant that deference became disregard, to some even scorn, once the word was only a word. The perils of a name.

"I heard you might be coming at some point, gentlemen," the leader of Silas said as he began to pace back and forth before them. "But breaking in like this, before dawn, just when we are putting this all to an end? A strange excuse for a commando raid. What did you think was going to happen?"

"That's simple," Feldon said. "We thought we could have a reasonable talk with the man in charge."

"Reasonable talk presumes reasonable behavior."

"There was no time, no other time…"

"Very true, congressman. We have come to the end of this time. Every time has its end. The bomb will be dismantled, the pieces shipped hither and yon, and Silas will turn its attentions to the norms of military discipline. We will push politics back out onto the streets and stairwells of public caterwauling. The army will reclaim the order it was always intended to champion." He stopped pacing and smiled to himself. "We must of course thank the public, the local public up north there, who have done us the favor of providing respectable cover for this one-act farce that you all dropped into my lap. The Soviets now only see a new town, or an amusing gesture in the direction of one, and they will no doubt proceed to ignore it just like the rest of us. Please thank Alicia Monroe for running interference for us."

This Morgan would not abide. He started toward O'Connell and shoved aside Jack's attempt to hold him back. "How about I write Alicia's name across that smirking face of yours, colonel."

The captain pulled out his gun again and took a few steps toward the General. Feldon and Jack both started pleading with everyone to back away. O'Connell, either from indifference or blind confidence, cocked his head and tilted his weight on one hip, as though he were about to study the underside of a museum sculpture hanging somewhere overhead. "We wouldn't want someone to take a shot by accident, would we general?"

Now Robson reached his limit. "Why don't you have your surrogate hand you that gun, colonel, and you 'take the shot' yourself. On purpose. If you can."

Despite the oppressive atmosphere their hearts labored under, and the dank and dirty chaos of equipment and disorder that surrounded them, and the precarious standoff that could with one misunderstood hand gesture or eye movement descend into slaughter, the four friends (Yes, they had, almost without realizing it, passed through to that invisible bond of familiarity and mutual forgiveness) felt lifted to a place above the absurdity they beheld, even though it was not clear they would yet escape being victims of it.

O'Connell turned and waved off the captain, then strode up to Andrews with what seemed like a new inspiration of defiance.

"I know all about the streaks voodoo you've been preaching, Andrews," he said. "And your ineptitude up there in North Dakota that led to your 'cosmo' moment. Nice job, wriggling free of incompetence by reciting mantras. People talk, you know. Nobody cares, but that doesn't mean they don't talk."

"I admire your lack of insight," Robson said.

"I don't care what you think you understand about life. You can't understand your way to food in your stomach. Good thing there's money in the bank to back up your philosophizing. And not caring matters. It keeps uselessness off my mind, and it shows you, or should show you, how little a sprinkle of satori dust means to anyone else."

"Forget what I believe or don't believe. You can't turn off that device. All of our arguing and insults are just dancing around that simple fact. Those two pollings are still happening, the noon one approaching in a few hours –"

"You abandoned it! All of you! And tried to hide it from everyone. What about those pollings! It could have gone off after any one of them. You have no say. Now clear out!"

He walked back to the cart, clambered up into his seat, and said something to his orderly. The cart purred up to them and came to a halt.

O'Connell looked at them in silence for a moment. Then he said, "That's right, chaps. We are going to turn it off at noon, just before the polling. We've been studying the routines, and we're confident that a simultaneous power cut and immediate extraction of the trigger mechanism, will silence it forever. The bolts are all undone, and a retraction device is clamped in place ready to yank it out at the precise moment, an infinitesimal hairsplit before the twelfth hour. Just remember, we are the ones taking the risk. If something goes wrong, we pay the price. You can drive back up to fairyland and evacuate your party before it even starts. Pity about all the hot dogs."

And the cart quietly turned around, and disappeared back down the tunnel. O'Connell's men started putting away their sacks and thermoses and prepared again for work. The emissaries from El Tajín gradually became aware that each of the four of them was staring straight ahead at nothing in particular, absorbed by the vacant immobilizing shock of knowing not what to do next.

The captain stopped what he was doing and looked them over. "Justice is served," he called out with a grin.

"Maybe so," Robson replied. "But don't be reassured by that. Justice is no one's friend."

One of the men started up the generator and turned on the compressor. He lifted and dropped a few of the hoses, then picked one up and began cleaning the end nozzle. The rattle and hiss soon became unbearable, and even though they had accomplished nothing, Robson and the others saw no choice but to leave. They turned to head back toward the opening they had come through, when suddenly the mechanical sounds increased to a high-pitched whine, and first Jack and then Morgan realized, a moment too late, what was happening. The man with the hose pointed the nozzle at them and shot out a roaring stream of concrete dust that smote and saturated them all with grainy acrid fury. Robson was caught on the inhale and fell to his knees choking. Feldon lost his cane and stumbled to the ground. Jack and Morgan managed to cover their faces but could do no more than shield themselves without moving.

The man released the trigger and relaxed his grip on the hose. "There's justice for you," he said, and all of them laughed as one. The man, emboldened by his comrades, looked as though he was about to pontificate further, but in that brief interval Feldon scrambled about until he found his cane and, gripping it at the bottom end, clambered to his feet and threw it underhand in a tight spin at the man with the hose. The brass lion handle hit him in the eye with such force that he dropped the hose and began howling with anger and pain. Jack tucked his arm under Feldon's and led the way through the tunnel and back out into the Action Room. They all staggered and hobbled to the elevators, and as the sliding doors closed they could hear the distant shouts of a few men heading their way.

They were up and out of the elevator, through the side exit door, and in their vehicle without a word, and they sped back out through the awkward unhinged opening in the gate that Jack had worked free. Robson found a few rags in the glove compartment and passed them around to wipe their faces and hands. But no attempt was made to clean the grime off their clothes and hair, which would have raised that much more dust inside the car. So they drove back north in silence, and the oppression of dirt, failure, and despair swarmed around them all, and gradually seeped under their skulls and engulfed every pulse of thought and feeling they were able to muster.

"As we came down the road toward the town here, the full parking lot and happy crowds overwhelmed us all to tears," Robson murmured, as though remembering a tragedy from decades past. "How could we face you all, much less raise ourselves to some sort of celebratory feeling. We could not. But we could not do anything else either. We had no say in our life. Jack drove around the parking lot, this time easing his way carefully through the rocky terrain, and came up and parked right there behind the bandstand. Strangely – perversely one could say – we all got out of the car at once and staggered out into the melee. Again, it was not a decision. It was just the only thing we could do." He looked at Monica. "What if you all had not been there?"

"We were there. Are, here."

He smiled. "My little Zen missus."

She pouted at him and tweaked his nose. "I'm not so little."

All the while his narrative was unfolding they had been aware of the distant pomps and toots of the bright brass horns and the low pulsing drum throbs from the other side of the green. A few moments went by and they now realized the music had ceased. They looked out the window and saw that the crowd was melding together in attentive order and moving closer to the bandstand.

They stood up to leave, and Monica was about to ask whether they should rearrange the couch when the majestic, mournful gongs several floors above them sounded out the ten hours since midnight in patient immutable measure. Instants after each tolling they felt a slight tremor down and up the building's framework. Robson watched as the crowd respected with stillness each round of the hammer, obedient perhaps to this call, however mechanical, to remembrance of time passing and to the ephemeral "now," whatever it for each man, woman, youth in this little plot of town was felt to be.

The tenth bell sounded, the walls and windows shivered gently, enough to tease a feather, and the crowd remained attentive and unmoving.

"It's almost as though we are all awaiting an eleventh phantom toll," Monica said.

"Strange how marking time stops time," Robson said. "An experience far removed from glancing at your watch."

"Let's stay far removed then as we get ourselves up to the stage. Keep hearing that eleventh toll."

She unlocked the door and gave a soft cry at the sudden rush of desert air. "Oh, it's so much warmer. I am going to melt, but never mind."

She took his hand and they hurried off, intending to steal around the perimeter of the crowd by way of the monument. But after they had gone only a few steps a shriek came from the center of the green, and a few voices shouted "Snake! Snake!" as mothers lifted children and men spread wide their arms to herd everyone aside. In a moment an empty circle materialized to reveal, of all things, Esther, with one foot planted on the neck of a writhing serpent, the whir of its rattle sounding like an eerie metal wand. She looked about her as though in search of someone, and catching the eye of her friends – who were caught within a triptych of fear, bemusement, and hilarity – she smiled and waved as though greeting them from across the room at a cocktail party. Robson flinched forward, about to rush to her aid, when Jack appeared out of the crowd with a shovel, and after a few deft turns and strokes he carried away the severed head and squirming flesh, a trail of excited boys chasing after him. A ripple of applause relieved the apprehension in the air, people began strolling back to their places, and Monica hurried over to embrace the heroine of the moment.

A pop and scuttle of static from the bandstand indicated that the amplifier had been turned on, and Feldon was already at the microphone tapping a few resonant thuds and asking for more volume, then less, then more again several times in response to the shrieks of feedback. Alicia, a bit embarrassed by the disorder onstage, was directing helpers to set out the folding chairs and arrange the podium with the stack of speeches, and water glass and pitcher, which meant politely working around Feldon until it was necessary to nudge him away entirely. He, unperturbed, raised his hands in mock indignation and, grabbing up the walking stick that someone out of the crowd had given him, stepped down in search of Ethel. Monica pinched his cheek as she and Robson passed up onto the stage.

They greeted Alicia with hugs and kisses, but behind her smiles the sorrow in her eyes was evident. Seeing what they saw, she did not wait for solace.

"Paul told me the horrors. I am so sorry, Robson. I hope you're not sick from inhaling that poison."

"I was sick at heart, Alicia, until this miracle of a town revived me. Perhaps it is good fortune that we've been forced away from despair. The dreaded moment we fought so long to delay is arriving in less than two hours, and standing here, at the cusp of an everything or nothing, stripped of the prayer to the false god of 'Never,' I feel an elation clean of all fancy, bare before the instant that will follow an unplugging, of no consequence or all consequences. We will probably never know the outcome: whether O'Connell toasts to our hysterics, or a Soviet satellite registers an unusual blip of fire."

"Cyclops blinks off either way," Monica said.

"Cyclops was always only a light bulb, sweetheart. The real Cyclops resides in us, in each of our entrails, lurking in perpetual half-sleep, just awake enough to glare at our refinements and scorn their ambition. We will always be wrestling this bedfellow of our torpors, but in this hour he has no say with me."

"Nor me," his wife said taking his arm.

"I am so grateful," Alicia said, "though I would not resent anyone's decision to leave. Feldon and Ethel, Jack and Esther, are working through the crowd now with the news. We'll give them a few more minutes to get out the word and then we can begin…with whoever stays. Here, let me show you your places."

The podium was centered a few feet in from the top step, and was flanked on either side by large dark green vases each holding an exuberance of gladiola singing tones of yellow, orange and white, a lively complement to the muted lace of flowery jewels adorning the bandstand framework. The amplifier and single large speaker sat on the railing near the stairway. Six chairs were arranged behind the podium where the speakers would sit to wait their turn, three each left and right of center so that they all were visible to the audience. Glasses of water had been placed on the floor next to each seat, and the water pitcher and another glass were placed on the shelf inside the podium.

As Alicia began going over the simple program, the three of them were distracted by the squeals and quirks of a very high-pitched male voice, coming from the direction of the monument. They all looked to see Paul Morgan and a younger man incrementally larger than the General in all proportions, walking across the green toward them accompanied by the rain and lightning of what seemed like an argument, the thunder of Morgan's bass rolling beneath the alto showers of insistence from his foil.

"This must be Bull," Robson said.

Father and son were soon close enough for their flashes of repartee to be heard whirling about the storm's eye of "memorize" and "you don't need help" and "if you forget, you'll remember."

The General became conscious as they neared the bottom of the steps that an amused audience was working overtime not to notice them, and he gently placed a hand on Bull's shoulder and gestured up to the stage. "Please, here they are. Alicia, everyone, my son, Bradford."

The gentle unassuming hulk mounted the steps and loomed over them as though Pale Moon itself had sidled up for chat. "Very honored to meet you, Madame Monroe – and Colonel, Mrs. Andrews…I have heard so much praise of you all," and there followed a few more nervous bows of politesse from the halting falsetto of this modest young man, his childlike voice and simple honesty attenuating the bulging power of his biceps and shoulders, barely contained within the seams of his knitted polo shirt.

"I want to explain," Brad continued as he noticed his father about to voice an explanation. "He wants me to prompt him during his speech…"

"Only the part I memorized…"

"Hey! Forget it. He knows it, you see, and I keep telling him that if he forgets, the forgetting will remind him. Don't you all agree?"

Robson considered that Bradford Morgan was rather used to receiving agreement from those around him, and not for the subtlety of his positions. But in this case he was quick to second this conclusion on its own merit.

"We always forgive the pauses, Paul. They won't stop us listening, so long as they don't stop you delivering. Stumbles set the ship aright."

"Remind me never to take you fishing, Andrews."

The ladies shared an eyewink of merriment over this male thought-tussle, when abruptly the distant sounds of car doors shutting and ignitions whirring brought everyone about to stare out upon a stream of visitors walking back down the avenue to the parking lot. Here and there groups and pairs ran ahead of the crowd and flung themselves into their vehicles, leaving behind a scorching churn of dust and panic. Alicia bowed her head and walked over to the far end of the bandstand. She stood and gazed at the monument, resigned, she felt, to a solitude that Fate had decreed long before her dreams of a savagery-defying haven had ever informed her life.

She was not permitted, however, to dally at the liminal gap between serious musings and the creeping shadows of self-indulgence. Her ears were soon tickled by the sounds of another public tête-à-tête, courtesy of the Whitings. Ethel could be heard complaining that brute honesty was best, her affirmations interrupted by her husband's futile counters that "brute" is not "honest." What added to this sideshow was, to the surprise of everyone onstage, the surge of "groundlings" that followed after them, members of the crowd eager to catch every word and gesture of this domestic parley.

"Oh my!" Alicia gasped as she walked back and took Monica's hand. For beyond the immediate circle around husband and wife, a still larger crowd milled about on the green, monument, and gardens, patiently awaiting the start of the proceedings. Robson and the General each privately took a count, and they were in agreement that upwards of five hundred had chosen to stay for the ceremony. And what was turning out to be the opening act continued right to the steps of the bandstand.

Feldon threw out his arms and wagged his walking stick at who-ever would give him ear. "She just said to people that a bomb could go off and we're all going to die. Discretion must be as old-fashioned as Nehru jackets."

"I was honest," Ethel said, hands on hips and still sporting a coat of pale concrete dust from cleavage to knee of her dark green dress. "And I dared them to stay anyway."

"You were fifty percent honest, darling, Yin only, no Yang…"

"Stop saying the same thing, silly man! You have kicked that can all the way up this palatial avenue. It's over, and many brave people are here with us."

Feldon appealed in vain to his friends, who could only find dif-ferent ways to smother their mirth. Monica smiled and reached out a hand. "Come along, congressman, we really should get started." And as she helped him up the stairs, she looked Ethel over and said, "I suppose there's a reason why you're still sporting that soot, my dear."

The congressman's wife tossed back her head in defiance and, placing her hands on her hips, rocked from side to side. "It's my badge of honor, baby," she said with feigned hauteur. Then she strode over to the sack that she had left on the steps, zipped it open, and took out the box of printer paper that it contained.

"I'm going to hand out your speech now, darling." And she looked out into the crowd and called Esther over to help her distribute the sheets.

Jack tripped up the stairs and gave everyone a warm grasp of the hand, Bull walked out onto the green, and all the speakers found their places. Feldon could not resist another tap or two on the mi-crophone, and the firm resonance made him relax and wipe his brow. He turned around to catch the eye of everyone seated behind him: Jack, Monica, Morgan, Alicia, Andrews. Then he took a full minute to look out over the crowd, as Ethel and Esther moved among them handing out the papers.

"Good morning, everyone."

"Good morning!" came back a cheery unison that erased the next words Feldon was about to say.

"Oh! I think I have to recover from myself." Sprinkles of laughter chimed about the quiet air. He paused to look at some of the individual faces, smoothed or creased brows and cheeks, modest attentive poses, eyes aware and waiting.

"My first order of business has just now become my second order of business, because first of all I want to tell you all how happy I am to be here, and to see you all here. That sounds like a platitude but I assure you, the platitude is true. And besides, the only other way I could express this feeling would be to go down there and give each of you a hug. So you see how merciful I am – you have all been spared! My second order of business, which was to be the first – and is the first really – is to inform everyone that, at Mrs. Monroe's request, we guest speakers are not to eulogize or reminisce about Jackson Monroe, the man whose life and unexpected death is the bedrock of this great new city of the West, and whose image so enigmatically keeps watch with sacred vigilance over its nascence. Alicia herself wants to say whatever there is to say, and we all respect her for that."

The titters and chuckles that accompanied Feldon's evident impromptu pronouncements gave way to an approving round of applause. He nodded a few times and then continued.

"As you may know, your current congressman is busy touring the factories of China. No doubt seeing whether he can ship over a few prefabricated supermarkets." A few knowing guffaws spouted here and there. "Sorry, sorry. Didn't mean to get political. Only to say you will have to make do with a former congressman. As you will with former commanders of Silas." He gestured to Morgan and Andrews, and more spontaneous applause rippled out in crisp, pleasing plashes. When it subsided he continued. "Yes, something about a 'former,' how he or she embodies for us the Janus persona of accomplishment and failure. How quickly that person becomes a figurehead, or image only: the world-weary warrior, with his leathery heart the strop to so many razored cunnings, the veteran of whatever arena he was tossed into, so knowledgeable of every twist and trick and foible of his discipline, more often than not as victim to them rather than master of them. And his accomplishments. We need only wait a span of months to witness the curves of approximation encircle them round, and what had seemed a breakthrough achieved or monument raised now joins the pantheon of pebbles, different colors or shades perhaps, new-found contours and cavities, but always after all another stone dropped along the single line of time's miserly mete-ings out. What can truly wrench itself above the plane of entropy?"

Feldon paused again to search for the ladies out in the crowd. The next moment he espied them just in front of the clock tower building. He smiled as Ethel held up the empty box and shook it a few times. He blew her a kiss.

"Let me apologize, friends, for that moribund deviation. That is not what I wanted to talk about, though I did want to call attention to the stock image, the cardboard cutout of what we see a person to be. And thank God for the trope, the idiom – without it, we would have nothing to shoot down, or work off of. What I want to talk about is contained in my speech there. I guess you all have a copy by now, or can share one with your neighbor?" And here a wave of laughter back and forth across the green, down the avenue, and up into the monument, gave him answer. "I see that you do," he said, and another roar of delight answered him from all around.

He took it all in for a few moments with a quiet grin, and then he said, "Okay, now hold them up. Hold them high. Let's see them all."

Hands shot up en masse, and a sea of white rectangles waved and gleamed in the bright desert sun.

"Very good. Now, one of you, please, read out the speech."

A few snickers were heard in the distance, and then the entire audience was smoothed over with a silence that lingered long enough to begin hearing the birds cavorting among the cypresses.

"Wonderful. I asked for one of you to read it, and you all did. How delicious it is, a little moment that exceeds one's expectations.

I would be perfectly content, you know, to stand here for the remainder of my allotted minutes with all of us in silence together. But in this logorrheic age of ours, the floor and crater of opinion gapes wide with an almost boorish opposition to any notion of a life without words. And it would be unfair of me, in fact, not to explain myself to you, when you have all so willingly gone along with this little sideshow of mine, taking in your hand an empty sheet of paper and accepting the gesture on its own terms. Whatever else happens today, I am grateful for that."

Feldon reached under the podium for the glass and took a sip of water. As he did so he registered some movement at the back of the crowd, and looking out he saw Ethel arrange and stand up on a crate. Their eyes somehow met over the gap of yards and heads, and she pursed her lips to him in a prolonged kiss. He toasted her with his tumbler, and she returned the toast with a phantom flute.

"As many of you know, I grew up in a large city. I took municipal buses to school for much of my childhood and adolescence. The early morning rides were always pretty quiet. Everyone, the grownups especially, was still rising out of their yawns and dreaming, with many, it often seemed, doing their best to stay nestled in those dreams until the demands of the day wrenched them away. Me and my schoolmates also did not speak much, partly because we did not want the adults overhearing our many important intrigues and, in my case, because I often dreaded another day of not really having done my homework the night before." The crowd murmured a soft appreciation. "I seem to be in a confessional mood today. Where will it lead… Anyway, one of my frequent experiences on those rides to school was looking at people's hands. Faces are more interesting, of course, more dimensional, but you can't scrutinize a stranger's face for too long without arousing some kind of creature inside them that forces you to look elsewhere. So I looked at hands. And here was the interesting thing. Except for the few reading a book or newspaper, the pair of hands rested in the person's lap. Try to picture that for a moment. We've all seen this: the slender hands of a pretty girl, the bejeweled fingers of a smart-looking shopper, the spots and veins on the dorsal side of a sickly elder, the thick dark calluses of the laborers, and many another nuance of wrist, nail and knuckle, all folded and resting in their laps. Hands in laps. Innocence at rest. It was for me a simple equalizer that made everyone look like a child, no matter their age or size. If I kept looking at those pairs of hands, I saw boy and girl after boy and girl; if I glanced up at their faces, well, you sometimes felt a body snatcher was at work. So I stayed with the hands, and as the weeks and months passed, I found myself riding the bus with a crowd of kids. Silent kids. Kids who did not know they were kids. There is something about that image of innocence that I have always wanted to emulate. Keeping my hands at rest in my lap or at my side – yes, actually doing that. But something else too, what I would call the cradling of innocence inside myself, the unassuming fingers laced right here, in my solar plexus, observant, calm, without the need for words or fidgets. And that is the meaning of my blank sheet of paper. The innocence inside each of us. Let us be that paper today. Let something be written upon it, upon our heart and mind. Not necessarily from the blowhards up here, mind you. From whatever comes your way today. Let us look and listen and feel, in attentive, childlike silence.

"And is there another way we can understand this childlike silence? There is–" Feldon gestured over the heads of the audience. "Our giant primordial guardian, under whose shadow we now stand, who demonstrates it for us whenever we trouble ourselves to notice him. He has been here for – for an eternity really, measured against our fleeting blur of flesh and verbiage, and has no doubt been called many a name, including 'those hills over there.' As backdrop to eons we know nothing of, we tacitly assume the foreground of those eons to be no more than a chronicle of desert creatures slithering, lurking, scrounging among the cacti. Why would it be otherwise? But instead of such a picture, of Nature at her most beastly, I want to assume otherwise, for now, for this moment. I want to see a man, a so-called prehistoric man, walking under the range's shadow right over there, just behind our majestic clock tower building. In the spirit of being a child, being blank, let us consider this prehistoric fellow and the first words he ever uttered. We often assume that prehistoric man first spoke because of something he saw, something outside of him. He points to a tree and says,...whatever he says. Of course, 'tree' is probably a bad example out here. 'Rock' more like. But if he picked up a rock and said 'Rock,' he then no doubt looked at the hand holding the rock and said 'Hand.' And then 'Arm.' And so on, up the shoulder, around the head, back down to the chest, thighs, and feet, naming each part as he saw or felt it. Meaning, his own body was also external to him, part of the wilderness just now passing from the unnamed to the named. Think of that, of such an experience. If we take it to its conclusion, he will have ended up seeing a stranger, someone he does not really know at all, yet someone he is always with. He is that stranger. And so that naming, and the separation it leads to, would carry him through a portal into a world he could marvel at but never really comprehend, because it was always something 'Other' that he regarded, a perpetual 'Other' that carried on his life without explaining, being able to explain, why here, why breathe, why exist. Since he had been spared the centuries of wiseacreing that have since followed him and his kin, he had no distraction from the theories, philosophies, and worships that crowd around our minds whenever we entertain such interrogatories. We also tend to think that prehistoric man, poor sod, lived, ate, breathed, and died in a world he did not comprehend. Maybe he did not comprehend it, but oh! for a far, far different reason than we had supposed! It was not the lack of inspired treatises or technical skills or scientific templates that beset his troubled days. In short, it was not what he did not know. It was awe. Unspeakable, incomprehensible awe. Awe of himself, he no longer someone he knew, and awe of the world, regarding image after impression after phenomenon as yet another stirring of a magic invisible hand. And where was he himself in all of this? If he was looking at that body, that hand, what was doing the looking? Emotions were likely to well up, aches of the heart, foments of uncertainty, and from these feelings, these confusions – or perhaps clarities, let us not underestimate our forebear – a word is formed, and spoken. Yes, this is how I picture it. His first real primordial utterance was not something he saw around him; it was something he felt inside of him. Out of the chaos of his heart, he uttered the words, 'I am.' Does not all language come from this? I speak because I exist, and if I lose my existence, I speak again to find it.

"And now, friends and companions all, if you will allow, I would like to bring new meaning to an old endeavor. Some of you may recall how, during the end of my last campaign, I abandoned script and walked out among you, just to see the individuals, the He's and She's, that make up what we call 'crowd,' though after my many years of addressing one, appealing to one, explaining to one, placating one, I am not sure that such a thing exists. You, each of you, standing next to each other of you, are not a crowd. You are just you. So let us meet again. Back then, that action of mine meant the end of my political career. Never mind that. Let us now think of our prehistoric friend, and the lonely discovery of what he finds to be his 'Other,' his own self. As I walk among you, consider me to be someone's 'other' – how I talk to you, how you hear me talk to you. But that Other, is Other to me too. We will stand side by side and marvel at the mystery that is our unknown and unknowable selves."

And so saying, Feldon took up his walking stick and began to step down into the audience. He stopped and pulled an orange gladiola from the near vase. He glanced back at Alicia and the others and said, "Please carry on. You know where to find me."

A sea of cheers greeted Feldon as he swam in among them. Jack, as the next speaker, walked to the podium and watched for a few moments as the breakers and eddies of arms and shoulders hugged and kissed the congressman, and gradually the currents took him to Ethel's side, she receiving his flowery gift with a smile, then the waves subsided and the mass of men and women rolled their flux of attention back toward the podium to await what would come next.

Jack's gaze roamed around the many faces near and far in search of his Esther. He saw how Feldon had used his wife to anchor him in the moment, and he sought the same from his belovéd. As was his wont, he decided to be methodical, and started scanning across the rows of faces beginning at the far end. But he only traversed a dozen or so when he was shivered into stone. At the back of the crowd a triangular-shaped head, eyes and nose tilted slightly upward, directly in line with him before and the clock tower behind, rose slightly above the entire mass of people and gazed in unblinking indifference at Sergeant Major Stephson. It was Spooner.

Jack remained motionless and let the urge to barrel through the crowd and grapple with his vulpine adversary course through him without reaction. His rigid posture began to relax, but when his imaginings began again to replay this scenario over in his mind, and his limbs started to freeze up, he decided it was time to act – to act in favor of his own serenity, and retrieve and hold onto the buoyant gel of innocence and joy that Feldon had just implanted in him, and in everyone else. He retracted his gaze to take in the entire audience before him, and in so doing realized that, despite the figure's cold unwavering vigilance, Spooner was after all only a speck on the horizon of this Sea of Love, the hint of menace noticeable yet all but engulfed by eyes bright and hearts untainted.

"Sweetheart," came a whisper, seemingly from Jack's breast. He looked down, and there was Esther, standing at the bottom step right in front of him. She gently rocked from side to side, and tilted back her head such that the full portrait of her soft lips and clear skin beamed up at him in loving affection. His eyes caressed her face and figure, and he drank willingly from his Flower of a Friend.

All of these impressions, of Spooner, the crowd, Esther, filled no more than a few heartbeats, but Jack suddenly wondered if he had been standing up there in mannequin muteness for interminable minutes. He cleared his throat and shuffled about the pages of his speech, though like Feldon he was not intending to read by rote, and pushed from himself a smile of unaccustomed breadth and said, "Good day, everyone."

"Good day," came back in a pleasing rondo.

"Like Congressman Whiting before me, I wanted to begin today by telling you something about my childhood. Specifically, about my given name. My name, is Jeroboam. Jeroboam Stephson."

He looked at Esther and watched her lips suppress the merry giggle that danced from her eyes. Some individuals in the crowd laughed, while many more made an indecipherable noise that registered the surprise Jack had anticipated.

"As I am sure almost no one here knows, Jeroboam was a king over the northern regions of ancient Israel almost three thousand years ago. As a young boy, knowing nothing of this, and not being Jewish, I contented myself with my formal name, or the obvious informal version, Jerry. I even tried Jero for a while, but I was always asked why I didn't have an Australian accent. Eventually my father told me that he was drawn not to the ruler, who sort of betrayed King Solomon, but to the name itself, which had a meaning something like, 'one who rules or cares for many people.' He was never precise about it, but he had hopes for me as a future guide or commander of some kind. I lived on in happy oblivion of any other implication or association, until in my teens I learned that several hundred years of culture and civilization had all but forced this king and his mixed legacy from the Stage of Human History in favor of a large wine bottle. I did not want to be named after a large wine bottle. So I went exclusively for Jerry, but this often led to questions about whether my given name was Jerome or Gerald or etcetera. I therefore turned to the formal sounding moniker 'J. David', which looked great on paper, but in conversation had everyone assuming my name was J-A-Y. I did not want that anymore than I wanted the wine bottle. Out of a sense of despair combined with the devilish desire to rouse up confusion, for a while I decided to call myself 'the letter J.' Right, I know. My pals at the base didn't care – I even got a name tag that said just 'J' on it, without a final period. A small triumph. But then I tried it out on the parents of my girlfriend. There we were, in the middle of Thanksgiving dinner, and her father says, 'So, Jay, how do you like military life?' and I said, 'My name is not Jay, J-A-Y, my name is The Letter J. Please call me, The Letter J.' Many a fork was suspended before many a mouth, and so ended a dinner, and a relationship, and this dalliance of mine. On my way home that evening I surrendered. I gave up. I had a name – I had many names – that I did not want. I gave myself a name, then gave myself a second one. But that was not true, that was just playing. I did not give myself anything – I mocked, I toyed with people, with myself. No name had adhered to me, not one of the names I had ever been called, from infancy to my years of brash self-importance, evoked in me that instant rush of recognition, that gapless flush from being called to, asked for, and my saying, 'Yes, here I am. Yes, this is me.' This I never had.

"Instead, I lived with a gap. Someone says, 'Private Stephson,' and, for however brief a moment, I hesitate. Who is Private... Ah, yes, it's me. Some old friends still wrote me letters, addressed to Jerry Stephson. I stare at the envelopes. Who? Did I ever have a bro... Oh, yes, that's me too. I even balked at a single letter 'J' sometimes, which produced in me the not unvirtuous habit of not reading license plates and other random letters. I do exaggerate, of course, in describing these mental states to you. Not because they are not true, but because they are only hints, dashed off brush strokes, at conveying to you the real experience – which is, as I have said, when someone addressed me, an internal gap appeared, an empty space inside myself wherein I am not anyone or anything, until the next moment I am. I had, needless to say, always considered this a malady. Yes, there was therapy. Yes, there were mantras, and prayers, and group hugs. But something about all of these pokes into naught could never replace the naught itself. Inside of me there lived something that was always nothing. And this nothing, rather than dissolving or getting filled up with wholesome psychological sanity, grew and spread inside of myself. To be expected, if you think about it. For how can 'nothing'... dissolve?

"So did I succeed in the end? Did I give myself what I wanted, needed? Is Jack my name? No. Jack is the name I gave to my gap. I decided not to name me – instead, I named it."

The sergeant major paused and looked out over the familiar audience. Familiar because everyone was now like him – resting in a gap of unknowing. He reached under the podium and took a long sip of water.

"Oh, it's still cool," he said. He took up the pitcher and refilled the glass, and placed them both back on the shelf. He knew what he wanted to say next, despite Alicia's request not to refer to Jackson. He looked over at the monument, the immaculate trim angles of black stone glinting heroically in full sunlight. And though he could not see the bust from this angle, he brought to mind the "conversation" he had had with him that fateful day and evening. He turned back to the audience.

"So people started talking to Jack, writing Jack, asking help from Jack. I watched him receive the requests, gather the impressions, engage his responses. And of course, all of that was me, I did all of that. I am not saying I ceased to exist; for lack of a better description, I would say I began to doubly exist. Jack was spoken to, and he replied and I saw his reply – and then I joined the reply and what followed from it. Jack sat down to write something, and I saw the stream of thoughts collect themselves around his hand holding a pen, and then I and the thoughts wrote down this stream. Or he drew or painted something, and the subject before him, or in his mind's eye, gradually he and I together lined, shaped, and shaded the likeness of onto paper or canvas. This state of mind served me well in the army. Commands are given, Jack receives them, and we assemble our mission and carry it out. Strenuous maneuvers and exercises are thrust upon us almost weekly, I see and feel Jack exert himself, and I am exerting myself and sweating and panting and there is this delicious feeling, that comes and goes, of seeing him experience this, this 'him' that is, after all, me. My new life, for such I called it, lifted me out of years of confusion, for which I was grateful. But by degrees it settled me

EL TAJIN, NEW MEXICO

into another confusion. And that was, this merging I have spoken of, whereby I see Jack receive an impression, and soon me and Jack are the same receptor and actor, we are one being standing before the moment's offspring. But this shift, which occurred every few seconds or minutes, depending on how often I experienced Jack as separate from myself, never felt like the 'merging' one hears tell of in sacred writings. It was not a merging into something greater than myself, it was more a returning to the norm. There was me and Jack, and then there was neither. I could say, 'then there was just me' – but that was the problem. The 'just me' was not someone tangible or real.

"We conclude at a certain point in our life that the plateau has been properly scaled. We had seen it early on in our childhood or youth – that escarpment of our wishes – that one level of superior living or understanding just above us but well within reach. We knew our goal, we made the necessary efforts, and through hard work, suffi-cient work anyway, and some amount of luck – the talisman of chance always having its say – we arrived, set up encampment, and carved out our nook of existence in mankind's endless halls and chambers of what is and what could be. And there we abide, and there we play out our days and nights. It is satisfying to arrive at a goal, and rest therein. I do not deny this. But I also do not deny, to those who experience it, the questions, and the seekings after, and, if it cannot be stopped, the despair, that comes from the unexpected pause over a daily habit to look about for the next highland – and to find that there is none, at least none apparently visible. Where can it be found? The question may come and go, but if it comes and does not go…therein lies the agony. In such agony I lived after repeated, endless moments of Jack and myself merging back to a sealed door of normalcy. And then, about two months ago, I met someone who changed all of this for me. It began by hearing an anecdote about him. He challenged a group of people in his company to tell him what increment of future time can never, by anyone, no matter how clairvoyant, be predicted. The answer: the very next second. A quiet thunderbolt exploded inside of me, unheralded and unobserved, for which I am eternally grateful.

That not knowing what is in the next second – this was my answer. A lot of time can go by and that one unknown second is still there, right in front of you, waiting for you. What was the threshold that needed to be crossed (the future that no one knows about)? In this case, the question is the answer. The new highland I was seeking appeared before me in the form of this threshold. I observed Jack respond to something, his involuntary thoughts and feelings unfurl. Instead of merging with this and acting upon it, I waited that one second more for what would come next, that unknowable instant that was the future becoming the present. Watching and waiting, which becomes its own unpredictive state of, let us say, 'beholding' rather than 'doing.' I hope you will all forgive me if that is not entirely clear, for I must go on. The next day I was able to have a conversation with him. He gave me another piece of this puzzle, which is, that nothing we can see is ours. The uncompromising conclusion that comes from this, is not to expect answers, happiness, from what we see and touch and so on. Look instead not at, but between. Between you and what you experience, what you behold. But – see what you behold, see what you see.

"I am so grateful for Feldon's little story of our prehistoric friend and his first utterance. It made me realize that that first utterance – 'I am' – is a continual calling forth. Not for once, but for any 'once' in which we feel it so. I would add then – with your permission, congressman – this 'I am' arose from the wellsprings of his heart, and was seen, recognized, out in front of him, in the gap between what was not his body and what was not whatever lay before him in that moment, such as, perhaps, the rude earth and its inquisitive fauna. 'I am' was called to, dwelled within, the fixed point between the two. There still he silent dwells, as ancient as Pale Moon itself and as newborn as the next whelping pup we hear cry out to us on the lonely prairie."

Exhilarating trembles enblazed his sensibilities as each syllable of speech departed from him. After his last words – words nowhere to be found on the typescript resting on the podium ledge – Jack wiped his brow with the back of his hand and looked down at Esther. She unmoving looked up at him, and he knew that she had thus remained from the start. A cooling breeze rose up of a sudden and meandered through the crowd with welcome caresses of relief. Jack was especially chilled owing to the perspiration that soaked his head and torso, but he smiled through the drop in temperature and said, "Thank you, one and all, for being willing to hear my personal odyssey. Not a little of it do I owe to this new village and the many promises it holds for our future, both personal and collective. Thank you again."

Amid the applause that followed Jack turned and nodded to his companions on stage, then walked down the stairs and put his arm around Esther. In the same moment Monica stood up and walked to the podium, motivated by the wish to look down at Jack and send him a loving glance. Which she did. And which he returned. She picked out her speech from the stack, tapped the sheets together, and placed them before her. She smiled her beautiful smile at everyone and began.

"Today, friends and neighbors, is a ceremony, a celebration. In particular, the celebration of a beginning. Many ceremonies are for lives completed and achievements past; or memorials to someone or some 'when' we believe must not be forgotten, though most of the details are. Perhaps this corner of earth and time will be accorded such a ritual of remembrance in futures unknown. For now, our music and words and gathering announce a vision incipient: realized in part and offered, to whoever wishes, to join in its continuation and completion, in its elaboration and deepening. Is this day itself the beginning, the first moment? No, certainly not. Can we say when that moment was? Again, no. All beginnings engender in silence, unheralded and unseen. Many an intangible increment we cannot measure will go by before the first stirrings – the darkling presage to a gestating life or idea – shimmer out from endlessness into our temporal tolling of birth, maturity, death. I am impelled to say, against my desire to not pontificate a worldview, that no sleuthing after cause behind cause behind effect will ever dissuade me from the belief in a Womb of Eternity, nurturing the yet-to-be spawnings that become and adorn our life, all lives. What can be said, with some certainty, is that when the idea is made manifest, or when the newborn pushes his way screaming into the air and light, that idea and that little being already have a past and a future. It often intrigues me how the reflex of analysis finds preferment in the eye cast backwards. I suppose many of you out there read biographies? Yes? Oh, quite a few. Me too. We turn to the first page and, most of the time, the author begins with the subject's childhood, or the subject's parent's childhood, or perhaps with a chronicle of the town or village the person grew up in. And then onward through time until the arrival at the stage of life when this person reached his or her apotheosis, the ripened years of what we acknowledge as the distilled 'being' that was this individual. Fair and reasonable; but to me something is often lacking in these trajectories, in this tacit 'understanding the present from the past.' Not infrequently writer and reader are puzzled – What was it about his past that drew him to that particular pathway? And here, it seems to me, the obvious is often missed. For, if you want to know what drew someone to a certain path, try looking at what he looked at. Try looking down his path. Look at his future, as he himself did, and had fixed himself upon. The future influences and acts on a person as much as the past. There are future events right now calling to each of us, influencing our days and hours, influencing our present. We can say more: that often, at a certain point in one's life, the future influences us more than the present, or the past. A future we see for ourselves takes hold of us and will not let us be until it becomes the present we dwell in. Which means sacrifice – sacrificing the past, maybe even sacrificing something of our present circumstances, that we may well weep over for many months. What makes us who we are?

"A wedding is another ceremony that marks a beginning. Again, not the real beginning – you will only find that in the look husband and wife share. They will live what follows from that beginning – they are that outcome and fruition, the ceremony not the fixing of what it will mean, rather an acknowledgement between them and others that something has begun. I married willingly, as perhaps many have not. I dropped what I thought I was and walked through the narrow gate of commitment without implication, and without looking back. Those first stirrings of love, of being drawn toward something just in front of me – this I followed and never considered a consequence beyond the union I so fully embraced. Yes, those first stirrings, how not to lose them, how keep near the insignia they imprint on what and who our heart conjoins with. Many have held me; I have had many relationships, lovers, but only one marriage. As a postulant to love and, let me say it, homemaking, I feel myself as pure a virgin as any young blushling pursuing the uplifts of her own naïve heart. I now listen to these uplifts daily; they come as moments of laughter, or dalliance of light on a dewdrop, or distracted whispers from a friend – I let them lead me into a quiet roam about a nuance of understanding that may or may not be voiced, incarnated: for such thoughts, impressions, that go nowhere save around the contours of my heart…maybe that alone is their purpose, and is enough of a purpose. I married not to be held every night, but to be held once and forever. How private and how public sex is. Our intimate playtime, our aches to love and be loved, curiosities too, let us not deny it. Our wish for children, a world of which men never really know, though women hope they will respect. We, men and women both, each assume the right to our personal needs and how they are pursued and satisfied. But justly or no, the world lays claim to our private sharing of pleasure. Disregarding society's mores is a social act, intimacy as much billboard as assignation – what is only, solely ours is also everyone's. They will weep at our banns and ribbons, and jeer at our afternoon motel trysts. If a person wants true, immaculate separation from the world's sins and glories, let that person never mingle with another, let their body be placed beyond the reach of open palms, soft lips, warm breast, most of all, beyond the glance and eye-glint that will contain it all. The private is public, unless your social statement is one of no entry, or dead end. Never mind that, forgive my sarcasm. Separations are not immaculate, but they are inevitable. I claim my modest share of pain and forgiveness in dramas such. Why, after all, is the private public? Because of the obvious, that we are all so much the same, all composed of the same cravings, idleness, and, to be fair, these uplifts I speak of. If you will allow me to presume a collective understanding, I would say the gentlest hints of joy, of comprehension, that enter and pass through us before we can en-cradle them with logic, are what take us where we hope to eventually reside, to something unnamable, something momentary – though who can say whether 'momentary' is not 'forever'–something so alive that its merest whisper, fragrance, is enough to rule us for days and months. Can you hear it, feel it, now? Can you? I say again, What makes us who we are?

"Time has been good to me. The passage of years has given me what I wanted, hoped for, and more. Most of all, it has given me the understanding that it is not –"

Brutal it seemed, the sledgehammer slam against that cast metal in the high tower, booming an ominous intrusion down, over, through the ears and patience of each person in that little town. A second echoing boom sounded, then rolls of iron thunder followed as third, fourth swallowed nature's music, sought a dinning invasion of every-one's attentiveness, round upon hollow round continued, seeming to strike and strike again, as though the air did battle with itself. But it mattered not. The goddess Silence never yielded dominion over her citizenry; gongs they heard but did not heed, fixed instead on the firm ethereal web glistening between themselves and the podium, a web of understandings divined, shaped, and shared by each modest orator on this day of modest celebration.

Monica herself did not flinch or change position, and treated it all like someone coughing at a dinner party as she was about to ask for the potatoes to be passed. While the aural fog of the eleventh gong could still be heard fading into the landscape, she continued – "it is not anything at all, that, despite what I said a few minutes ago about future influences, it is all borderline meaningless. How generous of Time to teach me this. Pater Chronos did his best to seduce me. He fed me morsel after morsel of affection, vacation, scholarship, flattery,

354   EL TAJIN, NEW MEXICO

rewarded me with sweetmeats of success and romance, preened my wishes and patted my desires, and ever sat at ease in his armchair right before my eyes, dangling forth the next toy and dollop of pursuit. I fed and drank freely of these delights for many years, until an unlooked for truth shuddered me to a halt, and then continued boring its white hot poker of unwelcome clarity into the crannies of my self-love. I was not consuming Time; he was consuming me. I was not being led into deeper fonts of joy and wisdom; I was being primped for my casket. How the Lord of Seconds Wasted had hoped I would not see this – though when I did see it he leered at my despair, for, quite rightly, what could be done? He leered at me for months, waited for me to give up my push against the onrush of oblivion, continued to shake the next pleasing rattle of diversion before my eyes for me to, once again, snatch as though by right and pocket as though I conjured it at will. What could be done? I could look backward, forever, as many seem to do. But Chronos sits there as well, with his open arms ready to embrace our nostalgia for a paradise we imagine we had known. Faced with this omnipresent carnivore I came to a standstill of tears, tears not wet, not seen, but nonetheless welling my heart, my thinking, with hot and searing confusion and despair. Such a grace it was. For through that emptiness, and the impossibility of turning anywhere for solace, I found the answer in, and because of, this standstill. In brief, I avowed to eat him, to eat Time. How could I do this? Because standing immobile in a secondless twilight, with my burden of near madness, an obvious truth awakened in me – he is not omnipresent. He smirked at me in my future and he coaxed me toward my past. But he had nothing to say of my silent present and its pains. Indeed, he was not there. So here I reside, as much as I can, despite his yanking and teasing, in the threadneedle oval of what this instant flashes at me, be it a gaze into the eyes of a friend – Hi Ethel! – or running my fingers through my hair and turning to smile at my husband" – which she did – "or, thanks to a droplet from eternity, to place my hand upon my womb and smile at what is and is to come. And not just me. Come on up here ladies."

Murmurs of delight spread through the crowd as Monica stepped out from behind the podium and held out her hands. Esther took one, and moments later Ethel the other, and the three women were side by side before the appreciative assembly. A young man called out, "The Three Graces," and Ethel (her dress now clean of dust) called back, "The Three Pregnant Graces, kiddo. Here we stand, all six of us." Esther leaned over and whispered in her ear, and Ethel laughed and called out, "Or, as my darling friend here says, perhaps the seven, eight, or nine of us!"

When the laughter and murmurs had subsided, Monica said, "Well, I suppose I feel a little guilty, breaking the news to our men in this way, but I trust the joys outweigh the peeves." "I don't feel guilty," Ethel called out, "because Feldon in his day often shared his juiciest nuggets of gossip before the marketplace of opinion. Besides, birth is hope, so here we stand, hope thrice adorned."

A fresh ripple of clapping began. Monica glanced at the clock and hurried over to Morgan. She took him by the arm and with mock aggression mimed pulling him out of his seat and leading him to the podium. Cascades of claps and cheers mounted and mounted, and whoever had been sitting or leaning against something stood at full height and roared their approval for the last great commander of Silas standing before them in the now high-risen sun. Esther and Ethel helped each other back down the steps. Monica walked over and kissed Robson, cheek to cheek whispered in his ear, then scurried over to sit in the General's place and took Alicia's hand.

The massive frame of General Morgan stood at the podium, head bowed staring at his speech, until the applause and cheers abated to a palpable charge of attentive anticipation.

A few moments passed in this state of electric silence. Morgan looked up and cast his gaze about the many bodies and faces around him. He pushed a smile from himself, not out of insincerity but rather from a need to depart from, somehow cast off, the implacable leader who had allowed no emotional intrusions to sully his steadfast stewardship. Now all was intrusion, all he wanted was to be penetrated, filled, confounded by beauty and the unknowable. His eye lingered over Jackson's monument and its flawless sheen. He glanced up at the clock tower. Aware that he seemed to be slipping into private musings right before everyone's eyes, he faced his audience with a now genuine, disarming smile and said, "We heard a delightful tale from our sergeant major over there about the trials of his identity. It inspired me in many ways, including the decision to tell you all – and everyone else I will soon come across with whom I have converse, intimate or otherwise – that from now on I wish to be called Paul, and only Paul. Paul is my first name, my given name, and now I want what was first given me to be all I embrace. I am not General, I am not Morgan, I am not 'Big.' No one is big, no one is more than a millifraction above zero in this strange world we have been cast into, though for reasons that become less clear the older one gets, the ego supreme refuses to give up his place at the top totem of our self-worth. To that point, the sergeant major gave us another lesson just before the commencements began when he cut up and carried off that rattlesnake. And brave work of the missus, too! It brought back to me an incidental remark of my Dad's: 'Do not kill a serpent and leave its tail.' As a boy I dismissed that comment of his, like so many others, as another statement of the obvious – and how many a word and comment from others do we not so dismiss, vain creatures that we are. Clearly now I see, the tail does not literally bite, but left behind it still exists – and so squirm the 'tails' of our ego, curling and aimless, but not departed, not ever intending to let their partial death leave us in peace. Only when that ego does not exist in totality, for however brief an instant, in any slithering incarnation, can I now feel that I truly exist.

"Feldon was right – this is confession time. These words I have just spoken are not on the printed page in front of me, and I find nothing to resist this self-aware, conscious flow that is taking each of us toward a recognition of what our inner struggles are and probably will be. I will assume that you all understand and agree, as much at least as to let me have my say. I suppose we can ask nothing more of the world.

"Yes, the world. The world of other people. I have commanded many a crowd, both orderly and chaotic. Chaos is easier, because wildness is willingly directed down a sluice of confrontation and massacre. A little more on that later. What I want to speak to now is the different silences I have been faced with by a crowd. Rows of soldiers in focused attention awaiting my next command; their silence is that waiting, that keen razor edge of expectation. Beautiful in its way, but how many times was I deceived into thinking I controlled those men and women just because I played my role and uttered that next expected command. They were ready to hear what I had to say – but after all, anyone could have said it, a myna bird in truth. The mover moves not – never forget that, especially you young ones here today. Then the silence that follows the many formal celebratory dinners back in Washington, with statesmen, politicians, wives and companions, and ever more generals, where a table of sated bellies and head-swims dawdle half asleep while I recounted another overly embellished anecdote of not quite courage and daring, a diversion the guests consume like the silver plate of truffles picked at and passed round. Awareness narrowed or nodding – such I lived among. Then the day came when I faced a crowd I did not know. Perhaps many of you were there, when myself and the congressman asked for your vote, present votes for him and future votes for me. My syllables teased the air about my lips and cheeks, but otherwise they had no effect. I faced a vacuum. I faced a void I could not begin to comprehend. It drank in what I said, it understood what I said, it understood who and what I was, and it saw no need to acknowledge any of it. As I eventually admitted, I did not have much to say. I did not have anything to say. That crowd shouted back at me a resounding call from immutable emptiness, and then vanished. I should have been willing to continue to talk to myself and brave out the indifference – that is the political art, after all. But I could not do it, and standing here today I can tell you how grateful I am for having been so thoroughly vanquished by you all that day. You stripped me of my epaulets of pride, and after a few begrudging months went by I was ready for zero, ready for the assent into the sacred commonplace, into the realm where simple reality lives in supplication to the unknown divinities that sculpt by removal whatever kernel of spirit we may in the end be.

"Sometimes the most elusive things are the most definite. The more a person hollers, the more likely the cause is something instinctive, incidental, unimportant. We yell at a bug and yawn at an avalanche. The freight train of neglect, of kindnesses ungiven and inspirations not followed, eventually barrels its way into and over our complacency – if we're so lucky. And about that commanding of chaos. One humid afternoon in the Vietnamese jungle I received orders for my squad to occupy a rise of land about half a mile northwest of our position. We could see it with the naked eye, a hub of a hill curiously bare of trees. I concluded the enemy would be waiting for us at the bottom amid the shrubbery. I had the men fan out in a pincer movement, and on my signal we charged into the wet foliage guns flaring, throats screaming, grenades afly. We reconnoitered at the bottom of the hill but found nothing except a few shattered palm trunks. We assumed the enemy had fled west, because that bare hill couldn't hide a parakeet much less a rifleman. I still had everyone surround the perimeter and climb cautiously, in case some kind of unexpected crossfire awaited us, though it seemed impossible given the distances from the nearest promontories. We arrived at the top, and it was clear that no one had been there at all. I looked and looked for some sign of hidden malevolence, but the only impression other than rock and grassy tufts was a gentle spread of wild orchids, quietly looking up at me with yellow and purple gazes. I was momentarily drawn into their beauty, but got back to serious things and radioed in our arrival. I began to think we had charged the wrong position, and asked where the nearest enemy redoubt was likely to be. And the embarrassing reply came. This was not an enemy stronghold, there was none for many miles. I had not been ordered to attack and secure, I had just been ordered to go up there. In one second, and for one second only, I glimpsed the absurdity of charging, fighting, destroying, occupying. There had been no enemy and nothing to fight. As I say, that second of realization came and went, and I was back to being the hardass warrior that ordered everyone to take up watchposts, unnecessity notwithstanding.

"But I never forgot those orchids, people. Years later I researched them and had a small greenhouse built in my back garden to house a few of them. They are one of my greatest joys today. So you see, all of those rounds of ammunition and exploding shrapnel, they were all expended so that now and then I could have a few quiet moments with beauty, beauty so joyful in itself, so magnificently indifferent to the sweat and anger of men and their concerns. I conquered no hill. I was conquered – by a flower. Though like I say, it took me years and years to accept that.

"Was that flower the meaning of that day? Was it the meaning of my entire tour of duty? Well, yes. Not the flower itself, but the unassuming innocence of it all, an innocence that Feldon so perfectly illustrated for us this morning. I am so glad I can now say to you that I too experience this innocence. It almost feels undeserved. As I never tire of saying, when it comes to relationships, I am a confirmed widower. I married my high school sweetheart, and we stayed together until her unexpected passing ten years ago. I held no one else before, and no one else since. Once and forever, right Monica? Not exactly the love life of a soldier, I know. More like that of a chaplain. Never mind. I loved and was loved. I mention this because I have one final segment of speech to impart, and then Paul is going to say farewell to the Grand Old Limelight, dubious corner of nowhere that it is. I am going to recite for you all a lullaby. My granddaughter taught it to me – yes, that's right, the child sang the man to sleep. I promised her I would learn it by heart, and though I believe I have, I will not really know unless I can say it to you all now, word for word, without a script, you, this wonderfully aware assembly willing to give their silence to another's moment in the sun."

Paul paused and straightened up to full height. To many in the crowd a curious caprice of vision unpacked in a few shuttering seconds whereby the mass of his shoulders and neck seemed to grow to outsized proportions, as though a wrathful gladiator were poised to challenge any disturbance to the ether-fine sense of sight and sound that everyone in El Tajín now partook of. Someone standing on the monument step could hear him take his next breath. And then the poem followed, a serene unhurried cadence of spoken music in the big man's murmuring benign thunder-tone:

> " 'Tis true, my child, we fight off sleep,
> When most we need to rest;
> Tomorrow brings you vows to keep,
> Tonight your stirring breast,
> Like dove-bird's wing,
> Still fluttering,
> Seeks further realms to nest.
>
> "So let your darling budded eyes
> Maintain their softened gaze,
> While you respire in tender sighs
> And watch the rainbow ways
> Of loves to come,
> And lovers hum
> Their sweet abandoned lays.
>
> "Your soft white hands, like petals calm,
> Upon the coverlet,
> With tiny nail and open palm,
> Seem in enamel set,
> Two half-op'd blooms…
> All Love assumes
> And knows we shan't forget.

"I see your yellow tresses lay
  A fan of golden thread,
They spread like spokes from sunlight ray
  A halo round your head,
    And at a glance
    They seem to dance
  As fairies streamers shed.

"Your breath now draws in measured song,
  The rise and gentle fall,
An airy note just heard among
  This room and silent hall;
    Your lips unspeak,
    Your ivory cheek
  Flushed with the angels' call.

"But though your blue-veined eyelids close,
  A filmy milk-white drape,
Your pupils wide, without repose,
  Two sentinels agape,
    Persist to see
    With clarity
  And let no dream escape."

Silence began to hear itself. As a drifting seabird arches out over the
sparkling ocean, and minute by minute we watch his merry dip and
rise along the airy waves, a span of wings soon diminishing to blot and
speck and pinprick and naught into a horizon he alone inhabits – so
lingered and departed the last syllable from the fervent breast of the
one-time warlord. Nothing wanted to move. Nature dared not tickle
a grass leaf. A crystal sheen of the Unutterable glowed about the rows
and rows of motionless bearers of this tremulous burden. If people
were breathing it was not noticeable. Life was living without life.

Everyone heard from above the tiny hollow click of the minute hand. Paul looked up and saw the finely tapered point of black metal resting at six. Thirty minutes, thirty minutes more, to the other side of everything. What was there?

In the next heartbeat Alicia stood up and walked to the podium. Out of respect for the tensile aura of awareness burning brightly from every pair of eyes regarding her, she made no show of herself but without ceremony handed Paul a small square-framed picture. No one could see its contents, but his happy smile was enough for all and sundry. He leaned over to her and whispered a quiet word. Then his muscular body turned about and in a few catlike steps sat back in his chair, Monica moving over to Alicia's place. She smiled and stroked Paul's cheek. He kept his head bowed and looked at his square picture, modesty settling over him like swan's wings folding in for glided pleasure.

Alicia looked out at the glow of audience stillness, and in the next second she was one increment of emotion away from being overwhelmed by face after innocent face displaying in relaxed awareness an unexpectant composure, like oil-on-canvas portraits suspended in their timeless detached gaze, each of them keen with the understanding that another impulse would arise into the present moment and equally keen in dismissing any presumption or covetous inclination to have a private pleasure or curiosity idly satisfied. Eschewing all preamble and feeling no need to rouse drowsing minds, as there were none, she began.

"The religions of this world, disingenuously or otherwise, omit a significant detail about the Afterlife. Nobody is going to hell. We were all born in hell already. There is no 'trying to avoid it' – there is only 'getting out of it.' The spiritual work implied, and in some cases overtly stated, in all sacred texts – despite the reassurances their clerical gatekeepers roseate them with – is the work to get out of hell, and not a self-congratulation that we are in the clear already by virtue of syllabic devotion. No small feat, since we have so easily grown accustomed to living among the pillows of complacency. Hell is that complacency, with all its attendant yawnings and naps and full stomachs, conceived as stopovers on the way to a paradisiacal satiety. Hell is our hate, and our jealousy, and our unhappiness, and you can speak up now and add to the list. Hell is our lack of feeling – 'I do not care,' as the touchstone of a person's life, is certainly effective, and keeps consequences at bay or completely shuttered from our sight…and as far as that goes, hell is also success. We are champions of sliding to the shafts and locking them in place, but well I know we best not congratulate ourselves for sitting on the floor with our backs to the door. Do we really savor staring at a concrete wall that much? Hell is our dreaming, that which never ever ends, the fantasies that swirl, often with enticement, just as often in grapples with phantom foes. We dream all day long, let no one here deny it, nor deny we are all in thrall to the deadliest of dreams – that we are all going to heaven, that we will all live forever. 'As what?' one must needs ask… Dreaming is its own end, and if we are happy with that, so be it. But do not expect a trophy for your 'lack-of' pains. It sounds like I am saying hell is everywhere and everything – the most innocent and the most abhorrent. I suppose I am. It also sounds like I am saying that hell is an internal state only that the world around us can take away, if only we were to turn our eyeballs about from their self-preoccupation. No, I am not saying that. Sure, the material world is our playground, and our enemy, and our museum and science lab. It is also hell, the hell of a deceptive permanence that is no less fragile than any straying whimsy we follow for the briefest of moments. Anything we can see perishes, much of it long after we are gone, so do not admire a slower death than your own, that of a granite boulder or redwood monolith. Rocks and bark are not gods. And do not believe that fashioning timber into house, learning into income, passion into family, and syntax into lecture buy us a ticket to anything beyond their own existent facts, frail as that existence is. Have we accumulated, or expended? Have we risen, or plunged, or never budged an inch?

"Jackson knew he was going to die this day, a year ago. I went looking for him that morning all around the gardens and orchard to bring him the news of the standoff with the army. Not something we had anticipated, and certainly had not organized. The spontaneity of defiance surprised me, and I feared for a moment when everyone might conclude the border between civility and violence did not exist. For some things only exist because we say they do. I found him inside, in his office. He was sitting on a footstool staring into the fireplace. There was no fire, of course, and I said so and began blubbering out the news – but he looked up at me and said, 'Everything that matters burns.' My concerns were gone, my concern for him replaced them." Here Alicia took up a pair of sheets that contained the story to follow. "He continued, 'The streaks...how strange they are. Not the phenomenon, though that too indeed. What is strange is having to be shown them. They occur, have occurred all our lives, but until someone shows them to you, you do not see them. And further, until you are told of the riches they contain, and the persistent need to let yourself fall under their spell, you cannot partake of those riches. Why is that? When they appear unheralded of a late afternoon, bands of phantom film spreading their welcome fingers, how often have we not, any of us, glanced up and with arched eyebrows remarked the odd spectacle of light, noted a sudden bloom of curious joy in our breast, then as quickly unregarded it all and returned to our forward or downward gaze at whatever we never really were concerned about. That is real hell, wouldn't you say, my love? The hell of ignoring what is before you? Perhaps much of what is before us is near to naught, but it is our naught, that which the world metes out to us in this Here that is the personal line of our own life. I cannot bear sometimes to think of all the simpleness I have ignored, never to return...for the miracles were ignored as well. By some pure accident I somehow did not let you pass me by, and you never knew that it was you, one unheralded spring afternoon, who taught me to see the streaks, and let them surround and carry me to myself. What is myself?, I asked during that twilit mesmer; and the lack of a reply drew from me the decision to let what I had ignored be who I would from then on be. I would become what I had passed by, killing all the selves that hurried somewhere hence to master something else, or not yet else. You see, my love, I tell you this now because the blackouts are too frequent. I will not survive this day. The breath comes too thinly. No, do not be alarmed, and please do cry. You do not cry enough. Let us go then out to Pale Moon and, as we go, inhale every marvelous little nothing as we move through it, and when we are out on that dry plain, which will soon enough nurture our new city, let us thank the sun, the Glory of the Witness, in his omniscient wisdom for disappearing eight to twelve hours at a time. Yes, disappearing, so that we can daily re-experience the cipher of His Light Ascendant – as the unknowable deity no doubt wishes us to learn it, morning upon morning, of that which may ascend at any moment out of the darkness on each of our brows.' "

Alicia put the sheets away and looked out at everyone. "And so we departed. He displayed a final burst of energy out the door, down the stairs, and into the car, such that I was lulled into a brief complacency that all would be well. And perhaps…all is well."

She choked back a sob and went quiet. One second of resolve to step down from the podium, walk to her car, and drive away came and went. She glanced out into the crowd, and in the midst of so many the caprice of coincidence had her lock eyes with Malvin. She had not known he was there. The Easter Island enigma of his implacable gaze looked back at her, sentinel of what she aspired to, lived for. The magic of last evening returned, and the remembrances of the wilderness talk, civilization and chaos, the blur of borders to what we may pass through…

"In the car Jackson spoke about what he called 'the next step' with the streaks – to partake of their riches without the phenomenon to prompt them. He said, 'The streaks teach so many things without us really knowing it. And teach most of all – not to be spectator only; spectators go home, jubilate, and rah-rah to sleep. No, we must become what we admire, what we learn from. We must rest in illumination, in undreaming, and let the darkness darken only itself.'

"Yes, everyone, we can internalize the streaks, as my friend Ethel told me this morning. And why? Because they are internal, they always have been. The amber light comes to meet us and we come to meet it.

"Back to hell. How do we get out? We stand before a door all our life. Every day, usually early in the day, I feel this threshold and the urge to cross it. Everything around me penetrates, a little, but never seems to go quite deep enough. We live one tantalizing moment away from something more solid, more open, more alive. Just one moment away, a moment that waits and waits and waits. And we wait for others to take us there, or wait for sudden shocks to jolt us past the ordinary…the crises and unrest that placidity adores. But why abandon the ordinary, especially when it may not be so ordinary after all. Love takes us across that threshold, and confusions, and quiet unheralded emptiness. You all understand what I am saying, because we are all standing on the other side of that doorway – right now. This selfless light pervading everyone, that we have created together these precious morning hours.

"As we pulled up on the outskirts of the circle that fateful day, down there where the avenue now begins – many of you were here then, so you recall the atmosphere – Jackson said to me as I was about to step out of the car, 'The citizenry have arrived. The bricks and trees and coffee shops will follow. But the real city we shall create, the "downtown" of this spot of nowhere, is standing here – on both sides of this face-off. For the moment, they do not see themselves or each other. But we underestimate the invisible. They, you, will see, see each other, and yourselves in each other. And that seeing, that place which sits between the space of brow to brow, is El Tajín. Lay the cornerstone there…' "

Alicia not so much paused as interrupted herself. She closed her eyes and heaved one trembling sigh. "Friends, we have so laid it. Thank you."

This last a whisper. As a violinist presses his bow lighter and ever lighter down upon a single string, both elongating and diminishing that final shimmering note, a note respeaking by its gentle fading the entirety of peaks and valleys, crescendos and dapples, staccatos and sighs, with which he had delighted his hearers, seconds bidding seconds to remain and expire in the same instant, so did Alicia Monroe's gratitude saturate the air and spread a waft of her respect and love about each man and boy and girl and woman.

Robson had been sitting upright on the edge of his chair ever since the speech went back to hell. Other than a finch or two dipping through the warm elastic air, no living being moved during the three years of silence that followed Alicia's last words – until the colonel bent over and took off his shoes. He stood up and walked down the steps onto the green, and gestured for the others on the podium to follow. Once together he formed a tight huddle with them and murmured something no one else could hear. The lightest ripple of laughter came from them in response to his private words, and then Robson hopped back up to the podium and an empty stage, and looked out and into the true city of El Tajín.

"One day, a few years ago, I sat behind my desk without my shoes on. The bare feet were airy and relaxing, even a bit mischievous. But the real charm of that day was my sitting. I just sat there, for much of the afternoon. A merciful gap in my schedule left me with nothing to accomplish, and some unknown stasis overwhelmed any impulse to do anything at all. I looked around, looked at myself, looked around again. Hours passed. In retrospect it was, unmercifully, a naïve respite literally minutes before a world of chaos carried me off to another life, lives, I never would have chosen to pursue myself. I am grateful for that chaos, and for that calm that preceded it. Because, friends, as I see it now – or choose to see it – those idle hours in my office were my tutor, and my talisman, instructing me what to seek out when circumstance seems to shut off all exits, and protecting me twofold from the injustice of life's willful misunderstandings and the injustice inflicted by my own self-condemnation. Self-attacks are the worst, don't you think? You need to sneak up on yourself a lot of the time, just to turn yourself off. And what a stubborn ass the body can be. If it weren't for a full bladder and empty stomach, it would be happy to spend much of the day emulating a stone. And in truth does. We all miss the obvious. We all know what to do. Hamlet said he didn't know, but really he did. He marveled at the question; but you know something – the charm of marveling at a question is that tantalizing unwrapped package which we call the answer; yet the charm of marveling at the answer far, far exceeds this. To know what to do, and to do it. This the great reward of living. Like death, for instance. The things we look for in death are actually to be found in life – including dying. The belief that we will achieve fulfillment when we die is the ultimate external conclusion, the body giving up the body to reward the body. And yet, ironically, this belief also acknowledges that the spiritual is not the physical – which begs a more challenging question: how to not be the body, in the body? When we yearn for something, even something tangible like the taste of a round red burgundy or the haunting chords of an elusive melody or a companionship lost to time or accident, we are yearning not for the body and appetites appeased, but for what was in that moment. We want the moment, not the body; we want the spiritual, not the physical. And we want new moments. Stop everybody. Just stop. Tilt your heads back. Like this. Come on. Keep your gaze up there – squint if you have to. Okay, good. Just one moment longer. Now bring your heads down. Oh yes, that did hurt a bit. Massage it. Oh, that's better. You kids out there did way better than us codgers. What did we just do? Mind what happened, then never mind. Don't look back at how a day began, or try to figure out the changes from episode to episode. The cause is not a cause. You know the trope – here, let me pretend I'm reading from a script: 'I overslept this morning and so my entire routine had me a quarter hour behind schedule leaving the house. I walked down the street and turned right instead of left, deciding to go to the post office before breakfast at the coffee shop. While going through my mailbox, who should walk in but Martha, who I had not seen in ten years. She was on her way to the airport but needed to buy some stamps…' and so on. We need less faith in cause and effect, and more faith in the moment's dictate, or caprice. Let's not look for explanations in a rewind – 'If that had not happened, this would not have happened.' A significant moment in our life, our day, encompasses what came before and after, but the before did not create the after. One could as much say that the bullseye hit the arrow. Destiny doesn't need weeks to decide a chess move, nor does She need to wait for us to walk into a wall – She will build the wall and give us the nudge right there and then. No, I do not mean to make light of tragedy. But we ourselves do this, by parsing over 'what might have been' – that time and place of all promise and no answer – until the impacts that matter melt from our awareness. We could propose that yielding to necessity, to what is true, is an art, but more often it is an impossibility. Ergo, impossibility exists. Unknown circumstance crushes us, and then we taste a morsel of the Fates' repast. Is it worth the pain? Well, decide, though there is pain anyway. Time creates pain. Our seconds fleet by, yet we can hardly bear a pause in the forward rush of our personal torrent. We say we yearn for tranquility…sure, provided it takes place at high speed. How do we learn to bear things? Do we learn? How silent the world is about itself. So much silence. This despite the reams of experiment and insight, cataloged and piled up, in the warehouses and caverns of learning. Knowledge is a lattice-work, not a solid: everywhere the holes of approximation, guesswork, assumption. Boil those away and the uninteresting fact remains – and in the end, we know what we do not need to know, nor want to know. We must make a distinction, between wanting intelligence and wanting to exist. Pursuing the one fails the other…so why be smart? Do you know the story of the invisible man? I think you all do, but I will tell you anyway. The story begins with people, people the invisible man met. They could talk to him, laugh at his jokes, sit with him at table, drink and recount ofttold tales, pay him money or offer goods and services, and receive the same in kind. Some loved him, many were indifferent or slightly

EL TAJIN, NEW MEXICO

amused, many more were wary, not sure whether respect or outright confrontation were the appropriate rejoinder to his predictable sarcasms. Then the day came, the strange day, when the invisible man was speaking to a couple, an elderly couple, they facing him on a busy shopping street, pedestrians walking by in both directions, and he was speaking and they were looking at him intently, trying their best to understand the question he was asking, because you see, he was lost, the town was unfamiliar to him, and he was explaining where he thought he wanted to go, and he watched their eyes, their crinkled faces kind and attentive, and suddenly the invisible man appeared, solid and definite, unheralded and nonchalant, and it was me – speaking to this couple. I continued speaking and saw my mouth move and my awkward half-turned stance, and I saw them seeing me and realized that what I now saw for the first time they had seen from the moment I stopped them to ask for directions, and they indicated the side street, not far from where we stood – I was quite near my destination after all – and I thanked them and turned about and started walking and disappeared again. And I could not see me. Then I tripped on the step leading up to the glass doorway I wanted to pass through and I saw me stumble awkwardly. And that has been my life. Disappearing under my own nose…the nose disappears too. Does it matter? Do we have to see us? I can't answer that, but I can answer something else. One early morning, in a bunker far underground, farther down into the earth than I dare think of ever going to again, I was sitting on a folding chair and pictured a priest saying Mass. Opening the missal, bowing before the altar, holding up the chalice, parting his vestments to kneel in prayer. He had done it many times – repetition and routine. And then this image, of prayer and chanting and gesture and supplication, of repetition and routine, struck me as something other than itself. Priests in their ritual hope for light unknowable, seconds or minutes of divine whispers, and their strict redoing of what has been done, learned and memorized and by now redone ad eternum so that memorization itself is forgotten, reduces who they are to a nothingness that has become only what it was taught to repeat and repeat and repeat and repeat and when you are only that and nothing more maybe you are ready to be occupied by something other than yourself, outside of everything you had ever hoped to be but gave up for the circle and posture of this repetition. And maybe he is so flooded, with Divinity, sometimes. And maybe not. This the high risk of effacing your own life. Yet though so few of us – none of us here today – are magus or pastor or monk, despite this we all somehow learn a similar lesson: What we do is also not what we do. I only knew this the day the invisible man materialized. Nothing made him appear, nothing made him blip away. Oh, and somehow that reminds me: I created time today. I walked out the hotel door before dawn this morning. It must have been the melancholy darkness that roused me from the usual stupor that comes with rising before one's habitual hour. I felt each step to the car, felt my hand on the latch to open the passenger side for my wife, gave her a welcome kiss, watched her settle in as I closed the door, I looked up at the coal-grey sky dotted with streetlamps near and starbeams far, sucked in a rush of cold dry air, placed my hand on the driver-door handle, settled into the seat, smelled the clean uphol-stery, inserted the key in the ignition – you see, friends, such a ha-bitual act of getting into a car and driving away happens in such a blur, as though it never happens, time ignoring itself. But if you see it, feel it, you make it. If I can create time, God can too. And probably does, for each of us. Maybe each of us should have been dead a long time ago, but He keeps creating more time for us. We die and are re-birthed by him, in that second between the motion of a breath. You can't really dispute this. We would not notice if it happened. Many of us may have been halfway out of our bodies save for the Generous Deity deciding we needed another day, or year. No one knows what happens within a single breath. We do know we are al-ways running out of time. Every day things will live and die, so every day we need to run in place. Running in place is not the best descrip-tion. I am trying to capture for us that feeling of time standing still but not time wasted. If time stops, does eternity appear? Or are both

EL TAJIN, NEW MEXICO

a trick of distraction? We can deny the existence of eternity – 'What we cannot see is not seeable' as a not so famous sceptic once said – but we cannot deny that time fails us, again and again. We anticipate a rewarding vacation, a finished project, a simple afternoon of rest, and so often time and its demands…demand something else. Those who accept the unseeable may say that eternity itself is the agent of disappointment, but for my part, whenever time fails us we must appeal to eternity–"

The untellable story, of a simultaneity of events taking place in one millisecond, between inhale and exhale, the pause ahead of the next merciful heartbeat, that electric flood of all cognizance blazing amid a naked clarity that brooks no lie or dissent, was now made manifest in Robson's gaze suddenly linking with his beloved Monica, a line of code dutifully rushing from clicking tape through electric wire toward its trigger core, Colonel O'Connell popping the cork on a well-chilled wet champagne bottle, Ethel placing tender palms against the cheeks of her Feldon, Alicia impulsively starting back up onto the stage, another line of code winking ones and zeroes inside the tower clock mechanism dancing toward the lever of bell and clapper, Jack and Esther teasing each other's eyelashes, O'Connell's aide-de-camp ramming home the steel lever that fired a single whir and snap, poles and hinges shooting back and pulling clear the thin metal firing box, a flood of blazing white clarity melting away for an unknown second every thought and impulse each citizen of El Tajín never cared for, so alive were they in their attentive unrest, with many a limpid unwavering look cast upon the foundress of this city, a city forever remembered in legend as the land that dwelt only in the present moment, that suffered and held an illumination born of clarity accepted, the mortal and the timeless understood; and in that moment, in the outer reaches of space, the Seven Sisters, eternally vigilant for a sign of their Eighth sibling, smiled as one as they saw Her wink up at them from that silent blue planet, a white star on a terrestrial breast shining through the swimming atmosphere, content to illumine only Herself and those who saw and knew Her.

ACKNOWLEDGMENTS

Thank you to Ruth Atkins, Ulrich Kaiser, Roger Kent, and Susan Luccini for reading the manuscript and offering their many insightful comments and critiques. A special thank you to Ruth, for her generous page-by-page commentary, without which this book would not be possible. Thank you to Radu Sava for his inspiring photograph, and to William Bentley for the professionalism he always brings to his book designs. And to my wife, Solee, for always keeping me honest.

Made in the USA
San Bernardino, CA
02 October 2018